OTTAWA REGENTS, BOOK ONE

RUBY RANA

To the heartbroken brown girls who are still hopeless romantics and secretly dream of a Bollywood love story.

And to any woman constantly underestimated, overlooked, and forced to shrink down to fit into a neat, socially acceptable little box: tear it up. Tear. It. Up.

CONTENT/TRIGGER WARNINGS

This book contains explicit language, some internalized fatphobia, microaggressions (directed towards the female main character by side/minor characters), sexual content, mild recreational drug use, and alcohol use. There are also brief descriptions of past bullying (verbal and physical) and past sexual assault and otherwise mature themes.

If any of these topics are a trigger for you, please refrain from reading or proceed with caution.

PLAYLIST

Wrecking Ball - Miley Cyrus

So Ambitious - Jay-Z, Pharrell Williams

Desi Girl - Vishal-Shekhar, Shankar Mahadevan, Sunidhi Chauhan

Burn - Ellie Goulding

Levitating (feat. Da Baby) - Dua Lipa

Heat Waves - Glass Animals

I Can See You (Taylor's Version) - Taylor Swift

Left and Right (feat. Jung Kook) - Charlie Puth

Meet Me at Our Spot - The Anxiety, Willow, Tyler Cole

All for Myself - Sufjan Stevens

Ferrari - James Hype, Miggy Dela Rosa

Good Thing - Ruelle

Attention - Charlie Puth

Save Your Tears - The Weeknd

Main Tenu - Rahat Fateh Ali Khan

Tere Vaaste - Sachin-Jigar, Varun Jain, Shadab Farib, Altamash Faribi

Come & Get It - Selena Gomez

Jag Ghoomeya - Vishal-Shekhar, Rahat Fateh Ali Khan, Irshad Kamil

CHAPTER 1:
AN ABSOLUTE LEGEND

LANDON

NOTHING FEELS BETTER THAN WINNING.

Adrenaline surging, heartbeat thundering over the blaring horns as the crowd's raucous banging on the glass blends into white noise. It's the highest of highs.

Don't get me wrong—I've lost my share of games. Missed hundreds of shots. Taken nasty hits. I don't get twisted over it, but nothing tastes sweeter than a win.

Good thing I don't have to worry about losing these days.

I'm living the dream. We stand undefeated—*top of the division*—in the postseason. Swept the last two rounds of the playoffs. Only one series stands between us and the final. Four games until the Cup. It's so close, I can practically taste the metallic champagne bubbles popping on my tongue.

Both of my palms press into the warm tiled wall of the shower as the buzz of the conference win wanes. I lather up my face and beard, hoping to wash away wracked nerves.

The white soap bar flies from my fist with a jolt when Wade reaches the top of the chorus with his rendition of Miley Cyrus's "Wrecking Ball", squawking over the steady patter of shower streams. One eye peeks open through the sudsy foam to the sight of him tilting his head back and using a shampoo bottle microphone. He hee-haws to hit the high notes. Something about getting wrecked. Which is what is happening to all of our ears right now.

A chorus of groans echoes from the team. I'm with them. It's fucking torture. You'd think we'd be used to our tendy's post-win ritual by now, but it's as bad as the first time we heard him sing. If you can call it that. The falsetto ends abruptly when Jaeger slaps the bottle out of his grip. "Dude! *Not* cool!"

"You're fucking embarrassing."

Jaeg's a grumpy shit, but who can blame him? After ten solid years in the league and five leading this team, our captain can pretty much do and say whatever the hell he wants if you ask me. Am I biased because he's my best friend? Maybe. But everyone respects the seasoned vet. Wade, too. Though he'd never admit it.

Wade picks up the bottle and chucks it at Jaeg, who swats it away like a mosquito. It lands outside the shower area and skips across the floor until it hits the base of a trash can with a thud. "That's not what your mom said to me last night." His head convulses, eyes rolling back. "Oh, Wade." He moans in a girlish pitch and humps the air. "Fuck me harder!"

A brutal shove from the broody d-man sends Wade slipping through his footing. We respond with scattered snickers. He catches himself, sliding over the film of water like Tom Cruise in *Risky Business*, belting out the first chords of "Old Time Rock and Roll" while curling up his lip like Elvis Presley.

"*Dun-dun-dun-dun-dun-dun-dun!*"

I shake my head and scoff, grabbing the dented soap off the tile.

"Whatcha lookin' at? Wanna piece of this, Landy?" Wade wiggles his hips, waving his junk. Man has the most unfortunate last name for someone so obsessed with his own prick.

I gag. "*Gluhueck.* You wish, Boehner."

He likes to remind everyone his last name's not pronounced how it's spelled, but it's fun to give him crap. It brings him down a peg. Sometimes.

Wade smirks and spreads his arms as he backs away, ignoring my retort. "'Cause you'll have to wait in a lineup like everyone else." Wrapping a towel tight around his hips, he goes through a series of body-building poses. His chest puffs and hands clench on either side of his head to flaunt those flexed biceps he's always sculpting. "It's the Bone Zone!" Then he leans forward, pulling his fists together. His pecs and delts strain as he grunts. "It's the Bonerrama!"

Derrick strides by on his way out, knocking his bulky shoulder into Wade's, and this time, he falls on his ass. "*Bro!*"

Jaeg flips him off behind his head while looping a white towel around his neck.

Wade wobbles to his feet like Bambi, complaints fading as he wrings the damp line of towel on his buttcrack and follows Derrick.

After a quick rinse, I wipe a foggy mirror clean to practice a pre-press pep talk.

Fucking crush it, Radek. We're gonna drink from Lord Stanley's Cup in no time.

I practice a humble but winning smile for the conference before pushing off the sink and tousling my hair dry. As dry as it can get with these flimsy locker room towels, anyway.

When I get to the dressing area, Wade and Fletch chuckle and snort as others chatter. The two huddle over a phone, probably watching a TikTok. Predictable. Fletch notices me walk in and smacks a turned-around Wade on the arm. They both send me looks over their shoulders. Schemers if I ever saw 'em.

Out of nowhere, the lights flicker and a familiar electric guitar riff— *the beginning of the Chicago Bulls team entrance song*—blasts over hidden speakers.

"Attention beauties and beasts!" Wade yells through cupped hands. At least his bottom half's dressed now.

I swear, if I have to look at his pecker swinging around one more time.

"Were you aware we're in the presence of hockey *royalty*?"

Fletch whoops and bounces on the balls of his feet in time with the drumbeat as it speeds up and intensifies. His arms pump the air like a true hype man, encouraging others to join this ridiculous stunt.

Wade points to me with both hands. "Landy with the Michigan!"

This fucking kid. I fight back a grin before slapping a hand over my eyes. Applause and cheers peal through the squared-off space. Fletch, Olsen, and Szecze crowd together, pretending to take pictures with their finger-cameras as Wade eggs me on.

"*Two* end-to-ends!"

Okay, I'll give him what he wants. He's like an overgrown puppy: excitable and overeager, but harmless. I nod, bobbing my head in agreement. Breaking into a strut, I pace behind a bench and hit them with a GQ model stance, lips pursed and looking off to the side with my hand on my chin. The guys holler back.

"The buzzer-beater!"

Hell yeah! That was me, too. I grace them with the Greek God: one bicep curled towards a fist and the other arm extended with a hand pointing to the sky.

"Hits so clean, he didn't need to take a shower!"

That bit makes me bust out laughing. More of the team circle us. Even Jaeger. Their screams rise as they jump, torsos in various states of nakedness slamming together in a mosh pit.

"Give it up for...The man! The myth! The LEGEND! Our very own... *Landonnnnn Radekkkkkk!*"

A tangle of arms vine around us, connecting in a giant, palpating embrace, and letting out a unified roar.

What did I say about winning? This is the best fucking part. Knowing you belong to something way bigger than yourself.

The guys go back to fooling around and getting dressed as the celebration peters out. Wade lets out an *ugh* behind me as I pull my arms through a crisp white shirt. He smacks a TV remote in his palm. "The fuck is wrong with this thing?" Alternating between pointing it at the screen and punching the power button, he squints and pouts.

"Need some help? Here." I offer a hand, but the man has pride.

"I got it, I got it!" It zaps on. "See? I told you—what in the actual *fuck*?" Wade elbows me in the back as I tuck the shirt ends into my slacks. "Is that what I think it is, Landy?"

"Eh?" I turn as the broadcast throws up an image, eyes blinking to focus. Holy shit. That's...

"A compromising picture of Ottawa Regents' Landon Radek with who appears to be the team's ex-publicist, Annalise Pall, was posted soon after the end of tonight's game. The team moves on to the conference finals of the Stanley Cup playoffs on Saturday against the New York Eagles."

"Your ass...is on...TV," Wade continues, mouth hanging open.

I can't stop staring at the partially pixelated photo on-screen. My heart drops to my ass. Yep, the same one that's on the ten o'clock news, bare cheeks smooshed into my living room window with Annalise's unmistakable o-face pressing into the glass over my shoulder, her feet digging into the back of my thighs. This is...not good. Fuck. Fuck me.

"I didn't know you banged the PR chick. Damn."

"Shut up, Wade." No need to discuss a drunk mistake with Fuckboy #1 over here.

"*Jesusfuck,*" Jaeger grumbles, shuffling up next to me.

The report amplifies as the rest of the team gathers close to the TV. They go quiet, joining in our shock, then howl with laughter, clapping hands onto my back and punching my sides like this is some sort of victory.

A weeping Annalise appears, sobbing and honking her nose into a tissue. The news runs a recording on a loop.

"He said he loved me."

The fuck I did.

"But he used me."

Fucking hell.

"Promised he'd get my job back if I slept with him."

Lying liar!

My jaw clenches so hard a headache arises. Hand tugging at my hair, I reach into the locker for my phone.

Wade flips through the stations. "Every fucking channel," he mutters. Not at all the publicity I expected after this game. "You're an absolute *legend.*"

"Seriously? Shut the fuck up, numbnuts." Jaeg to the rescue. He tips his chin up, tapping me with the folded toque in his hand. "You okay?"

"Fuck no."

My fingers tremble. Dozens of missed calls from unknown numbers appear on the display. As many voicemails, too. Even more texts. I should ignore most of them but...*oh, fuck.* The family group chat. I suck air through my teeth, dreading to see what's on the other side of the notifications.

Before I can tap on them, a hand grabs my shoulder and spins me around. "You're in deep shit, Radek." My agent Cooke grips one side of my collar and unhooks my suit jacket from where it hangs. "Keep movin'."

I forgot he was gonna be at this game. "I was about to call—"

"No time. We gotta get you outta here."

"But—"

He snaps and motions to a lollygagging assistant to pick up my gear. "The fucking wolves are waiting." He leads us away from the interview

.

room. "And we're *not* gonna feed them. We're ditching the conference. Here's what we're gonna do instead" —Cooke stops in his tracks and holds me by both shoulders, forcing eye contact— "you're gonna tell me fucking *everything* so I can figure out what to do about it."

I nod, gulping down the massive knot in my throat. It lodges itself in my stomach, where my heart now swings by a thread after climbing up from my ass. Which, by the way, is *still* on every fucking screen we pass.

"Throw these on." He hands me a set of dark aviators and helps me into my suit jacket before we're thrust into a sea of microphones.

Cooke stiff-arms through the swarm—*a handy leftover skill from his football days in the States*—pulling me through the blinding camera lights while shouting "No comment!" repeatedly until the car doors close around us.

My eyes strain as I wrench off the sunglasses. I cover them with a muted groan. The driver jerks the car forward and I'm instantly queasy.

The phone buzzes in my hand. It's another text on the family group chat.

DAD

How's it going buddy?

MOM

Really, Leon?

DAD

I'm trying to ease him in.

DELANEY

Pretty sure "easing something in" is what got him into this mess in the first place.

MOM

Laney! That is so rude.

14

DELANEY

Not as rude as having to see your brother's ass on the news.

MOM

Landon Eric Radek, what on earth is going on?

DELANEY

Ooooh. Not the full name! You're in big trouble now, buddy.

DAD

Let's all take calming breaths, shall we?

DELANEY

I knew you were a show-off but an exhibitionist? Tsk tsk.

MOM

You're not helping.

DELANEY

What? He's the one stuffin' that poor woman's muffin' in public.

MOM

Delaney Jo!

DELANEY

I'm sending you my therapy bill, hotshot.

MOM

Christ, Lane.

DELANEY

Off to wash my eyes with ammonia.
Goodbye.

DAD

Sure, sweetie. Stay safe.
Love you.

MOM

What is wrong with you? Are you
on drugs?

DAD

Marijuana is legal now.

MOM

I have no words for you.

MOM

Landon?? Honey. We love you. Text
back, answer the phone. Something to
let us know you're okay.

Reading the messages was a mistake. My head spins. I squeeze my eyes shut to make it stop. When we screech to a stop at the curb, I double over to put my head between my knees, trying not to blackout.

Cooke swings open the door, the stuffy summer air whooshing in to replace the cool temperature within the car.

Getting into the building should be simple enough. But I straighten too quickly. Or maybe it's the shock, incessant screaming, constant flashes, and horde of paparazzi between us and the double doors. My stomach lurches. Acid bubbles up. There's no stopping it.

This time the gag is real. "*Bleh-bleheurg—*" I don't make it out of the backseat before half-digested remnants of chicken carbonara—*damn those pre-game meals*—purge forward, ruining Cooke's polished Oxfords with a dramatic, projectile *splat*.

CHAPTER 2:
TWO HANDS AND A BOX OF TOYS

INDI

"READY?"

Gabe moves our pint glasses to the side and steadies her elbows on the wood surface. Across the table, Bea squeals, mirroring my best friend's position. I lean into the thick edge.

"One..."

Sheena whines. "Do we have to? I don't *wannnnna—*"

"Oh, unclench that sphincter, Mrs. Goody-Two-Shoes," I say, nudging her in the ribs. A small burp escapes through the corner of my mouth. "It's tighter than those ties Akhil uses on—"

Whoops. That's the beer talking.

"*Shhhhh!*" Sheena's whole face scrunches with her shush. "Indi!"

The girls burst into sputtered laughter. My oldest friend is smiling, though, so she can't be too mad. It's not like I announced she enjoys being choked. Which she does.

"This is *very* out-of-character for someone who *likes* being told what to do."

Gabe snorts, covering her mouth to prevent a spit-take. Sheena smacks me in the arm for the comment. I'm tipsier than I thought.

Bea slams her hand on the table three times, rattling the remaining peanuts in our basket. "Enough! Let's do this."

"Okay, okay!" Sheena brings her arms up to join us.

Gabe counts down again. "One...two...*three!*"

Bea and Sheena scream as we push the empty peanut shells off the tabletop, reuniting them with their fallen brethren discarded by those who used this booth before us. They drop to the floor in a crackling wave, sending us into a fit of giggles. We're easily amused. Or drunk. Probably both.

"I can't believe this is a thing."

"Don't look at us, Sheen. It's *your* city." Uh oh. Gabe's poking the bear.

"*Excuse me*! Chicago is *not* my city." Sheena flips her long, straightened hair over a shoulder, revealing a cute, shirred top with puffy sleeves and a delicate floral print only she could pull off. Inappropriate for tonight's plans, but very Sheena. Very cottage-core. "I'm from *Mississauga*. I've only lived here a year!" She holds up a sole finger. "We wouldn't have moved if Akhil didn't get the ortho residency at Rush."

Gabe swats playfully at Sheena's hand. "Get that thing away from me."

Sheena tightens her lips and kicks her under the table as the peppy waitress, Lori, walks up, hands tucked into her apron. "Another round over here?"

"Yes, please!" Gabe slides the goblet-style glasses over. "Two *Float Floats* for us" —she motions to our side of the table— "and two more *Off You Go's* for them." Bea and Sheena nod in agreement. Thank God Gabe knows good beer. I can spot a decent wine, but until today, I'd only had cheap cans.

"The summer IPAs are tasty, right?"

Gabe nods, making goo-goo eyes at the waitress. All this woman needs is someone to talk beerty to her. *Beerty*, I chuckle to myself. *Good one, Indi.*

"We're ready to order, too." Sheena clasps her hands over the menu.

"Sure! Go ahead."

"Okay, we'll have the cheese curds, pickle fries and nachos—*no beef*— and the Chicago poutine to start. And then we'll split the Blackened Po'Boy and Quinoa burger."

"You got it." Lori threads the bulky glass stems through her fingers, two in each hand, and tucks the menus under an arm. "I'll bring 'em out as they come."

"Thanks, Lori."

"Cheese curds? Pickle fries?" Bea's eyebrows rise as Lori walks over to another table. "God bless America!" She cracks open another peanut shell and tosses back their contents. *Tossing nuts. Heh.*

"I don't know. Ordering 'Chicago poutine' is like a crime against Canada, *Bea*nedict Arnold." I tilt my head. "Seems—*hic*—fishy."

"The only thing *fishy* is the Po'Boy." Sheena narrows her eyes. "I've been to Monk's before. You gotta trust me."

"I trust you." Bea pats her on the back. "Everything you ordered sounds good."

My drunk mind wanders. You know what else sounds good right about now? Orgasms. They should have those on the menu. This place would be packed.

Gabe snaps in front of my face, derailing my train of thought. "You dreaming of orgasms again?"

"Hey, now! I think about things *other* than orgasms." I've gotten enough crap on this trip since autocorrect screwed me over on the group chat with its brilliant text edit, "*Gimme a sex*," instead of "*sec*."

The three of them grin back at me. Sheena pulls her lips in. Bea's brows are on the rise. *Again.*

"Yeah? Like what?"

I've had two beers too many. "Y'know...law...*stuff*."

"Right, right. Law *stuff*." Gabe half-stands from the bench, opening her arm towards me. "Ottawa's brightest legal mind, everyone!"

"*Pfft*. Pipe down, you bat!" I pull her down by the arm. "I'm on *vay-cay-tion*."

"Yeah!" Bea comes to my defense. "Let her loosen up. She hasn't gotten off in forever."

"Whoa, whoa, *whoa*." I wave a palm around before pointing to myself. "I do *just fine*, okay?"

"Sure, sure. *On your own*," Gabe mumbles.

I straighten. I don't need this. I have dignity! I have pride! "Whatever. Who needs men?" Not me. I've got two hands and a box of toys. Dudes are bigger dicks than the ones they have dangling between their legs.

"I don't know..." Sheena shrugs. "I like mine."

Gabe crunches on a peanut. "I like mine, too."

Lucky bitches. Most men are trash. Or maybe there's something wrong with me. Oh, no. Danger! Don't go there. It's dark. Big sad.

"Can we change the subject?" I rest my cheek in one hand, fingertips drumming on the table with the other. "I'd rather *not* hear about how much *amazing* sex you're all having." Or discuss my lack thereof.

"*Oooh*! Food!" Bea claps then flattens a napkin in her lap. "I'm ready for my heart attack."

We ditch the shells onto the floor once more to make room for the appetizers and fresh beers, exhaling in unison after taking in the mouth-watering aroma of greasy bar food.

"A toast!" I lift a glass. "To the last night of our girls' weekend." They raise theirs, too. "We have so much to celebrate. To Sheena, on her fifth wedding anniversary."

"*Aw.* Thanks, babe."

I blow her a kiss and keep going. "To the lovely Behraz, for taking the plunge and deciding to apply to law school."

Bea takes a seated bow with a flourish of her free hand.

"To Gabe and her new assignment covering hockey next season, and to Kurt for putting a ring on it!" I grab her left ring finger and show it off to the others. They've already cooed over it several times the past couple of days.

My one sober brain cell works overtime thinking of these mini toasts. I deserve some sort of award for this performance. And the Oscar goes to... Indi Davé's last firing neuron!

"And to you for winning the Pearson case!" Sheena adds.

I've got enough alcohol in me to be braggy about my accomplishment. It's been a tough, busy few months. I brush a shoulder off.

"A-thank you. Cheers!"

She mouths a *love you* while our glasses clink and cheers echo. We all take large gulps of our IPAs. Stuffing our faces with those delicious carbs soaks up some of the alcohol.

"So, Gabe is covering hockey instead of golf and Bea's studying for the LSATs. Is Theresa sending any more high-profile cases your way?" Sheena wipes crumbs from the corners of her bright, red-orange-tinted lips.

"And where is Theresa? I thought for sure you'd invite her." Gabe bites into a pickle fry and squints at the tartness.

"I mean, we're cool," I say, picking at some cheese curds. "I like her. But imagine getting sloshed and talking about orgasms with your boss."

"Yeah, *imagine that.*" Bea rolls her eyes.

"Oh, *come on.* I'm not *technically* your boss. And even if I was, I'm not, like, a regular boss. I'm a *cool* boss."

"*Uh-huh.*"

I may have been pushing it with the cool part. But I'm not her boss.

"I'm serious! You're my *friend*. I couldn't ask for anyone better by my side at work."

Bea's lower lip juts out and she wipes invisible tears with the back of her hand before placing her palm on her chest. "I think that's the nicest thing anyone's ever said to me."

"I hate to break up this lovefest, but..." Sheena flips her wrist to look at her watch. "Don't we have a game to catch?"

The four of us turn into *whoo* girls for a minute, then call Lori over to wrap up the check. Hailing a cab is surprisingly fast, or maybe beer-time moves at warp speed. I don't drink the stuff often enough to know for sure.

Grey and domed, United Center appears as we pull up about a block away. There's bumper-to-bumper traffic in every direction. Crowds waddle toward the entrance. Red spotlights dance into hovering clouds. We *ooh* and *aah* from the sidewalk before heading in.

"Look, it's the Jordan statue!" Gabe extends her arm. "Quick! Take a video!" She manages to climb over the barrier and up, doing a slow squat against the metal-likeness of the legendary basketball player while we laugh and record.

"Hey!" Some bald beefcake in a black and yellow security jacket barks at us. "Get down!"

Bea whisper-screams. "Hurry up!"

Gabe escapes from the other side of the square base. We hide within the moving masses, wheezing through laughter and catching our breaths.

Through the doors, thousands of voices clamor over Jock Jams remixes. Red and black jerseys, blown-up vintage photos and other paraphernalia hang from the walls and sky-high ceilings.

"*Ladies*," Gabe intones. "Welcome to the Madhouse."

The arena is electrifying, and we get carried away, drinking far too much beer. They're fancy in Chicago. Budweiser? Have an eleven-dollar cup of Goose Island instead! And why is it so expensive? Probably because Mr. Goose Island puts crack in it.

After four—*or was it six?*—rounds, Bea and I pretend to make out on the kiss cam. Sheena sticks her tongue out and twerks in the direction of the unsuspecting bushy-mustachioed grandpa next to us when she's put on the Jumbotron as Cardi B's look-alike. Gabe captures everything on her phone.

The Chicago Fire absolutely crush the L.A. Suns in the background of our shenanigans. It's been a minute since I've seen a game in-person. *Years.* Not since university. And I blocked out most of university.

"So, they'll play Ottawa for the Cup?" Bea asks, swaying towards the exit, her arm looped into Sheena's.

Gabe nods and swallows a belch. "If the Regents beat New York. I'll see if I can snag seats there, too. Maybe club-level."

We stop in our uneven tracks at the outrageous, trafficky, honking clusterfuck, jumping into the first taxi that accepts all four of our drunk asses in the back. It's a feat, considering Gabe has legs for days, beer bloat is real, and Bea's giant knockers need their own seat.

My eyes drift closed as I get comfortable. "I might be able to get tickets, too."

"What she say? You're thunker than I drought," Bea drawls behind me.

"I'm serious. Theresa asked me to take a case for one of the players."

"What case?" Gabe leans over Sheena.

"You know that whole business about Landon Radek and the leaked photo of him putting his dick somewhere he wasn't supposed to."

"The juicy ass on TV?" Gabe asks further.

No need to remind me. I've been replacing that blonde's face with mine in special-edition nighttime fantasies for a whole week. The girls shriek simultaneously, and I'm thrown off the boob pillows.

"I didn't know they were doing something about it!"

"Don't go all reporter on me, Finch. I don't know the details yet, but *apparently*, it's all lies. Which is slander. Which is *illegal*." See? I don't think about orgasms all the time.

"Wait, wait, wait. *Landon Radek?*" Sheena pokes me in the side. "Landon Radek plays for Ottawa?"

I hum in response, resting my eyes again and dropping my head back. "Yes, Sheen. He's a forward for the Regents." She's not Sporty Spice. She wouldn't know.

"Landon Radek, the same guy you had a crush on in middle school?"

My eyes fly open. A collective gasp echoes in the cab. Even the driver, who, up until now, was mumbling into his Bluetooth earpiece, stops and gives us a look.

Bea rasps out, "*Whaaaaaaat?*"

"No. Fucking. Way. You went to school with Radek?" Gabe slaps my thigh so hard it stings through the denim.

"*Owwww!*" I push her away. "I didn't."

"Oh, right. *Sorry*," Sheena continues. "They played hockey together."

Bea and Gabe's heads swing from Sheena to me. "*You* played *hockey?*"

"I was *twelve*. It was *one* year—"

"How did we *not* know about this?"

"'Cause it's not a big deal." Middle school sucked old saggy balls. One of the worst times of my life. It's right up there with sophomore year of high school. Sophomore year of university is up there, too.

"I don't blame you for that crush one bit. Radek is a hottie boombalottie." Bea shrugs and hiccups. "Have you seen his playoff beard? And those blue eyes." She makes a gurgly drooling noise.

"I don't have a crush on him!" My high-pitched denial makes it sound like one word.

They respond with disbelieving hums.

I untangle my arms and cross them. "I hate you guys."

"The Regents' goalie is fine as hell, too. Have you seen his arms?" Gabe puffs up her cheeks and creates a bulky bicep with her hand in the air over her own. "Those bad boys should have their own post code."

"*Wow*. Does Kurt know about this?"

Gabe scoffs. "I have eyes. I'm allowed to look!"

"Not the jealous type, eh?"

"Nope." She shakes her head. "And I'd never *dream* of cheating on my baby."

"Baby?" My mouth pulls into a frown. "That's disgusting."

She sticks her tongue out at me.

"You know what? I hope you take him on," Bea cuts in. "Maybe we'll get to meet the team and work them up with our *womanly wiles.*" She peers down and fluffs her ta-tas together. "I wouldn't mind getting pounded silly by one of those *big*, muscly athletes. Think of the stamina!"

"They've got egos to match." I should know. Cocky hockey players have historically been my Kryptonite. But never again.

"I'll let you guess what else of theirs is *big*." Gabe pumps an imaginary dick in the air.

I am too drunk and horny for this conversation right now.

"Donovan is nice to look at," Bea rants on. "I wonder if he's packing?

Olsen isn't bad either."

Gabe and I side-eye each other at her admission.

"What? He's got the *roundest* peach ass."

"He doesn't have any teeth!" Gabe cackles, clutching her stomach as Bea shoves her into the door. There's no space for that in this sardine can of a taxicab. "Lookin' like a fuckin' White Walker with his albino ass."

"He has *teeth*!" My petite friend throws her tiny fists around, measly punches doing nothing but make us howl louder.

We argue over who's the best-looking on the team until we get to the hotel and annoy some other guests in the elevator with our drunken antics. It turns into weepy drunk goodbyes to Sheena, all hugging before we part.

There's something so melancholy about growing up. We build friendships over the years, only to have adulthood test them by time and distance. These girls are it for me, though. Nothing changes between us no matter how much time passes, or physical distance grows. And I'm so fucking grateful for them.

We're not sharing rooms—*thank God*—because all the hockey butt-talk wakes the sleeping crickets in my abandoned vagina. Luckily, I'm a planner. I brought a little something-something to hold me over. My mighty bullet boyfriend Magic Mike usually puts me right to sleep. Not this time, though. Overthinking the whole conversation about my nonexistent crush on Landon ruins my o.

God damn it. I *had* a crush. That's what pubescents *do*.

It's not like I followed his hockey career or something. Or watched his uni games at Michigan, or had his stats memorized when he got drafted and signed with Ottawa.

No, that wasn't me.

Nope. I *definitely* don't have a crush on him anymore.

Why the hell would I—*an accomplished, litigating, boss bitch, if I say so myself*—be hung up on a glorified meathead who sided with my bullies?

CHAPTER 3:
SMASH OR PASS

LANDON

FUCK MY LIFE.

I hauled ass my whole career for this chance. Didn't screw around at university. Laid low as a rookie and kept my head down for the last five years while the team built up. Focused on the game and the game only.

One slip-up. The *one* time I think with my dick, and it all comes crashing down. And the dogshit-covered cherries on top are the rumors around why I yakked. Gossiping dirtbags. They throw around headlines like "*Radek Addicted to Pills?*" and "*Regents Star on a Bender*" like being dehydrated wasn't a possibility. Worse is when they claim it's an admission of Ann's false accusations.

Four fucking games in a row I choked. Missed goals. Stolen pucks. Eating shit on the ice. Fighting when it got too frustrating then shitting myself watching the team tank from the sin bin. And the Cup slipped through my goddamn hands.

I scratch out the scribble on a paper napkin, distracted by ruminating anger. What was the beginning of a woman's face is now destroyed. Furious disappointment takes over the anxiety. So much for leading the team. I let them down. I let myself down. I'd much rather grieve in private, but here we are. Drinking away the pain while DJ Kumquat shamelessly mixes country with electronica.

The guys scatter throughout the nightclub's roped-off upper level. Their silent avoidance means they're pissed off but are civil enough not to give me more shit. Olsen and Szecze take shot after shot with a few busty blondes in skimpy dresses. Desperate for a chance. Puck bunnies, every single one.

A bored Fletch scrolls through his phone next to Wade, who grimaces at Jaeger. Our captain's got his girl seated in his lap. He was a bigger grouch before he started dating Skylar. She's fucking awesome. How she and Wade are best friends is beyond me.

Skylar coddles Derrick, mouthing what I imagine are sweet assurances with every caress on his jaw and cheek. He nuzzles into her neck, soaking in all her sunshine. The man's totally soft for her.

Wade glowers and makes a face when they start making out. "*Gross.*"

Jaeg's middle finger flies up from where his hand rested on Skylar's back. It turns and plants into Wade's forehead, the lone digit moving him away. The invader of personal space sets his drink down and karate-chops Jaeger's forearm before jumping to his feet and stomping over to the teammates knocking back drinks.

"Scotch?" Cooke, the light-footed sneak, shows up next to me.

I tuck the doodle into my jacket pocket, accepting the lowball glass. He claps a firm hand on my back as he sits, the amber liquid almost splashing out before I throw it back in one swallow.

"Don't worry, man. We're gonna hire the best lawyer on the hill to handle it."

"Lawyer? For what?"

"Wake up and read the news."

I stopped after the substance abuse allegations.

"They've got pictures of you with more women and Pall keeps adding to the story. Making you out to be some conniving playboy. Saying you're breaching the contract's family clause."

"*Ugh*, what a nightmare." My fingers rub into my face and jaw. "I told you. Whatever she's saying, it's not true." I dig out my phone. "Can't I call Annalise and clear things?"

"Fuck no, you can't! Are you *insane*? We need that lawyer. What Pall's doing, it's slander. Maybe defamation, too. You're losing money, your performance stinks while your reputation's dragged through the mud. Hell, the whole team is affected."

Twist the knife, why don't ya?

I hang my head. My dress shoes are suddenly interesting.

"Remember that whole scandal with Senator Pearson? With the aide claiming misconduct?"

"Vaguely."

"This is the lawyer who won his case. We can fight this. Smooth it all out. By next season, you're scot-free." He pats his hands clean.

I'm not in the wrong, but it doesn't look like this will go away on its own. And I don't wanna fucking deal with it anymore. "Fine. Whatever it takes."

"Thank you! She's gonna be here later. I'll introduce you."

She? Great. Just what I need. Another woman in my life.

"Actually" —he peers down to his phone and stands— "she might be here already. Lemme go find her."

Cooke leaves without another glance, passing Wade, who hones in on my sorry ass. Not now, man. Let me wallow in peace. He marches over and plops himself down, setting two beer bottles on the table in front of us. Wade pushes one over, but I shake my head in refusal. If I drink any more tonight, it'll be alone on my couch at home.

"You're fucking depressing."

I glare at him and rumble out my annoyance.

His eyes brighten, dopey, toothy smile shining in the black lights. "I know something that will cheer you up."

"You find a way to get us back into the finals? Or do you have a secret time-traveling machine that can undo the past two weeks? No?"

"Smash or pass."

"Aw, *come on*." I tut. I'm in no mood.

Fletch fumbles over and lands on the other side of Wade. "What's going on over here?"

"A good ol' game of smash or pass."

"Nice! I'll start. I saw these hotties. Where'd they go?" He rubs his hands together, scanning left. "There."

A petite, fair-skinned girl with bright red lips sips from a straw and nods rapidly, her ample rack bouncing every which way.

Fletcher points. "I like her. She looks feisty."

"Cute, but pass."

Wade rejects her, too. "Pass. Too little for me."

"You're both *stupid*." Fletch wrinkles his nose and leans back on the lounger. "I like 'em little." He grabs invisible hips in the air and lifts his crotch. "I'd sit her on my cock and spin her like a top."

Wade puffs his cheeks, chortling. "Yeah, *right*. You can't even fucking talk to her."

"I could talk to her!" Fletcher slurs, faltering as he straightens. "I'll go talk to her right now!"

"Alright, big boy. Let's see. I'll give you a hundred if you do." Wade stretches an arm, inviting him to go ahead. "Five hundred if you get her number."

"I'm going!" Fletch makes it to his feet and tugs at his jacket, twisting his neck in prep. "See? I'm going."

Wade shoos him with his hand. "Off you go."

Fletcher grumbles over his shoulder as he moves toward the group.

I frown and nod, impressed at how brave alcohol has made our shy teammate. "Whoa. He's really gonna do it."

"Wait." Wade's lip curls in the corner.

Fletch's determined strides stop abruptly outside the small circle of women. He freezes, then pivots right towards the bar, slumping onto the counter where he wags a finger at the bartender.

"Told ya. Chicken shit."

"Well" —I slap my knees, about to get up— "as fun as this was..."

Wade shoves me down. "We're not done. Be a pal, Landy. You may be out of luck with women, but I for sure ain't going home alone tonight."

I don't have the energy to fight him.

Wade motions back to the women. "What about the tall one?"

"Pass."

"You're a fucking liar. You wouldn't smash that? I can't see her face, but her body is fuckin..." Wade grunts out a series of *unhs*, drawing out a curvy silhouette with his hands.

"Do you know who that is, Wade?" I shift and squint to make sure. "That's Gabe Finch, the sportscaster. She's gonna be covering the games next year. And she's taken."

"*Psht*," he putters. "Taken doesn't mean married. Taken girls can be *untaken* when they see the size of my—"

My brows rise in warning. "She's engaged to Kurt Vaughn."

"The Toronto Towers center?"

"Yep."

"Damn, *fine*. Not Gabe Finch. You're such a cock block." He huffs then taps on his chin, seemingly in deep thought. Though I don't know what deep thoughts Wade Boehner could have. Actually, I have an idea, but I don't want to think about them. "What about the one standing next to her?"

"Which one?"

"Dimples. In the black onesie pantsuit."

Whoa. Who is that? "Onesie pantsuit?" That's not what that's called. It's a romper. No, a jumper. A jumpsuit? Fuck, whatever it is, it looks fucking good. Insanely good.

Full tits, little waist, *great* ass. She squats, for sure. Can't see her legs from the loose fabric of the pants, but they're as long as this fucking day. She's tall, but not quite as much as Gabe Finch.

Graceful fingers tuck her hair behind an ear as she smiles, coy and restrained. The ends brush across her shoulders when she turns to talk to the little one Fletch likes. Deep dimples pit each pretty cheek. Her eyes gleam, cutting across the room like daggers in the dark lighting, reflecting the purples and blues. My heart thuds away. She wets those full lips. Lips shaped like a bow I want gift-wrapped around my—

Wade elbows me, clearing his throat. "Yeah. *Wow*. Smash or pass, Landy?"

"Smash." I gulp down the hoarse whisper, staring like an imbecile. I can't blink. There's something familiar about her. Something familiar and comforting.

"Atta boy."

This must be what talking to beautiful women is like for Fletcher Donovan. I'm paralyzed in my seat. Can't budge. I'm fucking entranced by this gorgeous girl I have no business engaging with. I force my eyes to pull away. My hands wring between my knees.

I already kissed the Cup goodbye this year. No need to repeat the same mistake for the rest of my career. Nope. *No* women. Singular focus.

"I'm going home." And wanking myself to death.

Wade scoffs. "You're not gonna go over there?"

"No way. I got my hands full with the press on my ass."

"*Literally.*"

"Zip it." I jab him in the shoulder. "I don't care if she's God's gift to man, I'm not fucking around with *any* chicks this season."

CHAPTER 4:
SWORD FIGHTING

INDI

THERESA GIACHETTI IS *VERY* PERSUASIVE.

It's the only explanation I have for ending up in the VIP section of Persepolis on a busy Friday night to meet Cooke Wagner and Landon Radek.

"It's a hell of a contract, Indi. We can't pass it up," she said. "Plus, it's amazing publicity."

"Didn't we get enough publicity with the Pearson case?" I hated how exposing it was. I also hated how I had to break down another woman so a man could maintain his image, even if she was at fault. It haunted my feminist spirit.

"But this is different! That was politics. This is sports and entertainment!"

I sighed. "Can't you assign Thomas to it or something?"

*"Thomas is a dim-witted ass-kisser, and you know it. I can't give him this big of a fish. I trust **you**." She moved to the front of her desk. "I want you to succeed, Indi." When she leaned back against the edge, her voice lowered. "I'm not gonna run this place on my own forever, you know."*

If she's serious about making me a partner, I can't say no. I've been working my twenties away for an opportunity like this.

"Fine. I'll meet Wagner." But I won't like it.

"Yes!" She pulled down a fist in victory and strode back to her office chair. "Persepolis. Tomorrow night. Take your friends along. Drinks are on the client. I'll tell Nance to share the contact with Bea. Go get 'em!"

Wagner and I talk business for a few minutes. When he excuses himself, I'm more than unsure about the situation. And since I lost count of how many free drinks I impatiently glugged down to tame my nerves, the girls cut me off.

"If I'm gonna represent Landon Radek, he's gonna pay top dollar," I tell Gabe and Bea, pressing my finger into the opposite palm. They nip at their drinks and exchange approving glances. "It's not like he doesn't have it."

"So you're open to taking the case?" Bea jumps excitedly on the balls of her feet.

Landon may have tricked me into thinking he was some nice-boy-next-door back in grade seven, but that's ancient history. I won't fall for his charming act. Or brutal good looks.

"Nobody panic, *buuuuutttt*" —Gabe dips down to us, whispering behind a hand— "I think that's him. On the black couch in the gray suit." Bea and I idle half a minute before we cartoonishly peek around either side of our friend's frame.

Fuck me. He's better-looking in person. Like Chris Evans cloned himself, but the clone is taller and beefier and outrageously hot in a suit. Pathetic. I'm pathetic. Is he looking at me? Why is he staring? Act natural. My gut twists. Stuffing my face with Instant Maggi for dinner was a mistake. What am I saying? Maggi is never a mistake. Coming *here* was a mistake.

"I think I need to go home."

"Home?" Gabe asks. "We just got here! You haven't met—"

"Don't care. Gotta go. It's an emergency." I tug at their hands.

"Indi." Gabe grabs both of my arms. "Tell me you're not avoiding Radek."

"A *poop* emergency." The sweat beads on my brow and upper lip are convincing enough. It has them bee-lining behind me into a cab.

We stop at my place first since I'm the one with the supposed GI issue.

"Feel better, Indi!" Bea waves through the open window as the car peals away.

I rush towards the entrance and hastily wave back without looking.

A heap of unfolded laundry awaits when I enter the apartment. I throw my clutch on top and shovel the pile to the other side of the sectional so I, too, can become a heap on the sofa. My stomach gurgles, settling with the pressure of my weight against the cushion. I slip off the back of my shoes with my big toes, sighing out while unzipping this awful one-piece to unhook my bra and conk out without trying.

Horrible rattling wakes me the next morning. I fumble for the phone, ending its racket by unlocking it and squinting through mascara-clumped eyelashes at the screen.

THERESA

How'd it go? Did you meet Radek?

ME

I met Cooke Wagner.

ME

The client was unavailable.

Not entirely a lie. I *didn't* see Landon after I thought I caught him staring.

THERESA

I see.

Maybe she'll give me a break. It's Saturday after all. I groan and roll, expecting a plush embrace of cushion, but it's the wrong way. "*Wlah!*" Off the edge of the couch, I fall with an unceremonious thump. "*Ow.* My back is broken."

A low voice with a robotic lilt gives me permission to die.

Bane? Is this one of those inception dreams? I jolt upright from the rug-covered floor to see Gabe mouthing the rim of a coffee cup at the kitchen island. She hacks out a gravelly, villainous laugh. "*Muahahahahaha!*"

"You jerk!" I launch a decorative suede pillow from the couch in her direction. She dodges it. "You scared the shit out of me."

"You're so *easy.*" She looks downward at my bra-less chest and the straps slouching from my shoulders. "Rough night, eh?"

I zip back up to avoid giving her a free show. "*You're* easy!" Hissing at the too-loud volume of my own voice and lack of decent comeback, I sandwich my head between two rogue throw pillows. "I'm too old for this. How are you alive right now?"

"I'm a halfie. Dad's Swedish blood is mostly vodka."

"How nice for you." When I recline back to the floor with another groan, my phone buzzes again.

THERESA

Find another time to make it happen.

"*Ugh*, Theresa. Let me be."

"I thought you liked her?" Gabe rounds the sectional and steps over my ailing body to have a seat. The aroma of fresh, hot coffee lingers.

"I do, but that doesn't mean I wanna deal with her while my head is exploding. Also" —I shield my eyes with the inside of my elbow, wishing away the sunlight— "what the hell are you doing here so early?"

"First of all, it's 10 a.m. And Kurt stayed at his after a long day of training. He's working out today, too."

I peek from under my elbow at her sullen face.

"I got lonely." Gabe stares at the white lid covering her drink.

"Did you talk to him yet about moving in together?"

"No. There hasn't been a good time. "

This hangover needs to die so I can support my friend. My head pounds harder when I sit up and drape an arm over her knees. "Everything okay with you two?"

"Yeah, I think so. He's stressed out over the team not making the playoffs this year. And I haven't been around during the transition."

"Makes sense." I hum, rubbing her knee. "By the way, if I knew he was proposing, I would've taken pictures and showed up to celebrate after."

"I know," she intones, palming my forearm. "But he wanted it to be private. It was nice, just the two of us."

Kurt's alright, if not a little elusive. They've been together nearly three years and we've hung out maybe five times. I get that pro-athletes have demanding schedules, but he's hard to read. Gabe seems happy, though, and I don't want to throw a wrench in her happiness because of my general distrust of men.

"I'm glad you had a good time." I scoot my ass to lean back onto the bottom of the couch. By the lull that follows, she doesn't want to talk about it more. I don't push it. "*Please* tell me you brought me an iced latte."

Gabe reaches over and passes me a clear cup, ice crackling against the liquid and plastic sides on its way to my open hands. "With caramel."

"*Mmm, yes.* Come to *momma.*" I wanna put my face in a giant bowl of this stuff and stay there for the day.

There's a reason I don't drink often. Two and I'm done. Last night, I had eleventy rum and Cokes. After a few pulls of delicious caffeine, my stomach garbles out a whale song. "I need food."

Gabe smiles and pats my head. "It's so cute how you can't handle alcohol."

I glare back at her smug smile and pinch the flesh of her thigh.

"Truce! Truce." She winces and wrenches her legs away, holding up a hand in surrender. "Want brunch? My treat."

"Deal."

After a weekend of napping through the rest of that wicked hangover and folding laundry—*why is there so much?*—Sunday ends with the scaries for the incoming workweek.

But, as usual, I haul my ass to the office Monday morning, ice-cold caffeine in my veins and shooting outta-my-way Miranda Priestly-esque insults left and right to the lackadaisical summer tourists blocking foot traffic.

Radek's agent sends me an invite to some charity game the Regents are playing against a local beer league team. It's for the Community Food Bank. A noble cause. Management probably signed them up for it to counter all the bad press. I doubt any of those rich jocks care about the hungry.

Piles of paperwork in the aftermath of a previous case take me late into Thursday evening and I won't make it to the game in time. I call the agent to cancel.

"This is Wagner."

"Hi. It's Indira Davé from Giachetti Law."

"Ms. Davé! Good to hear from you."

"Sorry, Cooke. I'm still at the office. Is there a chance we can reschedule?"

"I'd like to meet if you're available. Giachetti told me you're a fan. Why don't you meet me at the CTC?"

"I don't know if that's—"

"The game ended but I can show you around, meet some of the team, and Radek, of course."

"*Eh*," I reply, hoping he hears my hesitation. "I usually have the client come to the office and speak with me in private."

"Oh, for sure, for sure. I'll get it on the schedule for next week. This is super informal, though. The guys are about to cool down and get clean. Come through the secure lot. I'll meet you there."

Before I can conjure up an excuse, he hangs up. I get why he and Theresa get along. Neither like the word no.

Time to put on your big girl panties, Indi. This is your career on the line. You can keep it together in front of brainless hockey bros for a few minutes.

The Porsches, Lambos, and Maseratis lining the staff lot make my Audi RS7 look like a junkyard salvage. This is where the zeros in those eight-figure salaries go. I don't care what Gabe said. They're overcompensating for something.

Cooke greets me at the security entrance, giving me a quick tour of the rink while the Zamboni cleans up. "And *this* is the locker room." He points ahead as we near.

It triggers memories I'd rather keep hidden. The taunts. The smell of sweaty gear. Ick.

"Ms. Davé?"

"Yeah." I shake it off.

"You wanna go in and see?"

"Is that allowed?" I've seen the renovated space on TV. They did a piece on the 9 o'clock news.

Cooke shakes hands and high-fives a couple of exiting players. "Sure. They've closed it off for the press these days, but you're fine. Though it can get a little hairy, *if you know what I mean.* Let's wait for Radek out here."

I don't mean to, but I scoff. Men's locker rooms don't scare me. This sexist nitwit doesn't know shit. I'm a grown-ass woman. My posture tightens. I unbutton and smooth down my blazer. "I can handle it."

His phone buzzes. Cooke shrugs and raises a skeptical eyebrow. "I gotta take this." He motions to the phone. "Go at your own risk."

Whatever. I'll introduce myself to Radek.

Two huge men come toward me when I enter. I recognize them from the roster: Fletcher Donovan by his ginger features and freckles and Theron Olsen by his pale blond tresses and burly stature. The latter groans and runs a hand down the front of his button-down, rubbing his belly, unfazed and unaware of my presence. "Dude, you should have seen the size of the massive dookie I dropped—"

Ah, yes. The pride and joy of Ottawa. Fucking fools. Their lazy saunter comes to a halt when they nearly bump into me.

"Gentlemen."

"*Jeez*—" Donovan at least has the decency to blush a bright red.

Olsen, on the other hand, sports a toothless grin. "Sorry."

Can't wait to tell Bea we told her so. I chuckle to myself. He doesn't look sorry. He looks like his last brain cell is as toothless as he is. I push past them.

An open entryway reveals jerseys hanging in separate cubicles. The smell—*oh, God, the smell!*—punches my nostrils. I blocked musty gear stench from memory. It's eighty-percent bacteria and twenty-percent pure evil. I suck in a sharp breath through my mouth, bracing myself before stepping through.

Heavy footsteps scamper about between grunts. "Take that, you jag!"

I roll my eyes, knowing almost for certain it's another set of fully-grown professional athletes behaving like children. Probably wrestling or something.

How wrong I am.

Landon Radek and Wade Boehner jostle about, completely buck naked. I freeze. They don't.

My brain short-circuits at the sight of those tight muscles: pecs and arms and abs and thighs and asses, flexing and straining as they chase each other, sword-fighting with their...*oh, my God.*

They're fully-grown, alright. Fully-grown penises. They fist the enormous things in their equally enormous hands.

The shock hits me like a bus. Or truck. A truck of fat dick. I'm shocked, and a little in awe. Those are *really* big penises. Maybe it's because it's been *way* too long since I've seen a live one, but the sheer size of them drives my pulse into a tailspin. Saliva pools in my mouth. And there are *two*. Gabe *was* right. Holy...wow. I'm a pervert. A disgusting pervert. I backpedal one step. My traitorous mouth chokes out a gasp.

Now they stop. My knees lock as Radek and Boehner stiffen and turn to face me. Heat creeps up my neck, searing the tops of my ears and cheeks. My eyes wander to Landon's chiseled jaw and broad, square chest. Twenty-pack abs sit between hips forming a delicious v, like an arrow directing my gaze right to the thick, perfect specimen in his palm.

My tent flaps twitch. Easy, girl.

Wade smirks in the periphery, his toned thighs looking like they could crush a watermelon. He bites his lip while giving me a once-over, still holding on to his third leg like it's the last breath of air on Earth. It might as well be.

What is air, even? What is breathing?

Landon cups his groin with both hands, eyes widening, studying me. "*You.*"

I can't tell if it's a question or a pointed accusation. His chest heaves, shifting the damp brown hairs hanging across his forehead. Those big, blue eyes narrow.

"It's you."

CHAPTER 5:
NOT NOW, HE-MAN

LANDON

MOM

Good luck tonight!

DAD

Sorry to miss it, bud.

ME

No worries, guys.

DELANEY

Here's hoping you don't trip and fall into any more vaginas on camera.

ME

Fuck off.

DAD

Too far, Lane. Too far.

DELANEY

Fine. Have a good game.

ME

Eat a dick, Delaney.

DELANEY

Don't mind if I do.

My older sister's not half as hilarious as she thinks. I toss the phone into my bag and slide on my helmet and gloves, giving Wade a mindless, pre-game chest bump before we head out of the lockers and to the rink.

Top Beer Cheese gives us a hell of a laugh. It's much needed. The whole team's been on edge since the Fire won the Cup everyone predicted would be ours.

Jaeger and I got Simon, the new publicity guy that replaced Annalise, hooked up with our contact at the Food Bank. We volunteer at their soup kitchen one or two holidays a year, schedule permitting. It's his project, if I'm honest. Jaeg grew up poor in a tiny Nova Scotia town and the man's made good for himself.

Skylar jogs towards Jaeger in the hallway after the game ends, brimming with warm smiles sunshine. "*Babyyyyyy!*"

His face lights up from its usual scowl. Jaeg tips his helmet back and spits out his guard, letting her jump into his open embrace, stick crossing her back while her limbs twine around the bulk of his pads.

"Hi, my sweetheart." It's an audible but low murmur. My guy is so far gone.

They peck a few times as he moves further down the hall, carrying her to the changing room. I turn and keep ahead to give them some privacy, but Skylar's muted giggles can only mean they're about to stick their tongues down each other's throats.

I'm envious. Dating and one-night stands are out.

Summer training is your woman now. Gonna tear that shit up.

Cooke catches me as I'm getting rid of my skates. "Landy!"

I groan and sigh while cracking my toes against the floor.

"Nice work out there!" He shoots me a cheesy salesman smile. "Hit the showers soon, hey? You've got a guest."

"A guest?"

"Yep. The sharp lawyer you're hiring. Giachetti told me she was the youngest woman to work in the Supreme Court."

Perfect. "What do I have to do?"

"Nothing yet. I'm about to give her a tour, then I'll swing by to introduce you." He tightens and straightens the silk knot in his tie before turning to the door and calling over his shoulder. "Amp up the charm, eh? She's kind of a hardass."

"Isn't she on our side?"

"Not yet, but we *definitely* want her to be." Cooke taps the top of the door jamb twice as he exits. "Be yourself. Play nice."

After peeling away my pads, I go to cool off on the bikes as Wade teaches Fletch and Szecze yet another TikTok dance for the team account. I get bored after their five-hundred-and-twenty-seventh attempt at coordinated twerking and hit the showers.

The heated, forceful spray soothes the tightness in my shoulders and lower back. Olsen snickers from the end of the row, collecting water in the skin of his nutsack. Yikes. An intermittent buzzing gets louder and louder. Next to me, Wade takes an electric razor to the pecker, his pubes free-falling to the floor in giant clumps before rolling away like miniature tumbleweeds.

"Manscape at home, Boehner." I reach out to shove him. He elbows my hand away. "Shedding it isn't gonna make *that* any bigger."

Wade turns off the wireless trimmer with a snort. "Am I giving you a complex, Landy?"

"Fuck no. Your green bean has nothing on He-Man."

"Green bean? Chinese eggplant's more like it. And He-Man? *Fuck*, you're ancient." He rinses off, lowering and lifting his gaze, then sends me a side-eye. "You wanna go? We can go right now." He palms his dick in a tight grip.

"Really? What are we, thirteen?"

"Loser buys winner double-doubles and Timbits of choice the whole season."

"Oh, it's *on*." I crack my neck both ways, pumping a fist down He-Man's length once, like the cocking of a rifle. "You'll have to remember I like the chocolate ones."

"Won't have to," he says, bouncing alternate feet like a boxer. "You'll be buying me ten packs of blueberry all year." Wade lunges, slashing at the air with his semi. "Take that, you jag!"

He's an agile little shit, escaping my attacks from every direction. I contemplate ending it by kneeing him in the balls, but a loud gasp cuts our fight short. We still.

For a second, I think I'm daydreaming, but Wade must see her, too, from that shit-eating grin forming on his dumb face.

Her. She was at Persepolis after that last loss.

Fuck, she looks good in a tight skirt. A skirt suit, no less. The surprise pales her tan skin. Her incredible tits rise and fall, their round tops peeking above the scooping neckline of her white top. A blush blooms across her face and my dick hardens again. Not now, He-Man. Not in front of the pretty lady.

Her eyes, a warm brown, widen as she darts them in a triangle between us. Me, then downstairs me, Wade, and back at me. And...*shit.* I'm gawking with my cock in hand. Both hands slap over my groin. It's not exactly a difficult task to hide, considering my balls have retreated into my guts.

"*You.*" Why do I sound like that? Pull yourself together, man! I swallow a breath, attempting to slow my pounding heart. My mouth is a bastard. "It's *you.*"

She backs away in quickened steps, disappearing behind the open entryway.

"We calling that a truce? And who the *fuck* was that?" Wade asks as I grumble curses under my breath and march over to my locker. "See how embarrassed she got?" My clueless teammate rambles on, "Shy girls are fucking *hooooot.* Freaks in bed, I tell ya." He turns his head, wiggling his eyebrows. "Think she'll give me her number?"

This fool went to Harvard, but I swear he's one of the biggest idiots I've ever met.

"You know what? *Go for it.*"

"Yeah?" His face lights up after pulling it through the collar of a white tee. "Where do you know her from?"

"I don't." I tug on a pair of boxer briefs, then push my arms through the sleeves of the white button-down I wore to the rink. "She was at that club." Wade shakes his head and shrugs like he doesn't know what I'm talking about. "When you said you'd bang Gabe Finch."

"*Ay-oh!*" He lifts a palm to get a high-five, sticking his tongue out between his teeth. I stop buttoning to roll my eyes, then reluctantly give it to him. "*Ohhhhh. That's* the girl you wanted to smash?"

"I want to smash *no* girl." I scoff back, tucking the shirt ends into open navy slacks. At this point, all women are bad news. "But I'm gonna see if I can apologize to her. And then I have to find Cooke and my—"

Lawyer. No.

"Oh...*no, no, no, nooooo!*" How did I not figure this out sooner? Fuck, fuck, fuck.

"Your? Your who?" Wade calls after me. "Finish the sentence!"

Scrambling to put on socks and hopping into my favorite cognac Wingtips, I fumble towards the door. It hits the wall behind it with a comic *wham.* A couple of the boys peer over their shoulders at the crash from where they stand with Cooke.

Good news: she's at the end of the hall and I can catch up with her. Bad news: she's with Cooke, too, confirming my fears. Her arms cross, pushing that already perky rack up and together. Snap out of it, Landy. This is no time to think about tits!

I puff out my cheeks, mentally prepping myself for the consequences of this brand-new dumpster fire. It's like I've got a target on my back for disaster after disaster. My strides slow as I approach. Szecze and Jaeg sidestep and back away, their faces cringing once they're out of Cooke's sight. And my lawyer. *My lawyer.* Who saw me naked as the day I was born.

My stomach twists. Her eyes are no longer soft, cheeks no longer flushed. They're flat, deadpan, the same as her expression. She shoots a stoic stare my way. How did she flip a switch like that? One second, she's blushing and flustered and the next, she acts like nothing happened.

"Radek!" My overzealous agent claps his hands together and waves me closer. "Get over here."

Her glance fires over from him to me, seemingly unimpressed.

I clear my throat. "Landon Radek," I say, extending a hand.

She doesn't miss a beat, returning a firm shake and polite, professional half-smile.

"This is Indira Davé."

Hold up. "*Indira* Davé?" And I thought her brown eyes couldn't get any bigger. They stretch when I repeat myself. "Indira *Davé*?"

"Yes, Ms. Davé was recommended by—"

She jolts at the surprised laugh I interrupt Cooke with.

I can't fucking believe it. *That's* why she looked so familiar. "Indi?"

CHAPTER 6:
EVERYTHING'S FINE

INDI

NOW I'VE GONE AND DONE IT. WHY DIDN'T I CLOSE MY eyes and run *immediately*? I should have apologized for intruding, for staring, but the *penises*. They were right there, so big and distracting. My palm slaps my forehead. This temporary lapse of judgment may have cost us a major client contract. Top-notch work, Indi.

Cooke smirks as I return to the hall, dropping his phone into his pocket. "You look like you've seen some things."

'Things' is right. *Plural*. Alright, play it cool, Davé. You could still bag this. Repeat after me: partner, partner, partner. My eyes relax and I straighten my shoulders, releasing the tension knotted in my neck. "Not really," I say, cool and composed. "Mr. Radek must have been occupied."

"*Hmm.*" He twists his mouth. "I swear he was in there." His feet shift against the low carpet, and he pulls out his phone again. When the door to the locker room re-opens, my breath hitches. But it's not him.

Two suit-clad starters emerge instead. Cooke beckons them with a sharp whistle.

"Derrick Jaeger. Blake Szeczin. This is the lawyer we're hoping will take Radek's case."

They nod as we shake hands. "Indira Davé."

Szeczin narrows his eyes a bit, dipping his ear in my direction. "Sorry. Say that again?"

"*Davé.* D-a-v-e—"

"*Ohhh.* Dave!" He cuts me off. "Why didn't you say that the first time?"

Excuse me? Absolutely not. "It's not *Dave*. It's *Davé. Duh-vey*. The *e* has an accent."

"Dave, Davé. Same difference, hey?"

I thought being undermined and unaccepted—*in hockey, university, law school*—was a thing of the past, sheared away by professional success and a significant glow-up. Old insecurities threaten to resurface, but I push them down. These jerks have no idea who they're dealing with.

Cooke stammers out a nervous chuckle. "*Uh*, whoa. *Err...*"

My jaw clacks shut, teeth shifting with a silent grind. "*No*, it's not. I'm sure you can understand, Mr. *Szeczin.*" If the world can manage to say Szeczin, this oaf can try to say Davé.

Cooke opens his mouth to apologize, but I hold up a hand to stop him. I don't need his pity or help. "It was nice meeting you."

Derrick Jaeger scowls at his teammate and shakes his head. "A real pleasure, Ms. Davé."

The door snaps open again, this time revealing the man himself.

Damn. I'm really gonna have to act like a put-together, professional human when he looks like *that* in a suit. I mean, I've seen him in his birthday suit, and this might be better. Okay, no. What am I saying? It's a tie. A tie? I'd use a tie on him. *Mmm.* No! Focus, Indi.

Landon's bumbling steps even out when he nears. The two others take their cue and make a swift exit. Cooke sighs out, seemingly relieved to end the awkward silence in this conversation.

"Radek! Get over here."

"Landon Radek." He holds out his hand. The same one he held his dick with.

This is fine. I'm fine. Everything's *fine.* I've seen your peen and I'm mature enough to move beyond it for the chance to make partner.

I put on the kindest smile I can muster as Cooke introduces me, ignoring the goosebumps coming to life from being this close to Landon. Wow, he smells clean. Like fresh laundry and citrusy soap. I could get off on that scent alone. No. You stop that. Bad, bad coochie!

"This is Indira Davé."

Radek's brows dip, face falling to a frown. "Indira Davé?" God, why? Is the deep timbre of his voice not torture enough? The way he says my name—*and correctly*. Gah. My pussy is sweating. "Indira *Dave*?"

The second time is worse. My pits are sweating, too.

"Yes." Cooke switches his glance between us. "Ms. Davé was recommended by—"

"Indi?" Landon says through a gasping chuckle, his worried eyes growing into surprise and shimmering with the bluest of blues. "Indi! It's me! Landon! We played together on the Lightning? In the U13 league back in Mississauga?"

Well, shit on a hockey stick. He recognizes me. But how? I don't look like the Michelin Man anymore.

I grew too tall, too quickly to be as graceful and controlled as the other ice skaters. The coach was more than discouraged by my height while petite peers voiced nasty comments about my too-full chest and chubby midsection. To my mother's disappointment, I quit.

Discovering my size was an advantage whenever I played a friendly neighborhood game, I begged to join the local ice hockey team. Being five-foot-six at twelve years old and fifteen pounds heavier than most of the boys, and agile from years of ice skating made me the perfect goalie.

Convincing the league was the first challenge of many.

My father, a tall, hefty brown man with black, shoulder-length hair and a full beard, poked a finger into the chest of a moon-faced league coordinator. "Bollocks!" His British accent was strong when angry. "There's nothing in the rulebook about not having girls on the team."

*"Listen. There are only **boys**—" he emphasized, "—on this team. There are other all-girl teams. It's easier to manage—"*

"Easier to manage?" Dad scoffed. "How is it easier to manage paying exorbitant fees when there's a perfectly good, sponsored team available?"

"But the lockers—"

He had a point there. I'd rather be buried alive than have to change with boys my age.

"Do the facilities not provide girls' locker rooms? If so, you've got bigger problems than me, mate."

The man threw his hands up, making his beer gut wiggle in a wave. "Girls can't keep up! Boys are rougher, faster—"

"Pardon?" Dad wasn't having it. "That's rubbish. You have no idea what she's capable of. Why don't you let her try out? If she can't 'keep up' with the lads, we'll leave." He folded his arms across a huffing chest.

Coach Alexei laughed when I shutout that one little shit named Bryce

Bennett. *"That's not beginner's luck, kiddo. That's skill. We could use a decent tendy."* *He tapped my helmet.*

The crease was my jam. Breaks between bursts of action gave me time to think. The looks of disappointment from the opposing team when they couldn't get a puck past me was thoroughly enjoyable. But the biggest bonus? Seeing Landon. I liked the way he skated, so smooth and effortless. I liked when he smiled even more.

At the time, I thought Landon was my friend, but he'd chosen Bryce and those jerks over me.

"Indi?" Landon asks again. I blink away the hurt and compose myself. The surprise morphs into joy as he flicks his eyes up and down. "*What!* I can't believe this." One hand reaches up to rub the side of his neck, a smile widening through his neat brown beard.

Cooke gapes in the fringe of my sight. "You two *know* each other?"

"Hell yeah! We go *way* back—"

How despicable. Acting all buddy-buddy, casually calling me by my nickname as if he had nothing to do with faking our friendship and participating in cruel jokes.

My belly knots with bitter memories I have no intention of revisiting. Seeing him naked was one excuse. Him pretending like we're long-lost pals is another. Theresa will have to find someone else.

This would've been easier to get through if he had forgotten me. If *I* could forget. But some scars never heal. They remain superficial, delicate enough for any passing blade to nick the tender flesh and leave a fresh wound behind.

I haven't gotten to this point in life by walking around with my bare heart on my sleeve. And I'm not starting today.

"I'm sorry. It's Ms. Davé. And you don't *know* me, Mr. Radek. We played on the same team *one* season, fifteen years ago." My icy tone slices through the glint in his eyes, their blue spark fading. I almost feel bad. Almost.

"Oh, *uh*..." Cooke's at a loss again.

"You'll have to excuse me. I've had a long day and it's getting late." I lift my phone to check for any notifications to pass off as emergencies. No luck there. This is what I get for not having a life. "Ms. Giachetti was adamant on meeting with you, but I'm not sure I'm the right person to represent you. I'll speak to her early next week and advise her to provide a more appropriate counsel."

I wish them a good night and turn on my heel, pulling the keys from my blazer pocket while searching for the exit.

In the privacy of my car, I drop my forehead against the top rim of the steering wheel. A series of thuds syncs with my chant. "Stupid, stupid, stupid." My hand pushes off the horn too hard and the loud honk startles me.

Knuckles tapping on the glass make me jump again.

A burly security guard lowers to mid-window and squints at me. "Everything okay, ma'am?"

"*Uh*, yes." I show him a weak smile. "Everything's perfect. I'm leaving."

He responds with a single nod and points. "The yellow arrows lead out. Have a good night."

It *will* be a good night, once I get home and crawl into a bottle of wine. Hell, I might call it a work-from-home day tomorrow and stay there the whole weekend.

With that exact intention, I switch out my pencil skirt and blazer for my favorite panda bear printed pjs and a ratty t-shirt from my university's debate team. The three days out of the office allow me enough time to practice the spiel I'll give my boss when I turn down Landon's case.

———

Fueled by double shots of espresso in my iced latte, I give Theresa the update in our Monday morning one-on-one. She stops the constant swiveling in her desk chair with a squeak.

"What do you mean, '*you don't want the case?*'"

"I meant exactly what I said. I did what you asked: I met Wagner, I met Radek. I'm not interested."

My boss studies me through the thin slits of her eyes, pursing her lips until an array of dimples form on her chin. She's sizing me up. Scanning for lies. "Did something happen?"

Yes! I saw his wiener! And it was no regular wiener. It was an *extra-large* wiener!

"No." And it's too embarrassing to admit we played hockey together, considering how our friendship had ended. "I'm not the right person for the job."

"*Oh?*" Her brow arches sharpen. "*You*, with a better record than most lawyers holding twice your experience, are *not* the right person for the job?"

"Come on, Theresa." My pleading tone has no effect on her.

"And here I thought you *wanted* partner," she says, clicking her tongue. Her head tips back to shake out the loose, walnut brown waves hanging over her shoulders. "Shame, really."

Damn ambition. Toss the feelings in the trash, Indi. You can do this.

I groan aloud, resigning to her manipulations. "Fine. Jeez."

"So you'll do it?"

"Yes."

"No. Backing. Out." She wags her index finger at me.

"No backing out," I parrot.

Gathering evidence is easy enough. There's a handful of photographs and hundreds of articles, but nothing on personal social media is substantive. Over the course of the week, I try to corroborate the different stories, hoping one of Radek's teammates will crack and give me something. They won't talk to me. They grunt and huff through my interrogations. Loyal cavemen, every last one.

Shuffling papers to one side of the mahogany desk, I squeeze my temples with the thumb and middle finger of one hand. This headache is the kind where I'd usually lock the door, tell Bea to hold my calls, and blow off some steam with a silicone pocket rocket, but my office landline beeps. I hit the speaker button with my elbow. "Yeah?"

Bea coughs out an *ahem*. "Landon Radek is here."

Here we go. Laser-focus. You're not here to make friends. You already have those. You serve Lady Justice. You win, you make partner. *Giachetti and Davé Law Associates* has a nice ring to it.

I push off the desk surface to stand and puff out a breath. "Bring him in."

The door clicks open to Radek's sparkling smile. How annoying and chipper. Bea blushes as she ushers him in, tittering through small talk. His eyes swim when they meet mine. Calm and inviting. Like lapping ocean waves on a sunny summer day. My heart flutters.

Ouch. I'm gonna need extra bandages for those scars.

CHAPTER 7:
LIKE POETRY IN MOTION

LANDON

THAT WAS WEIRD.

If she acted like the embarrassed woman who saw my big guy a few minutes ago, it would've made sense. Sure, we'd been kids the last time we played puck. No wonder she looked familiar the other night. Had it really been fifteen years?

This wasn't the Indi I knew. The shy, kind-hearted girl with sad brown eyes, hiding under hand-me-down gear and oversized clothes? Nowhere to be found. This Indi's all bangin' curves: perky tits, tiny waist, and a round ass I wanna sink my teeth into. The baby boner I had for her in grade seven has ballooned into a big boy boner. A man boner.

And she treated me like a stranger. I know the guys back then gave her a hard time, but it was different between us. I told her things I never told any of them. Things I hadn't told my family or closest friends until much later.

"The *fuck*?" Cooke throws up his hands before balling his fists on his hips. "*Unbelievable*. She can't do that!"

"But she did." A mindless reply. I'm too occupied with how her black skirt strains against that firm backside as it turns the corner. Her ass is like poetry in motion. I need to get laid. No, you absolutely do not, you dumb fuck. You and your hands are on your own.

"Giachetti promised me her best lawyer. If that's the best they can do..."

I hum, rubbing the bristly ends of my beard with my fingers. Maybe she's right and I don't know her. But I *knew* her once and a part of me wants to know her again. As a lawyer, I mean. As a friend. Not, like, *biblically* know.

Maybe when we're alone, she'll be the Indi I remember.

"If she's the best, set up an appointment."

"You sure?" His head shakes. "I told you she was a hardass."

"That's the kinda lawyer we want, right?"

———

The following Thursday, I scan up the brick front building facing the river down the way from Parliament Hill. It's one of the older ones in this section of the city sitting alongside newer, low-rise, modern condos with black window frames and glass balconies.

Giachetti Law Associates displays in gold, embossed text on the frosted privacy panel on the door of the suite, an ode to retro business entrances. I hit the bell. They buzz me in. We catch the attention of everyone we pass, in various stages of surprise and recognition as Marie, the receptionist, guides me through the short maze of desks.

The walk ends at Indi's secretary, who skitters about, straightening her desktop mid-chew of a club sandwich. She sweeps the mix of papers, pens, highlighters, used facial tissues, and a spilling bag of potato chips into a drawer. Marie's face goes from pink to red as her colleague jumps to stand, realizing too late that her camel-colored jacket's on inside-out. She shrugs it on the right way with a nervous smile.

It takes a second to place her, but she was with Indi at Persepolis. The woman Fletch couldn't talk to.

"Sorry," she says through a puffed-out breath. "You're a little early, Mr. Radek. I'm Ms. Davé's assistant. Behraz Irani."

We shake, a quick, delicate exchange as Marie passes me off. "Nice meeting you." I smirk a knowing smirk. This'll be great to rib Fletch with later.

Her fair cheeks fill with a blush. "I'm sorry, *this*" —her pointer finger circles in the air over her workspace— "is not the usual state of my desk. I was on lunch break and—"

"No worries. I'm not here to judge."

"Right. I'll let Ms. Davé know you're here." She whispers into the digital intercom before meeting me at the front of the desk.

Behraz is sweet. Her eyes, while a darker brown than Indi's, brighten and whir to life as we chat, her hands animating the brief conversation about her day and the nice weather. She giggles between every other word. I didn't realize I was *that* good-looking. Well, I *did*, but the ego boost doesn't hurt.

Through Indi's door is not where I'll get it.

She dons an unamused smile in contrast to the pleasant atmosphere of her office. Hints of cinnamon and cranberry intensify as we near her desk, reminiscent of Thanksgiving and Christmas at Babi and Děda's farm. Nostalgia warms my chest.

Ottawa's summer sun shines through the floor-to-ceiling windows, filling the room with a mid-day glow. Its rays reach Indi's big, beautiful sable eyes and transform them into the deepest pools of honey. Comfort washes over me in her presence once more, this time sending heated blood to my gut. And downward. For a second, anyway.

"Mr. Radek. Have a seat." And with her frigid tone, *poof*. Disappeared. The moment's gone, vanishing like her secretary behind the heavy wooden door.

Time to charm the pants off her. No, not pants. God, *no*. Not pants. Everyone in this room will be keeping their pants on. She's not wearing pants. Quit thinking about her without pants!

"Hey, Indi," I intone, reclining into the cream fabric of the small armchairs. I can be cool in front of my boyhood crush. Cool and casual.

The lower lids of her eyes twitch, obligatory smile straightening as she sits. Those long fingers lace together when bringing her elbows to the clean desktop. "Please. Ms. Davé."

Oops. That had the opposite effect for what I was going for. We'll try again. "*Aw*, Indi. It's just us now." I cross an ankle over my knee, getting comfortable and clasping both hands behind my neck. "No need to be so formal. How are you?"

"I'm *great*," she shoots back. Snippy.

"Looks like it. How ya been? Where ya been?" I maintain my grin. She can't keep up the ice-queen front forever.

Her nostrils flare. "Very busy, Mr. Radek. As have you, it seems."

Was that a dig? "Have I?"

She shrugs, her eyebrows jumping for a moment. "Clients don't visit with me for *fun*."

"It's a dirty job but someone's gotta do it." How can she not laugh at that? I'm funny! I'm funny, okay?

Indi's eyes roll closed with a sigh, black, lush lashes leaving a shadow on her cheekbones. Fuck, she's pretty. Be prettier if she was kneel—

She clears her throat. "*As you know*, this is a time-sensitive appointment. We bill by the hour. While I don't doubt you can afford it..."

"It's not a problem." My smile holds strong, determined to retrieve the real Indi. The one I caught the tiniest glimpse of in the locker room. "I don't mind taking the extra time to catch up with my *ol' friend*."

The tips of her ears tinge a rosy pink. If I was closer, I'd see steam swirling from them. Indi bends toward me, wearing a cordial smile. My heart skips, elbows resting over my knees as I instinctively bend forward, too.

"I'm not sure what you're up to, but let's get one thing straight: we played on the same team for a few months as *children*. It doesn't change anything. We're adults now. You are my client, Mr. Radek. I am your lawyer. Nothing more."

How wrong she is. It changes *everything*. Especially when she looks like *that*. And especially with how we left things. Why she won't admit our past friendship is beyond me. *Fuck*, if I'm not gonna find out. She wants to play games? I compete for a living.

"Ah, yes. My *lawyer*. Your boss couldn't find anyone more *appropriate*, eh?"

Call me twisted, but I kinda like how Indi's jaw ticks at the jab of her own words thrown back, chest rising and falling in patient breaths.

"Mr. Radek..."

It's a low, stern hint of caution, causing my dick to stir. Jesus.

"You've hired me because I'm the best at what I do."

"And because we're friends."

Her eyes simmer, controlled fury crescendoing as she blinks. Blink. Blink. Blink. "We're *not* friends." Okay, more than kinda like it. I absolutely enjoy winding her up.

"Sure, we are." Lawyers like to argue, right?

"Mr. Radek," she repeats with another sigh. I'd prefer her saying my name like that under different circumstances. "Can we focus on the case? I need you to be straightforward with me."

"I'm always straightforward."

"That's nice to hear." Her hand claps on the desk. "I have many questions, but I'd like to hear your side first."

Motioning over my torso, palms spread, I melt into my seat again. "I'm an open book."

"Great." She pulls a wireless keyboard from below her iMac. "Start from the beginning."

A more perfect moment to be a smartass couldn't exist if I planned it myself. I know what she meant, but I'd rather spend the hour chipping away at Indi's frozen heart than talk about last season's shitshow. I want her to be the person I saw at the club: relaxed, intriguing, with that sweet, subtle smile. It's ridiculous, but I *really* want her to like me.

"It all started when my mom and dad fell in love. One thing led to another..."

Her typing stops, head turning from the monitor in melodramatic slo-mo. I have to pull my lips inside my mouth to hold back, but my shoulders shake with laughter.

"Is this a joke to you? You find this funny?" Her dark, full brows pucker, that plump set of muted red lips tugging to one side. Every question after warbles as I imagine how outstanding the deep shade would look spread over and staining my coc—

A beige folder slaps onto the desk, jolting me out of my distracted, ill-timed fantasy. Indi slides over a page-size version of the infamous photo blasted on the news and countless online articles. "You find this funny, too?" My smile retreats.

I fucking *hate* that picture.

She hums. "Glad to see you're finally taking this seriously. If you will let me do my job, we can probably get this settled out of court. Now" — she taps a charcoal grey, manicured nail on the horrible image— "I don't want to assume, but there is *some* truth to this picture, correct?"

The accusation stings worse than when I got chewed out by Coach. And the GM.

"I thought you're supposed to defend me, *Ms. Davé.*"

"I'm trying to. But you have to be truthful." She pauses and leans back in her chair. "Did you sleep with Annalise Pall?" Like a hot knife through butter, her critical and unfeeling gaze cuts away at my remaining composure.

My teeth grind, the grating sound scratching against my eardrums. "Last time I checked, sleeping with someone isn't a crime."

"It's not."

"Then what's your point?" In the last few minutes, she's managed to hit every last nerve. Including the one that makes my main man swell up.

"You do understand the gravity of this situation, right, Mr. Radek? We can't claim she's lying on your word alone."

"Well, she *is*."

"Okay. Which part?" A curt, snide response thrown back, complete with crossed arms.

I stay silent, withdrawing. Indi quirks an eyebrow while we lock eyes before a new photo appears on top of the previous.

"What about Callis Key, the supermodel. Were you sexually involved with her as well?"

Callis's arm hooks through mine, mid-stride in formalwear at some post-runway event.

Another picture joins them.

"And Rayna Metzer, the popular Instagram influencer?"

My face is paralyzed in an awkward expression from the camera flash, our hands connected while I help her out of the limo.

And yet another comes along, a small pile of photographic evidence forming in front of me.

"Sierra Martin, the designer."

These are not super recent. They're practically ancient. Months gap between the photos of non-relationship relationships. It's embarrassing as it is and downright humiliating coming from the neat, tidy, successful perfection that is Indi Davé.

Does she actually believe what Pall said? That I'm some sort of manipulative mastermind who trades promises of favors for sex? I haven't had to put an effort for no-string flings, like, *ever*. They come willingly— *and literally*—and aim to please. She's right, we don't know each other anymore. And she's not trying to, unlike my pitiful ass.

I choke the shame and resentment down. It brews and boils as Indi's voice fades into a droning buzz. Thoughts of regret for agreeing to pursue this case burn my already-bruised ego.

"Mr. Radek?" Indi knocks her fist on the wooden desktop. "Are you listening to me?" Her finger stamps against the stack of pictures. "*This* is the narrative they've built. If it's untrue, we have to change it and I *will* make sure there are repercussions. But I can't do that if *you* don't tell me what happened."

My patience snaps. "Why don't *you* do your research, *Ms. Davé*?" Best lawyer, my left buttcheek.

There's no way in hell I'm discussing my sexual past or clarifying every female relationship in my life with someone who didn't bother to check on the dates of these photographs.

"*Excuse me?*" Her mouth parts and I'm too angry to wander to filth anymore. Fine, I'm still a little keyed up. A half-chub though. Not a fully.

I rise to my feet, buttoning my suit jacket. "I'm sorry, but how do you expect me to trust you when you can't give me a little respect?"

"I—" Indi's face blanches under that smooth, wheatish skin.

"I'm out. Send the bill. I'll sign the fucking check."

The door gives up under my incensed blow and Behraz hops to her feet, abandoning the rest of her sandwich, a string of mustard-covered lettuce hanging from the corner of her lip. Nosy employees eye me as I march out of the office.

It's a miracle I made it home without crashing. The Porsche took my wild swerves and gear changes through downtown like the gorgeous creature she is. My forehead vein throbs as I attempt to calm in the lot. Deep breaths provide no solace.

The unhurried speed of the elevator up to the penthouse irritates the fuck outta me. My fists crash into a couch cushion, driving in again and again until I'm sweating through my shirt. I peel it away, frowning at the missing buttons and rip in the underarm seam.

After a necessary ice-cold shower, I pull on some cotton shorts and find my phone. I want to run away. My thumb finds the favorited contact, line ringing in my ear as I crouch over the end of the bed.

"Hello?"

"Hey, Mom."

"Hi, sweetie. You doing okay?"

"I've been better."

"Yeah? Wanna talk about it?"

"Not right now. What are your plans for the weekend?"

"Nothing really. I'm off. Your sister's heading down from Toronto with the kids. Seth's out of town."

"Ah, okay."

There's a pause before Mom asks, "You wanna come home, too?"

"Yeah." I deflate with a sigh. "I do."

———

Gray painted brick contrasts the bright yellow door Mom swings open, dropping her shoulders with a sigh at my offer of a Timmie's double-double.

"You're the best son I ever had."

"Morning." We share a hug and exchange cheek kisses while I balance the coffee tray, the cup in my hand, and the weekend bag over my shoulder. I've been up since 4 a.m. to catch the early flight home, but the in-air nap and this medium roast have me ready for the day. "I'm your only son. It's too bad your firstborn is feral."

She smacks my arm mid-sip. "Be nice to your sister."

Fat chance. Laney is a pain in the ass. God knows how her husband deals with her.

"I got her an Iced Capp. That's more than she deserves." I crane my neck into each of the childless rooms we pass on the way to the den. Used bowls rest by the sink and cereal boxes stand on the kitchen table. Cheerios and Corn Flakes scatter the floor underneath. "Where is everyone?"

"Delaney's got the kids in the bath," Mom says, pulling the panels of her blue-striped robe closed and plopping down on the couch. "Seth went on a bachelor weekend fishing trip with his brothers. You know Daniel's getting married, right?"

I nod.

"And your dad's on his morning run."

Puffy bags wrinkle under her eyes with her next smile. It's a sure sign she had a twelve-hour shift the day before. While her job as a nurse at Henry Ford over the border in Detroit brought us to Windsor, I've told her countless times she doesn't have to work so hard anymore. But Mom's Mom.

"*Ah.* First shift giving you hell?"

"Could be worse. They're so short-staffed. I feel bad saying no."

I lean back and mirror my mother's position, propping my feet up next to hers and gazing up at the white ceiling while drinking our coffee together in a rare moment of silence. It's strange coming home as an adult, but also something peaceful in that almost nothing has changed. She and Dad still live together, despite being divorced for years. They're best friends, and while it may not be society's normal, it's our normal.

The security system beeps and Dad appears at the front door, jogging through the foyer and slowing as he nears.

"Landy!" He dries the sweat from his face and neck with the small towel hanging from his running belt. Spread arms greet me, clapping my back through the embrace. As always, he plants a kiss on my temple. "Love you, baby boy. Good to see you."

I let him have it. I don't get enough time with these goofballs.

He catches his breath, hands on his waist, t-shirt drenched and running shorts sticking to his thighs.

"Lookin' good, old man." I tease, laying a playful hook into his shoulder. Dad jabs me in the gut a couple of times in response. "How ya doin'?"

"Can't complain," he shrugs. "What about you? You got your mother and I worried."

"Eh—" My complaint gets cut short with the storming of tiny feet down the stairwell.

High-pitched shrieks crescendo in our direction before Sadie and Gunnar bound into my squatting form on the floor. I scoop them up, the little rascals, in each arm. They wriggle in my grip as I stand, giggling at the tickle of my fingers digging into their sides.

"Who are these big kids?"

"Put me *downnnn*, Uncle Landy!" Sadie arches and flails. I nearly drop her. She's fucking strong for a four-year-old.

"Down, Unku!" Gunnar parrots his sister. "Outside!" He points repeatedly to the patio door.

I send an inquisitive look to my mom, who agrees over her coffee cup, the lid now discarded. When I release them, they scamper to the back of the house and slide the glass door open, dancing and jumping across the pavers and into the grass.

Delaney ambles into the room with an exasperated sigh, jeans and tee dotted with splashes. She tilts her head to check on the kids, then smirks at me. Her arms move in a welcoming arc, stretching from her front to the side. "The manwhore himself is here."

My parents groan in chorus. "*Delaney!*"

I laugh and slow clap at her fucking hilarious joke, then stop suddenly to give her the middle finger.

"Alright, cut it out, you guys." Dad's attempt at reffing is fruitless.

My sister uncaps her finger like lipstick and taps on her butt pocket. "Kiss my ass, Landy."

I pretend to swirl mine in my coffee and flick the invisible hot liquid in her face. "Get fucked."

"*Landon!*" Mom scolds in a tired tone, rubbing her forehead with a hand.

Del uses an imaginary crank to lift her middle finger. "Don't need to. You're doing it enough to cover all of us."

"*Argh!*" I charge closer, ready to get her in a headlock. "You're such a—"

"*MOMMMMYYYYY!*" Gunn's squeaky voice cries out.

We all turn to the yard, where Sadie frowns and vehemently denies wrongdoing as her baby brother lies face down in the grass, kicking his legs. Takes after her mother.

Grunting into a fist, my sister then points two fingers to her eyes and then to me with her middle finger. "This isn't over."

"Eat shit," I mutter through my teeth, sticking my leg out to trip her as she marches by. She stumbles over her feet and glares back at me.

"I *heard* that!" Mom kicks my calf from her reclined position on the couch and I fall back to the cushions with a wince. "You're worse than the *actual* children."

"She started it!"

"I really don't fucking care, Landon. You two need to cool it."

Dad purses his lips and sucks in a breath. Mom cursing is a big deal.

I cross my arms and pout. "It's not true! I told you it wasn't true."

"We know." My father pats me on the shoulder from behind the couch. "You're not a serial dater, never have been. Lane's riling you up. The attention's not going away as fast as you thought, hey?"

I rest my head back. "Not at all. Cooke hired a lawyer and..." I didn't make the best first impression. "Do you remember Indi?"

My parents trade glances and clueless shoulder shakes.

"The girl who played goalie one year on the Lightning?"

"*Ohhhh*, I remember hearing about that." Mom taps her cheek with a finger. "What made you think of her?"

I huff out a dry chuckle. "She's my new lawyer."

"No shit!" Dad nods. "Small world."

"Right? I thought we were friends back then, but she...*I don't know.* She acted like I wronged her or something."

"What do you mean?" He corners the couch and sandwiches me between him and Mom.

"I met with her and was excited to have someone I knew on my side. She made it seem like we never knew each other. I kinda snapped."

"Son," Dad says with a shake of his head. "Lawyers are never your friends."

Mom peeks over her coffee. "Is she a good lawyer?"

"Supposedly one of the best."

Her eyebrow perks. "Then you should probably apologize."

"Yeah." I sigh. Probably. Definitely.

Mom squeezes my shoulder. "We all have our bad days."

Don't I know it?

"Apologizing wouldn't be the worst thing."

Before I get too lost in my head, Dad nudges me with his knee. "Hey, what are you up to today? I've got a tee time booked at the club with Stephen." He reaches into a pocket on his belt to pull out his phone. "He always enjoys time with you."

"Sure. Sounds good."

Spending the morning at the driving range with Dad and his boyfriend isn't what I had in mind when I came home to escape. But the earnest, eager look in his eyes has me folding. When it's this easy to make him happy, why wouldn't I?

The trip home is too short. Delaney and I act civil for the rest of the weekend. She hugs me goodbye after I help her get the kids in the car as they prepare to leave. "You're an asshole, but I love ya."

I squeeze and lift my sister off the ground, ignoring her protests. "I feel the exact same way about you."

"Yes, you're sweet like that." She pinches my nipple and I yelp, slapping the back of her hand. "Can't have everyone thinking we're too chummy."

"Right. Drive safe." My sister goes to ruffle my hair, but I block it with my forearm.

Mom and Dad pull their heads from either side of the backseat after giving their grandkids farewell kisses, then shut the car doors. Del stands between the driver's seat and door.

"And hey, don't let the news get to ya. They'll move on to the next dum-dum that screws up soon enough."

Mom facepalms with a groan, tone low with warning. Laney waves like Forrest Gump and shoots us an innocent smile.

I feel *so* much better now.

CHAPTER 8:
AHOY, CAPTAIN HOOK

INDI

HOW DARE HE? HOW DARE HE WALTZ IN HERE WITH AN easy, lopsided smile on his unreasonably handsome face?

The confident saunter while he unbuttons the jacket of yet another freshly laundered suit tailored to fit his broad torso and toned legs perfectly? Ludicrous. An invigorating citrus and fabric softener scent combo? It has no business floating in here to make all my essential organs throb. Especially not the one between my legs.

"Mr. Radek. Have a seat."

"*Hey, Indi.*"

Oh, God. I'm actually wet. Where the hell did Bea go? I can't be left alone with the charmer!

Landon sits and so do I. "Please. It's Ms. Davé."

His charcoal suit and white shirt underneath fit way too well, leaving nothing to the imagination when he leans back in the chair with his hands behind his head. And I mean, *nothing*. Bulky biceps bunch, stretching the upper sleeves of the suit jacket into round hemispheres. A cognac-toned Wingtip wiggles from where it hangs over his knee, the knit fabric of his pants straining to cover the meaty muscles of his legs and...*holy fuck*.

There it is again. The big one. His thing is *right there*, bulging and molded to his inner thigh. Is that how big it is at rest?

Mercy, mercy, mercy. I rein in control, keeping myself from fixating on it and holding his gaze instead.

"*Aw*, Indi. It's just us now. No need to be so formal. How are you?"

Formal? Your thunder-down-under is making this anything but. No, no, no. I won't allow either of them—*Landon or his huge wang*—to derail my thoughts anymore.

"I'm *great*." I know I'm being curt, but he's my client. There are boundaries. With anyone else, any level of informality wouldn't be acceptable. I shut down every attempt at his playful back-and-forth, replying to each quip with brusque remarks. He's persistent. While his flirting may work on more gullible women, I have zero interest. It's an idiotic physical attraction and has to end now.

The second I take the case file out and show him *the photo*, his face falls. The twinkling blue life in Landon's eyes fades, and an embarrassed blood-red brims the top sharp angles of his cheekbones. Good. That snapped him out of it.

The cut corner of his jaw ripples when I ask about his relationship with the publicist. Maybe I took it too far, but I honestly don't care if he's pissed off. Landon Radek doesn't get to come in here and waste my time while I'm trying to do my fucking job to save *his* public image.

"Mr. Radek?" My knuckles rap on my desk. A blank, lifeless expression on his face lingers for a few moments. "Are you listening to me?" I motion to the stack of photos. "*This* is the narrative they've built. If it's untrue, we have to change it, and I *will* make sure there are repercussions. But I can't do that if *you* don't tell me what happened."

His torso stiffens, jaw ticking and eyes reigniting once more. Not with roguish teasing though. It's unadulterated wrath, the fiercest blue flame. "Why don't *you* do your research, *Ms. Dave*?"

My mouth gapes. "*Excuse me*?"

Landon stands, hiding that broad chest with the panels of his blazer. Swiftest, smoothest button I've ever seen buttoned. I cannot be turned on by that. Confidence sags from my head. I lower my gaze. *Aaaand* there's his plonker again. It's still posted against his groin, but now above desk-level. *Gah!*

"I'm sorry, but how do you expect me to trust you when you can't give me a little respect?"

"I—" Brain no worky.

"I'm out. Send the bill," he grates through his teeth. "I'll sign the fucking check."

The entire office comes to a standstill as he storms out, stomping through every turn to the exit. Was I too harsh or is he mad I didn't fawn over him? Hey, someone had to give Landon Radek a reality check and I'm not sorry it was me. Life isn't all fun and games and fucking pretty blondes against windows facing main roads.

If he's stupid enough to get caught, he probably deserved it. Buy some curtains or something, asshole. I bet if I was a man he would have listened and told me the whole story. It's like he doesn't *want* to clear his name. I fold onto my desk with a sigh.

"No backing out," Theresa's voice echoes in my head.

Blow me, Giachetti.

Monday arrives too soon. Frustrated by how Landon ignored my calls and voicemails all weekend and growing bored of watching news clip after news clip and reading the same quotes on a bunch of different tabloid sites, I pack up my desk and decide a workout is in order. It helps clear my head. For a moment, anyway.

Tuesday is worse than Monday.

I typically don't let work get to me, but between Theresa popping her head in here every thirty fucking minutes to ask if I've gotten a hold of the client yet and Bea out sick with her annual summer cold, I'm about to lose my goddamn mind. On top of that, Cooke isn't picking up either. And the worst is I can't get the naked image of that stupid, big-dicked bastard out of my head.

By noon, the coffee urn is empty, I've stress-pooped five times, and my right eye twitches at the cadence of a strobe light. Even a Nutella sandwich doesn't boost the serotonin. I'm down to my last resort for relaxation.

As the office quiets for lunch, I peek through the door to watch for stragglers, then close it before shuffling back to my desk. The chair sinks under my weight when I lean over to unlock a drawer holding my personal belongings. I fish out a discreet satin satchel.

Ahoy, Captain Hook.

The palm-sized, c-shaped silicone toy rinses clean and pats dry without trouble. I return from the washroom to my seat and shimmy up my skirt. If Landon's gonna traipse about in my brain all day, I'll put him to work.

Get him out of my system once and for all.

I switch the AirPods to a favorite chapter of a smutty audiobook, but what really helps *move things along* is imagining Landon's full lips on my jaw, my neck, and chest, nipping and sucking the skin between his teeth. His rough hands scrape against my breasts, pinching the peaked nipples before grazing down, down, down.

I move the black lace covering the ladybits aside and shift under the desk, allowing the sleek Captain to slide past the exposed opening at the split of my legs. The bulbous end sits flush against the sweet sensitive spot inside as the outer lip makes contact with my tender and needy clit.

On my desktop, the phone app glows with fluorescent pinks and purples and I swipe across the screen, the intensity of the vibration and movement changing with the pressure of my fingers. My eyes close as the pleasure builds, head tipping into the back of the reclining chair. A shirtless Landon writhes above me, taut pecs and abs clenching with every roll of his hips. Shiver me timbers, Hooky.

My knees knock together as I squirm and whimper, tightening around the toy, a repeated refrain rasping from my throat. "Landon. Landon. Landon." The position, the endless circles...being so close to the edge feels *too* good. Breathless and gasping, all inhibitions melt away when I top out with a shudder and one last sigh. "*Landon!*"

Amidst the best orgasm I've had in weeks, the desk bumps toward me, wrenching my eyes open. My lungs expand with a gulp of thick air as a shimmery blue gaze, divided between awe and lust, stares back.

CHAPTER 9:
DREAMS DO COME TRUE

LANDON

MONDAY IS THE LAZIEST DAY. I'M TOO BUSY IGNORING calls from Indi's office, stuffing my face with the Twinkies from the bulk-size box I bought from Costco, and being annoyed my parents were right about apologizing.

The next morning, I nut up. "Ms. Davé, I'm sorry." I fix the collar of a pressed shirt, clearing my throat and squaring off my shoulders while facing the full-length mirror. "My behavior was highly unprofessional." A grumble follows as I unbutton the sleeves to roll them up my arms. "Sorry for my behavior the other day, Ms. Davé. I hope it doesn't affect our future professional relationship."

My fly gets a tug up with a wiggle, freeing my balls from an inner thigh and opt for these sick black and white Nike Air high tops to push my feet into before heading out the door.

The parked Range Rover takes up too much space on the street, earning me some obscenities from passing cyclists as I jog around to the sidewalk. Someone leaving lets me into the ghost town remnants of the law office. I stroll through and recognize Behraz's desk, despite its lack of strewn papers and food wrappers, but she's not there either.

"May I help you?" Judging from the lilt in her accent, she's Québécois. My head turns to an unfamiliar leggy brunette. "You play hockey, yes?" She smiles and flips her hair.

I hold back an eye roll. Sniff, sniff. I smell a puck bunny.

"*Uh*, yes. For the Regents. Landon Radek."

"Geneviève Martel." Her hand hangs limp in front of her. She want me to kiss it or something?

"*Geneviève*," I sound like a douche imitating her pronunciation, emphasizing the *viève* while awkwardly grasping her hand. "Do you know if Ms. Davé is in today?"

She scoffs out a series of annoying laughs. "She is, yes. *Always.*" Her finger points to Indi's door. "Likely eating a Nutella sandwich in her office, alone."

She still eats those?

My eyes narrow at her condescending tone, suddenly feeling protective of someone that I only used to know. Somehow meeting Indi again struck a match in the lightless, tucked-away corner of my heart. Her place in it sparks back to life. "Thank you."

In four strides, I'm at her door, my shadow taking up most of its breadth. I knock and wait.

"Ms. Davé?"

No response. When I peer over my shoulder, Geneviève has made herself scarce as well.

The doorknob meets my palm, hesitant and anxious to face Indi's potential wrath. It rolls open. "Ms. Davé?" I pop in, headfirst.

Indi sits at her desk, eyes closed, headphones in. Her suit jacket hangs over the back of the chair. Didn't take her for a power-napper. I repeat her name and she hums in reply with a shallow exhale. That's gotta be a coincidence. Maybe she's listening to one of those meditation apps. Her chest floats up and falls. *God damn.*

He-Man rouses from sleep at the swells of her terrific rack in that tight, sleeveless top. I toe closer, skimming over her upper half. She squirms. What is she doing? My palms flatten against the desk opposite her. Her index finger presses and swirls on her phone screen, bursting with color and faintly buzzing with every sweep. It's hypnotizing, drawing my torso forward until I'm hovering over and...*holy, holy, holy, fuck.*

Wrinkled skirt fabric gathers at Indi's hips, thighs spread, a bright pink arc peeking through the cleft of her legs. My mouth waters, feeling as slick as she looks.

That's her...*all of her.*

Any coherent thoughts turn to scrambled eggs as her knees pinch together, hiding her from view. And then she lets out the softest simper, followed by my name. *Three times.* The first time has me stiffening and my heart crawling into my throat. But the second two? They're gasps, a whined-out chant, stiffening something else entirely.

That's the hottest shit I've seen in...*ever.* Fuck. She's using a toy and pretending it's me. And on the clock? *Wowza.* Dreams do come true.

Instead of backing away, I stay jammed in my spot like a creep, gaping. My breaths slow like the current passing of time, tongue darting out to wet my lips, wanting to savor every second of this. I'd give my left nut to hear her moan out my name once more. Which is strangled by the underside of my painfully hard cock and the zipper of my jeans.

"Say it again," I whisper, "Say my name."

As if on command, Indi shivers, her voice wrenching out a sharp sigh. "*Landon!*"

My fingers slide, hands bracing against the wood to prevent my legs from buckling and climbing over that desk to have a chance myself. The force of my control lapses as I heave into the table. It jerks forward.

Oh, no.

Oh, no.

Oh, no, no, no, no, no.

Indi bolts upright, eyes and mouth wide, matching my dumbstruck expression and equally upright cock. One AirPod decides to abandon ship from her ear, free-falling to the carpet. We share a rushed intake of air, though I doubt there's any left in this room. Every bit of it has been sucked into my imploding brain and high-flying dick, hell-bent on poking out from its denim confines.

"*Aaahhhhhhhh!*" She lets out the most horrified scream.

By instinct, I scream back. "*Ahhhhhhhhhh!*"

Indi bounds to her feet, continuing the prolonged shriek. My knees decide to give up on life, sending me tumbling backward. The back-and-forth screeching keeps on, skyrocketing my heart rate as I backflip over a chair, scuttling across the floor towards the door like a crab and slipping with each step.

I scamper out of the empty office, knocking my knees into every desk corner and wall and hurtling down the emergency stairs, not looking back until I collapse onto my car.

CHAPTER 10:
MISSED EACH OTHER

INDI

IF IT ISN'T A RAGING DUMPSTER FIRE FLOATING DOWN A river of hot sewage.

Oh, wait. That's my life.

Mortified. Flat-lined. I'm actually dead. This is a dream, right? A lunch hour fantasy turned nightmare?

Nope, still my life. Guess it's over now. It was nice while it lasted. Goodbye, cruel world. You did me so, so dirty. Captain Hook decided to buzz off and flopped to the floor like a fish during the screaming match.

If I hadn't been so humiliated from Landon witnessing me moan out his name, I might have laughed at how he floundered out of my office like a bat out of Hell.

Slumping back into my chair, I struggle to lower my heart rate—*not flat-lined, after all*—and get back my breath by dropping my head between my knees. When that doesn't work, an errant paper lunch bag that didn't make it to the trash can comes in handy.

Footsteps near as I breathe into the bag, rapid pulse fading from its whooshing in my ears.

"Ms. Davé?" I emerge from under my desk as Geneviéve shoots up a perplexed eyebrow. "What are you doing?"

"Nothing. Throwing this away." My hand wiggles the scrunched brown bag before tossing it into the bin.

"I see." She hums. "Your client, Landon Radek, was searching for you."

"Was he?" I lift a shoulder with the nonchalance of an overconfident actor. "Must have missed him."

"But you were...*here*?" Her palms face up, mouth screwing in confusion.

"Mostly." I cough and clear my throat. "Perhaps I was using the facilities." She frowns.

My phone buzzes with a message from Bea. Perfect timing. "Is there anything else you need?" I point to the device. "I've got to take this."

She stammers out a denial and turns to leave.

Nosy. Get a life, Gene. "And close the door, please."

BEA

Everything okay at the office? Geneviéve texted the legal secretaries Radek came in looking fire

More like I came, he saw, and panic conquered us both.

These office gossips. Now what? I absolutely cannot tell Bea—*or anyone, ever, for that matter*—how Landon Radek caught me engaging in safe sex. At work, no less. The girls would *never* let me live it down. Even if I survived their taunts, forget about partner, I could be fired. No way I'm letting that happen.

I'm a lawyer. I know how to circumlocute. I can omit details. If I can do it to uphold law, I can definitely do it for self-preservation. I already evaded all conversations about the locker room DickflateGate in the group chat. My darling friends didn't suspect a thing. This should be cake.

ME

Didn't see Radek. Must have missed each other.

Three little dots dance on the left side of the screen before an incoming call materializes. It's Gabe. I answer.

"Hey, how's it going?"

"You tell me. Bea texted me Radek came in. Did he apologize for being a prick? Did you have to apologize? Spill the beans."

I shake my head, knowing she got all the tea, despite my best efforts to keep it under wraps. Behraz Irani is such a blabbermouth.

I brush off her questions with a scoff. "Okay, first of all...Hi, hello. How are you?" My brain cogs spin to life to figure out how I'm going to phrase this next part. "And second, I didn't *meet* with him."

"'Cause Bea said—"

"You can thank the office rumormonger for that."

Gabe tuts, disappointed.

"I know. Too bad. Would have made a juicy story." My face cringes at the choice of words, eyes wandering to the carpet where the wet, marooned Captain Hook lies lifeless. "And anyway, you know I can't talk clients with you. Especially not this one."

"But you already told us he was your client and what for..."

"Because that's public information, *available on newsstands and television screens everywhere!*" I announce with the contrived enthusiasm of an advertisement voiceover.

"Fucking lawyers." She whines. "You're no fun."

"Yes, yes. I'm very boring." A knotted shoulder muscle shifts under the pressure of my hand's massaging grip. "But you love me anyway."

"Got me there." She sighs. "What are you doing for dinner tonight? Kurt left for some team retreat."

"No plans. What are you thinking?"

"Wanna get takeout from India House?"

"Yes, please! Pick it up and bring it over around seven?"

"You got it. If I get bhindi masala, will you tell me what's going on with Radek?"

"Nope."

Gabe blows a raspberry in response. "Booooooo!"

"But you can help me brainstorm how to get on a problematic client's good side."

"Done."

When she hangs up, I snatch the neon vibrator off the floor and head into the en suite to wash it off before returning it to its satin home in my purse. You're in time out, Captain.

I flip open a pocket mirror to check my makeup more closely, hoping it's not smudged from sweat and tears. Of all the embarrassing shit I've been through, Landon Radek seeing me get off wins. How am I supposed to face him, much less work his case?

———

One bhindi masala, one shahi paneer, one jeera rice, and two orders of phulka roti later, Gabe and I are too full to think about anything but the growing food babies in our bellies.

"India House bhinda are good, but not as good as your mom's." Gabe gasps out a burp. "'Scuse me."

"Agreed. One of these days, I'm gonna learn her recipe."

"And then you'll invite your best friend over so she can eat it all."

We clink wine glasses and down large gulps before refilling them.

The bottle of Riesling empties as we watch a video of hit Bollywood songs from the early 2000's on YouTube, failing miserably to keep up with the elaborate dance sequences. I blame the restricting fabric of my blouse and pencil skirt and switch them out for a pair of soft joggers and a loose tank. It's no use.

"How did we do this regularly at uni?" I pant, palms on my knees.

"I have no idea." Gabe puffs out a breath and wipes her brow with the back of her hand. "Nothing like trying to keep up with old Aishwarya Rai choreo to remind you how old and out of shape you are."

I humph. "Speak for yourself. I work out four days a week."

"And it *shows*." Gabe smacks my ass when I straighten, her tongue peeking out between her teeth.

"*Owww!*" I rub the sting away. "That is so *rude*."

"Whatever. You liked it. That's the most action you've seen in years."

I flip her off on my way to uncork a second bottle.

Gabe's post-workout sweet tooth craving kicks in and she ransacks my kitchen cupboards, discovering the wholesale-size bag of Lindt melting chocolate wafers on a high shelf. My best friend requests a personalized candy bar for Kurt.

I giggle and snort, my inebriated, unsteady hand using tweezers to place bright white letters onto the setting milk chocolate. When they spell out 'Eat My Ass,' Gabe chokes, spraying her sip of wine back into her glass. The sprinkle job I complete it with is messy, but hey, so is eating ass.

"You're such a bitch!" She shoves me through a laugh, toppling me around the corner of the island to the floor. "I *knew* I shouldn't have told you he said no!"

My stomach aches, I wheeze so hard. "I can't—think of a better way— to convince him —*bahahahaha*!"

Gabe pokes me in the belly with her foot and continues to glare.

Feeling dizzy from cackling and that last glass of wine, I stay in place, sprawled on the hardwood as my chittering peters out.

"*Alright*, drunky." Gabe hoists me up with an outstretched arm. "Let's get you to bed."

We sway to the bedroom with my arm draped across her shoulder for support. "You're a good friend." I pat her cheek once before cupping her face with my free hand until it puckers. "I love you to pieces."

We collapse onto the mattress with a *fwoomp* and tuck our legs under the covers. Gabe nuzzles into the extra pillow. "You can show me how much by being the big spoon."

"No way. Keep those paws to yourself, Grabby."

Only a few minutes pass before we knock out. And I've managed to avoid discussing Radek.

———

Luck falls short at work the next morning. Bea's still out, my head's splitting and snooty Geneviéve is about as helpful as a cabbage. Landon and Cooke are still on the lam, it seems. Theresa's on vacation for the rest of the week, though, so my stress-shits have dissipated.

Each thud into the desktop makes my headache worse. How the hell am I supposed to apologize now? I fire up the iMac, welcoming three chocolate-covered espresso beans into my mouth before clicking open a browser. In one tab, I open the client's file. In another, I type into the search bar and write notes in the margin, and taking breaks from plotting to pray it works.

Radek's residential building is insane. Reflective blue glass and white steel frame the facade and towers over nearby structures. The elevator bank is decorated nicer than my whole apartment. Massive double doors of the penthouse run from floor to ceiling. Spindly bag handles dig into my clammy grip while waiting for him to respond to the bell.

Apologizing is a great idea. Exuding confidence has worked so far. He's the same as any hockey bro you've ever dealt with. No biggie. You will not melt into goop from embarrassment. You will not. You will *not*. One leaf of the grand door clicks open.

"Hi—" An impervious lump forms in my throat, snuffing out the words.

Landon Radek answers the door shirtless, every smooth muscle of his torso on display. A trail of trim chest hair between those square pecs leads to a set of unreal abs. Engorged veins in his forearms shift as he smirks and takes a bite of the Twinkie in his hand, never breaking our eye contact. Cream filling oozes from the other end—*and, wow, same*—before he laps it up with the broad, flat surface of his tongue.

I gulp. Guess I have new material for my stupid fantasies. I want this man to turn *me* into a Twinkie. More veins streak between the defined v of his hips and downward, the thin grey sweats hanging from them not at all useful in hiding the giant bulge at his crotch. Avert your eyes!

"I—" My voice croaks. The lump loosens when I *ahem*.

His smirk grows.

My shoulders level as I invoke some semblance of composure, overlooking his teasing. "I've brought a peace offering."

CHAPTER 11:
PRETEND NOTHING HAPPENED

LANDON

EVERY BEADY PAIR OF EYES IN THE ROOM GLUES TO
the eight-foot-wide TV screen on the wall. Fletch's foot bounces from the
floor. Wade murmurs curses. I twist a pinch of hairs on my chin back and
forth between my thumb and index finger.

There's a slight movement from where Olsen has his hand tucked into
his pants. His fingernails *scritch-scritch* against his skin. "What's taking so
long?"

Fletch glares and shushes while Szecze elbows Olsen. "Shut up and
wait." Derrick harrumphs. I turn up the volume.

*"Ms. Blautner, do you see the inscribed initials here, L.N.? They stand
for Leslie Nash, who was an early designer for Tiffany. How much did you
say you paid for this?"*

"My father paid five dollars sometime in the 1930s."

*"Remarkable. This well-maintained, original piece was blown in either
1914 or 1915 and we estimate its worth to be between sixty and seventy-five
thousand dollars—"*

Concurrent groans and grumbles resound as Fletcher jumps to his feet,
then drops to one knee, pumping his fist downward in victory. "Hell yeah,
motherfuckers!" He points both fingers in the air as if thanking Jesus in
the sky, then crip-walks around, gathering cash from the rest of us suckers.

"Asshole." Olsen chucks a large bill at him.

Fletch ends his gloating with a Harlem shake in front of Wade, who
gets up, turns, bends over, and farts in the winner's direction before
returning to his seated position.

It's bad enough he robs us blind playing poker on the road. But losing to him over Antiques Roadshow is a whole new low.

"Wouldn't be so sore about it if you'd listened to me." Fletch licks his thumb and pads through the bills. "Had to be a Tiffany."

Wade's phone dings and he fishes it out of a pocket. He looks at the screen then smirks. "Pussy calls."

Fletch wrinkles his nose. "You really stick it anywhere, eh?"

That earns him a hook to the chest. "Pussy is pussy. You should try it sometime, Donovan. Give your hand a literal fucking break."

Fletch curses and shrugs him off.

Wade spins on his heel to me. "Speaking of pussy, do I get your lawyer's number, or what?"

"Or what?" I glare. No way I'm letting him near her.

"The smart mouth?" Szecze straightens. "What'd I miss?"

"First" —Wade claps a hand on my back— "Landy here has a massive hard-on for her."

Leave it to Wade to blab. Under a tight grasp, my fingers crinkle the Budweiser label on the bottle in my hand. Shit. Deny, deny, deny. "I don't have a hard-on for—"

"Then she saw us with our dicks out in the locker room. Turns out they played hockey together as kids..."

"*Oooh.* The plot thickens!" Fletch folds his winnings into his sweats and rubs his palms together.

"...But she acted like an uppity bi—"

"Hey, now—" I cut him off. "No need to call her names. She was—"

"Yeah, I *definitely* got that vibe from her," Szecze adds. "Shoulda seen how bent she got 'cause I didn't say her name right."

Jaeg thwacks Szecze upside the skull. "It's not her fault you're a twat. Your name's fucking *Szeczin*."

Olsen lets out a dopey Patrick Star laugh.

"Anyway, I thought you went to apologize for being a prick."

I chug the remaining contents from the brown glass lip, biding my time until I figure out an explanation. Definitely can't tell them what I saw. I'll get a stiffy just by thinking about it.

"You did?" The boys huddle closer. "What did she do?"

Quick! Pass out. Act dead. Pretend nothing happened. Belching after the last gulp, I shake my head. "Nothing. She, *uh*, wasn't there."

I saw—heard something I wasn't supposed to. And now I won't be able to forget.

Wade brays out a sad trombone noise as the rest intone with disappointment. "*Wa-wah-wa-waaaaa.*"

"The plot *thinnens.*" Fletch surmises.

"How anticlimactic."

Nope. There was a climax alright.

Wade's phone beeps again. "Damn. Read it and weep, mouth-breathing vag-repellers!" He shows off the disgusting text on his screen, then turns and moonwalks to the door. "Gotta run."

"Same." Fletch gets up from the ottoman. "Thanks for funding the contents of my next bookshelf." He kisses the side of his fist after thumping it against his chest, then throws up a peace sign. "*Deucessss.*"

Olsen and Szecze clear out soon after, citing boredom. Jaeg is the last to go. He folds the half-completed beret he crocheted tonight into his hoodie pocket. "I'm headed to Skylar's. You gonna be okay?"

"*Aw,*" I whine. "But I was hoping *we'd* cuddle tonight."

Jaeger palms my head and smooshes it into a cushion. "Keep dreamin', Radek." Any attempts to kick or swat him off fail, but after about thirty seconds, he shows mercy and lets me come up for air.

"Ah, fuck off. I'm fine."

I'm not fine. Not ten minutes after Derrick leaves, I open a pack of Twinkies from the snack cupboard. Then another. And another. It's fucking pathetic. Three twin packs is my limit. For now, anyway. Number six makes its way to my mouth when there are knocks on the door. I clod towards it. The delicious aroma of a fresh burger and hot fries seeps into the foyer.

"Hi—" Her greeting comes to an abrupt stop when I pull the door open, smiling eyes fading into surprise.

Considering we both know what she *did*, it's a ballsy move for Indi Davé to show up at my place. She stands before the threshold in another one of those fitted blouse-and-skirt combos, a purposeful torment, for sure. The blush tinging the tops of her cheeks reveals the response to my bare chest. If she's here to distract me with her rack, I can distract right back.

I bite into the remaining Twinkie, licking away the leaking vanilla cream.

Her blush deepens, then recedes as she swallows. "I—"

She's speechless. Mission accomplished. Indi clears her throat. My smile widens. There are so many things I want to say but I'm afraid she'll think I'm a heartless d-bag. Then I'll never get to know her. And I *absolutely* have to know her.

"Can't get enough of me, eh?"

She straighten in response, dark hair swishing across her shoulders.

"I've brought a peace offering." Indi hangs a brown bag between us.

Another waft of grilled meat, toasted bread, melted cheese, and fried potatoes smacks me in the face. My mouth waters.

I lean against the door jamb and cross my arms, making sure to flex my biceps and shift my weight to one leg so she gets a prime view of the goods. "A peace offering or a bribe?"

She doesn't waver, keeping her eyes on mine and showing off the familiar restaurant graphic with a jiggle. "It's a Juicy Lucy from Chomp Burger. I read that it was your favorite in town."

She looked it up? Maybe sweet Indi is in there after all.

My smile eases and then returns. "Look at that. You *do* know how to do research."

Her nostrils stretch, letting a controlled breath escape. "Please, Mr. Radek. I'm trying to apologize."

Fuck. My dick rises to the occasion at the way she says please. Down, boy.

"*Hmm.* Not sure I can accept it yet." Pushing off the door frame, I move aside so she can enter. "Let's talk."

Eyes scanning through every space we pass, Indi follows behind. Halfway to the living room, she mutters under her breath. "It's fucking *huge.*"

I'm about to have some more fun. "It *is*, isn't it?"

The clacking heels on her feet stop at that comment.

"Five thousand square feet." I snort, peering over my shoulder at her ashen face. Why is it so easy to mess with her? "Most of it is outside." I point to the rooftop patios.

Indi keeps going when I pause at the corner of the couch, and she crashes into my naked back. That fucking blush reappears.

"Have a seat." I lower and recline into the sectional.

She searches for a spot, then sits, tucking one ankle behind the other. "Right, sure. Mr. Radek—"

"Landon." I ask for the bag with a beckon. She hands it over.

"Okay, *Landon*, I'm sorry for being so short with you the other day. It wasn't my...finest professional moment."

No shit. I've already seen your finest professional moment.

"I'd like to put the past behind us—" Her gaze lingers where my fingers mindlessly scratch my chest. "Could you put a shirt on, please?"

This is too good. I smile, teeth cratering the lower lip. "Why? Am I too *distracting*?"

Indi winces. It drowns under the loud thumping pulse in my ears. "*No*. It's common decency—"

"You don't have to pretend, Indi."

She throws me an exasperated look before rolling her eyes. "And what am I pretending about?"

"What you think of me." I rid dryness from the seam of my grin with my tongue, watching how her glance fixates on my mouth. "You *like* me. It's understandable. I'm very likable."

With the next deep breath, she casts out her admission like it's the worst thing in the world. "I don't...You're my client." Her lips tighten, trying and failing to keep her annoyance under wraps. "This is a moot point. But it's not a secret...that you're..."

"I'm...?" The man of your erotic workplace dreams? A God on Earth?

"...Objectively, physically *attractive*."

A muffled snicker releases from my throat.

"Way to put the past behind us," she mumbles, squinting at the ceiling.

As I pick up the burger, a loud growl warbles from her stomach. We sit in a moment of awkward silence, exchanging looks between the food and each other.

My brow wrinkles. "Have you eaten?"

"*Um...*"

"Here" —I scoot to the edge of the cushion— "we can share."

"*Er*, no, thank you. I'd like to focus on the case—"

"I'll cut it in half." I tear into the pack of plastic silverware and wield a serrated knife, hovering it over the domed wheat bun. "It's not a big deal."

"There's no need. I'm fine—"

My eyes narrow. "But you're obviously hungry—"

"I don't eat beef."

"Some fries, then."

Another groan sounds from her belly.

"Eat, then we talk."

"*Fine.*" Indi resigns, folding forward to reach for the fries.

Forcing her to eat in front of me was the worst suggestion I've ever had. Muted, pleasured noises emerge as she pokes every thin strip between her full lips. I chew on my burger faster to avoid doing the same. When Indi licks her fingers clean before wiping them on a paper napkin, I nearly choke trying to hide my insane boner.

"There. Happy?"

Happy? No, I'm not happy. I'm horny. My cock, the betraying bastard, thinks we're going camping and pitches a tent in my sweats. "Actually" —I fumble and almost drop the burger onto its wrapper— "I think I *will* go put a shirt on."

The next few minutes in my bathroom are spent switching from yelling at my prick to conjuring up the most disgusting things I can think of. Wrinkly zombie balls. Maggots on rotting flesh. Olsen's hairy ass.

He-Man goes down like a popped balloon, thank fuck. I throw on a shirt and jog back to the living room, parkouring over the back of the couch into a smooth landing. "Okay." I take another large bite, savoring the cheese dripping from between the medium-rare patty. "You were saying?"

"Yes. I'd like to have a fresh start." Her hand finds its way into her briefcase and removes a pen and notepad. "I know if we work together, we can get this case wrapped up quickly. All I ask for is total honesty."

I hum. "And I can expect the same from you?"

"Absolutely." Even this life-changing burger isn't enough to distract me from the way her tongue wets her lips. "Glad we're getting somewhere. Ready?"

"Go for it."

"I'll need a comprehensive history of every romantic and sexual partner you've ever had."

My rabid chewing stops, and I swallow the mouthful in one harsh stroke. "That's not a real question."

"I didn't ask, but I do need to know." Her notes grow as she glides a pen over the page, then looks at me. "I can understand this isn't easy to talk about. But the only way I can protect you is if I know the truth."

I don't mean to, but I scoff. Every time this topic comes up, my blood heats to a boil. It's fucking humiliating. And the last person I want to know about my gullible stupidity is Indi Davé.

"Landon?" She pulls out *the picture* from a file in her bag. "A picture is worth a thousand words." Her voice drops. "Though I doubt you were doing any talking."

My clenched jaw relaxes from its defensive position. "You know what? No, it's not. It's a picture—*a snapshot*—of what actually happened. It tells a story, maybe. But it doesn't tell the truth. Only I can tell you that, Indi. Let me know when you're ready to listen."

Her hands fly up. "I was—I am ready to listen!"

"I have a better idea." My face hardens. "You want honesty?"

"Yes. That's *all* I'm asking—"

"You first."

Indi tilts her head. "Me first?"

"How can I trust you when I don't know you?"

"Oh-kay," she intones, releasing her pen onto her notepad. "What do you want to know?"

Everything. "You want to know my sexual history?" I wipe my hands on a napkin, then ball it up and toss it to the coffee table. "Let's hear yours."

Her eyes brim with rage, widening and narrowing. "*Excuse me?* What—how is this relevant?"

"You want my trust and to know about my sex life so *badly*," I snipe. "Shouldn't be so hard to share yours."

What the actual fuck are you doing, you absolute shit?

"The hell, Radek?" Her cheeks go red again, but not in a nice way like before. "Haven't you embarrassed me enough? I came here after..." Indi gasps out a few humorless laughs. "*I apologized*, and it's completely unprofessional—" The pen snaps in her grip. She broke the pen. Uh oh. "This is...I don't need this."

The words rattle out before my brain can catch up. "Yeah? Then go. You're the one who showed up here."

She packs her notes and shoots to her feet.

I trail behind her to the door. "What happened to you, Indi? You used to be the kindest girl I ever met. We were friends."

Her stride cuts short before she pivots. "I'm not that girl anymore.

And it's been a long time since we were friends."

I wait for her to leave, resuming our positions on either side of the doorway, the same as an hour ago.

"You have no idea what it feels like to have people talking about you."

Indi glances up from the floor, voice returning to a soft quality. "Believe it or not, Landon, I do. I know *exactly* how it feels."

"Then you know how horrible it is when what they say isn't true."

Her lashes flutter as she nods, gazing at the floor once more before those sad brown eyes meet mine again, the sincerest I've ever seen them. "It's worse when it is."

Indi blinks a few times, fighting a frown, then strides away. She tips up her chin in pride as the elevator doors *ding* closed.

CHAPTER 12:
DON'T LOOK, OKAY?

INDI

DEALING WITH LANDON RADEK IS WORSE THAN I thought it'd be.

One moment he's being a pompous, flirtatious ass, the next he's sweetly offering his dinner. Then he switches back to being defensive and combative when I bring up the case. Like, I get it. You made a mistake. It's a mess and you're paying to get you out of it.

I stew on the elevator trip down to the lobby, marching across the tile while muttering to myself. Someone gives a disapproving hum as I pass the security desk. It's Timur—the same attendant I used the lawyer card on to get in. "I wouldn't go that way."

"Why not?"

He points at the tinted glass. A mob of photographers blocks the exit and the sidewalk.

"That's gotta be illegal."

He tuts. "*Technically*, not. The sidewalk beyond that first cement slab is owned by the city. It's public property. They don't teach you that in law school?"

My eyes deaden. "No, Ottawa's municipal code wasn't at the top of the Supreme Court's priority list." The jab takes down his arrogance. "So, what? They camp out there all night?" I prop my elbow onto the marble counter, resting my cheek in my palm.

"Guess so. Waiting for their chance." He shrugs and returns to his swivel chair.

"Is there another exit in the back or...?"

"Yeah, but there are a ton of 'em beyond the gate, too. Ready to pounce and take photos of any lady *guests*."

My nails strum on the cold stone. "Help a lady out, Timur. How can I get outta here?"

The guard clasps his hands under his chin, putting both elbows on the other side of the desk. "You can wait 'til morning. I'm sure your client could host you for a night in that spacious penthouse—"

"What's another option?"

His thick eyebrows arch to the middle of his forehead. "Sorry, ma'am. Mr. Radek can let you out of the garage."

"Can't *you* do that? Come on, be a pal."

"*We live in a litigious society, Ms. Davé.*" He uses my earlier language against me, tapping on his lip. "I can't without resident permission. Would you like me to let you back up?" Timur motions towards the secure turnstiles.

"*Ugh*! Fine. I'll figure it out on my own." Like always.

I shake my head at myself in the privacy of the elevator. This night is absurd. But I have to leave. I'll do whatever to butter him up. Faking it is easy.

Or I could give Radek what he wants.

He wants mutual honesty and trust. I can do that, right? I said I didn't need this case, but I definitely do. It's for partner. It's not like your love life is some treasured secret. It's a short and abysmal list. Be vague. No names or details. Get it over with, Davé. Then you can go home.

I knock.

An unemotional gaze replaces Landon's usual knowing smirk as he answers. "You're back. *Yay*," he deadpans.

"I'll do it."

"Do what?" He huffs, crossing his arms across that broad chest.

"I don't know why you feel the need to '*get to know me*' or whatever. But I have nothing to be ashamed of." I take a step closer, ignoring the white heat growing in the deepest part of me. We meet at eye-level with the help of my heels. "Do your worst. Ask me anything."

That sanctimonious grin of his returns. Landon toys with his lip as his eyes sweep down and back up, dark, pretty lashes—*totally unfair*—outlining those striking blue eyes. "You mean my best. I *always* do my best."

I roll my eyes and push past him. "You're *so* annoying."

"Hey now, that's no way to talk to a client." The door closes behind him with a clack.

"Too bad. You're the one who wants to get all chummy." Briefcase and heels discarded on the living room rug; I drop my ass to one corner of the sectional. "But we're gonna do this on my terms."

"Lay it on me."

"First, I'm gonna need some wine."

There's no way I can discuss this without liquid courage. Any other topic, I'd be confident. Wanna talk about legal precedence and procedures, chocolate molds, old Bollywood classics, how liquid eyeliner is superior to a pencil, or extemporaneously debate foreign policy? I'm your gal. Dating, relationships, and sex? Unless you're referencing fossils, friendships, and how sex is biological and gender is a social construct, not so much.

I draw another boundary. "Second, I'll share however much I want, then you have to answer my questions."

"Done." Landon scoffs out a single chuckle, rubbing his jaw. He tilts his head for a moment before jogging backward into the kitchen. Clanging bottles and clinking glasses echo off the high ceilings as I fold my legs underneath me, side-saddling against the couch cushion. Anxiety builds.

"Any preference?" he calls from around the corner, out of view.

I fidget, picking at some stray white lint on my black skirt.

"Do you have white? I can't, *uh*, stomach red. It makes me feel" — *horny*— "uneasy."

More clashing glass peals out before the faucet runs. For being Mr. Impatient, he's certainly taking his time. He emerges, dark green bottle in the crook of his arm and a wine glass in each hand, both filled halfway with a red liquid.

"Sorry." Landon shoots me an innocent shrug. "I ran out of white."

Oh, God. Breathe, Indi. Get the truth out of him and leave. I mean to sip at it but end up finishing the drink in a single go. Whoops. The dry, rich Cabernet coats the line from my tongue down to my stomach.

Landon smiles through his relaxed pull of wine.

I place the glass onto the coffee table and rest my palms on my knees, giving them a rhythmic drum. "Okay. Where to start, where to start?"

He refills the empty glass. "Do you have a boyfriend?"

"Not at the moment." I grab my glass again. Another gulp slides down my throat. "Never had one."

"Never? I don't believe you."

I twirl the glass in hand, watching the wine whirlpool. "*Fine*. I've had a few boyfriends."

Landon smacks his lips, roguish smile in full effect. "Were they battery-operated?"

I give him my best side-eye. "Suddenly you're a comedian."

"And you're a terrible liar, Indi." He sets his finished glass down and leans forward, steepling his fingers. "I can't trust you if you lie. You seriously never dated anyone?"

"I've dated occasionally." That's lawyer speak for rarely.

Landon shakes his head.

Wine sloshes in my belly with the next swallow. "What can I say? I'm a late bloomer."

A furrowed brow and wrinkled frown await me when I peek up from the wine glass and catch his gaze.

"If you haven't noticed, I've been busy being a young and successful lawyer."

He hums, pouring himself another. "It doesn't bode well for relationships."

"I suppose."

"Your turn!" I say, louder than intended, swinging my legs out from beneath me. The wine makes its home in my veins. "Lemme grab my notes."

Landon sighs and nods, thumbing through the scruff on his chin. "Sure."

"Tell me about Annalise Pall."

His chest expands with a deep inhale.

"She worked as the team's PR lead for a while, back when we first signed Boehner and Donovan. The owners wanted to boost ticket sales, wanted us on social media. We were friendly, I guess. I'd see her around the lockers or before press conferences. But apparently, she wasn't as good as they hoped and fired her after two seasons. They hired a new guy who is doing better, and the season was going pretty well. We never do this in the regular season, but in January, the guys and I went out to celebrate beating the Sky here at home. Wade left early with someone, Fletch got wasted and called a cab and

I was about to leave, too, but Annalise sat next to me at the bar."

Landon's fingers dawdle as he shifts his shoulders up and down before muffling words behind his hands. "*God*, this is so embarrassing."

"You're fine." It's the best I can do as consolation. "Keep going."

"We talked about the team and how she misses her job. I felt bad and bought her a drink. I don't know exactly when things changed, but..."

"But?"

Landon massages his forehead. "It got flirtatious."

I snort.

He reddens and reclines, crossing his arms like an insolent child. "Never mind."

"*Sorry*—I'm sorry." I clear my throat. "That's a funny way to say you slept together."

"Sure. Laugh away, Indi."

"I didn't laugh! Continue, please."

He grumbles, then stares at his hands. "We had too many. It was a mistake. I didn't mean for it to happen."

"Okay." My eyes wander to the panel of glass windows edging the living space before refocusing on my notes.

Landon catches me. "That was her idea, by the way."

I pull my lips into my mouth. "Uh-huh."

"What? It was!" He facepalms. "And I never said any of that stuff to her."

"Elaborate on 'stuff.'" My hand cramps.

"I never said I loved her. Hell, I didn't *know* her. That was the only time we talked for more than a few minutes and the absolute only time we had sex. I was drunk, but I never told her I'd get her job back."

"Are there any texts or voicemails? Any sort of verbal exchange where you discussed putting in a good word or...?"

"No. Nothing. Like I said, it was an impulsive thing. One night only." Tongue rounding out his cheek from the inside, he locks into my line of sight again. "It's not my style."

I cock a curious eyebrow, then lower it. "And what is?"

"I'm a one-woman kind of guy."

"What's the story behind these then?" Pictures of Landon with Callis Key, Rayna Metzer, and Sierra Martin splay across the coffee table.

"Callis was a failed date. Cooke set us up. I couldn't get her to pay attention to anything I said. She kept talking about herself between schmoozing with other industry people there." He makes a face, clearly unimpressed. "And Rayna was trying to hook up with Wade. Sierra and I dated. We were together all of university. Broke up when I got drafted. Her business only got popular after. That picture is from about" —he squints to study it— "three years ago."

"Why'd you break up?" Wooooow. Auntyhood has come for you.

"She wanted to get married. I didn't."

I scrawl more notes.

"We stayed friends, and she invited me to a show in Toronto. She's smiling in that picture because she told me she met someone."

I trace over the written timeline. "You're telling me between Sierra and Annalise, you didn't sleep with anyone?"

His fingers press into his forehead. "I went on a few dates, but it's hard to maintain a relationship. It's a busy life. And I'm not the guy they're making me out to be."

"No sex in six years." I scribble onto the paper. "Got it!"

Landon hides behind his hands. "Indi!"

"I'm kidding! *Jeez*. I didn't write that down."

"Do you believe me?" The genuine worry in his eyes has my heart teetering, creating a lull in the conversation.

"Yes." I don't want to, but I do. Maybe he's not a playboy.

A grateful smile softens his face. I knock back the leftover alcohol in my glass to stop from staring at the maroon tint staining his lower lip, those shoulders, strong arms...*Shhhhh*. That's the red wine talking.

The notepad closes with a muted slap. "I think that's enough for today. We can talk about evidence another time."

Sitting upright for so long without support has my back aching. I slump into the couch. Warmth in my gut blooms, hugging my insides like a fluffy down comforter. I search for a more comfortable position, turning to lie across the cushions and boost my feet to the armrest.

Landon mirrors me on the opposite side of the sectional, lacing his fingers together over his belly and gazing at the ceiling. His head falls to the side to look at me. "I'm still shocked, Indi. How have you never had a boyfriend?"

"No one ever wanted to be."

"*Idiots*."

My inhibitions are on vacation for the time being. I twist to a half-sit and smack my hand against the cushion. "*I* know! I'm a fucking *catch*!"

Landon chuckles. "Totally."

"You wanna know the real reason why Ms.Indira Davé is the youngest woman to work in the Supreme Court?"

"Absolutely."

"Hold onto your hat and boots, cowboy! I took every online class offered in high school so I could graduate early." I hum out a string of *mmm*s in disapproval. "University was supposed to be a fresh start. I kept my head in books and stayed away from parties. You'd think I learned my lesson." I lie back down, both hands palming the sides of my head. "I got paired with this ridiculously good-looking right-winger for a PoliSci class. Believe it or not, I had a reputation for being an ice queen."

Landon gasps and holds a stretched hand to his chest. "*No!*"

I wave off his dramatics. "*Yes*! And he somehow fooled me into thinking we were together. Everyone on campus knew it was a joke and wouldn't shut up about it. I couldn't deal and graduated the next year as a junior, then moved to Ottawa for law school."

"*Christ*, Indi." Landon sits up and drags his hands down his face before clasping the back of his neck with them and tugging. Visibly uncomfortable. Probably pitying me.

"Now I'm gonna die a virgin." It's supposed to stay in my head, but my mouth has a different plan.

"What?"

"What?" I echo.

"What'd you say?" He tilts his ear in my direction.

"Nothing." I've said too much. Maybe he didn't hear. Maybe he'll forget it by morning. "I should go." My legs veer off the edge of the couch and launch me upright, but it's too hasty, too quick. The room spins and my balance goes off-kilter. "*Whooooa.*"

Instead of falling onto the rug like I expect, I crash into firm swells of muscle. Large, warm hands grip my waist, steadying me from wobbly knees. A swallow descends the column of Landon's throat, his chest heaving from where I peer up through heavy lashes. "How're you getting home?"

Gulp. "About that, you're supposed to let me out from the garage. There's a ton of photographers—"

His crinkled brow doesn't like that one bit. "You're in no shape to go out there alone."

"*Psht*! I'm *fine*." I go to push him away by the chest, but my palms linger on the solid plane of flesh.

The warmth of his touch lowers to my hips, grip softening. "No, you're not. You're drunk."

"And? Drunk women go home alone all the time."

Landon's angular jaw ticks. "Not when they have a place to stay."

A series of exaggerated *ha*'s push out. "I can't stay here. That's incredibly inappropriate."

"Almost as inappropriate as you getting off to the thought of me at work." Stupid, mischievous smirk makes a reappearance.

As does a flaming sear on my cheeks.

Walked right into that one. "Shut up," I say through my teeth and a sneer.

Landon dips his head down, tannic breath skating over the crest of my upper lip, his mouth far, far, too close. "Make me."

I shove myself away again and this time, the bully releases me, letting me fall to the couch. "Fine! I'll sleep here."

Smug Radek looks more than pleased. "Let me grab you something." He disappears down a hallway before I can protest.

Great. This is great. You've outdone yourself. You're in wine jail for the rest of the month, missy. You're off the rails. You can't be drinking and having sleepovers with—

"Here." Landon holds out a pair of running shorts and a hockey jersey. "Sorry, couldn't find anything else that might fit. I'm in the process of redoing the closet and shit is *everywhere*."

"Thanks." I fold them over my arm and look around. "Where's the washroom?"

"Right there." He points at a door across the space.

When I move towards it, he follows behind.

"What are you doing?"

"Making sure you don't fall again."

"I'm *not* going to fall—" My bare, unstable feet squeak to a stop at the washroom door. Or lack thereof. "What happened here?"

Landon cringes. "Renovations."

I step into the half-bath. "Do you mind?" I say, shooing him away.

"Oh, *right*." He awkwardly pivots back and forth, as if he doesn't know where to go in his own home. "I'll just" —he puts up two finger-guns, shooting left— "be over there."

"Don't look while I'm changing."

Landon stills. His mouth parts and I expect a wry laugh. Because why would he look? The unwavering reprise he responds with reminds me of the same promise he made so many years ago.

"I won't."

In full gear, I sat on a bench by the exit doors after practice. Alone, as usual. It'd only been two weeks since I joined the Lightning. Practices had been rough. The guys hadn't warmed to me.

Coach strode by. "Holy hell! You stink, Davé! Whatcha doing out here? Hit the showers."

My shoulders retreated beneath their pads as I crouch, trying to disappear. "I'll shower at home."

"Your poor parents." He shook his head. "What's wrong with the showers here, eh?"

"Um, nothing. They're fine."

Coach narrowed his eyes. "They not clean?"

"They're clean."

"Then what is it?" His hands pressed into his hips. "'Fess up."

I sighed. "The...um, other girls. The skaters. They say stuff to me."

"Think you're hot shit, playing for the boys' team, huh, Frida Kahlo?" Some girl bounced her pretty, manicured brows at me in threat.

Mom refused to let me tweeze mine yet. If I wanted, I could have fought back and done some damage, but most days I couldn't gather enough courage to reply.

"I saw you watching Bryce Bennett. Stay away from him, fatty. He's my boyfriend."

Coach Alexei sighed back and sat next to me. "Alright, kiddo. Lemme tell ya. People will say lotsa things aboutcha—on and off the ice—but ya have to keep a thick skin, ya know? No one can make ya believe what ya know isn't true."

My gaze lingered on the stale gray carpet; head hung. "What if it is true?"

"I'll tell ya what." He clicked his tongue. "Once the boys clear out, you can

go in. I'll have Donna clean the corner stall."

"Thanks, Coach."

The stench ripened. A horde of my teammates with their gear bags and dainty, giggling girlfriends strolled by.

A few minutes passed before I plodded over to the lockers. My stick poked through the door, like a battle-ready sword. Silence meant it was empty. Still, I took tentative steps toward the showers.

The last stall smelled like lemon cleaning solution. Donna had done good. I turned to drop off the heavy pads and layers onto one of the benches nearby.

"Hey. What are you doing in here?" Landon tossed the freshly washed hair swooped across his forehead with a flick of his neck. "This is the boys' locker room."

"I know," I whispered meekly, hugging my belly to cover the drenched shirt sticking to me. "Coach said I could."

"Why can't you use the girls' showers?" Those blue eyes of his grew with concern.

My heart pitter-pattered.

The damp ends of my sweaty ponytail brushed the back of my neck as I lowered my head toward the glossy cement floor. "They hate me there."

"Want me to stand watch? Make sure no one else comes in?"

"Thanks." I pulled at the hem of my tee, detaching it from my skin to hide my flab. "Don't look, okay?"

"I won't."

With my back to Landon, I glance over my shoulder one last time. His back faces me, too, but when I slide off my skirt, I swear his eyes are on me.

CHAPTER 13:
BACK UP, RADEK

LANDON

I LIED. I HAD WHITE WINE.

Call me selfish, horny, whatever, but since I got a glimpse of the main event at her desk, I want more. I stop pouring, then run water into the sink to uncork and dump four of these five-hundred-dollar bottles of Chardonnay down the drain—*like some sort of maniac*—before grabbing a Cabernet.

Indi frowns at the color of wine I hand over.

"Sorry" —I give her my best puppy dog eyes— "I ran out of white."

I don't fish for more questions when she skims over the details of her love life. By the way she downs the first glass, she's nervous. I can't help giving her a little crap, especially when she hides behind white lies and sarcasm. Explaining the backstory with Annalise goes smoothly, except for getting sidetracked when she nibbles on her luscious lower lip while jotting down notes. I focus too long on the hem of her skirt, wishing it would inch up further.

Here she is, trying to be as professional as possible after seeing your dick. She's practically an angel for coming here with food and apologizing after *you* caught her touching herself while calling your name. Fuck, I can't think about that again. I'll get hard. I'm so screwed.

Somehow the tables turn and Indi fires shots at my sex life. It hasn't been six years since I got a decent tune-up, but I can't give her more fuel to judge me. Having a puck bunny dole out a quick handy or getting a blowjob after a night out isn't uncommon, but it's not me. Sierra wasn't my first or last, but I loved her. Best sex I ever had. Sex is only good for me when it means something. Annalise serves as a reminder.

When I blink out of the wayward train of thought, we've drained the bottle. I peep into it with a squinted eye, giving it a good shake. Indi reclines, more at ease. I lie down, too. She shares the tiniest bit more, but still protects herself. And then it makes sense. A hateful bastard impacted who she became, professionally and personally. Something inside me clenches into a tight knot until...*wait*. Did she say she's a virgin?

I dive off the couch to prevent her from face-planting into my floor. Her waist melts against my grip as I keep her upright. Indi's hands skate down my chest, leaving a warmth in their wake. My pulse quickens.

"I can't stay here. That's incredibly inappropriate."

"Almost as inappropriate as you getting off to the thought of me at work."

A perfect pink glow on the apples of her cheeks follows. "Shut up," she huffs.

I lower to her eye-level, giving in to the pull of those goddamn plump lips. "Make me."

Indi shoves me harder, and I drop her down to the sofa. The blush is now equal parts annoyance and demure. "Fine! I'll sleep here."

Fleeting relief is replaced by sudden anxiety. The girl of your pubescent dreams is sleeping over. You're a dumb, dumb son of a bitch.

She fiddles with her thumbs and pulls at the fabric of her skirt.

"Let me grab you something." Another stupid decision. Renovating means my closet has been scrapped and everything in it is nowhere near where it's supposed to be. I grab a practice jersey from my rookie year and a pair of shorts. They'll both be too big on her, but it's the best I can do. And how did I forget they took out the door to the half-bath to paint? Oh, right. Because the idea of Indi Davé staying the night has blown my brain to smithereens.

"Don't look while I'm changing," she warns. It's the same tone as when she snuck into our locker room to shower because of those horrible middle school girls.

"Don't look, okay?" Her eyes were so worried, unsure. They held my heart in a vice.

"I won't."

But I did. It was an accident, some sort of unintentional impulse to look over my shoulder. Indi peeled away a sweaty shirt and leggings, revealing strong legs topped with briefs and a white tank. Gray duct tape ripped from the fabric as she undid its wraps, setting her incredible tits free to their actual size and exposing the smooth flesh of her midriff.

Cradled in a sports bra, her chest was the first I'd seen in person. I forced myself to look away.

Molten lava churns in my gut. Her eyes are going to send me to an early grave. Their genuine insecurity makes my heart ache. Especially now I know the root of it.

"I won't."

I lied again. I looked. And what a fucking sight. Her shirt slips over her head, delicate blades of her back squinching with the single, sweeping movement of unzipping her skirt to reveal the rounds of her ass. When she pulls on my jersey, *Christ,* I want to toss her onto my bed and fuck her until she's so sore, I'll have to nurse her back to health myself.

Back up, Radek. You can't do any of that. She's your lawyer. And what happened to "no women?" She's off-limits. I wrench my gaze away this time, too, blowing a breath into the ceiling and willing my cock to soften once and for all. Indi's sleepy, rasped-out words don't help.

"Can I have a blanket or something?" Long, tan legs shift under my old hockey sweater.

"What?" Fuck, she looks amazing. Stop staring.

"Maybe *you're* the drunk one," she says, poking into my chest. "A blanket, please. So I can crash on the couch."

"D-don't be rid-ridiculous." This girl has me so twisted. "You can sleep in my room. I'll stay out here."

"*Your* room? Your *bedroom?* In your *bed?* Where you choke your chicken?" Indi snorts. "No, thank you."

I roll my eyes. "*Real* mature, Indi." My arms fold across my torso.

"The couch is fine." She slaps the air with a sputter, then twirls with her arms extended. "And don't you have like a *million* other rooms in this place?" It's cute as hell.

"The *three* other bedrooms are currently storing construction materials, or else I'd let you have one of those. And I'll have you know; the cleaners changed the sheets this morning."

"You're a pain in my ass." She finally gives in with a grumble, grabbing her briefcase and swaying aimlessly until I show her to the master suite. Indi steps through and turns to close it, a hateful fire in her eyes. "Goodnight."

I shoot her my best smile. "Night."

As soon as the door shuts, frustration has my hands running through the thick strands of my hair, tugging and mussing it up. *Fuck.* I'm going feral with the thought of her lying in my bed, wearing my name, my number twelve on her tight curved body. *Mine.* All mine. It's a fucking wet dream come true. My heart thuds in its bony cage, sending its heated contents straight to my dick. I need to lie down before I pass out or go into cardiac arrest. Or both.

One couch pillow supports my head as another hides my other head. I lift one corner to peek beneath it. "Go away," I whisper to my dick. "Why are you like this?"

I've reverted to my twelve-year-old self, sporting relentless boners for Indi. Memories of that year return in waves as I suppress all those dirty thoughts about my lawyer and overnight guest.

Most of the guys were horrible to her. Graham, Yally, Newt, and especially that little twerp Bennett.

One practice Bryce picked on her the whole time. He tripped her as she skated onto the ice at warm-ups and shoved her into the T-bar when she blocked his goal during scrimmage.

"Knock it off, Bennett!" Coach yelled.

"It was an accident! My skate slipped."

He always pulled shit like that to get out of trouble. Everyone knows you don't mess with the tendy and definitely not your own. We're supposed to be a team, but for some reason, Bennett was determined to make her miserable.

When he grabbed her paddle and slid it to the other end of the rink, she lost it. Indi skated up from behind as she tossed aside her gloves, then grabbed him by the collar. With an echoing roar, she knocked him onto the ice and pummeled fist after fist into his face. The rest of us watched on, stupefied at the unexpected anger from our otherwise silent teammate. Coach Alexei had to pry her away. Bryce Bennett sniveled like a baby.

After practice ended, I doodled on the back of a flyer while waiting for Delaney to pick me up.

Indi sat on the empty bench space next to me and raised her chin over my shoulder. "What's that?"

"Nothing really. You kicking Bryce's ass." I smoothed out the yellow sheet.

It was a quick sketch. Not my best work.

She smiled, then winced, her tongue skimming over the split in her bottom lip from when Bennett got a jab in. "It's pretty good."

"You like it, eh? It's yours." Pride surged through my chest at making her smile. I lived for that smile.

"No way! You drew it, you keep it." She wiped her nose with the back of her sleeve. "Frame it for when you're a famous artist."

"I'll be too busy playing puck for Toronto." That would make her smile for sure.

She lifted one shoulder with a roll of her eyes. "I don't know if you have what it takes to make it to the Show."

I nudged her elbow with mine. "Liar."

Indi elbowed me back with a soft giggle before a blue Honda Civic pulled up outside. She went wide-eyed, then heaved her gear onto a shoulder and shuffled to the door.

"See ya later, Indi!"

"Bye, Landon."

All of those post-practice conversations we shared while waiting for our too-busy parents on the bench. We *were* friends. There's no doubt. Then why is she acting like I'm the shit on her sneaker?

The A.C. whirs on, vent blowing frigid air onto my bare arms. I shiver and eye my bedroom door, wondering if I should go in there and grab a blanket. The clock on the wall beeps every hour.

At 4 a.m., I can't stop thinking about Indi and how she could be thinking about me, too, sliding her fingers between her legs and touching herself. In my bed. *Fuck.* This is a nightmare.

I get to my feet and advance into the pantry, grabbing the first bottle of alcohol I can find and taking an unglamorous swig. Whiskey burns the whole way down. I don't stop until the bottle's contents halve and my mind clouds over, erasing every last thought of her.

Sleep ends too soon with the sound of Indi's feet faintly thrumming across the floor. I suck air in through my mouth, dry and rough like sandpaper. A bubble rises from my gut, weak whiskey coating my throat.

The drunk stupor doesn't dissolve when I trace Indi's steps into the kitchen. She's more glorious in the morning light. The flawless curve of her ass peeks out from under my jersey as she reaches the tips of her toes and opens a cupboard. She can stay here forever if she's gonna look like that.

I groan, pressing the pads of my fingers into my eyes. "What are you trying to do to me?" I mumble.

She startles and sighs out her next breath. "Sorry, I didn't mean to wake you. I was getting some water."

"I was awake already," I swallow another lie, gagging on the taste of cottonmouth. It's like a raccoon made a home there and then died. "Cupboard left of the sink." The edge of the cool marble molds to me where I lean back into it, rubbing my eyes.

Indi finds a glass and fills it from the tap, peering over the rim when she brings it to her bowed mouth. I have never been so jealous of a glass. A long quiet moment passes as she finishes. This woman drives me batshit crazy. I brush over my jaw, nervous.

Tell her to stay. Tell her you can't stop thinking about her. That you want more moments like last night, when she cracked herself open a sliver and offered little pieces of her life to you.

"What's next?"

She cocks a leg, her back against the counter across from me, leaving the glass next to the sink. "Oh, *uh*, I'll start to take testimonials and see if there's any hard evidence..."

I don't mean to laugh. "I'm not talking about the case." Scratching a brow, I continue. "I meant us. Are we gonna pretend like the last two weeks didn't happen?"

Tell her you want to know what she likes—her favorite food, how she spends her free time—everything. How she wants to be held, touched, kissed. Tell her you'll do it all.

"Yes!" Her shoulders slump, relieved. "I thought you'd never ask. That's what we should do. Clean slate. We can move forward—"

"Move forward?"

Indi pales as I straighten and stalk toward her, the heavy traces of whiskey making me brazen.

"And how am I supposed to do that? When you're here" —my eyes scan over her— "in *my* house" —I take a step— "in *my* clothes" —another step breaks the distance between us— "looking like you're exactly where you belong?"

Indi breathes out a barely audible response. "What?"

Tell her your heart wants to collapse onto itself when she's around. Not a single inhibition in sight, I trap her between my arms, posting them on either side of her frame. "How do you expect me to forget what you sound like when you come?"

This is not what we discussed! That's it. You're on your own.

She shrinks away, pressing herself into the counter, her lips cowering into a frown. "I hate you."

"No, you don't, Indi."

Fuck, she smells like the best times of my life. Warm, cinnamony holidays during the coldest parts of the year. I wonder if she tastes like it, too. My control dangles by the thinnest of next-morning-whiskey-drunk threads. "You showed me *exactly* how you feel when you moaned my name in your office."

"*Landon.*" A surprised gasp gushes out, intoning with a chide.

"Yeah, just like that."

Indi's throat strains through a gulp of air. Her eyes dart across my face as we close in, the tip of my nose sidling next to hers.

"I want to make you cry out for me again. Just. Like. That."

Tears well, kissing the lower lids of her eyes.

No! That's not supposed to happen.

"I should've never stayed here."

Indi grapples with my forearm and escapes, disappearing into my bedroom, then reemerges in her clothes from last night. My head throbs. Her heels clack past the door.

I pushed her too far, came on too strong and fucked up again. *Ow, my head.*

An aggressive, crescendoing growl bellows from my chest as I grab Indi's glass from the counter and hurl it against a white cupboard. Air tugs from my chest, heaving in the aftermath of the shatter and I slink to my room, hoping to sleep away the deep sense of regret settling in my gut.

CHAPTER 14:
CALM DOWN, EVERYONE

INDI

LANDON HAD ME FOOLED LAST NIGHT, THINKING I'D misunderstood him. He's been messing with me from the beginning.

"Move forward? And how am I supposed to do that? When you're here, in my house, wearing my clothes, looking like you're exactly where you belong? How do you expect me to forget what you sound like when you come?" A hell of a smooth talker. I almost fall for it. "I want to make you cry out for me again. Just like that."

His boozy breath streams by my mouth, shocking me into reality. It's a fucking joke, some sort of cruel game, a competition to see who can humiliate me the most. I did a pretty bang-up job—*pun intended*—doing that on my own last week. But now, not only does Landon know my weakness for him, he's exploiting it. It's a repeat of grade seven.

Was it worth it? So he'd tell me the 'truth' about Annalise? I can't trust him. I don't even trust myself. If I stand here one more second, I'll either have a mental breakdown or tear him apart with my bare hands. Neither can happen. And I won't let him see me cry, either.

"I should've never stayed here."

His eyes twinge with what looks like pain. My heart seizes, but I break free from the cage of his arms, the defined veins snaking under my grip only adding to my ridiculous sexual frustration. Men like Landon smell desperation a mile away.

The mixed bag of thoughts dissipates as I pull on yesterday's work clothes and toss the borrowed jersey onto his bed. I'm tempted to set it on fire. Landon clutches his head, stumbling over his feet when I sprint towards the enormous doors. How much did he drink? I thought he had less than me. Stop it, Indi. You don't care about him. He can rot in hell for all you care.

I give myself an affirming nod in the elevators, adjusting the shoulder strap of my work bag as I step out into the main lobby. Timur isn't there and neither are the vultures outside. The security guard in his place waves two fingers at me in greeting.

Two blocks of stormy heel-walking later, I hop into a cab. My phone vibrates from inside the front pocket of the briefcase.

BEA

Hey, where are you? If you're not here in seven minutes, we're gonna lose our spot in line. Gabe's head is about to explode.

Oh, shit. Saturday brunch. I look out the window, trying to figure out where we are.

"Excuse me? Could you take me to Wilf & Ada's instead? It's on Bank Street and Arlington Ave."

The driver makes a sharp left, sliding me to the opposite end of the back seat as I attempt to tie my hair. There's no salvaging it though. The ponytail is messy and smells like Landon and his stupid sheets. The citrus and laundry detergent scent combo sets my hormones on fire.

We stop with a jolt, and I almost hit my head on the plexiglass panel separating the cabby from me. I tap my card and nearly fall onto the curb, in view of the queue of people circling the corner. Bea beckons with large swoops of her arm from the foyer window. I rush inside.

"Thank God, you made it!" She gives me a tight hug.

"Yep, I'm here. You're feeling better?"

Bea takes a large intake of air and releases it, showing off her ability to breathe. "Turns out it's allergies."

Gabe checks out my haggard appearance as I smooth my shirt down. "What the hell happened to you?"

"Not now," I whisper through my teeth, throwing polite smiles at the staff and other waiting guests.

For a tiny cafe, Wilf & Ada's does well for itself. It teems with life, especially on temperate summer weekend mornings like this one. We've learned to show up early and wear comfy shoes. I've done neither today.

A young, blonde hostess guides us to a corner table and Sammie, one of the regular servers, distributes menus and water. "Any interest in hearing the specials or should I guess what you're ordering?"

"*Oooh*," Gabe coos, clasping her hands. "I like this game. Let's hear what you think we're ordering."

Sammie taps the end of her pen to her chin and hums. She points it at Bea. "You'll have a Poutine Galvaude with a Mimosa."

Bea gasps and does a golf clap, handing back her menu without a glance.

"And I think you'll go for the Veggie Bennie and a Bloody Mary today," she says to Gabe.

"Spot on, Sam."

"Now, don't get mad," Sammie adds with a grimace, scanning over my wrinkled shirt and skirt. "You look like you had a rough night. Maybe Eggs in Purgatory and a Coffee Avec Bailey's."

I slide the menu off the edge of the butcher block to her. "Close. Iced coffee. Hold the booze."

She returns an assumptive smirk but doesn't know the half of it. Gabe and Bea turn their attention back to me when she leaves to put in the order.

Bea grabs my shoulder. "You're wearing work clothes!"

"Sleeping at the office again?" Gabe raises an eyebrow.

"No." What the hell am I supposed to tell them? "I..." Hurry up, brain. "...Spent the night somewhere else." Genius!

"Somewhere *else*?" Gabe asks. "Weren't you going to Radek's to make peace or something?"

I did tell her that. Crap. "Oh, yeah." I wave it off. "We're all good there. I bought him dinner and worked it all out."

You did nothing of the sort. This is not good. Not good, Indi. You're building a Jenga tower of lies.

Bea snickers. "Men are so easy. Feed 'em once and they'll do whatever you ask."

"So where did you go?" My best friend's eyes narrow.

Sammie interrupts with an apology and our drinks, giving me twenty seconds of sucking this coffee down before I have to answer. A runner outside the window swerves through the line of people waiting to have brunch. And then it hits me.

"I ran into this guy from the gym."

Gabe stirs her drink with a stick of celery, the ice clink-clink-clinking against the glass. "And what? Had a sleepover? You've never done that before."

She's right. I've never spent a night like that with any man. Landon's the first.

"And who is this 'Gym Guy,' anyway?"

"He's a guy." Excellent. She'll totally buy this. "We've been flirting or something, I guess. He invited me over, we had some wine and I had too much, so I stayed." Only one lie there.

"That's so dangerous."

"Alright, *calm down*, everyone." I hold up my hands. "I'm a grown woman and I can handle myself." This is not at all true. I'm a big dummy who's fallen into old, bad habits.

Bea takes a break from her mimosa. "Is he hot?"

Ah, yes. Behraz, my voice of reason. I roll my eyes. "Yes."

"Is he packing?" She prods, grinning over her glass.

I cover my face with my hands. "It is *way* too early—"

"That means 'yes,'" Gabe butts in.

"*Noice*. And you like him?" A complicated question if I ever heard one.

Head tossing back with a weary sigh, I admit my indecision. "I don't know, I have no idea what I'm doing." Landon turns my brain to mashed potatoes.

My legal secretary leans in, smiling with impish glee. "You gonna let him" —she waggles her eyebrows, then creates an *o* with one hand and pokes the index finger of the other through it, whistling once— "wet your whistle?"

Gabe chokes on her Bloody Mary and reaches for the napkin from her lap.

"Shut up," I hiss through my teeth and elbow her.

"What? There's nothing wrong with having fun."

"I agree," Gabe chimes in again. "It's time, my friend. I say, let the man play your vocal cords like a violin."

Bea cackles, pounding her fists lightly on the tabletop. "Do him! Do him! Put his crocodile in your swamp!" Eyes wide as they can be, my face reddens. It does nothing to deter their teasing.

"Swirl his meat tornado through your southern region!" Gabe twirls a finger in the air, making a quiet drilling noise. "*Vvvvvvvvvvvvvooo!*"

"Stuff his gyro meat into your slobber pocket!"

My hands fly up to my cheeks, hiding my eyes, mouth, and hopefully, the fiery blush. They muffle my discontent. "I hate you both."

Gabe slaps her knee with a silent laugh as Bea wipes the corners of her eyes and lets out a lilting sigh. "You love us." They high-five over the table.

Sammie relieves me of their incessant innuendo, and they switch it out for a persistent interrogation about this mystery suitor. Who doesn't exist. I give no details about his name or occupation, citing I'm not ready.

Gabe huffs. "What does he look like?"

I gaze at the upper edge of the window frame. "*Ummm,* athletic, strong."

"Not his body, you wiener." Bea smacks my shoulder. "His face, his features."

"Handsome," I say through a bite of egg. Infuriatingly so. "Tousled brown hair. Insane eyes. Dimples."

She slides down her chair, swooning. "He sounds dreamy. Like a Disney Prince."

I side-eye her theatrics. "Yes, well. I don't know if I trust him."

The light conversation blips. Gabe straightens, crossing her silverware across the plate with a gentle clank, and finishes chewing. "Really, Indi? *You* stayed the night with someone you *don't* trust? That doesn't sound like something you do." She takes a sip. "I don't know him, but I know you. I think that you *do* trust him, but you're scared. And that's valid. Though maybe it's time to test out the waters. Give him a chance, you know?"

Condensation from my coffee glass drips onto its coaster below. My lips wrinkle, pulling to one side.

"Not every guy is Kleinmann," she adds. Gabe is the only person in my life who witnessed the whole fiasco with me in-person.

I gulp in response, still staring at the growing ring of water.

Bea curls an arm around my drooping shoulders. "And if he turns out to be..." She twirls the butter knife in her free hand from an innocent hold to something much more violent and stabs the air, a sinister grin stretching her mouth. "You know who to call."

I shrug her off with a playful nudge, hot tears building once more. I haven't cried over men in years, and I've almost done it twice over Landon Radek in one morning.

Gabe waves the waitress back over. "Could we have the check, please?"

We're not quite out the door before the staff clears our table and another group takes over. Gabe gets in an Uber to get some work done in the newsroom, grumbling about one more golf tour assignment she couldn't slough off. Bea offers to drive me home, but she's already running late to drop her car off for servicing and I refuse to add to her chaos. I hop into another cab, pulling out my phone to avoid the chatty driver. A few notifications on a group chat with my sisters flash on the screen.

ANIKA

I truly hope you're dead in a ditch somewhere.

ME

Unfortunately not.

ANIKA

She lives!

ESHA

You're so fucking dramatic, Nik.

ESHA

Can you respond to Mom? She's about to have an aneurysm.

It wasn't going to be long before ignoring her was gonna bite me in the ass. It's only been two, no, three days, right? I check. Never mind. It's been a week. But I'm not sure I can handle another conversation with Mom pestering me about whether I've eaten and how work's going. What would I say? *"Work could be better, Mom. My new client is my middle school crush—by the way, he's now an outrageously hot, rich hockey player— who I hate. He also caught me masturbating in my office while moaning his name and now is making fun of me for it. Otherwise, everything's **great**!"*

ME

I'll call her when I get to my apartment.

ANIKA

You're not there? Where are you?

ME

Went to brunch with Gabe and Bea.

ESHA

What about last night? Mom said she called, and you didn't pick up.

ME

None of your business.

ANIKA

But I wanna know!

ESHA

Me too!

ANIKA

I'll ask Bea. Give you the updates later, E.

ESHA

Also, are you coming home tonight or tomorrow morning?

ME

I wasn't planning on coming home this weekend.

ANIKA

OMG YOU FORGOT

ME

???

ESHA

Didi! Karishma's engagement thingy is tomorrow! How could you forget??

Tomorrow? I flip over to my calendar app, and lo and behold, tomorrow is my cousin's engagement ceremony day.

ME

JK guys. I'll be home tonight, depending on traffic.

ESHA

Sure, sure.

ANIKA

You forgot ahah. Can't wait to tell Karish.

ME

Don't you dare!

ESHA

If you're not going to wear that green anarkali, can I borrow it?

ME

No.

ESHA

The gold lehenga then?

ME

No!

ANIKA

You always get the good ones and don't wear them.

ME

Don't care. Don't touch my closet.

I pack as soon as I get back to my place, skipping a shower and changing into sweats and a tee for the five-hour drive that might turn into seven.

If I'm lucky, I'll be home for dinner. Traffic is hellish as expected, but I preoccupy myself with the eventful previous week and Gabe's advice from the morning, ruminating and ruminating. By the time I pull into the driveway, I don't know whether I want to tell Landon the truth or drop him as a client without explanation. It's only when I lift my hand to knock that I realize I didn't call my mother back.

Her sixth sense beats me to it, and she swings the door open with an unimpressed smile. Mom's expression transforms into sardonic surprise. "Oh, ho, ho! *Aaye, aaye, Mallika-E-Hindustan!*" She bows and backs away, bringing an open palm to her forehead several times, the respectful greeting of the Moghuls. I'm surrounded by sarcastic assholes. "We're so honored you have graced our household with your presence."

"Very funny, Mom." I slip off my sneakers and toss the duffle into a corner of the entryway, hugging her with a playful side-squeeze. "I'm sorry I didn't call. It's been a crazy week."

My height towers above hers and she gives in, patting my arm from underneath.

"Always so busy," she whines. "Too busy for your own mother."

I kiss the top of her head with a silly sort of aggression. "I love you," I say with a smile.

She glares back. "Yes, yes, I know."

Dad ambles in from the back of the house. "Oy hoye!" A family of actors, we are. He lifts both arms, pointing his index fingers to the sky, and shakes his shoulders, breaking out into his best bhangra move. "Induji ghar aaye, Induji ghar aaye!"

The play-on-words has me cracking up and joining him, sandwiching my mom between us.

"Rahul!" Mom smacks Dad with the hand towel hanging over her shoulder.

Dad grabs one end and pulls her closer, swiping the tip of her nose with his finger. "Anjali!"

Gag. These two have always milked the fact that they share names with one of the most classic couples in Bollywood history.

My mother blushes and tugs the towel away. "Stop it, Rahul." She redirects her focus to me. "And you! Go wash up. I made pav bhaji." Before I can ask, she continues. "Your sisters will be home soon. Anika went to pick up Esha from the train station."

Over the running water in the bathroom, I hear Dad softly singing, "Induji ghar aaye, Induji ghar aaye!" Probably harassing Mom some more. There's nothing like coming home.

My younger sisters arrive soon after, giving me shit about where I was last night under their breath. Either my parents feign blissful ignorance or truly have no idea what's going on. I get to live another day.

After we clean up, I kick Anika out of her room for the night.

"This isn't fair!"

"Too bad, so sad." I shove her through the doorway. "Find something else to take a stand about. It's one night. I'm leaving tomorrow afternoon. Unlike *some people*, I have to work on Monday."

Nik scoffs, stomping her foot. "More reason for you to sleep on the couch!"

I shut the door and lock it.

"*Indi*!"

Esha grumbles from across the hall before her door slams, too. "No way, Nik. You snore."

"You're both jerks!"

"Oy, what's going on up there?" Dad's voice booms from the bottom of the stairwell.

"Nothing!" We yell back in unison.

It's rare for the three of us to all agree on anything, but we band together again the following morning when Dad complains about us taking forever to get ready for the party. I spend a little too much time scrubbing the smell of Landon from my skin and washing it out of my hair. The bathroom mirror is of no use, still foggy from the searing temperature of my shower, so I stand in the hallway, utilizing the floor-length mirror on the door to moisturize my face and comb out the wet waves. Nik and Esha flank me in the rooms on either side, using mirrors to blend concealer or apply mascara.

"What's the hold up, eh? We have to leave in ten to make it on time and you girls aren't dressed!"

"Go away, Dad!" Only my youngest sister can get away with talking to him like that. Spoiled brat. "Beauty takes time!"

"There's no beauty in vanity, my loves." He places his hands on his hips, standing behind me and pacing between the bedrooms.

Anika breaks into a sputtered laugh. "It's makeup. It's not that serious."

"*Aw*, come on, girls. Please hurry up. You're beautiful as you are."

"*Dad*! Go. Away!" Esha repeats.

Anika snorts. "Don't you need to help Mom pin her sari or something? Stop bothering us."

"I beg your pardon! We're gonna have a chat in the car later about respect." He wags his finger, a disgruntled rant about having some say in his own damn house trailing behind him as he trots down the stairs. Not sure what he expected after having three grown daughters and a wife in the same space.

We eventually make it out the door, dressed and bedazzled with jewelry and bangles, bindi and heels. Despite the in-fighting from the backseat and Dad driving like a wackadoodle, we make it to the ceremony in one piece.

I brace myself for the inevitable comments from the usual crew of Auntys.

"You're next!"

I sure as hell am not.

"How old are you? Are you looking for someone? My brother-in-law's nephew is a software engineer at Netflix in the States."

No, thank you. I'm busy. I've got my hands full figuring out how to not kill my client.

Small talk and fake smiles for a couple of hours, even if it is my extended family, takes it out of me. It's been a tiring day. A long week to end a long month.

On the drive back to Ottawa, I practice a conversation with Theresa. "I've been working too hard. I got Radek's side of the story, but I'm not on my A-game. Going straight from the Pearson case to this has been a lot."

Hopefully, she'll understand and give me the week off. Hell, it's summer. If she says yes, I might fly across the country to get away from Landon before I have to see more of him.

CHAPTER 15:
THE HARD WAY

LANDON

SOMEWHERE AFTER MILE TWO ON THE RIVERFRONT, the high-noon sun beats down with a fury. I yank my shirt over my head and tuck it into the back of my shorts. Between the alternating sprint workout Jaeg's got us doing and replaying how hurt Indi looked, I'm suffocating.

"Look sharp, Radek." Wade huffs when I almost kick a rogue duck on the path. "These fartlickers are kicking your ass."

Fletch putters through a laugh.

Jaeger decks Wade in the arm as we slow to a jogging pace. "It's Fartlek."

"Unhand me, goon!" Wade shoves him away, getting ahead to face us. He keeps up with a backward run. "What's your deal? Something's off."

"This girl's giving me such a hard time."

"Hell yeah, she is!" The idiot holds up his hand, waiting for a high-five. I don't give it to him, instead shooting him a glare. "Wait, what girl?" Uh oh.

Fletcher raises one of his ginger eyebrows. "I thought you were avoiding women."

Derrick snorts.

Wade rolls his eyes. "Not everyone has accepted permanent celibacy like you, Donovan."

Fletcher charges at him for that one. Wade jukes, spinning and evading capture.

"I was. I am! I...just met her." Good. Lie. That always helps.

"Where'd you meet her? You don't go anywhere," Jaeger adds. "Thirty seconds at eighty percent."

Motherfucker.

We dart forward, feet pounding against the asphalt, racing each other until the stopwatch beeps out. Our steps decelerate once more, giving us the chance to catch our breaths. Wade wins again, the little shit, but at least I beat Derrick.

I gloat. "That's what you get, old man."

Wade crosses his hands over his groin. "*Suck itttttt!*"

My mind races to conjure up an excuse on the spot. "The gym," I blurt. Awesome cover.

"Which gym?"

"Fit365."

"*Ahhh,*" Wade intones. "That's why you always wanna go there."

"You caught me." I throw my hands up.

Jaeg doesn't buy it. "What's her name?"

"It's a secret." A coy response, but the best I can do.

"You haven't talked to her yet?" Fletch asks, right before the stopwatch beeps out again.

The last thirty-second sprint follows, this one all-out at full speed. Sweat trickles down my spine, pooling at the waistband as the sun's intense rays continue their beating. It's over soon enough and we double over, our hands on our knees.

"You pulled a Donovan!" Wade guffaws.

This time Fletch catches him in a headlock, his face turning the same shade as the freckles dotting his skin.

Hands resting on my bare hips, I suck in breath after ragged breath. "I've talked to her. I probably shouldn't have."

"What about Indi?" Jaeg questions over these two yo-yo's grunting while wrestling in the bordering grassy patch.

"What about her?"

"You tell me. It seemed like you were down for the count."

"Don't be ridiculous. She's my lawyer. That would be fucked up." Sure, sure. "Anyway, she bought me dinner and apologized. Strictly professional." Liar, liar, your dick's on fire. I swipe my shirt across my face, then the back of my neck, and down my chest. Sweat beads return to the skin almost immediately.

Derrick seems to accept. We look over at our friends on the lawn.

Fletch straddles Wade's chest, using the tendy's hands to slap his own face. "Stop hitting yourself! Why are you hitting yourself?"

"Will you two fucking grow up?" Jaeg shakes his head.

They part after a few more pushes. Wade throws me a bro nod. "You gonna bang that gym chick or not, Landy?"

"Probably not." I stretch my bunched-up tee over my head, pulling the panels down until it looks like a nun's veil. "Maybe I should take Donovan's lead and embrace celibacy after all."

Fletch flips me off. "You're a twat."

"No lie there." Wade pats me on the shoulder. "But he's *our* twat."

We plop down under a tree, hoping to cool down in the shade. Jaeg and Fletch leave first. After about twenty minutes of failing to not think about Indi, I get up to hail a cab.

Wade opens one eye, peeking from under his arm. "Yo, what are you doing this weekend?" he calls. "I was going to Whistler, but my mom's having knee surgery, so I'm headed to Lac Saint Anne instead." He tuts. "Wanna go? Suite was booked and everything. Shame to let it go to waste."

"Thanks, man. I'm dying for some time away before dry land training."

"I'll have Trish send you the details."

"Later, Boehner. Stay out of trouble."

"That's funny." He props himself on both elbows. "I was about to say the same to you."

———

Wade's P.A. goes above and beyond, switching over the reservations to my name and booking the flight and a car service, and by Friday, I'm set to travel coast-to-coast. I've driven the route from Vancouver to Whistler before, but not having to pay attention to anything but the rocky cliffs, cragged coastline, and sea green waters is relaxing. Stalwart cedars and pines line the scenic highway and lead to the evergreens on the climbing ridges. In the distance, snow caps the lush green peaks.

Angled roofs and art deco windows make up the facade of the modern lodge-style hotel tucked into the mountainside. Crisp air, blue skies and panoramic views welcome us when we pull up into the circular drop-off. My thoughts clear while staring through the glass elevators. They hide nothing of the literal epitome of nature's grandeur.

Doling out a decent tip to the young bellhop for carrying my luggage and ski gear up, I tap my card to the reader on the suite door. I pass the living space and mini bar on my way to take in the breathtaking view, dropping my bags onto the floor with a loud thud and sharp sigh.

"Excuse me." Rustling footsteps and a voice grow louder from the bedroom of the suite.

Thinking it's a maid and there must have been some misunderstanding between the hotel staff, I turn to apologize. "Sorry, they told me the room was ready—"

"I don't need housekeeping, I just got here—" Her voice fades. A pause looms as we both freeze. "No. Absolutely *not!*"

Hair in messy, effortless waves and eyes fierce with fresh rage, Indi Davé clenches her fists at her sides and plants her feet as the brightest white sundress flutters around her. The square neck and fitted torso highlight that set of glorious tits, the subtle floral pattern starkly contrasting her less-than-flowery expression. I halt the stream of thought before it goes down the drain. Regret fills my gut once more.

"Indi..."

"No!" She holds up a finger, hands and expression syncing in frantic movements. "No talking. Who told you I was here? How did you find me?" Her body trembles, she's so upset. Another pause. "Tell me!"

I form an *o* with my mouth, pointing to myself. "Am I allowed to talk now?"

Do you have a death wish, Radek? Shut your yapper.

"Get out."

"But this is *my* room."

"Like hell it is. Get. Out!" Indi manhandles me, backing me towards the door. She swings it open and shuts it on my ass before reopening it and throwing my stuff into the hallway.

The trip to the front desk is tedious and pointless. I mutter on the solo elevator ride back up, preparing myself for patience, kindness, and sensitivity despite Indi's anger. My mind shuts off as I step into the suite again.

Indi reclines on the couch, feet on the armrest, her legs going on forever until the point where her dress bunches at their apex. She bolts upright, mouth parting in disgusted surprise.

I surrender my bags to the floor with a hopeful smile and innocent shrug. "Looks like they don't have any more rooms."

Indi glares back, seething. "You're fucking *joking*."

"I'm not. They're all booked up."

Her nose flares with a deep breath. "Leave, then. This isn't the only place—"

"They're full, too." I sit my ass on the armchair across from where she stands. "I'm stuck here."

With you. And I don't mind one bit.

"No, you're not. Go away." She motions to the door.

"Unfortunately, I am. There's a mudslide lower on the mountain. Can't leave until they reopen the highway."

"But I got here first!" She stomps one foot. It's adorable. Goodbye, Mr. Kind, Patient and Sensitive. The need to annoy her is back.

"So? It's a big suite."

"So?" she echoes, imitating me while making a face. "Where will you sleep? There's only one bed." Blush pink is the prettiest color on her. Prettier on her than anyone else I've ever seen.

"It's called *sharing*, Indi." I extend my legs, crossing them at the ankles and clasp both hands behind my head, fighting a smile as the tint on her face deepens and creeps onto the shells of her ears. "Some people in the world don't have beds."

"*Landon!*"

"Indi!" I mock with a smile.

"Why do you insist on making my life Hell?" She throws her hands up.

And I feel bad again. I was supposed to be apologizing. "Listen, I shouldn't have said—"

"Cut the shit, Landon," she snipes through a sneer, marching towards the door. "We're gonna get this figured out, but you are *not* staying here. My boss agreed to give me time off in exchange for keeping this case. I came here to get away from you. You won't fool me this time."

The last words disappear under her breath, likely so I don't hear, but I do. Fool her? When did I do that?

"Indi."

"*Shhh!*" Her finger presses against those flawless lips. "No more talking from you. Get your ass downstairs." There's determination in her sharp tone, and *fuck*, if I'm not turned on by it. "We're gonna have a chat with the front desk."

They're helpless against natural disasters and a busy summer season. I doubt a threat of litigation will change things, either. Indi is strong-willed, though. She wants to do this the hard way. Unfortunately for her, I play to win. And I'm not leaving this mountain without her telling me the whole truth.

"Good call, Indi. Let's go." I wave my arm ahead of her in the hall. "Ladies first."

CHAPTER 16:
BIG PLANS

INDI

LANDON DAWDLES ALONG WHILE I LEG IT FROM THE elevators to the front desk. Boiled blood pumps into every part of my body. The vein in my forehead throbs with vengeance.

"Good afternoon! May I help you?"

"Yes, *Antony*, you *may*," I fire back to the too-cheery, unsuspecting clerk, slapping my palm to the high countertop. "There's been a grave oversight."

"Oh, no. What seems to be the problem?"

"The *problem* is you've got us" —I point between myself and Landon, who leans his elbow on the marble surface, an unbothered smile on his face— "in the same room."

He buffs his fingernails against his black hoodie, inspects them with a frown, then winks at the front desk clerk.

"We're having a little argument," Landon whispers with an explanatory nod. He scrunches his nose before that dumb perfect smile returns to his dumb handsome face.

I scoff. The nerve!

Antony flicks his gaze to Landon, then me, quirking a brow. "Ma'am?"

"It's. A. Mistake." My eyes widen for emphasis, index finger jabbing into the counter, with every enunciated point. "I did *not* book my stay here with him." Temper quickly unraveling, I tense my jaw to maintain some sort of restraint. "We *need* separate rooms."

Anthony is unfazed by my anger. "I'm sorry, Miss...?"

"Davé." A galloping cadence strums out from my fingernails against the stone. My patience hangs by the weakest of threads, much like whatever's left on Antony's thinning hairline.

"I'm *so* sorry, Ms. Davé," he responds with rehearsed, rueful eyes. "I don't have a different solution than when I spoke to Mr. Radek before. We are *completely* full this weekend. We don't have any rooms available..."

"And how is that my fault?" My palm turns into a fist before slamming down. "I paid for this suite!"

"Funny you say that," Landon finally chimes in. "So did I."

"We can clear that right up for you." Antony clatters away on the keyboard. "Your weekend stay is on us. Enjoy your complimentary—"

"Are you listening to me?" I shake my head, moving my arms around in shaky circles.

"I do apologize, but my hands are tied—"

"Welp! You heard it from the horse's mouth." Landon straightens and claps his hands together. "Thanks for trying, Ant. We'll share the room." He hauls his gear over his shoulder.

I whip my head to my unhinged client. He must be out of his mind. "We will do nothing of the sort!"

Antony's confusion lingers.

"Sure, we will."

This asshole has the nerve to lead me away from the desk, his hand on my lower back. It flattens against the dip above my ass, his grip warm, firm, and insistent. I hate that I like how it feels.

"What? Stop that! What are you doing?" Fighting him is no use but I do it anyway. My shoes squeak, the flat soles losing traction over the flooring. A few inches taller and at least fifty pounds heavier, I'm no match when Landon's determined to torture me, even with one hand.

"Have a nice day, Antony. Thanks for all your help!" He waves and smiles at gawking passersby.

"We are *not* friends," I grate out. My attempt to elbow him is foiled by a set of skis. I hiss and rub the joint.

"You're making a scene," Landon murmurs.

The elevator doors open, and he pushes us through. When it closes, I wrench his arm away from me. He lets go.

"What is your problem, Radek?"

Pushing out a short, exasperated breath, he hits the button for the floor, then shoots me an annoyed glare. "I'm looking right at her."

"Me? You're the one who won't leave me alone!"

"Indi!" His voice rises and echoes off the steel walls, hands outstretched towards me. He lowers it in his next breath. "I'm *trying* to apologize."

"I don't give a—"

The elevator doors ding open again. A family of three stare back at us, cutting our exchange short. Landon relaxes and throws them a fake, polite grin as we rapidly walk towards the suite.

His fingers graze the crook of my elbow when I throw open the door and stride across the carpet. It's surprisingly gentle and irks me more. I escape from their loose grasp. "Don't touch me! Don't talk to me, don't look at me..."

"Indi." Landon puts his bags down, tucks his hands into his jeans, and tilts his head. Why is he looking at me like that? Like he's actually sorry. He's not sorry.

"Didn't I say no talking?" I pace between the bedroom and living area, calming my breaths as Landon studies the floor. Logic kicks in and I huff. "We're stuck on this stupid mountain. You said it yourself: this suite is big enough. Stay over there and out of my way."

His eyes shift to the right, a pained look in their blue tone. They match the sky outside the window. "Okay."

"Pretend I'm not here and I'll do the same for you," I rant on, peering around the bed for my purse. "You use this door" —my hand motions toward the one we walked through, then the one from the bedroom— "I'll use this one. We'll both do our own thing."

"I said 'okay,'" he repeats, head slack from defeat.

My jaw softens. My heart, too.

"God, you're annoying."

Landon adjusts his backwards baseball cap, leaving his hands on the visor. "And you're stubborn as hell."

"One of my finer qualities," I mumble, turning on my heel. Kicking my shoes off by the vanity in the corner, I keep going. "I'd be insulted, but I don't give a crap what you think."

He sighs and plops down. The room goes quiet except for me shuffling around the bed twice and the TV playing elevator jazz. Where the hell is my purse?

"Looking for this?" Landon lounges on the couch, back facing me, holding the gray handles of my bag above his head. He switches channels every few seconds with the remote in his free hand.

"Give me that!"

"Here you go—*oop!*" He stands and trips on the corner leg of the sofa, lobbing my purse and most of its content across the floor.

"What a *great* help," I reply, picking up my wallet, sunglasses, and a travel-size pack of facial tissues and tossing them into the open compartment of the rectangular purse. A half-eaten bar of Cadbury Dairy Milk and a dozen folded receipts join them. I eye the black cap of a lipstick by a panel of white baseboards and reach down to grab it. Which lipstick is this for? I frown, rolling the hollow cylinder between my thumb and index finger. Wait a minute.

"Interesting." The timbre of his voice deepens. Landon leans on the back of the sofa, spinning the item in hand, then twisting it to reveal a silicone rose tip. He squeezes the metal column, the discreet toy buzzing to life under the pressure of his thumb. His mouth pulls into the smirkiest smirk.

I gulp as my cheeks fire up.

"Big plans this weekend, eh?"

I close the distance in three livid steps, snatching it from his grubby clutches. "You know what? I'm not embarrassed. I'm not ashamed. But you know what I am? I'm *so fucking tired* of you giving me shit for this. So you saw me." The vibrating lipstick gets switched off, closed, and thrown into my bag. "Big whoop, Radek! We're both adults. I doubt either of us are unfamiliar with masturbation. I happen to like it and toys aren't assholes, unlike every man I've had to deal with today."

He opens his mouth to say something, but I slam the door separating the rooms shut, then backpedal and stoop down until my ass hits the mattress. The man is exhausting. I lie back and stare at the recessed lights, willing this headache to die already.

Hey, universe? Wanna give me a fucking break one of these days?

Ten minutes later, the TV turns off. Undecipherable grumbles subside as the door creaks open, and snaps shut. My fingers massage the gap between my brows.

I somehow nap through the late afternoon, waking only at dusk. A growling stomach forces me out of the room to grab dinner. Hair fluffed and strays smoothed, I head to the village and beg to whatever Supreme

Power out there that I don't bump into Landon Radek.

———

The following morning, I take a ride up the peak, both to get away from my thoughts and Landon. And especially my thoughts *on* Landon.

Sun beams on the onyx rock peeking through the sprawling, stark white snow of Horstman Glacier. It isn't as robust as a few years ago, but I'm grateful it's still here, considering how quickly it's melting.

My head tips back as I fix the askew goggles atop my head. A clear, azure sky and the cool temperatures turning my breath into clouds refreshing my mind. Tipping back a little too far has one ski slipping. I regain balance with the support of a pole.

"Careful," someone cautions behind me. "You could fall and get hurt."

I cringe at the sky, cursing my luck—*what happened to staying out of each other's way?* —before glowering over my shoulder at Landon. "I can handle myself, thank you very much."

"Prove it." He lines up beside me, a bright, toothy grin shining in the morning light in contrast to his all-black jacket and snow pants. "Race me."

"What are you, a child?" I lower my goggles, rolling my eyes underneath them.

"It's okay to admit you're slow." He sniffs. "Tell you what, I'll go easy on you." Landon flashes me another glittery smile.

"Really? You'd do that?" I fake a grateful tone. What he doesn't know won't hurt him. At least not physically. He could benefit from an ego injury.

"Of course, Indi. I'm a nice guy."

I crouch into position, keeping steady and straightening my skis. "Countdown or 'ready, set, go?'"

"I'll countdown," he starts. "Three, two, one and on 'go', we'll—*hey!*"

His protest fades behind me as I boost ahead. I whoosh forward, the wind whipping against my frame while I pick up speed.

"Indi, you cheat!"

I laugh out, not daring to look back and risk falling. He may be a professional athlete, but I love to win.

My limbs pump harder and harder, quads burning as I swerve side to side. A group of skiers lollygag on my left and I vine around them to hit the last leg approaching the lift at the bottom. I skid to a stop, shooting a gossamer of powdery snow to one bank and turning full circle to face the sore loser himself.

"What the hell was that? You hustled me!" He pants and rips off his goggles. "I want a redo!"

"No takesies backsies, Landon. I won, fair and square." I squint towards him, the sun in my eyes. "Will you leave me alone now?"

"Double or nothing." He breaks into an effortless smile, poking a playful tongue into his cheek.

I shake my head and hop on the lift.

Landon follows and gets in behind me. "That wasn't fair."

"Sounds like something a loser would say."

"You cheated."

"You said, 'go' and I went." I drape a relaxed arm over the bench.

"Fucking lawyers, man."

"Don't be a sore loser, Radek."

"I'm not a sore loser!" The pitch of his tone lifts to the next octave.

I snort. "Fine. One run." Hopping from the lift, I motion to the spot where we started before. "I'll let you do your little countdown, and we'll see who wins."

Landon puts his goggles back on. "*We'll see.*"

I make it down first. Again. He throws his poles and gloves into a snowbank with a roar. Tears freeze on my cheeks from laughing so hard.

When he's done with his hissy fit, he refocuses on me. "Best two out of three?"

The man doesn't want to accept defeat. Admirable, but also stupid.

"At this point, you owe me, like, a *million* dollars."

He trudges over where I brace myself by leaning over my knees. A humid breath floats between us when he lowers. "Keep smiling at me like that and I'll give you whatever you want."

My chuckles peter out into short gasps of disbelief, pulse thudding in my throat. I cough. It's dry, parched like everything else. I'm dehydrated: mouth, skin, eyes. Everything is bone-dry except between my legs.

"Wow," I croak. "Smooth. *For a loser.*"

A groan rumbles from his chest. "Best two out three—let's go, Davé."

Landon grabs the discarded gloves and poles and readies himself. "Or are you chicken?"

This third run, he gets ahead for a few seconds but loses an edge by swiveling to broadly. It slows him down enough for me to take the lead again. Another tantrum. More cursing.

I cackle as I climb onto the lift.

Landon is adamant. He gets on, too, and builds an argument to convince me to do best of seven.

"Bye, Landon." I hold up a pole as I jump off, then propel ahead without looking back at him.

"Indi! Get back here! This isn't over!" It echoes over the mountain.

The urge to smile grows and grows until I can't bear it. It leaves me smiling the rest of the day. And I kinda hate that the time with him is the most fun I've had in a while.

———

Landon's not in the room when I wake from a midday snooze. Or after I return from window shopping and a peaceful dinner in the village.

Wanting a better view of the mountainside at night, I curl into an arced sectional in the lobby. It's cozy. Fleece-lined socks and a cable-knit sweater sate my need for comfort. The fire flickers, crackling flames hypnotizing me as they lick at their wood fuel. This is what I came here for. Stretches of solace.

"Coffee?"

And it's over. My head drops to my chest in resignation before lifting to face Radek. I prepare for a snarky comment but am pleasantly surprised.

"It's an iced latte," he offers at a soft volume.

Can't say no to that. "Thanks." I grasp it with both hands.

Landon takes a seat but gives me space. "It's not poisoned."

I click my tongue. "That's too bad. I was hoping to end this conversation by any means possible."

"*Ha-ha*. You're hilarious."

"You walked right into it, Radek." Landon lets out a shy, boyish smile.

I shake the cup, rattling the ice around. "How did you know?"

"I saw the pile of these plastic cups in your office recycling bin."

He noticed?

"Figured you're addicted."

"Guilty," I say through a chuckle.

An awkward lull passes. He fixates on his coffee cup, tracing the rim of the lid with his finger.

"You don't have to be nice to me, you know?"

Landon shakes his head and looks over from the corner of his eyes. "What do you mean? I *am* nice."

"If you say so."

His shoulders slump as he sighs. "Why do you hate me, Indi? What did I do?"

Those damn blue eyes gleam in the firelight, drawing me into their sincere remorse. For a moment, I question whether I hate him at all.

"You really don't know?"

The last practice of the season made me never want to play again. I'd gone to pee before gearing up and when I returned to my locker, it was all gone. Someone had taken my things. Guilty sneers and scornful snorts echoed from the girls as they watched me search for my pads.

Coach was furious when I wasn't ready, and when I wouldn't answer his questions about why, I was forced to use disgusting backup gear and a wonky paddle. They'd been sitting for who-knows-how-long, reeked of stale sweat and piss, and didn't fit right at all.

My teammates seemed to be in on the prank. Landon kept smiling my way, deepening the wound of betrayal. Maybe he wasn't my friend after all.

After practice, I trailed behind as they sat on my usual bench. I thought maybe they didn't see me, but I was wrong. They saw me, but they didn't think I was in earshot. Or maybe they didn't care.

"Check out the fat ass on Jumbo Dumbo," Bennett said through a snicker.

Dumbo? *I reached for an ear, mentally measuring it.* I didn't think they were that big.

Newt shoved him. "You're jealous because she's got a bigger mustache."

The pads of my fingers brushed over my upper lip. Definitely fuzzy. That's it. I'm going home tonight and telling Mom that Dad said I could get it waxed.

"Aw, come on, guys." Landon separated them.

"Whoa. What's up, Landy? You like her or something?"

"No." Ouch. Good to know.

Bennett didn't back down. "I think you like her."

"Cut the crap, you dingleberry." Landon swatted them away.

"Indi and Landon sittin' in a tree," Newt sang. The rest joined in as Bennett made smooching noises. "K-I-S-S-I-N-G!"

I grew red at the thought and hid behind a sheet of wet hair.

"Shut up! I don't like her."

"I dunno, you seem to hang out with her a lot for someone who 'doesn't like her.'"

"No, I don't." Way to drive the point home, Radek. *"We wait for our folks at the same time. I don't like her at all, okay?"*

I didn't stick around for the rest of the conversation, but I knew the truth. Our friendship wasn't real.

CHAPTER 17:
AFTER THE STORM

LANDON

LOSING TO INDI ALMOST FEELS LIKE WINNING.

She's so endearing, kicking my ass down the mountain. I knew she was competitive but it's still so unexpected. *Fuck*, I can't deal with how her eyes crinkle when she laughs, loud and hearty while squeezing tears out of the corners. It has my hand reaching for my chest to keep my heart from stopping.

While the losing was real, I put on a good show of disappointment and frustration. I secretly love it and want more. More of her proud smiles, childish teasing, more of the blush on her cheeks left by the bite of the wind. Every wisecrack, every sassy comeback. I want them all.

This Indi isn't like twelve-year-old Indi. She's relaxed, carefree. Fierce as hell. A buried memory uncovers itself when I catch a stolen glance as she leaves the slope. It hasn't been fifteen years since we last met. How could I forget sixteen-year-old Indi?

The summer after grade ten, I went to visit before Dad sold the house and Laney moved downtown. Her summer internship took up most of her time and I ended up spending the days reconnecting with old friends and playing ball hockey.

One rainy afternoon, we headed to the ice rink where we used to practice regularly. When we passed the rental counter, Newt elbowed me and tilted his head towards the person behind it. "Check out the view." He pumped his eyebrows twice.

Ass up in snug navy work pants, a girl was bent over to organize skates by size in the cubbies on the back wall. I adjusted myself with a slight squat, pinching the groin of my sweats to get my dick to cool down.

"I'm shooting my shot," he said from the corner of his mouth.

My eyes wandered to the dry erase board hanging above, distracting myself from her magnificent lower half. It displayed rental rates, skate times, and the names of staff on duty.

"Indi D," I mumbled to myself. Hold on.

"Excuse me?" Newt called. "I'd like to rent some skates. Size 69."

I smacked his arm with the back of my hand. Idiot.

She shot upright and turned. A flagrant blush emerged on the apples of her cheeks as she tugged on the bottom of her polo. The embroidered logo of Mississauga Sports Arena on the left side of her chest only highlighted the full, perky tits concealed beneath them.

Her eyes grew then narrowed, darting between us. "A real genius," she said through curled lips, pointing at the tied laces bunched in Newt's fist. "You already have skates, dumbass."

"Hey, I'm a paying customer—"

"Shut up." I shoved him. "Indi?" Her gaze moved from Newt to me. "I'm—" Recognition brimmed in the browns of her eyes.

"I know who you are."

Newt clicked his tongue, winking and biting down on his lip. "You do, eh?" He slammed a palm onto my shoulder. "Hear that, Radek? We've got a reputation."

I rolled my eyes. "No, asshole. Don't you recognize her? It's Indi. She was our goalie on the Lightning."

She crossed her arms and looked away, twisting her mouth to one side.

Newt went slack jawed at the transformed girl standing in front of us. I lingered too long at the way her arms propped her rack up higher.

"Whoa. No shit. Indi? Wasn't she—" He puffed up his cheeks and formed a circular shape around his torso with his arms.

"Don't be a coward, Newton. Go on, say it. I was fat." She peered into the back office before lowering her voice. "Too bad I'm fresh out of fucks, so unless you'd like to get kicked out, get the hell away from me." Her hands flicked in two sharp shooing waves.

Indi had always been quick. Her chirps were legendary, but they were always subtle, muttered under her breath, which made them more surprising. This was direct, overt. And it stung.

"Forget about her, Landy." Newt hooked an arm over my shoulders as we turned to the rink. "There are plenty of fish in the sea." He motioned toward the various high school girls on the ice. While he flirted for the next two hours, I kept thinking about why my old friend was so unhappy to see me. She'd disappeared after the last practice without a goodbye.

Not feeling up to accepting Newt's invitation to the movies with a few girls he'd picked up, I didn't want to go back to an empty house either. Open skate ended and I stretched out in the bleachers watching the end of a rec league practice. Someone dimmed the lights after, not realizing I was there.

The Zamboni driver made his rounds before scooting off. "It's a nearly perfect one for ya." He said to someone behind the reflective glare of the glass.

"Thanks, Moe."

"For you, Indira..." He lifted a hand to receive a high-five. "Anytime."

Half a dozen pucks clattered onto the ice. In a couple of minutes, Indi appeared with a goal frame, sliding it to one end of the rink. As she leaned over the boards to grab a hidden stick, I laced up my skates, then waited while she sent a shot into the net.

"Not bad for a goalie." I skate up from behind, circling her. "Don't you remember me, Indi?"

"You're not allowed on the ice right now." Her eyes followed my path.

"Neither are you."

"I work here." She adjusted her grip on the handle, then sniped another puck into the net.

I tried not to smile wider, but she made it so hard not to. "Kinda an abuse of power, eh?"

She stopped dribbling and straightened. "What do you want, Landon?"

"So, you do remember me." I was full-on cheesin'. "I thought we were friends."

Indi scoffed a short laugh. "You thought wrong." She set off, charging towards the goal ahead.

"Come on, Indi." I pulled the stick from her hand as she skated back, then scooped up a puck, bouncing it on the blade. "Let's catch up."

Her eyes rolled. Typical. If I knew her—and I did—she'd never say no to a challenge.

I moved my gaze to the net. "I ask a question and take a shot. If I make it, you have to tell me the answer. If you block it, you don't."

She flexed her jaw to the side. Say yes. *She pivots toward the benches again, re-emerging with a paddle and gloves. I edged forward as she skated back to the crease. "Nothing above the waist." She squatted into position. "Deal." I swerved around to the center line with a puck. "You vanished. Why didn't you come to the end-of-season banquet?" Taking off from the middle of the face-off circle, I drove a wrist shot right between her legs.*

Indi's nostrils flared and she tapped the paddle against the ice. "There wasn't any reason to. No one missed me."

Ice sprayed to the left when I skid to a stop. "I missed you."

"Sure." She rose from the waist. "Is that all? I'd like to go home."

"Not a chance." I sped off to the middle again. "How come I never saw you around?"

Crossovers boosted my pace as I hit a slap shot that grazed over her right thigh and caught in the net. This time Indi grated her teeth and slammed her stick. "Be mad all you want, but you still gotta answer."

"We moved to Brampton."

I slowed to face her. "You moved and you didn't tell me?"

"That's another question." She crouched. "You'll have to make another goal."

Indi blocked the second slap shot away.

I tossed my head back and coughed out a single laugh. "Damn it. What do I have to do to get your number?"

"Number?"

I skated a circle around her before heading back to my starting point. "Your phone number."

Those brown eyes melted for a transient moment. "Why?"

"So I can talk to my friend whenever I want." The puck I let fly for fun pinged off the left post. "What's your number?"

Hunkering down one last time, Indi glided side-to-side. "Gimme your best shot."

I got too cocky, too sure I'd make this one, but she knocked the puck away in one smooth, reactionary swipe.

"Sorry." She beamed. Is this Heaven? My heart. *"Better luck next time." With that, she removed her gloves and skated off the ice.*

I yelled after her. "So you're saying there's a next time?"

There wasn't. Until now.

Solo runs down the glacier throughout the morning provide more clarity than the evening before. She wouldn't tell me when we were sixteen, but I gotta know what happened.

When I bring her my version of a peace offering in the evening, she's still prickly. And I'm tired of dancing around it. "Why do you hate me, Indi? What did I do?"

Her lips purse around the straw of the iced latte in her hand. "You really don't know?"

My shoulders rise and fall. "We were friends at one point."

"Friends?" Indi snorts. "Not sure that's what you call someone you harassed."

"I don't remember that." I shift from the couch to the ottoman, so we face each other.

She looks past me to the fire, its orange hues reflecting in the dark browns of her eyes. "You faked a friendship."

"I didn't." I leaned forward, setting my coffee down and resting my elbows on my knees. "I swear, Indi."

"But I overheard you guys after the last practice." Returning the same fleeting, softened gaze as when I asked for her number as teens, she holds my focus.

"Whoa. What's with you, Landy? You like her or something?"

"No," I lied. Yes. God, I like her so much. But I'll get crucified if I say so. *"It's not cool to talk about girls like that."*

"Indi and Landon sittin' in a tree. K-I-S-S-I-N-G."

"Shut up! I don't like her, okay?"

"I don't know, you hang out with her a lot for someone who doesn't like her."

"No, I don't." The second time I denied it, I was sure they'd buy it. "We wait for our parents at the same time. I'm being nice. I barely know her."

Landon, you jerk.

"Indi..." I inch forward so our knees nearly touch. "I didn't mean it."

She swallows and keeps her eyes down. "Sure, you didn't. Didn't mean to laugh after hiding my gear either."

My legs straddle hers at the edge of the couch when I scoot forward further. Her body stiffens at the proximity. "Please look at me. I would never."

Watery eyes peer back, and a painful lump grows in my throat along with an ache in my chest. "The guys told me you'd forgotten it."

Of course, she'd hate me. She thought I was in on it. "I'm so sorry I didn't know about them taking your stuff. And I shoulda stood by our friendship. I liked you more than any of them." Way more.

Hands clasped, I retreat and lower my head, hiding how glossy my own eyes have gotten. "I'm sorry. I was a stupid kid who didn't want to get made fun of."

Silence hangs between us, but it's no longer a heavy rain cloud. It's the stray, dreamy gusts of wind after the storm.

"Hey."

Her palm finds my forearm, resting there with the gentlest caress. It's the most tender moment we've shared in the past month. Goosebumps prickle my skin when she recedes.

"Thanks for apologizing."

Leaden remorse lifts from my heart, if only a little. A few more moments pass. I have lots of making up to do, and I'll start with making her smile.

"Thank you for listening. Now..." I down the last of my coffee. "Where's my apology?"

"*Pfft*. For what, exactly?"

"For that absolutely brutal beating you gave me this morning."

"No can do. It's not my fault you can't ski." Indi nestles back into the couch and mewls out a yawn. "Sorry, not sorry."

"Tired?" She nods. "Must be draining to be such a badass."

"It really is."

I stand and offer her my open hand. "I'll walk you back to our room."

A sarcastic smile lies crooked on her face, dimpling one cheek. My heart pitter-patters. "You mean *my* room. You're the squatter."

Her hand slots into mine as I help pry her from the cushions, and though the hold only lasted for a few seconds, I wish I hadn't let go.

We separate in the suite once more, rustling through changing clothes, water running as we brush and prepare for bed. One source of tension releases and gives way for another. My arm drapes over my eyes as I beg for sleep. An hour goes by.

"Landon?" Indi calls from behind the double doors of the bedroom.

I hum out a reply.

"Are you awake?"

"No."

"Okay. Never mind."

I roll to my side. "Do you need something?"

"Nah." Her sheets swish as she tosses and turns before we quiet again. "Landon?"

"Yeah?"

"I feel bad you're sleeping on the couch again."

I drop my arm and sigh out, ready to tell her it's okay when she shocks me with a question.

"Do you wanna sleep in the bed?"

With her? Fuck yes, I do. I kick off the sheet and jump to the door barring me from her. My hand wraps around the handle, turning it to peek in. Indi blushes next to the king-size bed, backlit by the lamp on the nightstand. Her pajama shorts frou-frou around her shifting legs. She toys with the loose, flimsy tank top covering her slender torso, thread-like straps hanging over the angled collar bones I'm suddenly dying to kiss. I gulp.

"You sure?" My voice takes a coarse form, too hoarse to be conspicuous.

"If you're okay with it. We're adults."

I bite the inside of my lower lip, muting a whimper. "Yep. Adults." Two steps and I'm at the foot of the bed, admiring how her teeth catch on that ample lower lip. I could die a happy man. "Does this mean I'm off your shit list?"

"Don't push it. But look" —she points to the pillows dividing the mattress— "it'll be fine."

"Right." I clear my throat. "Totally fine." I have control. I have restraint.

Indi slinks under the covers, pulling them up to her chin. I climb in from the side, lying on my stomach and curling my arms around a fluffy pillow. The sheets are clean, crisp, and smell like her. My cock thrashes. Stop it. Stop it right now.

Screwing my eyes shut, I imagine things that happen in bed that don't include fucking. Murder. Bed bugs. Birth. Farts.

"*Psst.* Where's your shirt?"

I squint through a single eye at Indi's unimpressed, rapid blinking, then smirk and shrug. "Lost it."

"Likely story." She snorts.

How is she so goddamn cute?

"It's a normal thing people do, Indi. I get sweaty. I don't wear one to sleep."

"Uh-huh," she says through another yawn. "Sure, yeah, normal. How would you feel if I was lying here without a shirt?" She's trying to kill me.

"Uncomfortable." I mumble and groan into the pillow, squirming against the mattress more to rid myself of this ridiculous hard-on. Thank fuck for that pillow wall. "Painfully uncomfortable." In my crotch. Stuffing my face into the pillow again doesn't seem to deter Indi.

"What do you mean?"

It's too late for this conversation. Tongue heavy and thick with sleep, I lie. "Nothing. Let's go to sleep."

"Okay." She twists to turn off the lamp and returns to her position, tucking a hand under her head. "Goodnight."

"Night."

Neither of us sleep. We jostle and huff to get comfortable. She bends and straightens her legs. I wiggle my hips and tighten my grip around the pillow. Her breathing slows and mine follows. When I think she's asleep, I let myself drift off.

"Are we friends again, Landon?" Indi whispers.

"*Mmm*, I hope so. I'd like to be."

She sighs through her nose. "We had fun as kids, eh?"

"*Mmhmm*." I snuggle deeper into the pillow, searching for comfort, wishing it was her chest instead.

"Do you remember when I beat up Bryce?"

I choke out a series of groggy laughs. "Yeah."

"He deserved it, the entitled shit."

"Totally." Fighting a losing battle with sleep isn't the right time to tell Indi how important she was to me. How important she *is* to me. But my mouth has a mind of its own. "Remember when I told you my parents were getting divorced?"

She hesitates. "Yes."

"You gave me your Nutella sandwich."

It's pitch black, but I hear her smile, then smack a hand softly to her forehead.

"I'm terrible at comforting." She makes a rumbly humming noise.

"No, you aren't. It was the best day during one of the worst weeks of my life." My lids drop closed, unable to stay open. This is horrible timing.

I wait for her response. When she doesn't, I figure she's snoozing already. I tell her anyway.

"I like you, Indi. Always have."

CHAPTER 18:
THINK ABOUT IT

INDI

SO MANY YEARS HAVE PASSED SINCE IT FELT GOOD TO be near Landon Radek.

It's not hateful or tedious, forced by Giachetti, or because a huge promotion is on the line. Having the choice is empowering on its own. And choosing to move beyond the past is freeing.

I ease to the edge of sleep when he mumbles, "Remember when I told you my parents were getting divorced?"

"Yes."

Meeting at the bench was our thing.

Mrs. Radek swapped attending practices for night classes and Landon's sister usually ran late picking him up. My Dad ran on IST.

Landon grumbled and threw his gear bag down before slumping onto the wooden slab.

"You sucked today, Radek." I took a bite from the corner of my Nutella sandwich. "What's your deal?"

"Got a D on my math test."

"Ouch." I swallowed. A gooey hazelnut and white bread mixture stuck to the roof of my mouth. "Your mom is gonna kill you."

His head hung to his chest.

"Well, it's been nice knowing you. R.I.P."

"How ironic. A D. D for dumb as a doorknob."

"You're not dumb, Radek. Not for that, anyway—" Another chunk of sandwich found itself in between my teeth. Very nice. Kick the guy while he's down.

Ignoring my sad attempt to make him feel better, he continued, shaking his head. "D for dysfunctional. D for divorce."

"What?" *I lodged the too-ambitious, mostly chewed glob in the pocket of my cheek.*

"My parents. They're getting divorced." *Landon's blank stare at the musty carpet was worrisome, his expression an unusual rain cloud for an otherwise sunny person.* "They like each other but they're not 'in love anymore.'" *Air quotes emphasized what I guessed was his parents' explanation.* "Whatever the fuck that means."

I hadn't the faintest clue what it meant either. My parents were disgustingly in love and didn't hide it. Focus, Indi. Give him condolences or something. No! That's for funerals.

"How do you stop loving someone?" *A sigh crept from his pursed lips as he closed his eyes and clasped his hands between his knees. Another question I had no idea how to respond to. His stoic expression remained for the next few placid moments.* "You won't tell anyone, hey?"

My head shook left and right, unable to form words. It was a little due to the shock of the news, but mostly because I suddenly had a fear of choking on a Nutella sandwich in front of my biggest crush while he spilled his family secrets.

"Dad came out." *Landon sniffled. Both of those darkened blue eyes dropped a single tear, their trails streaking down his sweet face.* "I thought they were best friends."

A normal friend would have hugged him, or at least patted his shoulder or something, but the faintest thought of our bodies touching made my tween hormones rage so hard I practically felt my period start. Never having seen a boy weep before, I sat stupefied, incapable of doing anything appropriate for the situation.

Landon sniffled again and wiped his face with the sleeve of his gray hoodie.

My gaze dropped to the food in hand. "Want my sandwich?" *I tilted it toward him.*

His face broke out into a lopsided smile.

"I only took a couple bites."

Landon chuckled. Worth it. *One of his eyebrows perked. That lopsided smile reached his eyes as their concern and gratefulness reached mine.*

"What about you?"

"I already ate the first one. This was my second." I dug a hand into my duffle and retrieved a round Pyrex filled with orange slices. *"And I have these, too."*

He swiped the sandwich. *"Thanks, Indi."*

Nothing more was said. When his sister pulled up and yelled for him, he gave her the middle finger, then turned to me with a wave goodbye.

"You gave me your Nutella sandwich."

I facepalm with a groan. "I'm terrible at comforting."

"No, you're not. It was one of the best days during one of the worst weeks of my life."

His next words warble as I doze off mid-conversation. Whoops. Something in my gut tells me I should've been paying attention, but sleep takes me under.

I loll awake in the middle of the night to find his arm breaching the barricade of pillows from underneath. A sneaky maneuver. The pads of his fingers rest in the palm that used to be tucked under my cheek. A subconscious twitch introduces them to the gaps between my fingers, not daring to pass through. I expect my pulse to climb and goosebumps to sprout against my skin, but the contact is warm and uncontrived. Safe. I let it be. I've already given him a few pieces and Landon can have this piece of me, too.

When I wake next, the pillows smell of Landon. I inhale them, slow and deep. Their cool, fluffy quality has gone heated and firm. My fingers brush over smooth, shifting ridges. A low, approving noise hums from them.

Wait a minute.

I gasp with embarrassed surprise for spooning Landon Radek while we were both passed out. Panic replaces any sense of security, raising my pulse to unhealthy rates. I attempt to remove myself.

His hands grip my wrists tighter.

"Five more minutes," he mumbles, voice gravelly with slumber. Landon wiggles the perfect rounds of his ass into my hips. His idle breaths change to light snores.

This time I'm victorious. The alarm clock on the nightstand reads 10:30 a.m. and I curse under my breath, hoping I can still make my mid-afternoon flight.

Luck is on my side. Landon snoozes through my hasty shower and doesn't stir when I carry my suitcase out to the living area to pack. And I mean packing in the loosest meaning of the word. Clothes create a disheveled mini mountain in the center. I flatten it so the bag zips up.

"Morning," he croaks, interrupting my huffing and puffing.

So close! Play it cool. But this man never wears a shirt. And why would he? If I looked like that, I'd become a nudist. Act casual. Nothing happened.

Landon yawns and rubs an eye with the heel of his palm, ruffling his hair afterward. He sighs out.

"It *is* morning. Did I wake you? I'm sorry." My words rush out, not at all playing it cool like I wanted. I'm back to being out-of-sorts when he's around.

"You didn't. I couldn't sleep anymore." Half-sitting on the back of the sofa, he shifts his weight to one bent knee.

I titter, nervous to be doing small talk after wrapping around my client like a spider monkey.

Palms dragging down his cheeks with immediate regret, he sighs again. "This is weird. Why is this so weird?"

My hands drum on my thighs. They have no idea how to act either. He knows. He knows I made him the little spoon. The first two fingers on each of Landon's hands massage circles into his temples, but he says nothing. I'm screwed.

My cell phone alarm beeps out. The handle of my suitcase clinks and snaps in its extension. "I need to get going."

"Wait!" Leaping from where he leaned, Landon mutters to himself before continuing. "Can we talk? About last night?"

Yep. Totally screwed. Deflect! "*Um,* sure." I tap my wrist. "I don't have much time though. The drive to Vancouver will take at least a couple hours—"

"Did you hear me?"

"Hear what?" That you wanted to snuggle for five more minutes?

Landon's tongue peeks out, lingering on a spot on his upper lip as his head drops back. "Shit. How do I say this?"

Indi, you crossed a line. You're fired.

"I can't stop thinking about you."

My eyes flutter, rapid and confused, cartoonish in their blinking. "*Psht.*" I slap the air. "I thought we were done with these types of jokes. You're so lame."

"I'm not joking."

"Uh-huh." I roll my eyes.

"I don't know how to make it any clearer." Landon straightens and takes a step, halving the distance between us. "I keep imagining what it'd be like to be with you."

My heart pounds when our eyes lock.

"And I think you feel the same." He cuts himself off with one of his infamous smirks. "You've thought about it, too."

He did literally catch you mid-O.

"Even if only in an *objectively, physically attractive* way."

"Nice touch, Radek," I retort.

He bends, tilting his head with a bow, super proud of himself.

"And so, what? Okay, I've thought about it." Correction: fantasized many, many times. "But we can't do anything."

"Why not?" Landon pouts and furrows his brows like a shar-pei puppy.

"*Uh*, hello! I could lose my job, for one. I could be disbarred" —I count on my fingers— "it's a huge liability for your career."

"I'll risk it." The sentence has a scary level of finality.

"Don't be a smartass." I slide to the right, but he follows, bracketing those strong arms against the wall to trap me.

"I'm not." His smirk disappears. "I like you."

"*Like* me? You don't know me." My arms flail. "We just became friends again, like, *yesterday*."

"And then you spooned me." The bastard knew! "I'd consider that more than friendly."

"That was an accident, a mistake. I was unconscious."

"Make more mistakes, then." When he takes another step, the mint on his breath gusts onto my cheeks. "Trust me, Indi. I know what I like."

"Is that so?" Arms crossing in defiance and disbelief, I stand my ground. He doesn't like me. Not like *that*. I'm a warm body. "And what do you like?" Other than pissing me off.

"I like your eyes."

"Original." I tap my finger on the opposite, twined bicep.

"I like your smile."

I prepare some snark, but he doesn't give me enough time.

"The sincere one. You get these moon-shaped dimples that are so *fucking* adorable."

I'm adorable?

"Actually, I like your sarcastic smile, too."

My insides are as molten as Landon's gaze.

"I like how your chin juts up when you speak with confidence" — the crook of his finger hooks under my chin and lifts— "I like how compliments make you blush."

Heat rushes to my cheeks, breaths ragged and shallow.

"Yes, *fuck*, exactly like that. *God*, it drives me insane." He sweeps a hand through his hair and tugs at the nape, dipping his head until our foreheads nearly touch.

Hands balling at my sides, I recoil into the wall, though there's nowhere to go.

"Going crazy wondering if that gorgeous blush spreads downward." His eyes rake over my shaky torso and he's right.

The blush does spread, hot blood going south. I hate that I'm wet.

Landon continues, dropping his fist above my head. "I like that you're sharp as hell. And I like your smart mouth." Wetting his lips, he lowers to my ear to whisper, "I have so many ideas about how to make it shut up."

A long beat passes while I snap out of it.

"*Wow.*"

At the bite in my tone, Landon retreats a few inches.

I do a slow clap despite sweaty palms. "You're as charming as you play on TV."

"I'm not playing anything."

His angry, pointy eyebrows don't change the fact that we can be friends, but not anything else. An unsure knot forms in my gut. I want to believe him. Past track records tell me otherwise.

"Are you saying you don't think this" —he points between our torsos—" could happen?"

"No, it can't. I'm your lawyer. You're my client." My chin tips upward, like he mentioned earlier. "And unfortunately, I'm not a hole to be filled."

The thirst between my legs begs to differ. There's a hole! It needs to be filled! Quiet, you. "I'm not some conquest—"

"No, not *some* conquest," the cheeky fucker says through a dry laugh. "You're the Holy fucking Grail, Indi."

I scoff. "I'm the conquest of all conquests? A fictional, medieval cup?"

"Yes. What? No, *er*, no! That's not—*fuck*."

I have to say, watching Mr. Cool-and-Confident trip over himself is rather enjoyable. His expressions go from horror to rue. "Can we go back to the part where I said I like you?"

Here's the thing about words. You can't take them back. Once they leave your mouth, the damage is done. Apologies can be accepted, but it's hard to forget the hurt. We may have rekindled a friendship, but I won't jeopardize everything I've worked tirelessly for so he can get rid of a dick itch.

"Say something, Indi."

I shake my head and grip the cold handle of the rolling bag. "I have to get on a plane."

Landon slumps like a kicked puppy, but somehow beats me to the door. He holds it open. "Tell me you'll think about it."

As if I'll be able to think of anything else. I can't get myself to promise anything aloud. So, I don't.

The scenic drive to Vancouver distracts me enough. Opening emails at the airport helps, too. By the time I've whittled the past week's pile down to pending tasks and yet-to-respond—*I'm an inbox zero-type*—the gate attendant calls for boarding.

The most welcome distraction, however, is Sheena's text coming through the in-flight WiFi. She made a last-minute, surprise visit to Ottawa to treat her brother and bhabhi to a weekend getaway for their tenth wedding anniversary while she watched the kids.

If I can count on anyone, it's her. She'll know what to do about this recent swerve into the hot mess express lane.

Her brother's house in Kanata is the first stop before heading back to my apartment. I catch her up on everything since I drank too much wine at Landon's: what he said the morning after, Gabe and Bea's advice, how we spent the weekend at the same ski resort and his proposition. Everything except for the part that it was Landon. And that I woke up the big spoon. Lying is becoming too easy.

"Bea really called it a slobber pocket?"

"I don't know where they come up with this stuff."

"Sobber pocket!" Sheena's two-year-old niece parrots her from the other side of the playroom. I putter through laughter and get slapped on the shoulder for doing so.

"*Great.* Now I'll have to explain to my brother where Nina learned that."

Wiping the corners of my eyes with my fingertips, I intone a sigh. "Good luck. Kapil is such a prude."

"Daddy pude?"

Sheena brings her hand to her forehead with an audible smack. "You're a horrible influence. And for the record, I think the girls are right." She shoos Nina away before continuing. "It seems like he really likes you. Be upfront with what you want and see where it goes."

"How can you be so sure? That he likes me?"

She lowers her voice to a hush. "Guys don't try that hard for a lay, Indi." She flips her hair over a shoulder. "What's the worst that can happen?"

CHAPTER 19:
A NICE GUY

LANDON

DERRICK JAEGER HAS A WEDDING BAND ON HIS LEFT
ring finger. Skylar beams beside him with the biggest, brightest smile as
only Skylar could.

"You got *married*?"

The vague text on the group chat asking if he could bring Skylar over
before the annual 'Twas The Night Before Dry Land' party didn't prepare
us for this.

Fletch lunges forward, pulling Jaeg into an unexpected hug. "Congrats,
man!"

Their smiles waver as Wade shoots daggers at each of them. The
swollen veins on his right temple wind like a snake, jaw clenching tight.
"What. The. Fuck?"

Fletcher retreats behind the couch, knowing to get out of our
teammate's way.

"When—how—where?"

I switch my gaze between the two guilty parties, mouth curled to one
side, baffled by this spur-of-the-moment decision. It's no surprise they'd
get married, but not yet. Not like this.

"We flew to Vegas over the weekend." Derrick pulls Skylar to his side,
clasping their newly banded fingers together and palming her waist. A
protective, possessive stance. Much needed from Wade's standing height
and building temper.

Skylar frowns, her brown eyes going darker and rounder than they
usually are. "I thought you'd be happy for me."

Wade ignores her, menacing eyebrows dipping while staring Jaeg down. In one large stride, he's nose-to-nose with the d-man. It doesn't seem to matter that he's two inches shorter and probably forty pounds lighter—*though seven years younger*—than our captain, who also happens to hold the third highest enforcer score in the league. "If this was your idea" —he stabs a finger into Derrick's chest and grits through his teeth— "I'm gonna fucking *kill* you."

"Whoa, whoa, *whoa*." I bound toward them but fail to separate their torsos.

"It was mine, for the record." Skylar wraps a petite hand around her best friend's finger and gives him a gentle shove.

Wade snorts and escapes her grip, then stomps off, withdrawing into my kitchen around the corner.

"Damn it. I'm sorry, my love." Her hand cups Derrick's jaw. "Let me go talk to him, okay?" He turns to kiss her palm and nods. She squares her shoulders and marches after Wade.

"Are you mad at me, too?" Derrick grumbles.

I exhale and face him. "No. I thought we'd get to be a part of it. Feel like I missed out on a really important moment, I guess."

He initiates an embrace. "I'm sorry, man. This is what she wanted. And I love her so much, I can never say no. I already had the ring."

"I knew it was gonna happen sooner or later." I clap him on the back. "Sooner is better, eh? How'd your families take it?"

"Good. They're already planning a reception-party-thing." He shrugs. "My only rule is that Skylar gets whatever she wants."

I puff my cheeks and heave my chest to fake gag, then mime swallowing the acid down. "We get it. You're in love. No need to rub it in."

"Quit being a jealous prick." Jaeg shoves me. "You'll be the same one day. Anything going on with you and that gym chick? Or are you still wanking yourself to sleep every night?"

"Oh, *uh*—" Still wanking myself to sleep every night.

A fist pounds loudly into the kitchen counter, interrupting us. Good thing, too. I don't want to deal with explaining what happened over the weekend to him while he's riding the high of a whirlwind wedding.

"*Walton Quade Boehner*! Will you grow the fuck up and talk to me?" Skylar sounds more like his mother than best friend.

Fletch cringes and hisses. "She used his full name."

Never a good sign. He, Derrick, and I poke our heads around the kitchen wall in a Three Stooges-style slow peek to snoop.

"You robbed me!" Wade cries, the arm he points at Skylar shaking through real, giant man tears. "*I* was supposed to walk you down the aisle after your dad died. You promised me! *Me.* I was supposed to get you blind drunk during your bachelorette party and cry like a baby when seeing you in a wedding dress instead of *right fucking now* after you've got a ring on your finger and changed your last name."

All rigidity leaves her body. "Oh, honey. Come here." She holds open her arms and rounds the island. It's a ridiculous sight, Skylar's petite frame comforting one of the tallest goalies in the NHL. Seeing our nosy faces, she waves us off, shushing and rocking to soothe Wade.

People can say what they want about our tendy: that he's a goof-off, an unserious jock, a fuckboy. It's all true. But we know what's underneath the armor. When you have his affection, he gives it his all. And he loves Skylar more than any other woman except maybe his mom.

We watch some black-and-white western on TCM until Wade and Skylar emerge, arms curled around each other's sides.

She releases him and skips over to Derrick, bending to whisper in his ear. They exchange quick kisses. "Have fun tonight, you guys. See you at home, my love." Skylar blows a kiss and Wade blocks the recipient by standing in the way, swatting it with his hand.

Fletcher blows a sharp whistle using two fingers. "Pass interference!"

Jaeg tackles Wade to the floor, and they jostle about until Olsen and Szezce get there. More congratulations follow and when the team's all there, I pass out boxes of popcorn and set the TV up for the Batman movies. The Christian Bale ones.

It quiets my racing mind. For the time being.

———

Three days of agility training and I'm already sick of it. If I ever see a pylon or orange cone on AstroTurf again, it'll be too soon. So much for focusing on summer training. Indi has taken control of my brain. Is it so bad I want her to hold me again like that night in Whistler? Her rack pressed into my back, hands on my chest.

Unfortunately, 'too soon' is two days from now. To forget that awful fact, on rest day, I head to the gym to do deadlifts and squats, needing to loosen the tightness in my hips. There's no rest for the wicked, though. Halfway through my squat set, Indi's swaying ponytail shows up in the mirror's reflection behind me. I abandon the set, excusing myself from the confused trainer spotting me.

I jog up to her. "Indi! *Hi.*" Even sweaty she smells sweet.

She startles, missing the mouth of the bottle she fills with the water fountain stream. "*Uh,* hi."

"Hadn't heard from you." I wheeze. "How are you?"

"Good, yeah. Really busy" —she gives a polite smile to someone passing us and moves out of their path— "sorry. Working hard, being your lawyer."

A single drop from the sip she takes slides down her chin, tracing the length of her throat and upper chest, only to disappear under her loose tank. It holds all of my focus.

"Did you get the emails from Bea? She was supposed to—"

I cut her off, motioning to a nook beyond the washrooms. "Have you thought about what I said?"

Indi pales, then reddens. "Listen..."

"Goddamn it." My palm rubs one-half of my face. "You're on my mind a hundred times a day."

A surprised gasp leaves her mouth. "*Landon.*"

It's my new favorite sound. Her blush deepens and deepens and my heart rate peaks.

"I know you don't *let people in.*"

A disapproving grimace joins her disappointed headshaking as she rolls her eyes. "That's what makes this a challenge, huh? How *fun,* right?"

Every accusation strikes like the snap of a whip.

"Not even close. I care about you."

I told myself no women this season. Yet here I am, ready to drop to my knees, begging for a chance with Indira.

"I'm not like those idiots who hurt you before, okay? Let me prove it."

A fleeting look of ache passes before she responds with another eye roll.

"I'm a nice guy, Indi."

"Yeah?" she leans in, narrowing her glance. "Haven't you heard, 'nice guys finish last?'"

Tongue darting out before my teeth tug at my lower lip, I stifle a teasing grin. My hand finds support on the wall. I drop my mouth down to the crest of her ear, and with it, my voice to a low murmur.

"That's because we let you come first."

Indi's lips part, the desired effect making the blush on the apples of her cheeks permanent.

"Say no and we'll never talk about it again." I push off the wall, wiping the chalky residue from the drywall onto my shorts. "Say yes and I'll do whatever you want."

———

A few more days of grueling drills don't provide respite from obsessively checking my phone. The turf burn on my leg hurts less than her rejection. I shift on the couch, lifting the scraped limb onto a pillow and lying back. When my phone dings I almost fall off trying to grab it.

GYM GIRL

Hi.

It's happening! Nobody panic.

ME

Hi.

GYM GIRL

I've thought about your proposition.

I'm too impatient to wait for the continuation of that statement. It could take minutes for her to type back.

ME

And?

Three little dots dance on the left side of the screen, excited as I am for her reply.

GYM GIRL

Have your doctor send the results of a full STD panel to my office. In a sealed envelope.

CHAPTER 20:
TAKE IT OR LEAVE IT

INDI

I CAN'T BELIEVE I DID THAT.

Knees curled to my chest, Afghan blanket over my entire body, including my head, I peer at the back of my cell phone through a gapped loop. My hand creeps to flip it over, then retreats under the shroud once more, as if the device is hot to the touch. I whine and force myself to re-read the message.

ME

> Have your doctor send the results of a full STD panel to my office. In a sealed envelope.

Wow, Indi. It's like you don't want to get laid. I don't. I mean, I do. Agh, pesky feelings. No, I won't let history repeat itself. I'm not that naive idiot anymore. We're gonna do this my way. If he doesn't accept, then he said so himself: we'll never discuss it again.

GYM GUY

> You got it.

GYM GUY

> Are you gonna talk to me in the meantime? Or should I continue to pine after you in silent solitude?

An unladylike snort escapes.

ME

You're ridiculous.

GYM GUY

A-ha! I knew you liked me.

ME

Now, now. Let's not get carried away.

GYM GUY

I didn't hear a denial. BRB dying a happy man. Indira Davé likes me. Can I tell everyone?

ME

Absolutely not.

I snicker at the doe-eyed Puss in Boots gif he sends me as a reply. I hate to admit it, but it's kinda precious how hard he tries to win me over. Giving him shit in return is fun and effortless. The whole thing turns into howling laughter as the digital razzing continues and ends with pleasant good nights.

A budding excitement spreads through my chest and gut. It's a too-content, dangerous feeling and gives me whiplash into caution. To make this work, I'll have to tread very, very carefully.

———

No matter how long I fixate on the crisp, white results paper, it doesn't change the truth.

Landon Radek is negative.

Whether he'll agree to everything else, I'm not sure. Fear tells me he'll think it's too much, that I'm not worth the trouble. But something in the hollow core of my heart hopes to prove fear wrong.

ME

> Got the results. Where and when can we talk?

The response is swift.

GYM GUY

> How about my place at 8?

My thumbs hover and dawdle over the screen. There's no going back after this.

ME

> I'll be there.

A hooded trench coat and dark sunglasses slip me past the loitering paparazzi unnoticed. The rain seems to have sent most of them packing. Security doesn't give me a hard time, either. Butterflies put on their best gymnastic performance in my belly as the elevator climbs to the top floor.

They don't calm when Landon opens the door wearing a relieved smile. A long-sleeved black tee molds to his shoulders, chest, and arms, the right size to show off every cut of muscle but loose enough that it doesn't look like he's headed to the gym.

"You're here." It's almost sheepish, the way he tucks his hands into those jeans, the way his eyes scan up and down in my direction. The light fixture above us makes them sparkle, bluer than usual and I swim in their welcome. His socked feet have my smile matching his.

Words are suddenly difficult to produce. I've arrived for battle, and he's already disarmed me. "Yeah."

"Oh" —he holds his hands out— "can I take your coat?"

I loosen the belt tie and set my work bag down to unbutton it, sliding it off one arm and then the other.

Landon closes his eyes for the briefest second before blowing out a breath. "Do you ever wear pants?"

"What do you mean?" I frown, inspecting my unremarkable pencil skirt. "It's summer. Summer is for skirts. It's too hot and humid for pants."

He smirks over his shoulder from where he hangs my trench in the front closet. "Are you telling me to take my pants off?"

"Shut up." I roll my eyes by instinct.

"'Cause I'll do it. I don't care. I have nothing to hide."

My smile widens as he nears.

"I did *not* say that." A sputtered laugh seeps past my lips.

"It sounds like you did."

"Okay, enough!" My hands fly up to nix the idea. "We're supposed to have a serious discussion."

"Right. Sorry." Landon's gaze switches from my eyes to my mouth.

The nervous swallow I take is like eating sand. Dry sand.

"Could" —I cough— "could I have some water?"

He grins like he knows its effect on me. "Sure."

After an awkward, silent stroll to the kitchen, I down the offered glass of water, as if the short, indoor walk was a desert marathon.

Landon leans back on the counter, much like the last time we stood in these spots opposite each other. His hands curl over the edge of the marble top. I rehearsed this part. An embarrassing number of times. It's written in my phone's notes in case I need backup.

"I have a counteroffer."

His brows raise halfway up his forehead. "Go on."

"There are rules." The glass in hand clinks against stone as I set it down and straighten, feigning confidence with stiff shoulders.

Landon hums. "Like?"

"Whatever we *do* has to be a secret. No one can know. Not friends, family, teammates, nobody. We can't risk anyone leaking it to the press."

He frowns and bobs his head side-to-side. "Makes sense. Gotta protect our careers."

"Exactly." I stand firm under Landon's steady, continuous eye contact, though my insides bubble like lava. "We won't be dating, so there will be no dates, handholding, or otherwise cutesy displays—public or private."

His expression dips at the last part, jaw ticking. He's not happy.

"There will be no sleepovers, no—"

"But we've already done that twice." He sighs, visibly exasperated. "Come on, Indi—"

"And that's why it can't happen again." My foot taps in the short pause. "If you're not in agreement, I can stop."

"I'm in agreement," he says through his teeth. "Please" —Landon motions with his hand— "keep going. I wanna know what else you have in mind."

"We'll only move forward with things I'm comfortable with."

"Of course."

"With my *inexperience*, I have a lot to learn, but..."

That sparks Landon's curiosity. "*Oh.*" He tilts his head. "You want me to *teach* you?"

An instant lump grows in my throat. "Y-yes." Pulling it down takes a second. "And no penetrative sex."

His mouth parts, but his face gives nothing away. Is he disappointed? Upset? "Is that all?"

Here comes the kicker. "No kissing on the mouth."

"What?" It's a breathy, verbal double-take, paired with narrowed eyes. "I won't be able to kiss you?"

I bite the inside of my cheek. Past insults float around inside my brain.

"What the heck was that, Indi?" Manu Varma wiped slobber from his lips with his collar.

"Me?" I whisper-yelled. "You tried to stick your tongue in my mouth!" Fifteen-year-old-me was mortified.

"Don't you know how to kiss?" Disgust splayed over his face.

"That was my first."

"No wonder." He sneered. "If you say anything to anyone, I'll tell 'em all how shit you are at kissing."

Safe to say that was the worst birthday party I'd ever been to.

At uni, Russell Kleinmann hadn't helped boost my confidence either. "Can we not kiss right now?" He pushed my pursed face away, evading my eager make-out attempt. "Lift up your top instead."

If trusting the biggest jackasses was a sport, I'd have a million gold medals.

When I refocus on Landon, his tone seems annoyed. "So, what? We'll be friends with minimum benefits? Get each other off *without kissing*?"

I shrug, hugging my torso.

"And what do I get in return?"

Uh oh. Danger! "What do you want?"

"You have to talk."

"Talk?"

"You have to tell me what's okay, what's not. What you like, what you want."

I almost forgot that I've given him hints about how my boundaries haven't been respected in the past. While he doesn't know half of it, I'm surprised *this* is what he wants from me.

"Fine, but I don't do kissing." I cross my arms, unwilling to budge. A heart can only take so much humiliation. I won't survive having Landon Radek call me a bad kisser.

"Well, I don't half-ass things." Landon steps toward me, mirroring my stance.

He won't get the upper hand. I'll walk. "I'm pretty sure the entire world knows that you whole-ass everything."

The stern downturn of his mouth breaks, twitching into a tight smile. "What is wrong with you?"

I shake my head and cover my eyes with a hand. "Too much to unpack right now." My eyes meet his again. "No kissing. Take it or leave it."

"Take it." The gap between us cuts to nearly nothing with his next step into my personal space, entrapping me between the two posts of his arms. "I'll take whatever you'll give me, Indi. And anyway" —his whisper cools the flame on my cheeks— "I can think of more than enough ways to make you come without kissing this pretty mouth."

I groan. "Do you *ever* use that thing for anything other than sweet-talking?"

"Yes." Landon flashes me an innocent, golden, sunshiney smile, but his gaze? Those eyes brim with icy blue waves of mischief. "But then I'd be using it for something much, *much* filthier."

Fear creeps into my thoughts again. Great. Now I'm hot, bothered, and unsure.

"Indi, I see those wheels turning in your head. Don't overthink this." His forearms flex into my sides as every one of our limbs crisscross. "I told you I care about you, and I meant it. I won't hurt you." One set of his fingers trails across my lower back, pinning my hips between his and the counter. "I accepted your rules. Can we start now?"

My heart and stomach backflip in sync. "Okay."

Goosebumps sprawl when Landon's calloused hand coasts down my arm and wraps around my wrist. He brings it to his mouth. "Can I kiss you here?"

I urge him on with a series of enthusiastic nods. The dusting of his pillowy lips over my quickening pulse gives rise to a second wave of goosebumps, but he continues the slow seduction. Touching. Asking. Kissing the crook of my elbow, the curve of my bare shoulder, the dip of my collarbone.

An unintentional gasp releases when he brushes his nose under my jaw. Landon smiles into the sensitive spot. "*Fuck*, you're a dream come true. I've thought about this for so long."

Pleasure blossoms and surges so fiery and quick, I can barely breathe.

He palms the back of my neck and asks to kiss the upper rim of my cheekbone and temple, every tender touch feathery and soft.

"A month isn't that long."

"A month?" Landon stills while inspecting my knuckles, then denies it, swiping his mouth across the peaked bones. "Try since I met you."

Fireworks go off in my chest. I don't stop him from placing my hand on his neck when lifting me onto the frigid marble counter. My legs flank his waist, clothed nipples puckering under the pads of his fingers.

"*God damn*, Indi. Tell me I can kiss you here."

"Yes." I arch into his mouth, head lolling back as he sinks to his knees. "*Landon*."

My fingers weave into the thick, brown silk threads of his hair, nails scratching into the scalp. He groans out an approval, face nuzzling into my belly. But he doesn't stop.

"Here?" His thumb draws a swirl on the inside of my knee.

I confirm with a squirm as he repeats himself over my inner thigh, inciting a permanent goosebumps revolution on my skin. The smug bastard smirks up at me through those ridiculously long lashes.

"Did all that kissing make you wet, Indi?" My skirt gives in to the upward nudging of his fingers on my thigh. "You gonna let me find out?"

I open my mouth to practically beg him to, but a foghorn goes off. It's the ringtone for Bea.

"Seriously?" Landon resists playfully when told to let go, cursing under his breath.

I smooth the bunched skirt as I hop down, ignoring the pooling between my thighs. The rushed pace of my legs have my heels clacking on the floor the entire way to my bag.

A breath puffs out, in preparation for not sounding wound up. "Hey, Bea. What's up?"

"Indi! Thank God, you picked up. My car broke down and Gabe is MIA. My parents are out of town and helppppp."

"Shit. That sucks. *Um*, where are you?"

"Wait. What are you doing? Why are you so out of breath?"

Crap. I eye over to Landon who mouths an unclear question. "*Uh*, nothing. The volume of the ringtone scared the bejesus out of me."

"Okay, good. I'm having the car towed to the mechanic. Can you come get me? I'm out in Navan."

"Navan? What the hell were you doing out there?"

"Battery dying, explain later! I'll drop a pin." She hangs up without another word, but her message pops up with the location right after.

I fire up the directions and wiggle my phone in Landon's direction. "Duty calls."

He gasps out a laugh. "No fucking way. You're going? *Now?*"

"Uteruses before duderuses."

"You're really gonna leave me," he whines, stepping out from behind the island to reveal the bulge extending across his thigh, "like this?"

Wow-wow-wee-wow. That is *something*. Lips pulling into my mouth, I fight back a smile. Doesn't work though, because little ol' me managed to rile up Landon Radek.

"You'll have to take care of that" —my finger waves a circle in the air, pointing at his crotch— "on your own. But this was *fun*." I lift a grateful shoulder before slinging my work bag's strap over it. "Thanks."

Landon catches up to me before I make it to the door. "*Fun*? There has *got* to be a better word for what we just did."

I hum in sarcastic wonder. "You think about that. Meanwhile, I gotta go rescue my friend."

"I'll definitely be thinking about *that*." His hand finds that perfect position on my lower back to draw me closer. "This works both ways, right?"

"What do you mean?"

"I get to call you whenever I want, too."

"I suppose. But I'm very busy—"

"Good." The opposite thumb traces the bottom outline of my lower lip. "One day, these are gonna be mine."

He likes a challenge, but so do I. Both of us have a lot to lose if this game goes awry. If it does, I refuse to walk away the loser. "Not a chance."

"We'll see." He drops a kiss into the corner of my jaw and murmurs into the delicate skin there. "Bet you one grand that someday you'll beg me to tongue-fuck your mouth."

I clear my throat. "*Uh-huh*. Good night, Radek."

"Night, Indi."

My body slumps against the back wall of the elevator once the doors slide closed. I clench my chest over my heart and take the ride down to recover and re-disguise myself with dark outerwear.

GYM GUY

Hot.

I climb into the driver's seat and toss my bag into the back.

ME

?

GYM GUY

The word I was looking for was HOT.

He's right. In the thirty minutes it takes to drive to Bea, I sweat up a storm thinking about Landon's clinging hands and how his lips left cloud-like kisses on my skin.

Guess I'm cooking myself with my vibrator when I get home tonight.

CHAPTER 21:
BANG, BANG, AND BOOMERANG

LANDON

A COLD SHOWER WASHES THE CONSTANT STREAM OF sweat dripping down my chest, back, and legs after a grueling training day.

The exertion is the second reason I need the icy temperature. Thinking about how Indi Davé let me kiss her everywhere is the first. My arms and hands felt so full when wrapped around her. Alone at night, they sparked with neglect, reaching for more of her long after she left.

Her skin tastes as good as it smells and lingers on my tongue, the memory of what we did leaving a permanent imprint. Those smooth, firm thighs squeezing my waist, nails scraping my scalp, *fuck*, the way she sighed my name. I almost didn't make it through speed drills.

I don't know why, but my gut tells me she doesn't quite believe I could want her like I do. Maybe she still thinks I'm in it for sex. But anything physical will never be just that with Indi. She's hollowed out a space in my brain and I'm keeping her there as long as I can. Hand lifting from the tiled bathroom wall to the faucet, I switch over to warm water.

"You're a fucking mess." Wade massages shampoo into his hair on my right. "I've never seen you so dazed during practice."

"I don't know what you're talking about," I mumble behind both hands, wiping away tepid droplets from my eyes.

"Unbelievable. You're totally hung up on Gym Girl."

"I'm not hung up on—"

"*Bullshit*." He scoffs. "At this rate, you're gonna end up wanting to wife her up or something. Move on, man. No pussy is that precious to hold out for—"

"Who said she was holding out?" I adjust my teammate's shower head so shampoo suds run into his eyes.

"*Gahhh*! The fuck?" His scream dribbles soapy water into his mouth, and he spits, blubbering curses.

On the other side of me, Fletcher laughs in awe, lathering up a shoulder, then scrubbing across his chest. "How'd you manage that?"

A smirk lifts my lips in one corner. "It's called charm, Fletch." I curl an arm around his neck and rub my knuckles into the top of his skull. "I've got tons of it."

He knocks an elbow between my ribs and his fist flies into my side before escaping my grip. "Get off, asshole."

"*Oh*, I plan to."

"So, wait..." Wade's expression only conveys confusion. "Why are you still thinking about her? Hump and dump, bang, bang, and boomerang." His finger guns fire away.

"We're trying something."

His lips purse. "*Oooooh*. Like butt stuff?"

My hand smacks him upside the head. Idiot. "No, not butt stuff. We have..." How do I put this? "...an arrangement. There are rules."

"*Ahh*" —he doles out a slow nod— "I get it now. One of those safe-word, red-room, BDSM-contract thingies."

That elicits another slap, this time to the back of his stupid, immature head. "I swear I can't talk to you about anything. Not everything is about sex."

"If you're gonna quote Wilde, at least get it right. 'Everything in the world *is* about sex but sex. Sex is about power.'"

Fletch mimics a whiny baby voice, scrunching his nose on one side. "*Myah-myah-myah, 'I went to Harvard.'*"

Wade lunges forward, stiff-arming past me to shove the instigator.

I twist the faucet shut and go to dry off, leaving them to duke it out and wishing Derrick hadn't left early to do whatever newly married men do. The locker room towel sits snug on my hips as I throw up middle fingers to the two shitheads as a goodbye.

They stop beating each other up to flip me off in return.

It's only been one night, but I miss Indi. Impatience has me fishing my phone from a duffel pocket to text her.

GYM GIRL

Hey.

A smile splits my face at the simple message. This must be what it's like to be wooed.

ME

Is this your version of wyd?

GYM GIRL

It's 2 p.m.

ME

And?

GYM GIRL

And I'm at the office.

ME

Hasn't stopped you before.

GYM GIRL

Shut up.

I expected her to say that. This shit-eating grin stays put.

ME

Sorry, I'm jealous it wasn't me.

She types, then stops. Types again, stops again. This repeats three more times. Finally, the text pops up.

GYM GIRL

You said I had to talk?

ME

Yes.

GYM GIRL

Last night was intense.

ME

Yeah? Tell me more.

A sharp slap pulls my gaze away from my phone. Clad in her usual all-white scrubs, Helga wrings her hands, readying them for work. "Radek, you're up!" her deep voice booms. My shoulder tenses at what's coming next.

She shrugs when I ask her if I can bring my phone in with me, but Indi doesn't respond through most of the massage. Whenever my hips are tight like this, I wonder if Helga enjoys piercing my glutes with her elbows a little too much. Breathing through every rotating jab only helps so much. The therapist eases up, cracking my back with the pressure of her thumbs straddling my spine. My phone buzzes on the foot stool below my face port.

GYM GIRL

It was a lot. I'm kinda freaking out.

My heart clenches. "Helga?" I strain through the question. "Mind wrapping up? I think I'm good for today."

She frowns and nods with a harrumph, ending the incessant kneading and clearing my skin of oil with a steaming hot towel.

"Thanks. Anyone after me or can I use this room for a few minutes?"

"Nah, you're the last. You know what to do," she says, pointing at the robe hung on a hook for me and the bottle of water on the side table. As soon as the door creaks closed behind her, I scramble for my phone, sheets still wrinkled around my private bits. My hands move to call Indi. The line rings.

She answers by clearing her throat. "Indira Davé."

"Do you want me to come there?"

"It's nothing serious." Her voice runs low, husky, and trepid.

Something's wrong. I jump down from my seat on the massage bed. The sheets hang from the tabletop, waterfalling to the floor.

"I don't care. If you need me, I'm there." I wait through the pause leading up to her response, pacing a circle around the room as my pulse rises.

"Yeah?"

"Yeah," I say through a short laugh, stopping my feet. "That's what friends do. We're friends, right?"

"We are."

A deep breath blows out from my chest. "Wanna come over tonight and talk about it?"

"Can't. I have a work dinner."

"Tomorrow night?" I offer.

"It's girls' night. I can't bail."

"You're really making me work for this," I tease.

She mutes a chuckle, lowering her voice to a whisper and waking my dick right the fuck up. "Don't be so needy, Landon."

"What? I wanna see you." Another pause breaks the cadence of our conversation. "Indi? You there?"

"Yes. I...don't think anyone has ever said that to me."

"Too bad for them." My hand palms the muscle connecting my neck and shoulder, pressing into it out of nervousness. "I'll say it again if it means it'll happen. I wanna see you."

"Two nights from now?"

"Works for me." Neither of us hang up. "Now tell me why you're freaking out."

Indi sighs. "I'm not used to being touched. And definitely not like that. I'm more used to..."

Intrigue flashes in my mind. I think I know, but I want her to say it. Out loud. To me.

"Finish the sentence, Indi." A door clicks shut behind her quickened breaths.

"Touching myself."

Fuck. I push my arms through the sleeves of the fluffy terry cloth robe, sandwiching the phone between my shoulder and ear while tugging the panels around my torso and knotting the tie to keep them in place. "So, what do you want me to do?"

She hums out an uneasy whine.

"Indi," I intone in a stern warning.

"I don't know."

"You have to tell me what you want. You agreed." A final pause follows as clothing rustles on the other end of the line.

"I want you to...*watch*."

The last word has my cock rising from half-mast to full glory. Walking in accidentally was hot enough, but her *asking* me to? I might actually lose my shit.

My jaw ticks, mustering dominance from the caveman part of my brain. "Tonight. Not tomorrow night, not the night after. *Tonight*. However late the work-dinner-whatever thing goes. My place."

"Your place."

Indi floats through my door a few minutes after 11 p.m., wearing the same dress as that first day in Whistler. The tiny pink flowers on the white fabric pale against the deep blush on her cheeks and darkened berry lips.

"I'm here, Radek!"

Wedged heels make her long legs longer. They clop across the hardwood, cutting the distance in a few, determined strides. She throws her brown purse onto an armchair and does a fluttery spin, not unlike my heart. How she manages to look sweet and muck up my thoughts with filth at the same time is beyond me.

I walk over, feeling sorely underdressed in sweats and a plain t-shirt. "Hey, Indi." Leaning on the back of the sectional, I beckon her, hand outstretched. "Come here."

Unsure, she steps between my feet. I pinch a pleat of fabric to bring her closer, forcing her to touch me. Indi doesn't protest when I move her palms over my chest and settle them on my shoulders. My hands stroke up from her hips to the dip of her waist and back down again.

"Is this okay?"

She nods. I can't help but smile wider when she relaxes into me, the increased contact warming my skin. Her round eyes gaze back, sucking me into their dark depths for a moment before alcohol breath releases from her bowing, parted mouth.

I raise a brow, questioning her sobriety. "Had a good night, eh?"

"I had a glass of wine with dinner," she admits. "I'm not drunk."

"Was it red?" My tongue pokes out between my teeth. Please, please, please say it was red.

"Maybe."

My fingers wander through the delicate fabric of her skirt. "This is a nice surprise. You wore it in the mountains. I was starting to think black was your favorite color and I'd never get to see you in it again."

Her brows dip, mirroring her frown. "Black isn't my favorite color."

"No?" I tighten my hold on her, enough to make a difference without being aggressive. She doesn't notice or doesn't mind. I'll stay like this as long as she'll let me.

"Nope. It's garnet, in case you were wondering."

"I *was* wondering, actually." My imagination runs wild with the idea of red lace against her bare, brown skin.

"And this" —Indi interrupts my runaway train of thought, making a face while peering down at her chest— "is what I get for letting my friend Sheena choose things for me."

It's too tempting not to take the offer of her forehead, so I risk it and place a short kiss there.

"Peer pressure is bad, kids," she rants on. "Never cave to trends... *heyyyy.*" Her eyes grow in shock, then scrunch with a rapid shake of her head. "We said no cutesy stuff."

"You don't like cute, huh?"

We can get not-cute real quick if she wants.

Indi gasps when my hands dive to grab the pert rounds of her ass, dick twitching under all the fluttery fabric gathering between my legs. Her hands clench my shoulders as I bury my face into the arc of her neck. She feels so good, I choke on my words, groaning them out in a hoarse murmur. "How about, 'turn up your skirt and show me how you use that rose-shaped lipstick?'"

Her wine-blush flares, reaching the tips of her ears. "I don't carry that with me *everywhere.*"

"But you have these." I circle her wrist and raise it to run my thumb across her fingers. "That's what you wanted, right, Indi? To touch yourself for me?"

Throat tensing through a swallow, she recoils slightly.

Not wanting to waste a second to allow any sort of snarky reply, I lift her by handfuls of that ass, turning to drop her onto the empty armchair. "Time to live up to your promises." My inner voice gets ignored over the horny one telling me to forge forward. "Lean back and spread those legs for me."

Indi obeys, reclining and pointing her knees outward.

I backpedal to the sofa across from her, lowering to sit, keeping my attention on how her hands ball her skirt.

"You like when I tell you what to do, Indi?"

"Not usually." She gnaws at her lip.

My chest vibrates with a chuckle. "What else do you like?"

"Encouragement." The dress material inches up at a torturous pace.

Encouragement? I can do that. I'll throw on a skirt and shake pom-poms if that's what she wants.

"*Fuck,* look at you." More and more of that flawless skin appears. "What else?"

"Landon, I'm soaked."

"No use for those panties, then." I take a harsh gulp. "Take 'em off."

Narrowed eyes hold mine in a vice as she removes them from her legs, flinging the nude fabric across the floor with her shoe. Widening her position, Indi strums her fingers up her inner thighs, flipping up that floral skirt to expose herself to me.

"Now what?" Her chest heaves, the sound of our asynchronous ragged breaths volleying back and forth.

"Play with it." I lean forward and wet my lips, resting my elbows on my knees and steepling my fingers. "Show me how you like to play with it."

One slender finger swipes through the cleft, prying her apart and showing how right she was. That dark pussy of hers *is* soaked. Her arousal glistens in the dim canned light from above as she smears it over her reddened clit. "Like this?"

My footing nearly slips when she rubs circles into the hooded flesh before prodding into herself. She bites on her lower lip, stifling a pleasured hum before her middle finger joins.

"Just like that."

They delve, in and out, in and out, slow, and steady.

"That's a good girl," I grit through my teeth.

Indi whines out an approving noise in response. They disappear and re-emerge again and again, faster, and faster, her hips bucking with the hypnotizing speed. She winces and squirms as I goad her on. The squelching sound is enough to flatline my heart.

"*That's a good fucking girl.*" My fingers roughly scrub over my mouth, muffling the words. Restraint unravels like a loosely tied knot.

Her feet in those heels arch further, toes curling under the broad strap.

"*Landon!*" she moans, head tossing back, lashes fluttering.

The breathy cry from Indi's lips drains whatever blood was left in my brain straight to my cock. The poor bastard fights for his life within my jeans. "Eyes open. On me."

She jolts upright with another sharp gasp. Her thighs quiver and clamp shut around the hidden hand, my name gushing from her gaping mouth again as she peaks.

I struggle to breathe. I'd be shitting bricks if my balls weren't cramping at the lack of release.

"*Fuck me*, Indi." If she even thinks about my dick right now, I swear I'll come.

Indi's body goes slack as her high peters out. "That's against the rules. I'm a rule-follower, Radek." Her raspy, satisfied giggle slaps a smile onto my face. "*Hmm*"— she removes her fingers from her coated pussy— "I should probably get cleaned up." Glazed, glossy fingers scissor the air, connected by the swooping threads of her climax.

Smile erased, I scramble forward to kneel at her feet. Ready to worship at the altar of Indira Davé. There's no place I'd rather be. I might stay here forever.

"Me. Let me." My voice comes out strangled, mashing the words together in my haste. I'm pathetic and I don't care. "You gonna let me have a taste?" I shrink back to my haunches as she inclines forward.

Her pupils dilate, reflecting my desperate image, playful smirk lilting up the crease of her lips. "Only one way to find out."

"Anything," I say through a groan. "I'll do anything."

Don't come. Don't come. Don't fucking come, you absolute prick.

Her clean hand cups my chin, thumb brushing over my lower lip.

"Beg."

CHAPTER 22:
OKAY, SHELDON COOPER

INDI

HAVING THE UPPER HAND WITH MEN IS SOMETHING I'VE experienced only in an academic or courtroom setting. Any intimate relationships—*if they can be called that*—left me powerless. I got crushed by the same guard I let down.

It's different with Landon.

The way he accepts the drawn boundaries is disarming. It's an unfamiliar level of safety and security. I didn't think he would agree to all my demands. Instead, he shows care, restraint. Dominance, too, but in a way that's all for me. He may have been talking, but I'm in control. Rash. Empowered. Landon's on his knees, and I want to push him to the brink, exactly how he pushed me to mine.

"Beg."

Thin blue rings replace the endless azure of his eyes from the widened, blown pupils. My knees separate when his hands drop, broad palms wrapping the backs of my naked ankles in an insistent grip.

"Please."

It's nearly inaudible. He doubles over, kissing the bony joint under my shoe strap.

"*Please*." Agony laces the plea.

His fingers wisp around the curve of my calf, plush lips brushing over the invisible arc. "*Please*."

Thumbs circle both inner knees before the ghostly echo of his mouth grazes the skin.

"*Please*, Indi. Just a taste."

I expect goosebumps, but the contact is too warm, too electric. Heated blood rushes to every spot he connects with, surging wildly at the lowest point between my legs. I swallow down any lingering hesitation and bring my hand to him. The pads of my fingers sit on his lower lip for a few seconds until I push them past the parted seam.

"Suck."

Landon's wet, warm mouth welcomes me with a rumbling, chesty moan, striking pins and needles against the pads of my fingers. His eyes fall shut, lash line shading his handsome face. Hollowed cheeks highlight the sharp angles of his jaw as my fingers pass over the flat surface of his tongue.

I'd be a puddle on the floor if it weren't for my heels planted into the rug. My breath trembles with poorly contained restraint.

I want to believe the new height of trust means something, but I wash the thought away. It's too hopeful. We're using each other. We keep it physical, and it can't be anything more.

Landon releases my fingers and collapses onto my chest, hands scrambling from my knees upward. "*Goddamn it, Indi.*"

The gruffness in his voice sends delicious shivers down my spine. He gasps out humid breaths onto my bare skin. I count them to distract myself from how hard my heart thumps underneath. Four. This man breathes four times before detaching himself and forcing eye contact. Those blues dart back and forth, gleaming, piercing into me.

"You're gonna ruin me."

A smugness takes over my smile. "I bet you say that to all the ladies."

He scoffs out a laugh. I don't know how he does it, but Landon carves windows into the walls I put up. His half-smile fades. "There are no other ladies."

I can't let myself believe him when he says things like that. We're just friends. I won't serve up my heart on a plate. That's why there are rules. We don't kiss, we don't sleep together, we don't catch feelings. We don't do anything beyond what we're doing. Easy peasy.

"Sure, Landon." I fiddle with my dress, smoothing it out. It's fiddly, and definitely *not* a tactic for me to brush off his statement. "It's late. I should head home."

He stands when I do. My brain clouds at the sight of the massive bulge on his thigh. *I* did that. Little ol' no-one-likes-me Indira Davé brought panty-melting, golden boy Landon Radek to his knees. And now he's following me around his penthouse like a loyal puppy.

I rinse and soap up my hands in the kitchen sink. Landon watches, shifting his gaze between my hands, eyes, and mouth.

When I return the towel after drying off, he flips my wrist and drops a metal ring into my palm. "The key fob for the garage doors."

My lips part. "Oh." He seems unfazed, crossing his arms and tipping back onto the counter, relaxed, except that hard-on *cannot* be relaxing.

"It's easier than risking getting caught. When can I see you again?"

"I, *uh*..." Not tomorrow. I'll never hear the end of it if I cancel on the girls. "Sunday?"

Landon clicks his tongue and rejects the idea. "I have two-a-days then. And the boys are coming over for dinner and game night after."

I scroll through the calendar on my phone. "We have a meeting scheduled for Monday."

That signature smirk reappears through his brown stubble. He bends to me. "Are you suggesting we mess around at your office? How naughty."

"That's not what I..." I gape at the playful suggestion.

"If you want to get bent over a desk, Indi, all you have to do is ask."

My face fires up at the thought.

Landon's tongue pokes at his dimpled cheek. "You're thinking about it, right?"

"No, I'm not." But it's too quick, too soft, too bashful of a denial.

"*So* are."

Hair shaking from my straightening shoulders, I attempt to retrieve some composure. It's impossible because Landon brings his mouth to my ear. "Is that what you want, Indi? To be ass-up while I pound into that untouched pussy?"

"No," I choke out a squeak.

Landon's smirk turns completely sinister. "See ya Monday."

Sweat beads across my nose and upper lip from how flustered he leaves me. I dab them away with a tissue from my purse in the cab on the ride home. Grateful for the silence the cabbie provides, I sigh. It's short-lived. My phone buzzes in my lap.

GYM GUY

> My hand and cock are gonna be raw
> from remembering how you played
> with yourself on my couch.

Good. Great. I didn't really need a new fantasy to fixate on. As I exit the cab, I thank God it's pitch black out. And for easy-to-clean leather-covered seats because this dress definitely needs to be dry cleaned.

———

My pen taps a point onto the next item on the list.

Clad in a stark white button-down and gray slacks, Landon scoots forward in the chair across from where I half-sit my ass on the edge of the desk.

"We'll need text message records from your service provider."

His hands wander up and down my extended legs, tracing the calf and teasing the skin with feathery strokes. I wiggle. It does nothing to stop him.

"Will you cut that out and pay attention?"

"How do you expect me to do that" —Landon halts the soothing contact as his palms reach the backs of my knees— "when you're wearing this tight skirt and these heels?"

"You can start by keeping those hands to yourself."

He pouts. "I prefer you keeping *your* hands on *yourself.*"

I smack his shoulder with my writing pad.

"The text records, Radek."

A groaning whine emits through his frown. "There aren't any texts. I told you."

"That's why we need them. To prove there is no basis for the alleged promises you made."

"*Fine.*" He agrees with an exasperated sigh. "I'll have my PA send them over."

"Thank you."

"Can I go back to thinking about what your fingers did and where? It's all I can focus on right now." Those ridiculous blue eyes travel to my hands and lower belly, then back up again.

"That's *all* you can focus on, eh?" I drop the notepad onto the desktop and grip the edge on either side of my hips.

Landon's face lights up with a shiny smile. "I bet I can do it better."

I putter. "Doubt it. I've been doing this for ages."

The intercom beeps twice. Landon kisses a spot above my knee before I propel myself upright and round the desk to answer.

"Hey, Bea."

"Your five o'clock is here."

"Take 'em to conference room A. I'll be there in a minute." The line clicks off. I drop the receiver.

"So?" He rubs his hands together. "What's on the table? Other than your perfect ass."

I shush him with a glare. "If you don't keep quiet, we're gonna get caught."

As I gather files, he leaps up to wrap his hands around my waist, while something *else* firmer than his grip digs into my hip bone.

I gasp. "I, *um* "—I clear my throat— "I have another client meeting."

Landon doesn't budge, keeping his hands and dick in their places against me. "But *I'm* your client."

"You're not my *only* client, I'll have you know." I shove him with the fist clasping the brown folders. "Now go away. I'm busy."

———

The slotted time with Mrs. Garten snails on, despite it being her last meeting with us.

The setting sun leaves my office dark and shadowy. I flip the switch and jolt from the sight of Landon behind my desk. My hand rubs my chest to calm my skyrocketing pulse. "What the *hell*, Radek? You scared the life outta me."

He swerves the chair back and forth, keeping his elbows on the desk and his hands fastened together.

"Were you here this whole time?"

"Yep."

"What on earth were you doing?"

"Imagining all the ways I could have you here."

I ignore the chill that flits down my spine. "You're in my spot."

"Okay, Sheldon Cooper. There's plenty of space."

"Seriously, where am I supposed to sit?"

Landon traces the outline of his mouth, outlandish smirk stretching. I can't sit there. That's his face.

The arrogant jerk laughs at my growing blush. "One day, Indi. But not tonight. Tonight, your seat is still empty." His hips rise as he glances at his lap, clasping his head behind his neck.

"Smooth."

"The smoothest."

"Does Bea know you're here?" I back up a few steps, locking the door behind me.

He shakes his head. "No one knows. Now, sit your perfect ass down so I can get you off."

Mindless, tentative steps take me toward him.

"What if you can't...?"

"I'll probably run into oncoming traffic." Landon tugs at my silk shirt, untucking it as he pulls me closer. "If I do it better than you, then..." His arms twine around my torso as I lower and slide the files away. "*God*, you smell incredible."

One hand cradles my throat and I tilt my neck for more of the encouraging touch.

"I need to kiss you here again." Landon draws a quarter-sized circle over the most sensitive spot below my ear. "Can I?"

I nod, unable to put together any sort of words under his hold. He worships the delicate skin, those pillowy lips caressing, tongue sweeping, mouth sucking and teeth nipping, sucking and nipping, sucking and nipping until I melt like putty. My grasp on the desk slips.

"Show me how you like to be touched."

I stifle a moan, my nipples going taut when he curses and groans in response. "*Fuck.*"

He follows as I unbutton my shirt then grab his wrists to move his hands over my bra-covered breasts. "You're flawless," he says through a heavy breath, squeezing firm handfuls. "Fucking *fuck*."

I writhe, head dropping back as he continues to devour my neck, lashing his tongue again and again. Our fingers lace when I push his hands down, using them to inch my skirt up. Showing him where I really want him to touch me. They strum up my inner thighs, parting them over his hard quads below. He shifts, grinding against my ass, mumbling another *fuck* under his breath as I move his fingers over my damp panties.

One index finger guides his to draw the fabric aside. The slow swipes through my wetness have me losing my mind and I can't stop, craving his thicker, longer, stronger fingers inside me. His fingertip grazes over my clit before prodding at the soaked entrance. Our fingers slide in without a struggle.

"You feel so fucking good." Landon buries his head into my neck, tensing underneath me.

I press his finger down into the triggering spot. He presses harder, circling and circling.

I tremble and simper. "Right there."

My hand goes limp and retracts but urges Landon by the wrist to keep going. His sole finger pumps in and out until a second dips in, eliciting a muted moan from both of us. "You're taking me so well, Indi. Such a tight fucking pussy."

I whimper and judder. "*Please*, Landon."

He grunts as the pace and pressure amplify, stretching and scissoring me. "I wish you could see what I'm seeing. How fucking gorgeous you are when your dripping cunt's desperate to come on my fingers."

Rapid curling against my G-spot sends a garbled noise up my throat, threatening to turn into a scream, but he claps a hand over my unhinged mouth.

"*Shhh*," he hisses, breath teetering through gritted teeth. "'*If you don't keep quiet, we're gonna get caught.*' Do you wanna get caught, Indi?"

I wince and deny, deny, deny.

"Good girl. Then use me. Use my fingers to fuck yourself."

Rocking into his hand, I place his thumb against the needy bundle of nerves. "*Landon.*"

He groans into my shoulder. "You have no idea what you're doing to me."

Another moan gushes out in response as I ride his hand, holding on by the wrist. My free hand bunches the fabric of his slacks at the thigh, pleasure rocketing through me.

"Feel for yourself." He leads the clenched hand to the apex of his legs, skimming it over a rock-hard ridge.

I gasp at the warmth, the girth, the fucking sheer size of it under my palm. It grows with every stroke.

"*Fuck*, Indi." Landon leaves harsh sucks below my ear. "Take it out if you want."

There's no time to think or overthink. We're already scrambling to unbutton and unzip his pants with one of each of our hands, his other hand still inside me. His cock springs out, eyeing my surprised expression from the close-up view. It twitches and reddens, veiny and angry as it winks out a pearl of pre-cum.

Landon wastes no time stealing from my wetness and slathering it over his length, giving it a pink sheen. "Go on," he suggests. "Touch me."

His hand envelopes mine, the ring of my fist barely fitting around his heavy cock as he pushes into it. He growls and groans into my ear. "I'm gonna fuck your hand now. Fuck yourself with mine."

A string of my confirming *yeses* whisper out as we buck and grind, syncing into a galloping rhythm while suppressed, tortured sounds—*mine against his hand and his into my skin*—continue until the peak approaches. His mouth doles out unceasing, tongue-filled kisses. Combined with the speed of his thumb against my clit and fingers hammering in and out, I shatter into a million fragments, a cry dying within my throat as tears form.

My hands stretch to find support as I fall forward against the desk, inadvertently abandoning my grip around Landon. One last, shaky groan from behind precedes the hot streams of his release onto my back, soaking through my shirt and searing my skin.

My senses return. I laugh through the remaining high as Landon reclaims my midsection with his limbs, pelting kisses over my naked shoulder and neck.

"Fucking *phenomenal*." He chuckles back, his palm spreading the liquid further over my blouse.

"You're ruining it. This is silk!" I detach the sticky fabric and rebutton the front, then fumble to find my footing while shrugging on a blazer to hide the evidence. My dry-cleaning bill keeps getting bigger.

"Worth it." Landon tucks himself back in. How does it fit into pants? That thing should have its own pair of pants. "I totally won."

"You owe me a new shirt, Radek," I snap. "We never decided on betting terms."

"I'll think of something."

We stagger our exits. He takes the side stairwell to evade questioning. I use the elevators to leave through the main lobby, waving security off with a polite smile.

The next morning, a courier delivers a package to my door as I get dressed for work. I open the black box and unwrap matching tissue paper to find a white silk shirt with a handwritten note. *You're welcome*, it reads.

When I go to try it on, a card careens to the floor, revealing another scrawled note on the back: *I won, fair and square. Can't wait to collect my prize.*

CHAPTER 23:
SIMON SAYS

LANDON

FUCKING FANTASTIC.

Twenty out of ten, highly recommend fingerfucking your hot-ass lawyer in her office. Cannot recommend it enough. Best hand job I've ever had. And Indi did it while squeezing the life out of my fingers. They'd gone numb from the lack of circulation.

Two-a-days are brutal but not as torturous as having that night on a loop. A quick dip in the cold tub has my cock and balls shriveling to nearly nothing. I gotta stop thinking about how her warm hand fisted me in its tight grip. How soft and sweet Indi felt on my fingers. How her clit pulsed under the pad of my thumb. How balmy her skin gets, how she glows as she unravels.

Fuck. I'm so, so screwed.

I shake away the memory, launching my legs over the side of the tall aluminum basin. The boys brawl in the background as I leave for home. An empty bed will have to do.

Downtown traffic is abysmal in the summer. The streets teem with those who extend the after-work happy hours into the nightclub scene. I idle at a red light, irritated and impatient, when Indi texts.

GYM GIRL

Got the phone records. Thanks.

GYM GIRL

For the shirt, too.

Remembering how I stained the first one puts a smile on my face.

ME

I'll buy you a million shirts if it means you'll let me do it again.

GYM GIRL

Not necessary.

GYM GIRL

But I have another idea. Let me know when you're free.

Stopping only to have the concierge take my gear up, I drive past the penthouse to get to Indi's apartment, feeling like nothing short of a stalker by looking up Trevor's notes. He'd called Bea for her home address so I could have the shirt delivered. Dark sunglasses, a black baseball cap, and a hoodie are a perfect disguise as I slip past the front desk unnoticed.

A clamor rings out behind the door after I knock. I want her to be surprised. I want her to know if she needs me or wants me around, I'll show up every time. The door flings open, and I jolt back as something wooden swings at my face.

"What the fuck!"

Indi freezes but keeps the cricket bat in her grasp.

I lower my sunglasses.

"*Landon?*" she whisper-yells, turns her head in both directions down the hallway, then pulls me through the threshold by my sweatshirt collar. "What are you doing here?" She closes and locks the door lightly, setting the bat in the corner.

"Wishing for death, it seems. *Jesus.*" I shove the glasses into a pocket and drop the hood back.

"You could've texted or something." She rumples her gray sweatshirt in one hand and tugs at the hem of her matching shorts, ankle-socked feet shifting against the floor. The idea of her feet being cold is so adorable. "A heads up would have been nice."

"And miss out on getting maimed?" I have no control over my smile when I'm around this girl. My hands pull her into a hug, and she gasps. "Not a chance."

She rolls those big brown eyes. "Don't make me use the cricket bat again."

"*Brrrr*. I'm shaking in my boots." I fake a shudder. "But really? A cricket bat?"

She gives a weak shove to my chest, plotting her escape. I tighten around her.

A disapproving shake swishes her straightened hair across her shoulders. "Compliments of my dad. He gave it to me when I started living alone. It's supposedly heavier than a baseball bat."

The cap on my head is an asshole and the bill knocks into her forehead when I lean for a peck on the cheek.

"*Ow.*" Indi slaps the hat down, so it covers my eyes. "This is what you get for trying to be cute."

"Trying?" I lift off the cap and flip it around. "I *am* cute."

She pretends to gag but her blush tells me she's not unaffected by my charms. My hands lower from her mid-back to cup her ass—*how does it fill my palms so perfectly?*—and steal a kiss from her jawline. "And I think you know what happens when I'm not being cute."

Indi sighs out but tenses.

I pull back, not wanting to make her uncomfortable in her own home. "This is a nice place."

"I mean, it's no penthouse."

"Penthouses are overrated." I squeeze her sides. "You wanna show me around?"

"There's not much to see," she says with a spin, extending her arm to the right. "Kitchen, living room. Bedroom, washroom, bedroom turned into a home office."

I slide past her to inspect the living area. Dishes drying on the rack and soaking in the sink. Decent size sectional, a coffee table covered in unopened mail. Indi sprints to the bedroom door, shutting it and cutting my view of the pile of laundry on her bed short. Her uneasy smile makes my heart flip.

"Sorry, it's a mess. I told you; you should've told me you were headed over."

"It's not a mess." Nothing is dirty, just cluttered. The TV is paused on an unflattering frozen image of a dancer. "Were you watching something?"

"Not really." Indi scrambles for the remote and shuts it off. "Background noise while I work."

A strange pattern emerges on the last scan of the main room. My eyes dart around to the sound of *Psycho* theme music. Dead plants scatter the space: in the corner, on her bookshelf, on side tables, and a line on the windowsill.

"Damn, Indi." I lift the wilted limb of what was once a vine. "This is like a greenhouse graveyard."

Her face reddens. "I'm a busy woman, okay? It's not my fault they don't wanna live."

I click my tongue, feigning disappointment. "It's always the unsuspecting ones that turn out to be serial plant killers."

She hisses through a cringed smile. "It's not a great track record. This" —she points to the white orchid in the kitchen— "is the only thing that sticks around. And only because Gabe comes by every week to drop ice cubes in it."

The couch cushions hold firm as I drop back onto them with an uncool *plop*. "You mean Gabe Finch?"

"Y-yeah? How do you know—?"

It's my turn to blush. "We were told she's gonna be press this season and, uh..." I scratch under my ear. "I saw you at Persepolis with her."

"You saw *me*?"

There are those pure, sincere eyes again. *Fuck*. Their innocence shouldn't rile me up, especially knowing they're not innocent at all.

I've always seen you, I want to say. "You two are close, eh? How'd you meet?"

She joins me on the same branch of the couch, folding her knees to the side to face me. "We roomed together at Waterloo. She played basketball for the women's team."

"I don't think I knew that. She was an athlete?" One of my hands goes rogue and reaches out for her thigh. It glides up and down, a light and mindless touch.

"Yeah. Really good, too. But she didn't want to go pro and move too far away from her dad."

I hum back.

"Who are you close with on the team?"

"Pretty much everyone. We're like family. We spend more time with each other than our own. It's crazy." I pause. "Jaeger and I have been playing together the longest. He's my brother. Wade and Donovan are solid guys, too. We have our fights, but there's no way to avoid one another. It forces all of us to get along. It's a good time."

Indi scoots closer. "Seems like it. I can't believe you guys have a game night."

"You should see these dorks in action."

"Dorks?" Her eyebrows pop up. "I wouldn't call the Regents' starters 'dorks.'"

"Then you'd be wrong." I slouch and nuzzle against her arm stretching across the back of the couch. "I've never met a group of bigger nerds."

"Really?"

"Take Sunday, for example. We used to have a poker night, but Donovan is too good and robs us blind, so we've banned it until the regular season. We played reverse charades. The whole team, except one, has to coordinate and act it out together so the remaining person can guess correctly."

Eyes blinking up a storm, Indi shakes her head. "I have no idea what you're talking about but go on."

I chuckle, recalling how we had to put Jaeg and Wade on different teams. Wade is still pissy about him and Skylar eloping.

"Jaeger is a broody, grumpy bastard and hates losing. One of the terms was synchronized swimming. He and every defenseman flitted and traipsed around like ballerinas, miming front and back strokes and flips and dives. It was *ridiculous*."

Indi stifles a laugh.

"And Wade is a goof-off, but he can't stand losing either. He and Fletch were the most enthusiastic of the group trying to act out 'riding a carousel.' They made *whee!* sounds, giddying up on fake horses as they rose and squatted. I almost pissed myself."

Her teeth chew at her lip, making her shy smile lopsided. "That's actually really sweet, Landon."

"Sweet?"

"You have a bond that goes beyond athleticism and machoism. It's sweet."

My eyes dart between hers, in disbelief at how soft she is under all that snark and sharp wit. A blanket of warmth surges across my chest. I don't think anyone gets to see that side of her, at least not often. And I do. How lucky am I?

"Are you hitting on me, Davé?" I inch my mouth closer to hers, not caring that she won't meet me there. "I can be very, *very* sweet."

Those eyes roll, a sassy smile peeking through. My dick has been on his best behavior so far, but I don't know how long that'll last with how close her lips are to my face.

"That reminds me, remember what I said about my idea?"

"*Mmhmm.*" Her arm is smooth against the bristles of my stubble. I kiss it because I can.

"Promise not to laugh?"

I tip my head back to refocus our eye contact. "I'd never laugh, Indi. Promise."

She pulls her lips in between her teeth. "Can I kiss *you*? Here, I mean." Indi taps my cheek twice.

"You can literally kiss me anywhere you want to."

Indi draws a long swallow before her nose presses into my skin. A tender dusting from her soft lips sends the butterflies in my gut into my heart. My eyes draw closed. "Was that okay?"

I nod through a broken breath. "More than."

"How about here?" Her thumb taps below my jaw.

"Yes, please."

Body shifting for a better angle, she cups the opposite cheek with her hand. Her mouth connects with the mind-numbing spot beneath my ear before the tip of her tongue—*fuck me, that tongue*—meets my neck. When she sucks and draws in the skin, I shiver, digging my fingers wherever they settle. Into Indi's hip. Into her firm thigh.

"Did you like that?" she asks in the sexiest, husky tone.

I'm too keyed up to tell whether it's on purpose or not, but my cock is behaving badly now, swaying like a drunken sailor. "Y-yes. Don't stop. *Please.*"

Indi works the spot over and over, doubling my dick size. "You like playing games, Landon?"

I'll never get over how she says my name. I'm so hard I could cry. My head nods furiously as her palm slides down my neck and chest, stopping to tuck her fingers under my sweatshirt, barely missing the upright rascal. I wince. They strum across the ridges of my abs, goosebumps sprawling across my chest and tightening my nipples.

"Simon says, 'take your shirt off.'"

My eyes shoot open, all semblance of innocence wiped from Indi's gaze. The hoodie and shirt get wrenched over my head in an eager swipe and I send them across the room.

She sighs and studies me. Absorbing. Admiring.

I motion to her torso with a tip of my chin. "You, too."

Hesitation flashes across her face, the red on her cheeks flushing redder and redder. Her tongue clicks, rejecting my suggestion. "Close your eyes until Simon says."

"*Fuck*, Indi." I do as she says, because these are her rules. A low rustle sounds out before I hear something drop to the sofa. Without sight, the rest of my senses are in overdrive, a runaway train of filthy fantasies coming to life.

Her lips reattach to my neck, hand skating up and down my naked chest. Trim nails catch in the short chest hairs between my pecs, then scrape against my nipples. They pucker in response. I moan out her name, desperate for more.

Indi gasps. "Is that good?"

"Oh, my God. You have no *fucking* idea. Keep going."

That hot mouth and punishing tongue sweep over my neck, my shoulder, painting a line of open-mouthed kisses down my chest. It stops at a pursed peak, swiping across the hard flesh before grazing her teeth on it.

Her bare tits fall into my lap.

"Fuck." My eyes stay shut out of respect. "You weren't wearing anything underneath?" I wanna see her in this position: kneeling, mouth on my body, full rack within reach. I need her to fucking touch me already.

Indi must know, because her hand moves south, palm flat against the solid shaft in my sweats. But she doesn't wrap around it. She rubs and strokes and rubs while sucking on my insanely taut nipple.

"*Please*, Indi." Kissing is one thing but getting rubbed over my clothes is the stuff of my boyhood wet dreams. Add in Indi moving my quivering hands to cup and grope her tits. There's no going back. My hands blindly search for her. "Let me see you."

"Simon says, 'open your eyes.'"

They stretch at an incalculable speed to take in that glorious rack, tits round and supple and enough to have me committed for life. I groan, thumbing the dusky nipples. "You're so fucking beautiful. Look how perfect you are in my hands."

The knot of pleasure rooted at the base of my spine builds again when she restarts the stroking, pace climbing. One shameless moan strings together with another and another and another as she doles out the torment. "*Fuck*! I'm gonna come, Indi. I'm gonna—"

My hips jerk, fingers pinching those pebbled nipples as my feet curl inside my sneakers. Her high-pitched, whining moan sends me over the edge, exploding into my pants with a trembling groan.

Indi's naked chest vanishes as she slides her shirt back on.

My breath heaves from my lungs, chaotically trying to regain a normal rhythm. "You're brilliant. You don't need me to teach you. That was so good."

The pride on her face fades. "For a virgin, you mean." Her eyelashes flicker as she glances down, shadowing the top rim of her cheeks.

"For anyone." I pull her into my lap and cradle the back of her neck. She won't look at me. "Hey, stop that, okay? I don't care. You have boundaries. I won't push them unless you want me to. We're friends, remember?"

Friends, friends, friends. Goddamnit. I can't be *just friends* with Indi. I leave a kiss on the tip of her nose. "You're so special to me."

"What?"

"You've always been special to me." My forehead falls to hers. "You're the only person who I told about my dad coming out. I didn't tell others for years. You made me feel safe. You *make* me feel safe," I correct myself. "I trust you now like I trusted you then."

She returns a solemn nod.

"I'm not lying. You make me feel so fucking good." Placing a lingering kiss in the crook of her neck has her melting into me. "If you don't believe me, you can stick your hand down my pants and see for yourself. It's a disaster zone."

Indi's shoulders shake with laughter as she hides against my neck. "I did do that, didn't I? We're like teenagers."

"Whatever. It was fucking *hot*."

She gushes at the compliment.

I slap her ass twice. "Now, up. I have to clean up this mess you've made."

When I return from the washroom, Indi leans against the back of the couch, barefoot. The lack of socks makes her legs look even longer.

"All good?"

"One more thing, before I forget." I straddle her feet with mine. My hands plant themselves on her hips. Her hands find my forearms. "When do I get to collect my winnings?"

"We didn't make a bet." The little smartass makes a face, tilting away from me.

"Well, I'm not leaving here without it."

Indi narrows her eyes. "What do you want?" I peer over her shoulder at the height of the couch.

"Bend over."

CHAPTER 24:
FINDERS KEEPERS, LOSERS WEEPERS

INDI

LANDON SAID YES WHEN I ASKED TO KISS HIM. SAID I could kiss him anywhere. First green flag.

Second green flag? He liked it so much he came on himself.

I've never felt a level of adrenaline as high as when he shudders beneath me. His skin tastes like a hard day washed away by soap and clean laundry. Every muscle tightens under my touch and when I mouth a pert nipple, savoring it like I'd want for myself, he moans my name. Pleasure pools below, contained only by these worn grey shorts.

Those bare, square pecs ripple and ebb, leaden breaths gusting over the crown of my head. Engorged veins snake up his arms from where his hands grip one hip and the opposite thigh. The strong sinews of his neck stretch taut, fighting restraint as he begs to see and touch me. When I let him, my nipples shrink under his thumbs, ending their ache while building a new one between my thighs. And, *holy wow*, does the man know how to work my praise kink.

Landon's cooed encouragement in the low timbre of his whispers makes my heart pump faster. My toes squirm, sweaty inside the short socks, my feet not the least bit cold after this heated exchange. I run over to my bedroom and toss them in the hamper while Landon's in the washroom, doubling back to practice some sort of cool pose while propped against the couch. How does he make it look so good? Now, what to do with my hands?

I drum on my thighs, then hug my torso and finally settle on furling my hands over the top of the sofa. Landon walks through the washroom doorway and strides back to me.

"All good?"

"Just one more thing, before I forget." Landon steps into my space, outlining my feet with his. My stomach tightens with anticipation. He palms my hips, and my hands lift and land on his strong, veiny forearms. They thrum under my fingers, matching the steady beat of my heart. "When do I get to collect my winnings?"

I perk a skeptical eyebrow. "We didn't make a bet."

"Well, I'm not leaving here without it." Those cerulean eyes flicker and grow, as mischievous and playful as the quirked corner of his smirk.

And you won't have to, my pussy cries. *Shut up, you.*

I glare back. "What do you want?"

"Bend over."

A scoff coughs out. "*Excuse* me?"

"Sorry." Landon's tongue darts out to wet the rosy peak of his perfect Cupid's bow. "Simon says, 'bend over.'"

"You're not Simon."

"Says who?" He frees one hip from his grasp. That smirk grows to an absolutely devilish grin, all playfulness draining from his face.

"Says—" I get cut off by the nine-inch wand Landon retrieves from his pocket and taps on my sternum.

"I found something *super* interesting on the washroom counter, Indi." Tap. Tap. The line of muscles flanking my throat tenses as he moves the rounded head over my breast. "What's the saying? Finders keepers, losers weepers?" His thumb presses into the power button, the charcoal grey toy fluttering and bobbing to life.

I take in the shallowest breath of air, eyes wrinkling shut as both of my nipples purse under my shirt.

Landon drops his hand. I exhale out relief, but it's short-lived, because my near-empty lungs resume their ridiculous waver as he draws a languid line down the middle of my body, past my belly button, lowering and lowering until there's nowhere lower to go. His lips murmur onto mine. "Now bend over and let me see that pussy cry."

A rapid spin has me ass-up over the back of the sofa.

"Spread those pretty legs wide." Landon taps both ankles with his feet as his hips line up with mine. I listen. "Good girl."

His fingers climb the stiff tendon on my inner thigh, the vibrating, pulsating silicone mound following their path and waking goosebumps across my skin. He growls when hooking a finger into the inseam of these stupid shorts. "*Fuck*, you were naked under this the whole time?"

The wand prods circles over the split of my legs, purposefully missing the needy spot. His other hand flattens over the curved slope of my backside, smoothing and soothing. "These shorts are annoying." He pulls aside the fabric to expose me.

"Landon." I mean to scold, but it sounds more like a beg. "You're gonna stretch them out."

"We'll have to get rid of them then."

There's no use protesting. I'm already a quivering mess.

With Landon's harsh yank, my shorts puddle to the floor. I scream out a whimper when the globed tip of the wand rolls over my clit and a sharp jolt of pleasure rocks through my lower half. My jaw drops open, hands fumbling for support in the plush cushions.

"Who do you think of when you use this, Indi?" His mouth sears the question into my skin, free hand pushing my shirt up to skim over the ridges of my spine.

The punishing, increased speed of the hammering has me blubbering. "*Oh, my God.*"

"Wrong answer." Landon bumps up the frequency again.

My head tosses, back arching at the fiery surge of pleasure.

"Try again. Who do you think of?" His firm hold on my hip guides them through a grinding motion, urging and goading my approach to the brink.

"*You.*"

He kisses the base of my backbone, trailing his lips up, still holding the wand against the tender bundle of nerves. "Say my name."

"*Landon!*" I choke out, eyes watering from how hard he's throttling my clit.

"Sounds so *fucking amazing* from that smart mouth of yours, Indi." His hand reaches up to palm my nape, fingers squeezing the galloping pulse at my throat. It elicits a writhing, desperate simper. "You're gonna make me come again with those goddamn noises."

The orgasm rips through me with a blinding flare, knees buckling and thighs juddering as the thought of him coming burrows into my brain. I don't have a chance to go limp before Landon drops the wand and plunges two long, hard fingers inside me from behind. I pant, unable to pull any more air into my burning lungs.

Feeling so full and stretched, I clench around him as he thrusts faster, deeper. His knuckles bow into my G-spot, the aftershocks seizing my already sensitive walls and hurtling me towards another peak.

Landon groans. "Fuck, *yes*. Soak my hand."

Endlessly moaning through a slack jaw, my hips swing back and forth on their own, bucking to chase the second high.

"Take my fingers. Wanna see that wet pussy come for me."

His name dribbles out of my mouth, much like the arousal down my thighs. My feet squeak against the floor, slipping while seeking friction in an entirely different part of my body.

Between Landon knuckling the spongy flesh inside me and thumbing my clit with a delicious amount of pressure, my eyes roll right into the back of my head. The couch cushion muffles my shrill scream as he continues his stroking, extending the climax until my ears ring.

With my back to his solid chest, he pulls me upright, enveloping me in his warmth. Landon's hands brush away the sweaty hair from my shoulders. "So good."

It's a gentle sweep as he stitches soothing kisses from the shoulder blade and up my neck. His arm crosses my chest, a calloused palm settling around my throat and squeezing. "Adding this to my list of views to get off to. You're so beautiful coming on my fingers."

A brain malfunction throws up an error message, disabling me from shooting back a snarky response. He turns my head to face his glazed fingers, forcing me to watch as he licks and sucks them clean with a heady moan. My thighs press together but Landon pries them apart, bending to tug my shorts back on without releasing me.

Reaching around, he cups the cleft of my legs, spreading the evidence of my arousal and pushing the fabric into the wetness. "Winning is everything."

Landon drops a sweet perky peck on my cheek, then grabs his shirt from the floor to wipe my forehead dry before purring into my ear. "Simon says, 'don't take a shower and dream of me all night.'"

When the door snaps shut behind him, I topple onto the couch and embrace my new life as a useless, barely human blob.

———

The following morning, I rap my pen against my desk, keeping the phone receiver in place between my ear and shoulder. "Bea?" I call through the open door.

A kerfuffle of shuffled papers and a crash later, she rushes into my office, boobs jiggling with every step. "Pall's lawyer is being super evasive. This is the third time his secretary's got me on hold for more than ten minutes."

I hang up.

"Very sketchy."

"Yep." I put the pen down. "Plan B."

"Trick them into a meeting?"

I cluck my tongue and fire a finger gun. "Bingo."

"Got it." She scribbles down a note and hugs it to her ample chest. "One question, though."

"Sure. Go for it," I reply, mindlessly checking my cell phone. Landon's messages blink back.

GYM GUY

> Did you do as Simon said last night?

GYM GUY

> Remembering what your lips felt like
> on my neck has me losing my mind.

GYM GUY

> Please tell me I can see you tonight.

It's possible I slept without showering and fantasized repeatedly about how good he made me feel. Heat blooms on my cheeks and in the deepest part of my belly. I shiver.

"Who's got you all flustered?"

I flip my phone face down in an embarrassed, clattered scurry.

Bea frowns and narrows a suspicious eye in my direction.

"Nobody. It's Gym Guy."

"*Ahhhh*, yeah." She hums and nods. "A good ol' work sext."

"Please stop talking."

"Get it, girl." Her shoulders dance in a wave.

"Right, well. I have *lots* of work to do." I click around the computer screen and open a Word doc to type gibberish into. She can't see my monitor screen anyway.

"One more question."

My head drops back with a sigh. "What?"

"Why did Radek send a shirt to your home address?"

Fuck me. I jerk up and shake my head. "He ripped the silk one I had on the other day when he came in." Ripped is a nice way to say he Lewinsky'd it.

Bea's eyebrows lift to the middle of her forehead. "Ripped it? Holy *shit*. Like in half?"

I pshaw. "Don't be dramatic. His keys snagged on my sleeve and tore it at the seam. He felt bad and sent another as an apology."

"But why would he send it to your place? Why not send it here, to the office?"

"And have everyone question me the same way you did? You forget he and I are friends." *Friends.* The word leaves a bitter aftertaste. "Can't have anyone questioning our professionalism."

"Fair point."

"Thank you." I give her a tilted nod, then shoo her away. "Off you go. We'll brainstorm how to get Pall cornered before threatening a court date after lunch."

Bea turns on her heel and marches off, tripping on the edge of the rug before she exits through the door. I flip my phone over to re-read Landon's text. We'll have to be more careful.

Tonight. He wants to see me again. Tonight?

In a short week, we've already tasted each other's skin and used our hands and a toy to finish each other off. There's only so much left to do before lines blurs and rules get broken and I'm unprepared. Unprepared for how quickly things have progressed, and unprepared to revisit experiences that I'd rather keep forgotten. I tap out a reply.

ME

I'm swamped at work. Maybe in a few days?

Bea returns from a coffee run with Nutella-filled croissants. Our brainstorming session flies off the rails and ends in us conspiring to skip work one Friday and take the train to Montreal for the weekend. My phone buzzes at the same time her alarm rings.

"Saved by the bell!" She leaps up. "I gotta go pick up my car from the mechanic."

"You haven't gotten it back yet?"

"Tell me about it. I've been promised it's fixed this time." She backpedals across the office, checking the floor to avoid tripping again.

"Alright. See you later." I wave her off before checking my cell again.

GYM GUY

Is everything okay?

GYM GUY

Talk to me. Tonight. Over dinner.

Can't say no to food.

ME

Sure. 7?

GYM GUY

Your place? No paparazzi there.

ME

Sounds like a plan.

After ditching the pencil skirt and blouse from work for an oversized black tee and plain jeans, I pick through my fridge for possible dinner options. It's scant and I'm not a great cook. I've been known to burn a boiling pot of water. I thumb through the pantry. A family pack of my emergency Maggi stares back. Guess we're ordering in.

Fifteen minutes later—*five minutes before seven*—I trot over to answer the soft knocks on the door. Landon barrels in, closes the door behind him and grabs me. One arm wraps around my waist as his other hand trails up the back of my neck, threading through my loose hair. He hums out a sigh, lowering his head into the corner of my jaw and planting a tender kiss there. Even softer is what he whispers. "*God,* I missed you."

My hands land on his warm, firm chest, pulling him close by the sweatshirt material before traveling up to circle his shoulders. What was it we were supposed to talk about? Something pokes me in the belly. And not in the hot, fun way.

"Ouch! What is that?"

"Fuck, sorry." Landon pulls away and sticks his hands into either side of the kangaroo pocket. Two baby cacti in mini clay pots stand upright in his palms. "They reminded me of you."

"What?" I let out a confused laugh. "Sorry, that was rude. Thank you. But also, what?"

"Yeah." He sets them down on my dining table and returns to me. "You can't seem to keep plants alive. Maybe these will get a chance. You have a lot in common" —his hips pin me against the edge of the kitchen island— "they're prickly on the outside" —his lips caress the shell of my ear— "and wet on the inside."

I lay a sharp, but playful smack to his chest, unable to withhold an obnoxious smile. The blow is ineffective, and Landon continues the onslaught.

"What do you say, Indi?" His mouth sucks the skin stretching across my collarbone. "I came here to eat. So let me eat."

CHAPTER 25:
YOU'VE REPLACED TWINKIES

LANDON

INDI'S TEETH NIP AT ONE CORNER OF HER PLUMP LOWER lip. Soulful, unsure brown eyes framed by the lushest, darkest lashes I've ever seen plead at me. "About that, can we talk?"

Fuck. I knew it. Something's wrong. I felt that pit of my stomach grow when she said she didn't want to see me for a few days. A few days? The only thing getting me through today was knowing I'd get to see her. I wouldn't last a few days.

I loosen my hold on her, begrudgingly giving her the space she wants. "Did I do something?"

"No, I don't know," she says through a sigh, shrugging and crossing her arms. "I need time to think."

My chest thuds with a quickening beat, fear planting a seed in its core. "You don't wanna do this anymore?"

"I didn't mean—" Indi shakes her head, screwing her eyes shut. "I need a second to figure out how to explain. I've never been on the opposite end of this, you know?" She plays with her hands. "I'm still getting used to the fact that you wanna hang out with me at all, much less all the time."

My fist furls against my thigh, knuckles cracking. How could anyone hurt this delicate soul?

"Well, get used to it. Why wouldn't I? You're freaking great."

The downturned twist of her mouth shows she doesn't believe me.

Seeing Indi so vulnerable breaks my heart. This side of her is so sweet and innocent, but the Indi confident enough to make me beg? That's the one I want her to be.

"Come here." I tug her close by the elbows, uncrossing them only to tuck and recross them within my hoodie pocket. My hands clasp together on her lower back, fingers twining.

Her eyes flutter down when I drop a kiss onto her forehead. I tip up her chin with a finger to force her gaze. "I'm enjoying the hell out of getting to know you again. You're fun."

"Am I?" She lets me peck the tip of her nose.

"Super fun. Are we okay?"

Indi returns a shy nod.

"Good."

Her shoulders relax with her next breath.

"We gonna stand like this the whole time or you gonna invite me to sit?"

"Let's stand." With her face hidden against my chest, as good as it feels, I can't gauge her seriousness.

I whine and mutter under my breath. "But my feet are going numb."

The little smartass head-butts my sternum. "I'm joking, dumdum."

There's my sassy girl. Wait, *my*? Hell yes, *my* girl. I'm already attached and that's probably reckless, but I don't care anymore. *Too bad,* says my heart. I want what I want. And what I want is Indi.

"Oh, ya are, are ya?" I bend my knees to scoop her up by that tight ass of hers. She winces and holds on by the shoulders. "Wise guy, eh?"

"The wisest."

My hand slaps one buttcheek for it. Indi gasps before I lower to the couch, keeping her in my lap. "You like that?"

Her cheeks pink. "No comment."

A smirky smirk is here and here to stay. "You mouth off, you get spanked. I don't make the rules."

She scrunches her nose. "Not sure I like when you're bossy."

Hand reaching around her neck, my thumb finds the drumming pulse at her throat. "Pretty sure ordering you around is what made you scream my name last night."

Her chest rises and falls at an excited cadence as my free hand pinches the loose shirt away from her torso then slides over her denim-covered thigh. "And what's all this? I thought summer was too hot for pants?" Mischief wanes from her eyes. "You hiding from me, Indi?"

"Maybe." Her jaw tenses.

"It won't work." The pads of my fingers wander back up her leg, sneaking under her shirt, seeking the delectable stretch of skin across her stomach. "I've always seen you. I see you now like I saw you then."

Indi yields, melting into my touch.

"You can't hide from me, and I don't want you to."

Her forehead dips to my chin.

"Know what I think?"

The rigid column of her throat flexes. "What?"

"I think you've been a giver for so long you don't let yourself take. It scares you."

She softens further, opening her chest and widening her straddle around my thighs with a rocking motion.

I ignore my stiffening dick and take the chance to slot her against me, crowning her with my limbs like the queen she is. "But I'm gonna give," I say through my teeth, nuzzling against her jaw. "And you're gonna take it."

She breathes a shaky hum through her nose, eyes drawing closed. I smile against her neck, each lingering kiss longer than the last, my hands collecting every tiny reaction from her goosebump-pebbled skin.

"Touch me, Landon." Indi releases my shoulders and coaxes my hands to her thighs, guiding me between them by the wrist. "Here."

Fingers tracing the thick seam of her jeans, I rub gentle circles where she says.

Her hands twitch, tightening their grip on me. She swallows. "Harder."

Harder? I definitely am. The stifling sweatshirt fabric has me sweating and I yank it from my chest from the back.

Her hands, so fucking warm and soft, roam up across my bare stomach before climbing over my chest and to my forearms. "Inside," she demands in a whisper.

I pull her collar aside to lick the stretch of bone, pants button coming undone with minimum effort so my hand can slip underneath. Indi grinds into my fingers when I glide over the wet patch of her panties, stroking the split of her covered pussy up and down. Unhurried. Up and down.

Her hands fondle her chest over her tee, but I swat them away to roll us to the side, helping her recline for better access. A sports bra appears when I bunch up her tee. I tut before kissing down one strap. "More hiding."

Her nipples poke through the fabric, pleading for my attention. Indi gasps again when I snap the bottom band up, exposing those glorious fucking tits, tiny nipples the same shade as her dark pussy. I maintain the slow pace of my hand while mouthing one side of her chest, leaving it with a harsh suck before mirroring the movement on the other side. The circles shrink, honing into her clit, her restless hands and legs squirming as the speed increases.

"*Landon.*" Her moan has me bucking into the side of her hips, desperate for friction.

"Say it."

Her lips purse before parting. "Make me come."

"Ask me. Politely." My voice comes out as rough as the frantic movements of my fingers. "Good girls have manners. Say please."

When she doesn't, I stop. Indi quivers and whines, lifting her hips to use me. I pull my hand away entirely and slink down to my knees.

"Damn it. Landon!"

The open panels of her jeans fold in my palms, the edge of her black panties wrinkling under my fingers, but I don't move them away yet. "Beg me for it."

She shifts, attempting to wriggle out of her clothing herself. "*Please.*"

"Please what?" I drag the denim and lace down an inch.

"*Please* make me come with your mouth."

"Atta girl." Everything on her lower half gets wrenched to the edge of the couch and with it, her hips. I slide her pants off her legs and nudge her knees apart with my elbows, sopping cunt at my eye level. My cock doubles and throbs. Impatient prick. Shoo.

Mouth grazing that line of muscle on her inner thigh from her knees inward, I stop to bite on the trembling tendon.

"I'm obsessed with this. Your smooth fucking skin." I breathe her in. "How you smell: sweet, spicy."

That cranberry and cinnamon tastes better than anything I could've dreamed up on my own. I suck more skin between my teeth, nearing her wetness.

"Obsessed with how you say my name. How you beg." It's a goddamn miracle I'm speaking at all. My brain tailspins, dizzy and entirely overwhelmed with what I'm about to do. "Obsessed with this warm little pussy."

My lips meet her hot, inviting flesh and I lick upward to split her ready cunt apart with a groan.

She fights for air through a choked scream and anchors her hands in my hair. The painful strain at the roots from her sudden tugging sends jolts of pleasure from the base of my spine to the tip of my needy cock.

"*Fuck*, Indi. I'm obsessed with you." I flatten my tongue to swipe across her arousal again, savoring every fucking drop. "You taste" —I lick slower the third time, pushing into her pulsing walls with the tip— "like winning."

Indi's back bows off the sofa, hair a scattered mess over the gray upholstery, tits pointed toward the ceiling as she tears at my scalp. Her moans goad me on. I treat her clit like her nipple. Lapping, flicking across, sucking the life from it.

"Right there. Don't stop," she gushes.

My hand lets go of her thigh to squeeze the firm flesh of her breast in a signal to get her to focus. "Eyes open, Indi." The right words roll off my tongue like she does. "I want you to watch." Fingers digging into her skin from spreading her legs wide, I keep her in place. "Watch while this sweet cunt takes me."

She listens, dark, widened eyes fixating on where I am and what I'm doing.

"Landon, *yes!*" Her feet thrash against my sides.

"Doing so good, Indi. Give it all to me. Need you to come."

Low moans from my chest spark her cries of pleasure as I wreak havoc on the best pussy I've ever tasted. Devouring, ravaging until my nose, lips, chin, and throat are covered in her.

Indi seizes everywhere, toes clawing at my thighs when I pull her clit into my mouth one last time, going lax as she finishes with a judder.

Her body jerks as I clean her with my tongue, that perfect cunt still red and sensitive. She replaces the grip on my hair with tender strokes eliciting a deep hum. "*Fuck*, Landon." Indi's head lolls, eyes lidding, struggling to keep consciousness.

I push up off my knees, propping her head up by palming her neck.

She sways, a sleepy giggle escaping. "That was—"

"The best thing I ever had in my mouth."

Indi gapes and watches through hooded eyes when I lick her away from my lips, filling myself on the leftovers from my chin.

"You've replaced Twinkies as my favorite thing to eat." I press a kiss into her throat, trailing left under her jaw before looking down. I'm in a damn state.

"Fucking hell, girl. Look at what you've done." We both glance down at my blood-filled cock poking up past the waistband of my sweatpants. "Look how hard you've got me from all that begging."

Her slumped body and limp hands against the couch won't be helping me this time.

"Tell me where I can come. It's gonna be so quick." My hand tugs the elastic down, length hardening further as I pump, twitching with a vengeance.

Indi doesn't say anything but her eyes motion to her naked tits.

"Fuck *yes.*"

Barely three seconds of vigorous beating off has me going temporarily blind, my cum spraying on her skin in white hot spurts. She moans again, humming while I smear the stickiness in a cross-shape, up and down between her chest then across her nipples, marking her. Like an animal. *Mine.* My mind chants the possessive refrain, eyes studying her groggy, smiling response. *Mine.* I thought I'd seen her before, but this Indi? The more I see, the more I want.

I clean us both off with warm, damp washcloths before redressing.

Indi curls her knees to her chest, balling against the couch cushions. "So much for eating dinner."

"Some of us are greedy and have dessert first." I kiss her temple while taking my seat next to her, hand resting on one of her knees. Something cuts across my ass through the ridge where the cushions meet. I lift my hips and fish around to remove it.

A black book with painted purple flowers called *Hate* is what I retrieve. I fake ignorance. "*Oooh,* what's this?"

"*Oh, my God.* Gimme that." Indi tries to swipe it. I pivot away.

It falls open to a page with a red tab, an entire paragraph underlined and five exclamation marks in the annotation. A giant smile stretches across my face while reading the excerpt. "*Indi,*" I intone with a fake scold. "Holy shit, you like this?"

"Shut up." Her eyes glare at me. "Give it back." She beckons for it with the opening and closing of her hand.

"I will *not*." I roll and stuff it into my sweatpants pocket. "I'm keeping this for later." I need to take notes.

"You're the worst." She pushes my shoulder, jabbing the side of my thigh with her foot.

"I'd argue I'm the best at making you come hard in my mouth."

Indi sighs and cuddles into the couch again. "I don't have the energy to fight you right now."

"That's also from coming in my mouth."

She rolls her eyes at my smug grin. "Yeah, well. I'm still hungry."

The rapping on the door has me on my feet to answer. I sign the bill, tip the delivery guy, and grab the bag, the smell of freshly grilled food trailing into Indi's apartment.

"You already ordered something?" Indi unfurls from her spot and sits up. "When?"

"Before I got here. They said it would take an hour." I take a rogue fry that fell into the brown bag and bite into it.

Indi raises a skeptical brow.

My smile goes dopey as I chew through a chuckle. I shrug. "Tonight could have gone a few different ways. But you'd still need to eat." I place a paper container holding her burger into the cradle of her cross-legged lap. "This one's yours."

Indi blinks at it, then flips it open. "This is really nice of you, but I don't eat—"

"It's a meatless Juicy Lucy from Chomp Burger. I hope you like it."

"Is it new? They didn't have it on the menu before."

I pop open my box, too, grabbing the burger with both hands. "I had them make it for you. I know the chef."

"Of course, you do."

"Come on, try it."

One eye squints as she picks it up and inspects it. "Okay, here goes." Her teeth sink into the burger, surprised by the cheese that flows from the middle. "Oh, my *God*," she moans. "This is so good." Indi keeps humming and moaning through each bite.

"You better cut that out. You're making me hard."

Her noises halt with a sputtering cough, fist knocking into her chest to clear the stuck food. Indi shakes her head and hand, trying to communicate but unable to respond.

"What's that? Yep, that's where I came."

That earns me a slight shove, but she tilts her head toward me, bumping my knee with hers. The awe in her gaze makes my heart and stomach go all gooey.

I want Indi to look at me this way forever. Starry-eyed. Happy. Sated. And I want to be the reason for it.

CHAPTER 26:
TELL ME TO STOP

INDI

EVERY SLICE OF MYSELF I GIVE TO LANDON IS BIGGER than the last. I thought it'd make me weaker, smaller, but each one makes me feel more whole. More complete. More comfortable than I have been in this aspect of my life in, maybe ever.

And he manages to do it while donning those insufferable smirks and murmuring devilish words in my ear. Or inconspicuously flirting in public. Like now.

He lounges in one of my desk-facing chairs, manspreading and tapping his thigh to bring my focus to his schlong. Landon fixes his bright blue eyes on me, as if preparing to eat. Maybe eat me for lunch. No, no. It's too risky in the office. Focus, Davé. Focus.

Bea sits in the chair next to him, jotting down notes. She giggles and blushes when he throws charming smile after charming smile at her. Time to wrap this appointment up.

"Here." I drop a brown file onto the side of the desk closest to him. "You need to review those statements and then sign the last page."

Landon leans forward to grab the folder and winks at me when Bea's busy testing out her dying pen, scribbling, and tapping it manically on the corner of the page. He hands her a new pen from the holder on my desk before relaxing back and tipping his chin toward my assistant. "You like watching hockey, Behraz?"

Behraz? Since when are they on a first-name basis?

She straightens with a coy gasp. "Of course!" Even if she was playing cool, the excited rippling of her boobs would give her away.

"Yeah? I could hook you up with some tickets this season. Y'know, since you've been such a *great* help with this case."

Bea beams in response. "It was nothing, I—" Her words halt, smitten smile disappearing when seeing my unamused expression. The blush on her cream-colored cheeks goes crimson.

"You, too, Ms. Davé." Landon smirks back. "You can have the best seats in the house."

He lifts his groin, pretending to adjust his position. His dick jumps up, like a captive dolphin breaching the water on cue for an audience. Unbelievable.

My eyes widen. I silently reply for him to cut it out while Bea fixates on removing a long black hair stuck on her pant leg.

His first two fingers create a subtle, sideways *v* across his lips before that cruel pink tongue pokes out to lick the gap between them.

Stop, I mouth. But my thighs clench. He does it again.

I'm wet.

"Bea!"

She jolts out of her daydream at the sudden rise in my voice.

"I could use some coffee. Mind going out to grab me one?"

Slowly getting to her feet, she sends a tentative glance between Landon and me. I slide open the drawer of my personal belongings and dig out a card, handing it to her over the desk.

"Would you like something, Mr. Radek?" she asks through batted eyelashes.

"No, thank you." His googly heart-eyes smile up at Bea as she heads toward the door. "Not from there, anyway," he mutters under his breath.

"Sorry, what was that?" She pokes her head around the corner.

If I could, I'd kick Landon in the shin.

"Get yourself one, too," I say through a titter. "My treat, eh?" She accepts the save with a nod and closes the door.

"*Finally.*" Landon leaps up to round the desk.

"Finally, what?" I narrow my eyes at him, arms folding in defiance.

"Finally, I get you alone in this tight dress." His knees push mine apart as he palms the flanking armrests, eyes motioning to the drawer next to us. "You got any treats in there for me?"

I snap my legs closed, crossing one knee over the other. "You think I'd let you touch me after you flirted with my assistant?"

"Jealousy is never a good look." Landon kisses the tip of my nose. "But it's pretty cute on you."

I wipe it away, quirking a brow. "Pretty cute?"

His humid breaths fan over my cheek and jaw before his mouth reaches my ear. "Pretty cute that you think I'd want anyone else after tasting you." He shakes his head. "Nah. Downright *adorable* that you don't realize you're the best I ever had."

For whatever reason, it does nothing to dampen the fire of jealousy, instead stoking its sudden blue flames. All playfulness drains from the mood. It's not like I didn't know he'd been with others before me, but hearing him say it out loud like that? It's a painful reminder that I'm another number in the queue, while he's seen more, had more of me than any other man.

My teeth clack, the muscles in my jaw aching from tightening so hard. I reach for his file and shove it into his chest. "Sign the damn doc and send it back as soon as possible."

"Aw, come on, Indi." He laughs, angering me more. "I was *joking*. Trying to throw Bea off. If I flirted with you, she'd know something was up."

"Right." I swivel my chair the other way, wiggling the mouse to wake the computer from its slumber. "Get out."

"*Indi.*"

"Did I stutter?"

"You're such a pain in my ass, you know that?" Landon's nostrils flare as he tucks the folder under his arm. "This conversation isn't over."

"It is for me."

He huffs and turns, cursing quietly about stubborn women before snapping my office door open and closed.

I rub the tension knotting in my temples when he leaves, banging my head against the desktop. Is it too much to hope my head splits open and relieves this damn headache?

Bea fumbles in mid-headbang with a drink tray, placing it in front of me and removing the paper from my drink's straw. "Ta-da!"

"Thanks." I take a sip and sigh. "Salted caramel?"

"It's so good, eh?" She returns my card from her blazer pocket before sitting down and taking a pull from her own iced drink.

"Freakin' delicious."

Mouth pulling to the side, Bea clears her throat. "I'm sorry."

I stop drinking. "For what?"

"For flirting with Radek."

"Oh, *uh*..."

"I know you have a thing for him and it's *totally* unprofessional."

Uh oh. "I don't have a thing for him."

"No?"

I scoff, hand swatting the air in denial. "*No*. We're friendly, but I have Gym Guy, remember? But I suppose flirting could be seen as unprofessional."

"*Ah*, man! I didn't mean it. This is probably gonna sound bad, but I was doing it on purpose."

"On purpose?"

"Yeah, because..." Bea tries to capture the straw in her mouth without looking. It evades her at every angle until it pokes into her upper lip. She winces. "I *kinda* want tickets to some games to see Donovan play." Surprise, surprise. "Don't judge me!" she whines. "I have the *hugest* crush on him."

"Me? I'd never judge you for that." Regret sinks into my gut for thinking badly of my friend. My *friends*. Right, friends. Wow, I *was* an asshole. I owe Landon a hell of an apology. Friends fight, friends make up, right?

Bea sighs, relieved. "Thank God. You're the best boss ever, Indi."

"I'm not your boss."

"Speaking of," she sings. "Mind if I take lunch early? I gotta go pick up this bike I bought."

"You bought a motorcycle?"

"No, a bicycle. My car's dead."

"*Bea*," I scold. "I thought you got it fixed."

"Yeah, me too." She shrugs. "The mechanic charged an arm and a leg, and the old clunker wasn't worth it. I sold it to him for whatever parts worked." Bea sucks the last of her drink with a rattle. "Needed to pad my account to pay for law school next year, anyway. And a bike will help keep me in shape. I'll get rid of my gym membership to save some more cash."

"Sounds like you're getting things figured out." I haven't seen Bea think so far ahead about anything before. Pride fills my chest, followed by a fleeting sadness. "What am I gonna do next year without you?"

She rejects my puppy eyes. "Die, probably."

I snort. "Probably."

"*Eh*, you'll be fine." Bea backpedals with open arms. "I'll still be around."

I let myself mourn for a moment after she's out of sight, then keep my mind off both losing Bea and figuring out how to appease my other *friend*.

————

The sun sets as I arrive at the back entrance of Landon's building. A large garage door whirs open as I tap the key fob to the reader. I pull in and drive up the ramps to the top floor, reusing the fob to lift the barrier gate arm.

About a dozen cars line the side against the wall. I pass a white Porsche, a red Ferarri, a black Range Rover, and a blue Maserati. Does he own all of these? I shouldn't be shocked. There are others hidden under protective covers. I park in an open spot and stride towards the hallway door, the warm light of the penthouse lobby contrasting the fluorescent glow of the garage. I mean to knock, but instead wiggle the handle. It's unlocked. I twist it and enter, sliding my heels off in the foyer as noiselessly as possible.

A shirtless Landon stands at the far end of the kitchen, crouched over the island. It's quiet except for the scratching sound of his pencil's vigorous strokes. He doesn't seem to hear me approach, continuing his drawing.

"Hey." I sidle up next to him and softly slam the side of my body into his. "Whatcha drawing?"

Landon straightens and folds the paper, hiding the outline of a face when he shoves it into his pocket without a second glance. "Now you're talking to me?"

"I'm sorry I snapped." I press my cheek into his shoulder.

He grunts but allows my hand to rest on his forearm. My fingers trace the raised veins trailing up into those defined biceps. They flex under the light touch.

"Do you even like me, Indi?" Landon maintains the hang of his head and motions toward my grip on his arm. "I know you like *this*, but sometimes I wonder if you like me at all."

What's this? Mr. Confident himself, Landon Radek, has insecurities about whether *I* like him? My heart sinks into my belly. You suck, Indi. You've been a shit. Say it.

"Of course, I like you, Landon." I tug at him. "I'm not good at any of this. Flirting. Being affectionate. Or sweet and charming. That's what *you're* good at."

He peers down at his shoulder where I rest my chin.

"I'm learning from you, remember? And failing miserably."

"Not failing." One bulky arm wraps around my lower back as he melts a kiss into my hair. "I'm sorry for flirting with Bea. I didn't think you'd be so upset."

"That's not why I went off. When you said I was the 'best you ever had,' I lost it. It's stupid, but I hate that you've been with women before me."

His lips curl in one corner. "So, you *were* jealous."

I roll my eyes, but the words clog with emotion. "It sucks knowing you've experienced the same thing with other women, when you're the only one that's—"

Landon interrupts by grabbing my wrist and bringing my drumming pulse to his mouth, kissing it before leading my palm across the stubble of his cheek. "The same thing? This is nowhere near what I've had with anyone else." He slides my hand down his neck, the firm square of one pec, and further south, swerving so his back digs into the counter edge and our hips slot together. "When I say you're special to me, it's not a line, Indi. I mean it."

I don't know why my stupid brain can't accept it. "I want to believe you, but—"

His hand pushes mine down against his bare abs. Smooth, rounded, lickable abs. He stifles a content hum. "Believe this." Landon pulls my hand over the hard bulge in his shorts. "It's like a rock."

The thick shaft expands under the contact as my fingers accommodate its size.

His voice drops to a gravelly hush. "I walk around like this all fucking day. I can hardly get through it with the taste of your sweet fucking pussy on my tongue."

My thong is fucking ruined at this point. I take a gulp, heartbeat wild and erratic, blood descending deep into my core. Leave it to Landon to switch from being sweet to dirty at a dizzying rate. It's dangerous how powerful he makes me feel. Rubbing him over the mesh jersey fabric of his shorts, I drink it in, eyes locking with his as he fights for control.

"You like the thought of making me so hard it hurts, Indi?" The hand on my lower back drops to the bottom hem of my dress. "If I reach between your legs, what will I find?"

"Only one way to know for sure." I push his hand up to palm my ass, then slide from his hold, sinking to my knees. Yesterday I was unprepared. Today, I'm throwing caution to the wind. "Can I apologize first?"

I stare up through my lashes, cherishing the hand wrapping around my neck. Landon breathes out a ragged groan when I pull down the waistband to release his cock. It's bigger at eye level. Way bigger. Fear flashes in my gut.

"I wanted to kiss that mouth before I fed it my dick," he laments. "But if this is what you want, it's yours." The pad of one thumb caresses my parted lips. "You can take it." It's a gentle encouragement, not a rough demand like before.

"You can take it." Kleinmann said. I'd been stupid enough to think what we shared was love. "Spread your legs."

"Don't you want to, like, touch me more?" I lay back on the dorm bed, pointing awkwardly to my lady parts.

"I didn't realize you were the sex expert here, Indi," he said through a sneer, palming his condom-sheathed dick in his hand. "You're wet enough." Russ neared, shifting on his knees. "Ready to take this big cock?"

I balled fists into my pillow, bracing for impact, but as we connected, he went soft. "Fuck. No. Damn it, Indi! What did you do?"

"Me?" I sat up. "I didn't do anything."

"That's the whole fucking problem." He tore off the condom and jostled his limp dick, stroking it back to life. "Make yourself useful and spit on it." My mouth suddenly went as dry as the other place I was supposed to be wet. Russ groaned. "Fuck it." He spat. "See? Not so hard." Yeah, not-so-hard. Like your erection. "Wanna make it up to me? Suck me off." He brought it closer to my lips.

"I've never done that."

"I'll show you. Stick your tongue out." So desperate for his approval, I listened. "Lick. Like a popsicle." I did. "Yes," he moaned. "Open that mouth wider or I won't fit." I don't know. Looks like you'll fit fine. "Now suck."

Before I got a chance to, he shoved it past my lips, taking full control. His hands palmed the back of my head as he sped up, harshly fucking my face without warning. "Fuck, yes. You like that? I bet you do, you little slut."

I choked through every godawful thrust, tears of humiliation streaming down my cheeks. We never talked about degradation. "Take this dick. Take it like the dirty whore you are." I gagged, my throat swelling around his tip. "Oh, fuck, I'm gonna come."

He did, and I threw it up. On him. The salty liquid disgusted me as much as what he did.

"What the fuck, Indi? You're supposed to swallow."

I wiped my mouth and scrambled to cover my naked body with a sheet. "You called me a slut. A dirty whore."

"This is what I get for fucking around with a virgin." Russ rolled his eyes. "It's called dirty talk. Everyone does it. I can't believe you're giving me shit after your dry cunt couldn't keep me hard." He reached for his phone and cursed again, gathering his clothes, and pulling them on.

"You're leaving?" I shrunk further into the shroud of the bedsheets.

"You expect me to stay?" He scoffed. "Get over yourself, Indi."

Landon waits for a response. I unzip my dress, slipping the sleeves down my arms and baring my torso. The stiff fabric pools around my hips, like the pleasure between them. I want him to see me. My hand circles around him to support the weighted length of his cock, engorged head leaking pre-cum. I lick the tip in one, slow, upward swipe. His head sags back, hand cradling my neck with a squeeze, throat going taut through a moan.

"You're perfect." The artery bound to the column of my neck pounds under his tenderly grazing thumb. More of his arousal seeps out when I hum. I spread it over him with a tight pump.

He lifts his head with a gasp, meeting my gaze as I mouth him. "So fucking perfect."

I pause for a second, flooded with his adoration. It washes the bitter emotions away when I pull more and more of him in.

"Every inch, just like that." His thighs judder when he hits the back of my throat.

I gag with a cluck.

"*Fuck.* Tell me to stop, Indi."

I don't. I take him in, again and again, stroking the veiny underside with my tongue and dropping my hand from the trunk of his dick to let my mouth do the work.

"You're taking me so well." He twitches between the suction of my cheeks, every muscle in his body wound up, visibly straining for release. My own pleasure climbs as his hips surge forward, piloting how deep and fast he wants to plunge into me. Tears form but they don't fall. Landon groans and removes himself from me.

"Baby, if you keep going, I'm gonna come."

My throat is sore, hoarse from being filled by him, unable to produce any reply.

Baby? If he doesn't come, I might. My hands do the talking for me and fist the base of his length, bringing it to my lips once more.

"Oh, *fuck*. You want me to?"

I nod, seeing my reflection in the darks of his eyes.

"What a good fucking girl."

My stroking and sucking sync with his rumbling groans before I offer the flattened plane of my tongue as a place to finish. His knees buckle as his orgasm hits, knuckles going white around the edge of the counter.

I may never get over him falling apart while moaning my name, those gorgeous sweaty strands of hair hugging his forehead. Or the way he tastes like Heaven. A sweet and salty drop hangs from my lower lip. Landon swipes and pushes it back in with two fingers. His heaving chest chases after rapid breaths.

"When I come in your mouth," he says through his teeth, "I want you to take it all. Swallow it all, you hear me?"

My head nods, blinking away the rest of the receding teardrops.

"Good girl."

"Landon?" I savor his grip on my neck.

"Yeah?"

"Next time, paint my throat."

He pulls his shorts up and smirks. "Anything you want, baby."

"Why did you call me that?" My knees anguish against the harsh surface of the tile.

"Call you what?"

I force down the unsure lump with a gulp, afraid of the answer. "Baby."

Landon wrenches me upright, spinning us around to place me on the counter. He doesn't let go of the lush pressure against my throat until he uses the same hand to sweep across my cheekbone. "'Cause you're so precious to me."

I melt into him.

"Can I keep calling you that?" He assaults my skin with those soft lips, dotting my shoulders, chest, and neck with tender kisses while he redresses and zips me back up.

"Yes," I rasp out.

"Good, 'cause I don't wanna stop."

My heart is in so much fucking trouble.

CHAPTER 27:
BREATHLESS AND HORRIBLY, IMPOSSIBLY HARD

LANDON

ONE MONTH. FOUR WEEKS OF BRUTAL CONDITIONING for speed, agility, strength, and stamina to train for the oncoming season. Indi and I apply those skills to the bedroom. And the living room. And the kitchen, too. We've christened every goddamn surface in our apartments.

It's not a competition, but if it was, we're tied. I thought I was addicted to Twinkies, but they're no match for Indi.

"...I already told Sky she can have whatever she wants," Jaeg says, fading me out from my thoughts. "But she wants my opinion on everything."

A deep, humid breath huffs from my chest as I stifle the boner uncomfortably lining my cup. It's a good cover.

"I love the little stink, but I couldn't care less about what flavor the cake is. It's fucking *cake*."

In tandem, we shift the weight between our legs, switching one skate for the other across the boards.

"Chocolate, vanilla, red velvet, I don't fucking know the difference. I don't remember what I ate for breakfast. It goes in, it goes out. And cake?" He trills through blubbery lips. "As long as it's sweet and soft, I'll shove it into my mouth like good fucking puss—"

"*Oooooh, big stretch*," Wade interrupts with a loud groan, announcing his presence while doing the splits behind us. He bounces his hips while glancing over his shoulder, nose crinkling into an ornery smirk. "If this ice comes around in nine months asking if you know me, no, you don't."

I grimace and give him a thumbs down.

"*Booooo!*" Gliding onto his back, Wade windmills his legs one after the other, like a stripper, while beatboxing a jazzy tune.

Jaeg rolls his eyes.

Dissatisfied with our non-response, Wade rises to his feet and skates behind the forwards on the other side of the rink. Picking up speed, he throws up his right hand and the opposite leg into the air as he passes.

"Give 'em the ol' razzle dazzle!"

"Idiot." Jaeg scowls.

"What's up with him?"

Our tendy is a showman but it's rarely directed at Derrick. The poor dusters and second string usually bear the brunt of his shenanigans.

Jaeger grunts. "'Skylar's letting him MC the reception. He's excited to be involved. Prolly his way of apologizing for being a jackass the past few weeks."

The next time Wade whizzes by, he switches to the left hand and right leg and waves his gloves with jazzy-handed pizzazz. *"Razzle dazzle 'em!"*

"Enough!" Jaeg bellows, using his stick to trip Wade. "We're good, okay?"

He embraces the fall, landing on his side onto the ice and striking a Jane Fonda exercise video cover pose, a hand supporting his helmeted head and one knee bent, splaying apart from his straightened leg.

"Now quit screwing around."

Wade wobbles to his feet and hugs Derrick from behind, then skates away, calling for his paddle.

"It's like babysitting a fucking toddler."

His ridiculous display catches the attention of the other guys, distracting them from practice. The captain yells for everyone to cut it out.

I smack his arm with the back of my hand. "It's only the first day back on the ice. They're pumped. Let 'em have this."

"Fine. Is offering to make one of those ridiculous dance videos at the end enough incentive?"

We pull our feet back to the frozen surface and head to the other end of the oval.

I salute. "Aye, aye, Captain."

Jaeg whistles and calls the boys over, going through the day's drill order before we end with a scrimmage. He lets Wade talk to the social media manager about what to do for today's TikTok.

Today's assignment: act out different versions of sliding on the ice. Wade calls out the poses as the social media intern records.

"Twerk!"

A surprisingly difficult thing to do in gear.

"Put those bubble butts to work, boys!"

Olsen and Szecze put on a weak performance, but enough to entertain. Derrick, Fletch, and I get some decent booty bounces in, but Wade takes it through. "Don't get mad, get deep." He sticks his tongue as he squats and twerks, doubling the speed as his ass nears the camera before swerving to the side.

"Kung Fu!"

Most of us do karate kicks and ninja jumps with kiai. Fletch gets adventurous and does the crane from Karate Kid.

"Swimming strokes!"

We mime front crawls, back, side, breast, and butterfly strokes. Wade does a doggy paddle. Which fits, considering he has the energy of a golden retriever puppy.

Jaeg and I have to catch our breath afterward for a few moments, hands on our knees. He shakes his head and squirts the remaining liquid from a stray water bottle into his mouth.

"And the fun's not over yet." I go vertical before leading us off the ice. "We've got press, too."

Luckily, it isn't formal. Starters, coaches, and the GM sit at the front table behind mics, the PR team flanking us on both sides in case they need to step in. Staff wears their matching branded pullovers while we lounge in hoodies and sweatpants. A dozen reporters and their cameras wait for the chatter to subside.

I space out when they start with Coach, asking about this year's strategy. Wade kicks my ankle after a minute to snap me out of it. He flips his hat backward with a crooked smile. I pull mine over my eyes, hoping to avoid attention.

A long arm rises between two shorter ones. "Gabe Finch," she says, brushing her hair away from her shoulder and face. "Canadian Sporting News." The brown freckles across her nose and cheeks contrast her fair skin.

Wade's jaw goes slack, eyebrows reaching halfway up his forehead.

He tilts toward me to whisper. "*That's* Gabe Finch?" I nod. "*Fuck,* she's beautiful."

Ms. Finch's face goes red in response. Cheeks inflamed. Eyes furious. The rest of us fail to silence our titters. These mics are super sensitive, and everyone fucking heard.

"Did you hear that?" Wade asks no one in particular, but stares at the equally horrified reporter.

Fletch tucks his head under the collar of his sweatshirt to hide secondhand embarrassment. I shake with laughter as Wade slaps his hands to his face, then attempts to slide under the table. I don't think I've ever seen him so embarrassed.

Olsen and Szecze guffaw while Jaeg snarls and rubs his temples. The press laughs about it for a few minutes but gets over it and moves on. Neither their questions nor our responses are unexpected. They've been rehearsed, citing hard work and improvements over the summer, and how we'll keep our heads down and focus clear for the oncoming season. No one asks about Annalise. Back by the lockers, my phone buzzes in my bag.

GYM GIRL

How'd the press conference go?

ME

Got lucky.

GYM GIRL

You're welcome.

ME

You did that? How?

GYM GIRL

I'm really good at my job.

ME

Nicely done. Also, I'm learning lots from your book.

ME

Though I didn't need it to know how much you like having my hand around your neck.

GYM GIRL

I'm not much for jewelry, but it does make a nice necklace.

GYM GIRL

What else?

ME

Some things are better experienced.

GYM GIRL

There's an oral exam.

ME

Tonight?

GYM GIRL

Your place?

ME

I'll be waiting, baby.

———

By the time I get home, I'm riled up to the point of pain. I end up rubbing one out in the shower to avoid nutting in my pants the second Indi walks through the door.

She traipses across the apartment, feigning innocence but exuding pure sex. "Hey."

A pleated skirt in the darkest shade of blood red swishes around her lower half, flaring and receding with every step. I imagine how it'd look draped across my thighs. What it'd be like to have her ride my cock as long and as hard as she wants. Taking me however she wants.

"Landon?" I peer up from that sinful skirt to the bratty, knowing look in her eyes.

"Come here," I command, wrenching my shirt over the back of my head by the collar with a single hand.

Indi stops in response, going doe eyed. A pursed smile—*tinted the same color as her skirt*—tugs at one corner of her lips when I approach, the strides slow and steps calculating. She backpedals at the same pace. "*No!* Landon…"

Holding up a finger and giving me her best stern tone doesn't work this time. I lunge at her. She laughs and breaks into a barefooted sprint across the living room, veering off to the side with a squeal.

"Just wait a second!"

My arms capture her waist and hoist her over my shoulder. The smartass delights in the rough gesture. "You like being thrown around, Indi?"

"You tell me, Radek. You're the one that's been studying."

I flip up her skirt and slap her exposed ass cheek hard enough to leave a handprint. "That mouth's always getting you in trouble," I state, walking us to the kitchen. "It's only quiet when it's chock full of my dick."

Indi responds with a gasp before I toss her onto the marble island, bare thighs landing with an audible smack. She doesn't let go of her tight grip on my nape and holds my hips captive between her legs. "Are you ever gonna say 'hello' like a normal person?"

I kiss the adorable wrinkle of concern between her eyebrows. "When you stop teasing me, maybe." My lips stroke down the slope of her nose, the curve of her cheekbone, and the angled edge of her jaw. "I've been waiting patiently."

She clings to me as we exchange excited, pleasured hums, giggling when I undo two buttons from her shirt to trace the top rounds of her tits with the tip of my nose. Taking a breath of her in sends me spiraling into a moan. "You always feel so fucking incredible."

Indi pulls me from her chest by tugging the roots of my hair. "Pop quiz, Landon." Her eyes flick to the counter behind me. "Is that wine?"

I don't have to look to know. "It is." I put it there. Like bait.

"Can I have a taste?"

"Fuck yes, you can." I loosen my grasp and turn to grab the bottle. The biggest fucking smirk stretches across her face, dimples cratering into her cheeks as I pour us both a glass. Her tongue clicks when I hand it to her. "What happened?"

One of her full brows lifts as she wets her lips. "And you were gloating about knowing what I liked. I asked for a *taste*, Radek." My eyes narrow at the glass in her hand. "Watch and learn." Indi takes a large sip, then palms my neck in a swift swoop to draw us close.

My lips part in surprise and awe, but the pad of her thumb urges me to widen. She tilts my head back by tipping my chin.

Hovering over me, Indi spits, releasing the rich, astringent wine onto my tongue and coating the back of my throat. It goes down warm, a reminder of the heated temperature of her mouth, leaving me breathless and horribly, impossibly hard. This girl's the hottest fucking thing I've ever experienced. I kick myself for reading about this and not remembering. I won't forget next time.

I tremble as she wipes away a rogue drop of wine with the same thumb, then brings it to her stained mouth to suck it dry.

Teeth clacking as my jaw clenches, I keep our faces slotted together, tempted to crash our mouths together. "I wish I'd never agreed to not kissing you."

"Why?"

"Because it's literally all I can fucking think about." Having pieces of Indi will never be enough. I want all of her. Every smile, every laugh, every kiss, every gasp, every moan, every scream. I want it all to be mine. Her to be mine in every possible way.

She rumbles out a hum. "Too bad. You failed the test."

We battle for control, hands on each other's necks. Mine, holding her to me, and hers, keeping us apart.

"I fucking *hate* when you tease me." Silence fills the next few seconds as her eyes dart between mine, dark pupils growing to replace the rich browns of her eyes.

"Prove it." It's a sultry challenge. "Show me how much you hate it."

A humorless laugh escapes from low in my chest. I press my forehead into hers, gritting my frustration through my teeth. "Take your clothes off before I fucking *rip* them off."

Her stomach growls in protest, breaking the tension. Indi clamps her eyes shut, cheeks going pink with embarrassment.

I rub a palm over her belly. "You hungry?"

"I guess so." She frowns. "Sorry."

"Don't be."

"Are *you* hungry?"

I return a wicked smile. "I'm *starving*, baby."

Indi predictably rolls her eyes. "No, like, do you want to eat?"

My head nods to a rhythmic beat. "I'm telling you; I can *definitely* eat. Right here. On this kitchen island. I can eat all night long."

"*Landon.*" She squirms against the counter, knocking her knees into my sides.

"Okay, okay." I make it sound like I'm giving in, but who am I kidding? I'll put up with anything she throws at me. My hands caress her back in large, swirling half-circles. "I'll feed you and then I'll *eat.*"

Indi ignores the suggestive tone. "Can we order Indian?" She pouts, pleading. "I haven't had it in a while."

"You can have anything you want."

She gifts me the widest thankful smile. I couldn't ask for anything more. Except for maybe a kiss.

Forty minutes later, Indi teaches me how to tear chapati into pieces and use them to scoop up the spiced okra we ordered. "Bhindi masala from India House is the closest thing to my mom's bhinda nu shaak." Her knees sway off the edge of the couch. "One of these days" —she wags her index finger at me— "I'll have her teach me."

It's in these brief seconds that I get to see the real Indi. Passionate, sweet, open. These moments with her, *fuck*. My heart spills over and I wanna ask if she feels it, too. Someday, I'll grow the courage to do that without the fear of losing her. Until then, I'll cherish and collect these memories in the greedy pocket of my heart.

CHAPTER 28:
PLAYING DEFENSE

INDI

MY FINGERS LAY AGAINST THE EDGE OF THE TABLE, A sneaky answer to the question abruptly interrupted by the peppy waitress refilling our waters. Gabe and Bea stop their gaping and rapid blinking as the glasses bubble to the brim. I shoot a polite smile at our server.

The gaping resumes when she leaves, but there's no more blinking. "*Four* times?" Bea huffs. "In one night?"

I lean forward and the girls do, too. "In an *hour*."

Gabe's eyebrows fly to the middle of her forehead before she reaches for her icy drink. Bea uses the menu to fan herself and loosens the flowy chiffon fabric of her blouse to allow airflow.

"And he used" —I clear my throat— "*help*."

"Which one?" Gabe whispers.

"The Dongshow."

My girlfriends gasp in chorus. I'd been raving about that vibrating dildo and its magical ability to pound out orgasm after orgasm ever since Sheena's sister-in-law gifted it to all the bridesmaids during her bachelorette weekend.

"I *know*. I never thought it'd be better having someone else use it on me."

"You lucky bitch." Bea places her cheek in her hand. Her dark brown eyes go all dreamy.

"Kurt would *never*." Gabe tuts. "He gets so jealous."

Of a dildo? Red flag #293708374028374.

"*Ew*," Bea blurts.

I kick her under the table, scowling before focusing on Gabe's downward expression.

"I thought you said he does...good."

Gabe shrugs. "It *is* good. Doesn't mean it couldn't be better."

Neither Bea nor I have any words of solace.

"*Anyway.* This is about you and Gym Guy. I still can't believe you haven't..." Gabe makes a slurping sound as she inserts two fingers into the hole of her fist. "Or caught feelings."

"I mean" —I lift both shoulders—" that's why there are rules. No expectations, no feelings."

"Uh-huh." Gabe quirks a disbelieving eyebrow.

"Seriously! It's all in good fun." Right, good fun. It has nothing to do with how he showers me with affection, or calls me baby, or sends me filthy, needy texts, or how those calloused fingers press roughly against my cl—

Bea snaps in front of my face. "*Hellooooo?* Anyone in there?"

Gabe shakes her head. "You're a goner. You may not have had the dick, but the dick got you."

I know she's teasing, but I can't help but deny it. "Hey! That's not—"

"Don't look!" Bea cuts my protest short and scrambles to prop our menus upright.

Gabe peeks over her menu and I make the mistake of glancing over my shoulder.

"I said, *don't* look."

All six of the Regents' starters stroll through the restaurant, led by a blushing, giggling hostess.

"*Ugh.* I hate that guy." Gabe shrinks down below the top edge of the thick page.

Bea keeps her voice at a whisper behind the menu wall. "Which one?"

"Wade Boehner. He embarrassed the hell out of me at that press conference." Her mouth warps into a sneer.

"I'd let him get away with murder. He's so pretty," Bea states, her gaze lingering.

I mumble my agreement while trying to ignore them.

"I bet his dick's massive."

Landon's eyes hone in on mine, smile going full-on smirk before he winks. My pulse sets off into a sprint, but I glare back in warning and pretend to squint while browsing the menu.

"Donovan is way hotter, though."

Gabe pulls the corners of her lips down in surprise and bobs out a series of nods. "Never thought you'd go for a ginger."

"Me either, but he's *incredible*. His voice" —she mimes drooling and gargling—" is so soft and deep. There's this shirtless interview of him in the locker room from last season and you bet your sweet little titties I recorded that shit. I've lost count of how many times I've watched—"

"Wait," Gabe talks over Bea. "Did Radek wink at you?" Her brows furl as her eyes shift to mine.

My heart plummets into my gut. "Doubt it," I say through a snuff, sending the shakiness in my breath away. "I don't think he knows I'm here."

"You're not gonna go over?" Bea eyes me suspiciously, too. "He's our client, after all."

"And I'm off the clock. If he wants to say hi, he can. I see enough of him at the office." And after hours. And in my dreams.

"Okay, *jeez*. Weirdo." My legal secretary gives me the once over, those big, beady eyes searching me up and down.

Gabe clasps her hands together in a muffled clap. "Back to the point at hand. You and Gym Guy. You've been rockin' each other's boats for" —she counts on her long, svelte fingers—" over a month now. Deny it all you want, Indi, but you two care about each other."

My jaw twinges. I do care about Landon, but that's what friends do, right? Friends care for one another. We also happen to enjoy each other's company. "I promise. We're messing around, not playing house."

Gabe and Bea both throw their arms up in surrender.

"Fine, whatever. When are you seeing him next?" Gabe is so nosy these days.

"I don't know." My voice rises to a higher pitch. "It's not like we have a schedule or something."

"I wanna meet this sex god." Gabe picks up her phone from the table. "Maybe we can make a trip to Fit365 tomorrow. Try to see Mr. Orgasm in the flesh."

Confidence wavers through the next stammered-out sentence. "I don't know if he'll be there."

"Maybe not." Gabe sends me a determined grin. "But maybe he will."

———

No excuse works on my friend. After hours of back and forth arguing over text, Gabe picks me up from work, citing she could really use someone to shoot hoops with.

"You're engaged to a professional basketball player!" I don't know who I'm kidding with all this protesting. I'm already sitting in her car. "Can't he play with you?"

"He played with me last night." She sticks her tongue out before taking a left turn. "We got into it. I was so sore this morning, it took me like thirty minutes to get out of bed." Her hearty laugh ricochets within the confines of the Jeep. "Men are so easy. All I had to do was say how your guy gave you four o's, and suddenly it was go-time. Kurt is competitive as hell."

"And somehow that wasn't enough of a workout for you?"

Gabe pats my thigh. "One can never be *too* healthy."

The gym floor is packed by the time we get there, post-workday rush in full swing. She bends to tie a shoelace against a locker room bench, then straightens to tighten her ponytail.

I admire her exposed midsection. "Damn, girl. Look at those Janet Jackson abs."

"It's all the" —she thrusts her pelvis— "you should ask Gym Guy to take you for a ride. I bet he would."

I dissociate for a second, questioning why and what I'm holding out for. Bea's right. I'm a weirdo. A weirdo who's gonna die a virgin. All because I can't get over what stupid Kleinmann did.

"Hey."

I blink back to reality.

Gabe squeezes my shoulder. "It was a joke, okay?"

I nod.

"If you're happy with what you're doing now, I'm happy for you."

An exhale exits my nose. "Thanks."

"But I'm also your best friend and nosy as fuck." She claps twice and motions for me to get to my feet. "Hop to it. Let's go find Gym Guy!"

Gabe's investigative skills are on point. She scours the cardio equipment, weight machines, and free weight section, scanning between the men who match the vague description I've given her before and my face to get a reaction. I don't have to fight it because Landon's not here. Lucky me.

"Too bad. Guess we'll have to play HORSE and go home."

We dawdle on the way to the basketball gym. Gabe peers through the glass windows overlooking the indoor pool and through the occupied squash courts.

"You look more suspicious than anyone else here, you know that? Will you chill?"

"I will *not*." The door to the half-courts slams open under Gabe's heavy hand. "I'm on a mission."

I grab the last basketball from the rack and toss it at her. "It's a failed mission. Get over it."

"There's still time. Who knows? He and his buddies might be ballers."

"Yeah, definitely *not*," I mutter to myself.

Gabe dribbles the ball, then stops to turn on her heel to make a shot. It drops in without touching the rim. She does a side-to-side hip roll. "*Swish, swish.* Nothing but net."

When I bend over to pick up the runaway ball, the metal door slams open and closed.

"Well, well, well. What have we got here?"

I bolt upright.

Landon Radek and Wade Boehner wear the smuggest smiles as they saunter in.

Gabe crosses her arms.

"Didn't expect to see you, Davé." Landon's nonchalant tone is annoying.

"Small world," Boehner says.

"Something like that."

Landon hums. "There aren't any balls, no empty courts. You ladies mind sharing?" He lays on the charm thick in Gabe's direction.

She's not paying attention though, too busy glowering at Wade.

"Nice seeing you again, Finch." He squares off with her, which is saying something, considering Gabe is six feet. Wade is still taller by a few inches.

"Wish I could say the same for you, *Boner*."

He rumbles out a laugh. "Don't play."

"Why? Afraid you'll lose?"

What the fuck are you doing, Gabe?

Wade raises his eyebrows and looks over to Landon and me, who stand awkwardly outside the three-point line while watching their aggressive exchange. "Do we ever lose at ball, Landy?"

"Nope." He pops the 'p'.

Cocky bastard. I beg Gabe with my eyes not to step up to the challenge.

"You're going down," she says through a dry laugh, beckoning for the ball between my hands, but keeps a hard stare on her opponent. "Two-on-two. First to eleven. Nothing dirty." Her head whips to me. "You cover Radek. I'll whip Pretty Boy here into shape."

"You think I'm pretty?" Wade pulls out a beaming smile at the compliment.

Gabe rolls her eyes and slams the basketball into his chest. "Back up."

"But—"

No one listens to me. Wade and Gabe are already fighting for the ball. Landon stands behind me and tugs the back of my loose grey shirt.

"You look beautiful," he whispers.

I'm too pissed off to deal with the butterflies flying from my stomach to my chest right now. "Shut up," I say through gnashed teeth. "As if winking at me at Avec wasn't enough. You wanna get caught?" One step halves the short distance between us.

"They're busy."

"*Yoooo*, Landy! Help me out here!" Wade somehow stole possession and tries to pass. Gabe isn't having it, but he's still trying.

"Not that busy."

"Quit chatting and cover him!" Gabe yells.

"You heard the boss lady."

I lower at the waist to push Landon back and extend my arms overhead, waving my hands around like a manic monkey. Between my anxiety of being caught and flailing like a starfish in heat—*do starfishes go through heat?*—sweat covers me, sticking the cotton shirt to the skin beneath it.

"This isn't at all how I imagined your arms above your head." His voice against the curve of my ear draws a shiver up my spine, making my hips buck. "And stop pushing your ass against my crotch. You're making me hard."

"It's called defense, Radek." I bump him away again, inadvertently making contact with the big guy below. My insides clench.

"Not the way you're doing it."

Gabe smacks the ball out of Wade's hands, regains control of it, and makes two points. "Take that!"

I run three steps to high-five her and before we can get too self-assured, Landon and Wade run circles around us. In an extra-exuberant, macho display, Wade dunks the ball with one hand.

"I'm M.J., baby!" Wade puffs out his torso with a grunt and flexes his arms before the boys bump chests.

Gabe answers with a flawless lay-up. We slap our hands together in a double-high five. Though I have nothing to be proud of. I've contributed almost nothing to this game. Other than frustrating the daylights out of myself. The back and forth continues until we're ahead by two points.

My friend-with-extra-benefits passes the ball overhead to his teammate. Gabe's defense is good enough for both of us and drives Wade back away from the net. I spin around so that my back is to Landon's front once more.

His hands palm my ass cheeks and squeeze. "I told you not to rub that perfect ass on my dick."

"I'm playing defense!" I whisper-scream through gnashed teeth.

"No, you're making me *post up*."

"That's *so* not the correct term."

"Believe me, baby. It *is*."

My knees wobble and I step away to stabilize.

Gabe groans as Landon drops in a three.

I roll my eyes at him. "How did you get good at basketball?"

"I thought you knew, Indi." He jumps and mimics attempting a shot with both of his hands in mid-air before falling back to land on his feet. "Hockey players are good at *everything*. It's all in the wrist." Landon's voice dips under his breath and blows past my ear. "Need a refresher?"

"*Ay*! Are you two done dicking around?" Gabe asks through panted breaths, hands grasping her hips. "We *cannot* let them get this next shot in, Indi."

"Hey, what's that on your chest?" I shout over to Gabe, who tips her chin down.

Wade gets distracted as she adjusts the straps and bottom band of her sports bra. My plan worked. I'm a genius!

Wade and Landon groan in slow motion. I dribble the ball a few steps to the other side of Gabe and call out for her. She picks up the ball and it bounces off the backboard before dropping through the basket.

We share a laugh and perform Will Smith and Jazzy Jeff's handshake from "The Fresh Prince of Bel-Air," gloating and jogging away backward. Wade whips off his shirt and chucks it onto the floor. Landon bites down on his lower lip and smiles, shaking and dropping his head back.

Gabe's halfway out the door, but I don't miss the way Landon mouths, *"my place, now."* The breath I gulp down almost chokes the air out of me.

"As satisfying as it was to beat those jerks" —she hooks an arm around my neck— "it sucks that we didn't run into your Gym Guy." Gabe holds the locker room door open for me.

From the corner of my eye, out of view from my friend, Landon shoots me an impish grin as he heads to the gym exit.

"Yeah, totally sucks. Maybe next time."

CHAPTER 29:
AGAINST THE RULES

LANDON

THE MINUTE THE ELEVATOR BELL DINGS, MY PACING stops.

I whip the door open. Indi startles at the slamming sound but doesn't get a chance to react before I yank her in by the nape. It's a miracle I don't trip over our feet while shutting the door and pinning her to the adjacent panel. Her throat pulses against my palm, the excited pace hardening my cock in record time.

"You're a fucking *tease*." I push my hips into hers, our bodies so close we exchange shallow breaths. "I need your wet fucking pussy in my mouth." The grinding of my teeth grates in my ears. "Right now." My free hand travels down the curve of her ass and cups the space between her legs from behind. The clingy fabric bunches in my frustrated grip.

Indi gasps.

"I wanna strip this off you. Can I?"

Her chest heaves against mine. "I'm sweaty. I" —she gasps again when my mouth sucks the delicate, salty skin on her neck between my lips— "should" —my teeth graze over the same spot— "shower."

I raise my head and wet my lips, forcing eye contact. "I don't mind when you're dirty." That gorgeous fucking blush fills her cheeks, but she doesn't protest. "Let's go." I loosen my fist and swipe at the seam, rubbing her through the spandex with two fingers before lifting her by the ass and hooking her knees over my hips.

Indi buries her fingers into the hairs at the crown of my head. Her elbows dig into my shoulder blades. The whole walk to the bedroom, she giggles at how she holds our mouths apart.

When I launch her onto my bed with a bounce, her sweet little face flashes with pleasant surprise. Eyes wide, mouth agape, but turned up at the corners. It's a priceless expression. Indi's legs splay open when she props herself up by the elbows.

My hands furl around the band at the top of her pants, my face still hovering over hers. "Your ass looks so fucking good in these, but they have to go."

She bites down on her lip and nods.

All that banter makes me want to fuck the sass right out of her. Smooth, brown skin replaces the black stretchy fabric as I wrestle it from her, flinging her sneakers and socks over my shoulders from my kneeled position at the foot of the mattress.

When my palms move up her legs, fingers squeezing at the firm flesh, her head drops back. Indi's throat tightens with a moan when my lips follow their trail, kissing, nipping, and tonguing the entire trip up. I groan upon approaching the tense muscle of her inner thigh. "I can't think of anything better than you in my bed."

One of her hands creeps into my hairline and tugs, ending the fantasy and drawing a simper. The flimsy damp lace covering her feels rough against my tongue and I nudge it aside, exposing how she's just as worked up. "*Fuck*, look at you."

I bury my nose and mouth into her, savoring how sweet she smells and tastes. A soft moan slips from her pulled-in lips, her hips bucking when I skip over to the other thigh instead of gorging myself.

"*Landon*," she whimpers and pulls at my head, but I keep it down. Focused. Eye on my prized, soaked girl. "I have to tell you something."

"Can it wait, baby?" My teeth sink into the tender flesh of her thigh. "I'm about to eat."

Indi's back arches when I split the seam of her slick pussy and smother it with my mouth again. My tongue dips into the warmth once. Twice. Ready to flatten and lap like a thirsty dog. Nothing can stop me.

"My friends know about you!" she whines at a higher-than-normal pitch.

"What?" I push off my haunches and slink over the bed, shifting all my weight into her frame. "I thought this was supposed to be a secret." Fear rips through my heart. Did she do this on purpose?

It dissipates with the brush of her hand against my jaw, thumb stroking the cheek stubble. "They don't *know* know."

No. This isn't Annalise 2.0. This is me and Indi.

"They know you exist."

A wry chuckle huffs past my lips. "Of course, they know I *exist*. I'm Landon Radek, ruggedly handsome, beloved right-winger for the Ottawa Regents."

"Don't forget humble." Her eyes draw an arc as they roll. "I meant they know that I'm, we're" —she waves a pointed finger between us— "you know."

"They know you and I...?"

Her eyes snap shut as she shakes her head. "Oh, *no*. All they know is that I'm doing stuff with *someone*." Indi drops her hand from my face to cover her eyes.

Nooooo. Leave it. I liked it there. That's its home. Don't you want your hand to have a home? Go to your home, hand.

"They're such busybodies. I ended up giving you a code name and told them I met 'him'—*which is you*—at the gym to get them off my back." She lifts her pinky and ring finger, those umber eyes peeking out under the shadow of her hand. "We call you Gym Guy."

"That's funny." I pry her arm away and place her hand back on my idiotically smiling face. "I made up the same excuse when the boys figured out something was going on. They don't know it's you, either, but they call you Gym Girl."

Indi's chin tips up to release a belly laugh, cheeks dimpling with that sparkly grin of hers. "We're so immature."

"Oh, yeah?" Both of her wrists cross under the clinch of one hand as I stretch her arms to their furthest extension above her head. "We can get adult real quick, if you'd like." My hips roll and grind into her spread legs, cock stiffening further at the slow, dry hump attempt.

Indi squirms and writhes beneath me, a breathy, validating moan gushing from her throat.

"*God*, I want you naked."

Defiance and mischief glint in the question of her eyes. "I have a better idea, if you let me go."

"And what's that?"

"I'll shower."

"Together?"

"Not *together*," she rejects the suggestion, but doesn't miss a beat before offering another option. "You can watch."

Fuck. Okay.

She squeals when I leap up and throw her and her attitude over a shoulder before running into the washroom. Impatient hands rip her shirt away and unzip her sports bra from the front, her perky tits falling into my ready hands. I caress them before Indi denies me.

Taking her time, she explores every ridged muscle of my torso while lifting my tee. Goosebumps rouse to life at her light touches, shrinking my nipples down as far as they can.

My fingers hook into her panties and drag them down her legs. I look up at her from the floor and Indi willingly steps out of them, her hands on my shoulders. She glides them across my traps and delts, studying them through a narrowed gaze. "These are more defined than they used to be."

I don't think I could stop it if I tried. "I wanted to make them a perfect spot for the backs of your thighs. And knees. Ankles are welcome, too." She doles out a playful slap to my cheek before I get upright and motion with a nod toward my groin. "Your turn."

The little rebel pokes a single finger into the mesh shorts material over my bulge.

I wrap the finger in my fist and bring her painted nails to my line of sight. "You changed the color. Nice." The mint green is quite the change from the harsh grey and dark red I've seen before on her. My thumb grazes the knuckles below them.

"I had a nail appointment during lunch." She tests out the feeling of our clasped hands, then retracts, slipping out of my grasp. "Cut that out, Radek. It's against the rules. No holding hands."

Head shaking in disbelief, I sigh in surrender. She wants to stick to the rules. I'll stick to them with her until she's ready for more. If she's ever ready for more. In the meantime, I'll give her a run for her money.

"Right, sorry. My bad. You wanna hold my dick instead?"

CHAPTER 30:
STRIP ME BARE

INDI

SPARKS CRACKLE AND FIZZ BETWEEN OUR FINGERS AS Landon's hand finds mine. Every fine hair on my arms stands upright, tugging at the skin they're attached to.

The steady drumming of my heart dives as an anxious thought creeps in. Crossed lines are so far behind us we can't see them anymore. I'm comfortable being buck-naked in front of him, but it's too terrifying to think of Landon as anything more than a trusted friend. We're ignoring the consequences of the entirely illegal and risky agreement: the *f*-word. Feelings.

I tear my hand away. It felt too good, too calming. As if it wasn't tempting enough to have his eager mouth below mine. How warm the yearning in the cyan blue depths of his gaze is when I touch his cheek.

We can't. Getting each other off is detached. But kissing, hand holding? It *means* something. He's taken so many of my firsts, but I've had none of his.

"Cut that out, Radek. It's against the rules. No holding hands."

Landon gives in, sighing and letting me go. I don't know how or why he puts up with it. "Right, sorry. My bad. You wanna hold my dick instead?"

All the blood in my body splits between my face and the lowest part of my belly. I agree with a silent nod.

"Good, 'cause I need you to fucking touch me." His hand guides mine, molding to the clothed shaft as a breath hisses through his teeth.

My voice lowers to a husky whisper. "Can I take your shorts off?"

"Please." Desperation laces with want in his hooded eyes and groaned-out response. The elastic sticks to his damp skin and I use my nails to get under the sweaty waistband. Those tight boxer briefs leave nothing to the imagination. My mouth waters at the height of the pitched material. Through the thick frame of my upper eyelashes, I catch Landon in a heated, impatient stare.

"Do it. Strip me bare."

One haughty tug peels the spandex away from the large, toned sheets of muscle on his thighs. The delicious *v* of his hips flexes as my hands pass over it. I squat to drag it down the rest of his legs and gulp away the nerves when his cock bobs. Not sure how I forget that it's always bigger this close. Straightening to push Landon against the bathroom counter, I grab his wrist and shape his hand around the base. When I lean in, our chests press together, my nipples brushing against the broad, firm planes of his pecs. "Touch yourself for me."

I move his hand in languid strokes before backing away, separating our bodies. He stills when I open a drawer. "What are you doing?"

The fleshy, veiny dildo I left here the other day emerges and I measure it in my grip. It's surprisingly similar in length, girth, and weight to the prime specimen attached to Landon. My tongue wets the lower seam of my lips. "Letting you watch," I say with a smirk.

"Oh, *fuck*." His movements restart as I backpedal to the pane of glass encasing the massive shower area. The water steams quickly as I wash off Long John Silver in preparation. A hot cascade continues behind me.

Landon's legs angle away from the vanity for support as I suction the toy to one of the hexagonal marble tiles on the floor. "Can you see me?"

"Yes." His reply comes out strangled, fist tightening around his favorite limb, the head red and engorged, length leaden in his hefty hand. "I've always seen you, Indi."

I breathe, shunning the butterflies fluttering between my heart and stomach. "Keep watching."

Knees straddling the dildo, I wiggle and hunker down, sliding over the firm, rubbery shaft. The head slips in without resistance. I choke back a moan while easing in the length, gasping at how full it feels before shifting off it again.

"*Goddamn*, baby. Don't stop," Landon groans.

A quick squeeze around the base has the toy buzzing to life. I sigh, sinking onto it again. My hands and knees squeak and slide while I find a rhythm, widening my stance as my hips lift repeatedly to urge the orgasm out. The vibrations curve my back into an arc when I pick up the pace, prodding the silicone tip into my g-spot. I moan out without inhibition, bracing a hand behind me.

"*Fuck*, you're flawless," he rasps. "Perfection."

Landon pumps himself at the same incredible cadence as the decoy shaft plunges deeper and deeper inside me. Every thrust I take drives me closer to the edge. Switching to a slow grind, the toy contacts the most sensitive spot at my front wall. I chase the high by speeding up once more.

"That pussy looks so good getting fucked. Are you imagining it's me, Indi?" The mirror behind him fogs, steam kissing every inch of its clean surface. Dripping, matted hair clings to his forehead, sweat beading all over his beautiful naked body. The sinewed muscles of his neck and shoulders strain from the impending release. "Tell me you want it to be me."

"*Landon*." His name rushes from my throat.

"Play with your clit," he demands, and I obey, unsticking my hand from the clammy tile to rub the neglected, tender bundle of nerves.

A wince escapes despite me biting down on my lip.

"That's it, baby. Scream it," Landon pants. "No one can hear you from here."

I give in and cry out, eyes screwing shut, the knot of pleasure unraveling as my orgasm hits its peak. White blankets my vision for a few seconds before my eyes reopen, hazy and groggy to see Landon rumbling a drawn-out groan, his toes curling and back arching forward away from the counter. Every marvelous muscle tenses as he releases over the floor. I come again at the glorious sight of him coming so hard.

"What a fucking *mess*, Indi."

We catch our breaths through satisfied giggles, riding out the aftermath of the climax. Landon steps in after I shakily get to my feet. He smirks over his shoulder when I peer over mine at his round, pert ass.

"It's super unfair that your ass is nicer than mine." Each cheek gets a pat and a playful squeeze.

Landon soaps up his chest and shoulders. "I'm a professional, baby. I tone this for a living. But if you're fishing for a compliment, I'll give it to you." His voice muffles behind his hands as he rubs his face clean. "Your ass is my favorite ass." His smirk grows.

A giant lump forms in my throat. My thighs clench, seeking friction for the tiny nub of throbbing flesh between them.

Landon turns off the water and leads me to the wall with a gentle push of his outstretched palm on my belly. He bends and removes the dildo from the floor with a cartoonish *pop*.

"Turn around and lemme hit it from the back."

Twenty minutes later, I stroll back into the living area swathed in Landon's fluffy, oversized robe, giddy from an orgasmic daze. A stupid smile plasters to my face but drops when I fish out my phone from my gym bag. Messages on the family group chat await.

MOM

Madam, please consider this my formal request for an audience with Her Royal Highness Queen Elizabeth over the telephone. I have the honour to be, Madam, Your Majesty's humble and obedient servant, Anjali Davé

DAD

Good one, love!

NIK

Yuck

ESH

HELPPP

One of Landon's arms furls around my waist, his bare torso searing my skin through the Turkish cotton. The opposite set of fingertips brushes the ends of my hair away from my neck, tucking them behind an ear. His lips post a kiss where his fingers trail off.

Warmth bursts in waves through my chest.

"What's going on?"

I sigh. "My parents being dramatic as usual."

"Yeah?" He repeats the delicate sweep on the other side, continuing those soft, honeyed kisses on my clean skin. "What're they like?"

"Disgustingly in love." I turn off the screen and place it back on the counter. "And always needing my attention."

"My folks were never like that."

My heart frowns at the trace of sadness in his otherwise unbothered expression. "Your parents weren't lovey-dovey, like, ever?"

"I mean, they held hands and kissed or whatever, but it's hard to tell as a kid."

I grimace to myself, recalling all the times my folks were so publicly sweet to each other that it could have given me a toothache. Sickening.

"Hard to tell what?"

My body pivots to study him better. I let him keep his hands wherever he wants. One settles on my lower back. The other roams across the crook of my neck and into my hair, scratching my nape with his trim nails. I flatten my palms over his shoulders.

"Whether people are truly in love or not." Landon locks his gaze on mine. "You're lucky to have a good example."

"Yeah, right." I lower my eyes, fiddling with the short hairs in the middle of Landon's chest. "Unfortunately, it's not hereditary." My parents' ideal adds to the longing for something better.

Cupping my chin, his eyes flit from my mouth upward. "You deserve it all, Indi. Someone to love and dote on you. Someone to be the best friend and partner you could dream up."

My heart lodges itself in my throat and won't go away, no matter how hard I swallow.

Silence cuts through the air like a hot knife. I should've gone home already.

Landon draws a line at the rim of my jaw with his thumb. "Stay the night."

"I shouldn't."

He chuckles and hangs his head. "Worth a shot." The counter edge jabs across my back as he shifts, locking his fingers above my ass to bring us close. He nudges my nose with his. "I'm gonna be on the road soon. You gonna miss me?"

His too-sure, knowing smile is too easy to mess with. Can't let his ego balloon. "*Nah.*"

Landon pouts at my denial, his concerned brows wrinkling together.

"Between Magic Mike, The Dongshow, Long John Silver, the rose toy, and my little red lippy, I'm covered."

Landon's jaw goes slack. "Take it back."

"No."

Landon pinches my sides with his grasp. "Say you didn't mean it. Tell me nothing and no one makes you feel as good as I do."

"What's this?" I tease. "Do you have a praise kink, Radek?"

"I don't know, maybe." His head dips, resting his forehead against mine. "Stay and find out."

"*Landon.*"

"Please, Indi?" Those ridiculously blue eyes swirl and plead.

And how am I supposed to say no to that?

"Only until you fall asleep."

"And what if *you* fall asleep?" A mischievous smile plays on his lips.

"Not happening."

"But what if? Fifty bucks says you'll be passed out before midnight."

"Mr. Confident, huh?" I tilt back and cross my arms, but Landon doesn't release me. "I'll do you one better. If I fall asleep here, I'll wake you up by sucking you off."

"Deal!" His eyes brighten with hope, but he shouldn't be so excited. I had a latte with an extra espresso shot before leaving work. We shake on it. "One more thing. I have an early morning skate tomorrow. If you're in bed when I leave, you have to wear my practice gear."

The thought makes my stomach lurch. "*Yuck.* But fine. Can I have something to put on instead of this robe?"

"Got you covered."

Wearing clothes that smell like him is dizzying. Climbing into his bed is as worrisome as the last time. Having him lying beside me is unreal.

"Cuddle with me," he whines. "I'll let you be big spoon again."

I huff. "It's like you want me to leave."

"*Noooo!* Don't leave," he whines again, his eyes drooping with sleep. "I have a bet to win."

"You mean lose."

"I said what I said." Landon positions my arm under his head and throws his weight onto my torso. He nuzzles into my neck and moves my other arm onto his muscular back. "There. Isn't that nice?" I trace the rippled, solid panels of muscles.

It is. "Go to sleep, Landon."

The next time I blink, the sun's out.

CHAPTER 31:
ABSOLUTELY ATROCIOUS DISPLAY

LANDON

RUSTLING SHEETS CUT MY INITIAL CYCLE OF SLEEP short. I lazily blink up at the ceiling, then roll to my side, seeking another comfortable position. My arm refuses to move, plagued with a strange weight.

My lips pull into a drowsy smile. Indi slept here. In my bed. With me wrapped around her. Looking like a fucking angel, so tame and kittenish in comparison to her fierce waking life. My hand brushes the span of Indi's back while I peck kisses onto her forehead, her eyelashes, her cheeks—all the places she thinks are too cute when she's awake.

Her mauve-pink lips twitch, releasing a soft hum.

God, I want to kiss her.

My heart twists knowing I can't steal it like this. One more hour, one more day. As long as she'll have me. What am I saying? She already has all of me.

I return to my place on Indi's chest, ear down. Even through the thick hockey sweater, her heart's stable beating soothes away any lingering anguish. She lets out another hum. Lean fingers swirl through my mussy hair, her nails scratching my scalp in a moan-inducing pattern. The feather-light pressure makes me shiver. Goosebumps sprout across my exposed skin first, then the blanketed bits, too. Then something else sprouts. *No, no, no*, I scold my dick. For once, he listens, and I lull myself back into relaxation to the steady drumming of Indi's pulse.

"*Landon.*"

"No more chicken tenders. I can't."

A husky giggle follows a stifled snort as my dream sequence dissipates. "Landon. Wake up."

My eyes pop open. With a knee on either side of my stomach and hands planted above my shoulders, Indi hovers over my torso. The knitted jersey—*my jersey*—hangs away from her body, giving me the most insane view of her tits through the collar. I swallow, the dry texture of my mouth and tongue almost as painful as how hard my dick's getting.

Indi's smile simmers through a blush when she looks up from the canopy created by my main man. "Morning, glory."

Tousled strands of her hair fall from the deep, uneven part, hiding half of her face. I push them back, the dark brown silk between my fingers cementing the idea that this whole night wasn't some sort of wet dream. My knuckles warm when making contact with her heated cheeks.

"You stayed."

She pulls her lips into her mouth and holds my gaze, uncertain eyes searching mine. "Is that okay?"

I rasp through a sigh. "You're the best thing I've ever woken up to."

"Not yet." Her right hand lowers onto the solid peak at my groin.

I tense and gasp.

"I might have broken a rule, but I always hold up my end of the deal. And it's time to play the pipe." Indi slinks down, crawling backward, scraping her nails down my naked flesh until she reaches my shorts.

"Isn't it, *um*, 'pay the piper?'"

Her eyebrow quirks. "You wanna argue with me about technicalities or you wanna be sucked off?"

"S-s-s-second option." My hoarse stutter couldn't sound more desperate.

A crooked smirk dimples her cheek—the left one, the one with the deeper pit. My pulse skyrockets in anticipation. Her fingers hook into the waistband to release my already leaking cock. I groan when she spreads the stickiness down the shaft, her fist getting tighter as I harden.

Indi sways over the tip, teasing the fuck out of me with the seam of her lips. "Put your cock in my mouth, Landon." Those round eyes dilate as she licks them in preparation. When she locks my hands onto her nape, my dick weeps harder.

It takes no effort to slide past her full lips and I whip my head back against the pillow as she sucks around the swollen crown.

"*Fuck, fuck, fuck...*" I chant like a madman when she takes more of me between her cheeks at the most unbelievable pace while stroking her tongue on the underside.

Indi gags when I'm in too far. *Goddamn*, the gagging. Every gushy *cluck* tightens the coil of pleasure winding at the base of my spine. It's gonna have me busting so soon. Too soon.

I launch my head upright to witness this perfection in real-time. The way her saliva dribbles out and coats me has me dizzy. I thought Heaven was tasting her. Wrong. There's nothing as glorious or holy as Indira Davé mouthing my cock at the crack of dawn.

"*Baby*," I groan. "You're fucking gorgeous with your mouth full of my cock."

Teardrops bead in the corners of her eyes from how deep I've delved into her throat.

"You take me so well."

She moans in response, and it takes everything in me to retreat from the brazen thrusts. Balling my grip on her hair, I force eye contact.

"I love when you give me control," I grit through my teeth with another punishing thrust, "'cause you're the only one" —I knock into the back of her throat again— "who makes me lose" —another thrust— "all semblance of it."

Her whimper buzzes through my clenched balls. If I don't finish in two seconds, my dick's gonna burst into flames. I don't stop the manic movements, the rhythmic sloshing from her throat driving me to the brink. I writhe against the sheets, legs tremoring as jolts of pleasure roar at the edge of release.

My torso lurches, every muscle in my body taut as I explode with an embarrassing, loud groan. Stars cartoonishly circle in my vision. Indi keeps me in her mouth, gulping the cum and drawing me in with languid pulls while I'm still shuddering and sensitive in the aftermath.

Returning from the high, I soften on her tongue as she smiles back at me, batting her eyelashes. My breath settles from its erratic tempo. The sheets cling to my bare back, fresh sweat surely leaving behind a stain.

Indi snaps the waistband of my shorts back up with a giddy laugh, then falls back to my bed with a sigh. I roll over her and off the mattress after I pelt her neck with impatient kisses. She squeals and buries her nails into my scalp and shoulder.

"*Ouch*," I intone. "You're gonna leave behind marks." My lips float over hers before I push off by the forearms. "Unless you want everyone to know."

She lets go, her open palm landing on my ear with a *fwump*.

"Get off," she commands, lips fighting a smile.

"I already did."

She rolls those unimpressed eyes.

"*You* scored." I extend my left arm to her face, miming a whistle blow with the other, then imitate a foghorn sound to signal a goal. Indi attempts to jostle me off, but I plant my hips onto hers.

"Obnoxious." She laughs.

Yes! I make Indira Davé laugh. My chest swells with pride and I flex, balling my biceps and making my pecs bounce.

"Absolutely atrocious display." Lingering fingertips on my abs tell me differently. My stubborn girl can't admit to liking my ridiculous ass.

"Alright," I conclude, rolling her to the side to lay a clap to her perfect ass. It jiggles in a controlled wave. "Any more banter and I'll have to shut you up again and there's no time. I gotta get on the ice."

Indi sputters and dives under the covers. Cute aggression builds but I resist the need to squish her, instead smooshing a harsh kiss to her sweet, clammy forehead. "Let me get you some water. Stay as long as you'd like."

Indi downs a large glass before she yawns and turns into a hamster ball under the summer blanket. I loiter at the edge of the bed, not wanting to leave, but unprepared to get chewed out by the GM or Jaeg for being late.

———

At practice, Wade being his quirky self draws more attention than usual.

"What the fuck is that?" Olsen snickers and pulls the hood over Wade's eyes as we head to the lockers. "Wearing' a fucking hoodie under your gear?"

Our goalie tears off his shoulder pads and points to the 'RIPPIN' WRISTERS AND BANGIN' SISTERS' text on his chest. "Why don't you ask your sister?"

The big oaf shoves Wade into Szecze, who shoves him back to Olsen.

The playful volley suddenly erupts into an all-out brawl, pulling in more than the necessary parties. Jaeg and I end up prying the dog pile apart and order them towards the showers to cool off.

Derrick grabs the perpetrator by the neck with a warning. "Back to therapy you go."

When Theron Olsen gets amped up, it's like Thor and the Hulk had a love child but dropped it on its head more than a few times. Anger management is the only way to keep collateral damage under control.

"Professional fucking athletes, my ass." The grouch grumbles. "I'm too old for this shit. If I don't suffer an aneurysm by the end of the season, it'll be a fucking miracle."

"You're gonna be fine," I affirm. "They're probably stressed and taking it out on each other."

Jaeg snorts.

"They'll get over it on the ice. We're family. Brothers fight. Brothers make up."

Not that I'd know what that's like. I've got a Delaney. She's up my ass about some goddamned strawberries.

DELANEY

Did you get the strawberries yet?

ME

It's fucking 8 a.m., Del.

DELANEY

Get your ass moving! The kids and I worked our fingers sore to pick you the last batch of the season.

DELANEY

Ungrateful shit. I hope they rotted on the way.

ME

Aww, you're so sweet.

ME

Go fuck yourself.

DELANEY

Sure thing. That's Seth's favorite.

ME

Morning. Ruined.

I forget all about my disgusting sibling upon seeing the darling in my bed, stretching her arms over her head and pointing her toes, stifling a high-pitched whine. Cutie. Indi winks at me with a sleepy smile as I approach. I rip the sheets off, ignoring her protest and yanking her out by one arm and the opposite leg. "Hey!"

Over my shoulder she goes, like an unwieldy burlap sack of cranberries. I grab my gear bag in my free hand on the way to the terrace and plop her into a patio chair.

"What the...?"

I squat to unzip the bag. Indi's face warps with repulsion as the stench hits. "A deal's a deal, Davé."

After dropping shoulder pads over her head, I secure shin guards to her legs, slide gloves over her shaky hands and slap her helmeted head for good measure. She's speechless, gasping and heaving for clean air. Her gagging now isn't nearly as satisfying as earlier in the morning. I set a timer on my phone. "Five minutes should do the trick."

Indi ends up so sweaty she has to shower again. Her fist knocks into the glass before she wipes away the steam, pointing at me with a feisty curl of her lip. "You're so paying for that, Radek!" The mirror in front of me reflects her making a slicing motion across her throat with a thumb.

Shooting her a glance over my shoulder, shaving cream topping my cheeks, I wave my razor in her direction, pretending not to hear the threat. "Press your tits against that glass for me."

"In your dreams!" she yells over the water stream.

"In my dreams, they're pressed against my dick," I mumble, pulling the blade under my jaw.

She turns off the water and pokes her head through the shower entrance. "What?"

I shrug and feign innocence. "I didn't say anything." The words stop when her wet, naked frame steps out. *Fuck.*

She catches me staring with my mouth gaping and glares. Indi wraps herself in one of the large towels from the bathroom linen closet.

"Goodbye," she sings, backing away.

"Goodbye?" No way I'm letting the little smart-ass leave like that.

Scrambling to finish shaving without cutting my jugular wide open and welcoming an early, bloody death, I rinse my face and chase after her with grabby hands, slipping on the floor in the trail of her wet footsteps. He-Man swings around like a drunk, blind bastard, slapping my thighs with every hurried stride. I catch up and lift her onto the kitchen island, keeping her in a firm grasp against my bare torso.

She knocks the side of a fist into my hardened chest and wiggles her hips to get free. "I need to get dressed." Indi's uncooperative flailing knocks over a basket, covering part of the counter with rolling strawberries. "*Shit.* Sorry."

"It's okay." I wind an arm around her waist.

Indi softens with a sigh and stops fighting.

"Now I can tell my sister I got these. She sent 'em in the post." Fisting a few strawberries from the counter, I lean over the island to the sink, keeping a spread palm atop her thigh. The sensor-driven faucet detects my waving hand and runs water over the fruit.

"Your sister? Delaney, right?" Indi kicks her legs from the marble edge, one after the other.

"You remember her?" My heart. I'm tempted to rip it out of my chest and offer it up like vepřo knedlo zelo, complete with hot dumplings and pickled cabbage on the side. Here, have it. It's yours.

"Just her name. You used to whine all the time about how big of an asshole she was." She teases, shoving my shoulder. "And that she drove like a maniac."

I scoff, shaking the water from the strawberries in hand. "Not much has changed. She's still a lunatic driver and still an asshole, but now has a husband and two kids."

"You're an uncle?" Her eyebrows fly to the middle of her forehead, the grip on my forearms feeling less like she's pushing me away and more like she's bringing me closer.

I let her.

"They're blessed with the best." My gaze shifts from my hand to her eyes as she watches me bite into a perfectly ripe strawberry. Sweet, soft. Juicy. Not unlike Indi's wet puss—

"Very cheesy," she replies with an eye roll. "Not cocky at all." Her finger jabs my pec, then flicks the nipple, making the rounded muscle jiggle.

"If you want me to make that smart mouth shut up, just ask."

Indi's breath hitches, eyes widening.

"It's not my dick, but here. This'll do." I push the narrow bottom against her lips. They part without any further command.

Her eyes flutter shut as she chews and lets out a content hum. "Oh, my *God*," she moans, sending a false signal to the needy prick between my legs. "That's delicious."

"They're Ontario strawberries. Hand-picked." My thumb catches a drop of strawberry juice and pushes it back between her now-berry-stained lips. The suggestion isn't lost on her. Her pulse thuds on the surface of her skin beneath the hand still planted on her upper thigh. "More?"

I offer another. It elicits a similar response.

"I better stop." Indi toys with her lower lip.

"Why? I have plenty."

A blush fires up across the ridge of her cheekbones. "I'm getting turned on."

I can't help that stupid, knowing smirk stretching across my face.

"I don't see a problem." I lean in, hoping to kiss her neck until she's squirming for mercy, but Indi puffs out an aggravated sigh and hides her face in my chest.

She shakes her head like she's battling something.

"This is ridiculous. One minute, we're talking about your sister, the next..." her voice muffles against my flesh.

My cock deflates. "Come on, baby," I lament. "I don't wanna talk about my sister."

Indi's head pops up. "*Shit*! Nik is coming to town this weekend." She escapes me by jumping off the counter, then marches back into my bedroom. "Has some interview on Monday. I got an earful from my mother the other day for not planning the stay better."

"Nick?" Who is this Nick?

"*Nik*. Anika, my little sister." Her hands tug on her panties under the towel, robbing me from another naked viewing. I whine. "I have to entertain her the whole weekend."

"*This* weekend?" I jut out my lower lip. "That means I won't get to see you until next week?"

Indi turns around to hook on her bra. But I wanted to see booooooobs. "Yeah, I guess so."

"Does that mean you're not coming to my game?"

"In Montreal?" She pushes her legs and slides her arms through a black dress that appears out of nowhere, then points to the zipper. "Help a girl out, Radek."

"You packed this?" I smooth a hand down her back after zipping up, then glide it across her stomach from behind, holding her perky ass to my crotch.

She captures my gaze in the full-length mirror propped against the wall. A naughty grin tugs at my lips. "Indira Davé! Did you plan for—?"

"Calm *down*," she replies, fluffing her hair. "I keep extra clothes in my gym bag because I'm a loser who sleeps at work sometimes."

I shush her, spinning her around to face me. "Not a loser but listen: Come to my game." My hand squeezes her waist twice. "Watch me play."

"I don't know," she intones. "It might look suspect."

"No, it won't. Please?" I give her my best puppy dog eyes.

"We'll see."

That means no.

Indi pats my wrist and tugs my arm away, doubling over to dig out red-soled heels from a cloth bag inside her duffel. As she gathers her things, I follow behind like she'll vanish into thin air if I don't keep her in my sight. Keys jingling in hand, she waves me off from the open elevator.

"Hey, Indi?" My hand stops the door the moment before it closes.

"Yeah?" One last shot.

"You looked fucking *incredible* in my jersey."

Indi flushes immediately.

"Wear it to the game and I promise we'll win."

CHAPTER 32:
VERY EMERGENT, VERY CONFIDENTIAL

INDI

I MUTE THE PHONE, PROPPING THE RECEIVER BETWEEN
an ear and my shoulder to beckon my secretary through the door.

"Bea, write this down."

The button unmutes when pressed again.

"Marshall Langley."

She jots down the number I repeat to confirm with the young man on
the other end of the line. Thank God for clueless interns.

"Appreciate all your help, Grant."

Bea gives me a thumbs up.

"Sorry to cut this short, but I've got a client waiting. Thanks again!"

She high-fives me the minute I hang up. "What does it mean?"

I recline in my chair and strum my steepled fingers like an evil
mastermind. "I won't know for sure until I talk to Langley, but I'm fairly
certain he was paid to take those pictures."

Behraz lifts both of her brows. "You think Pall's behind it?"

"Wouldn't put it past her," I say, clicking my tongue and swerving
the chair to and fro. "Set up a meeting with Langley. Tell him you have
something juicy on Radek."

"Got it." She salutes and acts out a stiff march before turning on her
heel. "Pall's lawyer is still being a shit, by the way."

"Forget about them for a little longer. We need some more statements
and then I'll hit 'em with the threat of court. She'll agree to a meeting, then
bam!" I smack my palm against the wooden desktop. "Knock 'em dead.
Tear apart every single allegation. Radek's lost money on this. Hell, the

team could have won the Stanley Cup if he had been on his game." Knit blazer sleeves on my elbows squeak when I lean slightly forward and wring my hands into a tight fist. "Gonna drain that greedy well dry."

"*Brrr*!" Her shoulders shudder. "Sometimes I forget how savage you are. Damn."

"I like to think it's for a benevolent cause. But who knows?" I shrug. "No one is above the law."

Bea throws me a confirming nod. "One more thing. Is poutine okay for lunch? I'm on my period and if I don't get some greasy, cheesy fries with gravy in my belly, I'm gonna go feral."

"Poutine's fine." My eyes wander to my phone, distracted by the notification from Landon's renamed contact. "Let me know when you're back."

GYM GUY

What are you up to?

ME

Making some serious headway in your case. Why?

GYM GUY

Need to see you. Now.

ME

At the office. Swing by. I'll catch you up.

GYM GUY

Come to the Au Lait two blocks west of there. I'm getting you an iced latte. You'll leave to get coffee and return with a coffee. It's a foolproof excuse.

ME

Can't you tell me via text?

GYM GUY

It's an emergency. Confidential.

ME

I'll be there in 10.

I peer in from the cafe window.

Landon takes a selfie with the baristas, doling out fist bumps with that sunshiney, charming smile. He looks fantastic in a blue suit, bright white button-down crisp against his chest. The way his blazer molds over his broad shoulders and his slacks cling to the meat of his thighs has my mouth-watering. He catches me gawking and excuses himself.

Toasting his coffee cup to a fan walking by, he wordlessly passes me the iced one. I almost spit out my first sip when he switches spots with me so he's closer to the road. I've seen Dad do it a million times when he and Mom walk side-by-side. It's protective. Gentlemanly.

The entire stroll down the street plays out in slow motion, like something out of those serials my sisters love or the cheesy, guilty pleasure Bollywood movies I can't seem to stop watching. Landon's beautiful from the side, too: kind eyes, sharp jaw, and those sweet dimples peeking through every pull from his coffee. My heart does a series of flips.

"Turn left," he murmurs the directive from behind his cup.

The closed lunch cafe in the alley is bare and dimly lit, despite the nearly noon lunch hour. Landon's hand on my lower back has my posture straightening from its warmth. He uses it to guide us into the next right turn and parked a hundred feet away is a black Range Rover, tinted windows too dark to see through. The fluttering butterfly moment vanishes. "Am I being kidnapped?"

He shushes me through a chuckle, his crooked smile pitting a dimple in his cheek. "Just get in."

The doors beep to unlock before he pulls one open for me, the inside spacious as expected. Landon puts his coffee in the cupholder between the front seats and settles beside me.

"So, what's this all about—?"

He cuts off my question by grabbing the latte from my hand and dropping it next to his cup.

"Hey, I'm still drinking that!"

Strong hands lift and prop me into his lap without warning. I gasp, my arms flying to his shoulders for stability.

"Drink it later," he demands, splitting my legs so they straddle him before tightening his hold around my torso and pulling me close. "I'm about to get on a bus with twenty men who I'll be spending most of the weekend with. I won't make it through without this. Need you."

There goes my heart again. A cardiologist would have a heyday. My insides melt whenever he says *need* like that, all whiny and longing.

He nuzzles into me with a deep breath.

"*This?*" —I struggle to breathe when his lips press against my neck, the wispy kisses changing to tender sucks— "was the confidential emergency?"

"*Very* emergent," Landon groans, grazing his teeth across the delicate skin. "*Very* confidential." His tongue laps over the sensitive spot below my ear where he nipped.

My hips inadvertently shift forward, eliciting a pleasured hum from him and sparking goosebumps over my chest, nipples shrinking down to the point of pain.

He moves his hands, sliding them from my knees and up my thighs before cupping my ass and squeezing. His forehead drops to my collarbone. "Today, of all fucking days, you had to wear pants."

I snort. "I wasn't expecting to see you."

His head tips up, full lips pulling into a knowing smile. "Are you saying those tight skirts and dresses are for me?"

"N-no, that's not what I—"

"Indira Davé." Landon drops his jaw in fake surprise and disappointment. "How naughty and *unprofessional*."

My hand meets the swell of his shoulder with a thwack, lips tightened into a line. "I am *very* professional, as you know."

"I agree. You're a pro." His hips rise, bouncing the hardened contents of his pants into the seam of my slacks. My pussy cries for attention.

"I have to get back," I whine, fighting the temptation to slip Landon's hand down my pants and finish me off. "And don't you have a bus to catch?"

Landon pouts and head butts my shoulder. "I don't wanna."

I take his face in my hands, the stubble on his cheeks and jaw scratching my palms. "It's only preseason, Radek. Get your grubby mitts off my ass and your head in the game."

"Are you gonna be there?" His arms return to their curled position, elbows hooked at my waist. Glossy blue eyes scan my face, pleading. "I'll win for you."

"For me? Win for yourself, okay?" I let him go with an encouraging pat. "You've worked too hard to get where you are."

Landon grabs his chest like he's been shot. "You've killed me. Cutthroat lawyer Indira Davé is my personal cheerleader."

"Don't get used to it. Fans are fickle." I swing my leg behind me to dismount from his lap.

His touch lingers as we separate, the searing sensation not fading as fast as it ignited. Landon sighs. The condensation from the coffee wets my fingers when I retrieve it from the console. I hop out, but double back to peek through the open door, tipping the plastic cup toward him.

"Thanks for the coffee, Radek."

Bea clops toward me as I approach my office.

"I went to grab a latte!" I announce preemptively, holding up the proof.

"Oh-*kay*." Her mouth twists, hand held out to me in slight bewilderment. "*Anyway*, you got a delivery." Face now lit up; she stifles an excited noise. "It's on your desk."

"From who?"

Her grin turns downright evil, eyebrows bouncing as we walk into the workspace. "I'll give you one guess."

A black gift box tied with white ribbon sits on my desk. The Regents' crown logo is embossed in gold onto the upper right corner, and looped into the bow is a matching tag with my name on it. My fingers pull one loose end of the bow, unraveling the tie before I lift the lid.

"Oh."

"What is it?"

I pick up the envelope sitting atop a hockey sweater before using a nail to cut it open. "Tickets to tonight's game in Montreal." Goosebumps wake under my blazer.

Bea's lips turn into a pursed *o* as she sucks in a breath. "Let me see." She takes the envelope from my hand and flips through the tickets. "They're for private box seats. And there's three!"

My head goes foggy as I lift the jersey, flipping it to see the number twelve and Radek's name stitched onto the back.

"*Whoa*," Bea adds.

"What's going on here?"

I almost drop everything when my boss appears in the doorway.

Bea answers before I can. "Radek sent Ms. Davé fancy suite tickets to tonight's game in Montreal and a jersey with his name on it."

I'm dizzy from how fast she blurts it.

"Very nice," Giachetti sing-songs. "I hope you're going. It's good for client rapport."

If only she knew what kind of rapport we have.

She pumps a fist across her chest in an uncharacteristic manner of encouragement. "Show the client we support him." Theresa turns to leave. "I'm sure he'll appreciate it. You might have fun."

"Right. Support. *Fun*." And what am I supposed to do with my annoying little sister? I tap the tickets against my palm.

Bea gasps in realization. "What time does your sister get in town?"

"Her train gets in at three-something."

"That works out perfectly then. You can pick up Anika and..."

I glare back at her bright-eyed, scheming face. "Not my idea of a quiet weekend at home."

"Aw, *come on*, Indi." Her hands clasp together as she begs. "Please, please, please, *please* take me! You know I've been *dying* to see Donovan play. *Please, Indi.*"

"*Ugh.*" I slouch down into my chair with a squeak. "And how do you suppose we get there? The buses and trains are probably fully booked now."

"We *did* talk about spending a weekend in Montreal." Bea wiggles her hips in a happy dance. "Road trip!" She continues the silly dance as she shimmies back to her desk, knowing that she's convinced me.

GYM GUY

You got my gift.

GYM GUY

Wear it.

———

Six hours later, I stand in the window of SAQ Centre's level three luxury suite, flanked by my sister and my legal secretary. Bea has on her Donovan jersey—*her way of manifesting a meet-cute*—and pops one of those mini hamburgers into her mouth. Anika chugs a fresh beer.

"Slow down, will you?" I pry it from her. "We have all weekend and if I send you to that interview hungover, Mom and Dad will have my head. They're only warming up and you've already had two."

"Bea, tell my sister to be cool for once." Nik elbows me away and continues to ravage her beer.

"Yeah, Indi. Be cool." Bea's got her crazy leering eyes on the rink below, ignoring me entirely. "Do they hump the ice like that for the ladies or is it an actual stretch?"

Nik's cheeks pink and she fans herself. "I have no idea, but it's *so* hot."

"*Shhhhh*! There are other people here."

"Who are these suits?" Bea waves her pint behind us.

My voice climbs to the next octave out of frustration. "I don't know! Keep it down."

These two ignore me again, sighing from content as they watch the team skate around.

Landon kneels on the ice next to his captain as they stretch, chatting and laughing. His mouthguard hangs from the corner of his lip.

I finish the glass of wine from the bar and when I look down again, Radek's looking back. Face breaking into a victorious smile, still chewing on that damn mouthguard, his gaze lowers to my chest. One of his gloved hands taps on his jersey, a silent gloat that I fulfilled his request. He keeps his eyes on me and if I had blinked, I would've missed it.

Landon Radek mouths, *hi*, getting to his feet as the countdown begins. All warmth from my face flows southward, pooling in my gut and beyond. The lights go dark in time. I pray so fucking hard that no one saw any of that. Especially the two fools I'm with. They scream like banshees when the Ottawa starters skate out.

To avoid saying or doing anything stupid during faceoff, I stuff my mouth with these incredible fries. They're served with mayonnaise and it's a game changer.

"This is highly entertaining," Nik comments at how Radek and McCrimmon—*old teammates from uni*—fight over possession while chomping on my fries. "I'm gonna have to watch more hockey."

"Yeah, right. You never came to any of my games."

"I was, like, *nine.*"

"So? Gimme that." I snatch the empty basket from her. "Great, you finished them all."

The rest of the first period flies by with some fast plays and decent attempts, but no one scores. Landon catches a break right before the end of the second period. He speeds across the ice and takes a quick wrist shot. The puck clangs against the backboard and sets off the siren. The horn bellows out.

Half of the audience groans while the Regents fans burst into raucous cheers. Landon points his stick up to the crowd as he skates in an arc around the rink. His eyes lock onto mine while screaming, "Yours!" before the on-ice team wraps him into a hug.

Blood floods my cheeks. I knock back the remaining wine in my glass as the players disappear behind the boards for intermission, the ringing in my ears louder than the period-ending buzzer.

"Did you see what Radek said?" Bea asks Nik. "Yo?"

"It looked more like '*Yasssss!*' to me."

They wait for my opinion. "I have no idea. I spaced out." I manage to evade their scrutiny. Soon enough, the girls cackle at the mascots falling on their asses while doing sack races across the ice. I'm back to eating my feelings. My phone beeps mid-bite.

GYM GUY

You came for me.

259

GYM GUY

(That's what she said)

ME

Very mature.

ME

And my boss made me.

GYM GUY

Meet me after the game.

ME

No can do. Bea and Anika are here, too.

GYM GUY

I saw. Get rid of them.

ME

But we're supposed to go out.

GYM GUY

Make up an excuse.

GYM GUY

You in my jersey has me losing my goddamn mind, Indi.

I cross my legs, attempting to curb the throbbing between them, but can't help myself.

ME

Should I wear Wade's jersey next time?
Can't have you losing your mind.

GYM GUY

There's gonna be a next time?

GYM GUY

And no fucking way you'll wear
anyone else's jersey but mine

My brain flatlines. *Mine.* I click my phone off in a haste, shoving it into a pocket and swiping at my upper lip and brow.

"What happened? Why are you sweating?" Nik narrows her eyes. *Shit.*

"This thing is so hot," I huff. My hand plucks at the jersey.

"Who were you texting?"

Bea smirks and does that stupid eyebrow waggle of hers. "Probably Gym Guy."

"Not *everything* is about Gym Guy."

"Then who was it?"

"It was Cooke. Cooke Wagner. Radek's agent. Asking me to attend some after-game thing."

Bea gasps. "You have to go!"

"*Nah.*" I loop my arms around their necks. "I'm here with my girls. I'll tell him we'll meet another time." My face switches between theirs, eyeing their reaction. "And anyway, what will you two do if I go?"

"We'll be *fine.*" Bea pshaws and pats my sister's back. "I'll show Anika here a good time. And you can join us after."

I hum. "Are you sure?" 'Cause I really wanna see Landon lose his goddamn mind.

"Hell yes!" My sister throws both fists above her head.

"I'm sure you're disappointed."

She's not hiding her eagerness to drink endlessly without my watchful eye.

"*Fine*," I surmise. "I'll go to the thing and then meet up with you wherever you are."

ME

Where am I supposed to meet you?

———

The arena clears as the game ends with the Regents' winning on Radek's sole goal. Nik blows drunken kisses my way, her arm hooked in Bea's. I fidget with the jersey length while waiting for Landon's PA on the ground floor.

Trevor finds me and waves, then hands me a lanyard and leads us past security. "He's still doing press," he says, leading us down a long hallway. The kid extends a hand by a set of heavy velvet curtains. "But he asked if you'd wait here."

"Did he say how long it'd be?"

He responds with a shrug. "Shouldn't be too long."

Ten minutes later and not a soul has passed me by. Curious to see what's behind them, I pull one panel of the curtain aside. The now-darkened arena comes into view. I look left, then right, and worm my way through.

Only the rink is well-lit. The Zamboni whirs across the ice in calculated, hypnotic turns.

"Lost?"

I gasp and jump back a step as I turn. "Oh, *uh*, yeah."

Sutton McCrimmon tilts his head as he studies me.

"It's my first time here." He's not quite as tall as Landon, but built like a fridge, and better looking in-person than his foster photo. I almost look dainty next to him. "Silly me and my lack of direction." A nervous laugh slips from my mouth.

He hums. His walnut brown eyes give me a once-over. "You look really familiar."

"Me?"

"Sutton McCrimmon." He extends a large hand.

"Nice to meet you." I politely return the greeting, but his grip lingers, eyes flattening to slits. "I'm—"

"No, let me guess. I've seen you somewhere."

I don't mean to, but I giggle. Mostly out of disbelief that men think this line works, but partly from how flustered I am having a good-looking stranger hold my hand.

"I'm *positive* we have never—"

"Have I seen you on TV?" He points and nods. My palm goes clammy still clasped in his. "No! A model?"

The ladylike smile on my face wavers. "Definitely not."

His teeth graze the seam of his lips, tongue poking into his cheek. "Huh. You should be."

Something in my gut twists.

McCrimmon tuts. "So, first time here, eh? I could show you around." Mouth curling into a smug smile, his free hand reaches behind me to turn us to the ice. It only contacts the jersey before he's interrupted.

"Sutt," a voice booms by the curtain, echoing through the empty venue.

Landon Radek takes one calm, restrained step after the other toward us. He unbuttons the blazer of the same delicious suit he wore this morning, eyes on mine, so dark and gleaming they could light me on fire and devour me whole. And not at all in the way that I enjoy.

"Landy!" McCrimmon finally releases my hand and stretches his arms to his sides.

A muscle ripples in his jaw. "You met my lawyer."

Sutton's mouth goes slack.

"Indira Davé," I croak out with a forced smile, waving like a gangly teen.

"Damn." He continues to ogle while Landon side-eyes me, then shifts the annoyance to his once-teammate.

His tongue skims over the full curve of his bottom lip.

McCrimmon picks up his anger and steps back.

"Ms. Davé. A word?" Those four words fly out, so sharp that their edges cut my skin. But they don't burn like the pads of his fingers set on my lower back, as Landon ushers me to the exit.

CHAPTER 33:
OFF-LIMITS

LANDON

THIS AFTERNOON IS OFF TO A PHENOMENAL START.

The medium roast from Au Lait—*a far cry from the usual Timmie's*—hits the spot. I got to see my girl and didn't get pulled over while speeding through downtown like a maniac to catch the bus.

Everyone else is already boarded when I jog up the treaded metal steps. Wade hands me a rightfully earned box of chocolate Timbits and a cup of black coffee. No snark today. Jules eyes me as I pass, offering the bunched-together white paper straws in his grip. Even rooming with Jaeger for the season won't ruin my day. I choose one and it's a normal length. I'm safe from his hog-like snoring. No such luck for Wade. I snort to myself while putting in AirPods.

It's a fucking miracle the boys don't haggle me or draw my focus away from tonight's game. An empty seat next to Donovan is the best choice. He's got his headphones in and lost in yet another novel. Quiet and busy.

Performance anxiety spikes as we approach Montreal, but dips after we unload, dress down, and kick around a soccer ball. The usual clowning around always helps to ease the nerves.

Jaeg seems to sense my unease when we warm up.

"Doin' good?"

"Yeah." Forearms parallel to the frozen surface while holding the stick, my knees bounce and slide, stretching out my hips and groin. "Trying to put last season's shit behind me."

The corners of his mouth tug down.

"You?"

"*Fuck*, man. This reception is getting out of control." The lament pairs with a shake of his head. "Skylar got selected to be a trainer at the Winter Olympics in Beijing."

"No shit? That's so sick."

"Right? I'm proud of her, y'know?" His voice softens for the briefest moment. And then it's gone. Jaeger grunts. "They're asking her to get there in November for all this prep-training."

I smile a knowing smile, poking my tongue through my teeth. "Guess No Nut November won't be a problem for you."

"Shut the fuck up," he grumbles, but he's fighting a grin. His elbow knocks into mine. "Sky wants to move the date up. And make herself crazy to get it all together."

"I hate to say it," I reply with a shrug. This'll piss him off, for sure. But who knows? Maybe it'll make the old grouch smile, too. "That's what you get for having Fat Elvis do the wedding."

A throaty, stifled laugh follows. "You're a dick, you know that?"

I straighten from the stretch. "And you're a—"

The words go belly-up. I almost lose my mouthguard when my fleeting gaze over the crowd falls on the glass pane of a level three suite. My heart soars, beating at a feverish rhythm. Butterflies between my gut and heart band together to threaten a collapse.

She's here.

Indi Davé towers above us like a hockey goddess, wild brown waves framing her face. And she's watching *me.* The usual torment of her snug-fitted skirts and dresses has nothing on that black and gold jersey. Adrenaline stokes the fire, surging until all noise fades except for the pulse thumping in my ears.

As if on purpose, Indi shifts, giving me a view of the impeccable curve of her ass in those jeans and the number twelve on her sleeve. *My* number. All fluid in my body nosedives into my crotch. The breath in my throat hitches. Something in my bloodless, oxygen-less brain snaps. I want her out of that jersey and in my bed. To kiss her senseless while pumping my cock so deep inside that sweet fucking pussy—

"Radek." Jaeger pops the bubble of my fantasy. "Wake the hell up. The fuck is wrong with you? Didn't you hear? It's time to go."

A cloud forms and dissipates from my faltering exhale against the cool air. "Nothing. I'm good."

I can't help the smirk splitting my face while adjusting my jersey. Her chin lifts how it always does when she asserts control, but this time it's from restraint. Of which I have none because I mouth a silent *Hi*. The sexy blush that reddens her face in response makes my dick stir against the cup. Her frame disappears into the dark as the lights dim and the Jumbotron announces the countdown. But the damage is done. Knowing Indi's there gives me all the motivation I need.

The adrenaline rush quiets when McCrimmon skates to a stop next to me at the edge of the circle. It's nice to see my uni teammate, but the competitive streak between us hasn't died over the years. I nod. "Been a while, man. You good?"

"Long time, no see, pussy."

I want to face wash that smug look off the arrogant bastard's face.

"Last time I saw your ass was on TV. Giving the business to some leggy blonde."

"Jealous?" I chirp back. "I figured you'd at least be warming beds with all the time you weren't on the ice."

He returns a humorless chuckle. "Fuck off."

My head motions to the bench. "Does your coach even know you're out here?"

"You wanna dance, Landy?" He unfurls from his bent-over position. The puck hasn't dropped and this asswipe's ready to fight.

I shake my head. At the sound of the whistle, we both chase the puck, taking turns shoving each other into the boards. Coach tilts his head at me with a disapproving smile when I get called for cross-checking. I hold out my arms in a shrug before we crouch down around the circle again.

The game is all defense. Neither team can get past each other's goons, and no one scores through a frustrating first period.

Wade gets the brunt of it in the locker room. He deserves it for poking the bear. "You look tired, Olsen. Here, have some of my crackers."

The defender glares back and replies by spraying water from his bottle in Wade's face.

"Get the fuck away from me. We're out there bustin' our balls and where were you, eh?" Olsen shoves Wade.

I suddenly have a headache.

"Jerking off the crossbar?"

Jaeg growls. "I swear to fuck you'll both get benched the rest of the game if you don't shut your fucking traps for one goddamn second." He smacks Wade upside the head. "You're in timeout. And you" —he grabs Olsen by the ear— "go call your mother and apologize for being born. Ask her to teach you some manners."

They storm away to opposite ends of the locker room.

"At least you can tell Skylar you're ready to have children," I say, squinting at the tartness of the mustard packet I pull between my lips.

He snorts. "Score next period and I will."

It's a nearly impossible feat, every play as fruitless as the last. The refs call offsides every other minute like they're getting blowjobs for it and I'm about to break my twig in half. Finally, I see a window and steal the puck—*from McCrimmon, no less, which makes it that much better*—and rush to the net. Their tendy hunches down but isn't prepared for this. In-stride, I rip a wrister and it flies right through the five-hole.

The Regents fans swell with a cheer and there's that adrenaline rush again. It's back with a vengeance and doesn't give a fuck if I publicly dedicate this one.

"Yours!" I bellow, cellying around the rink with my stick in the air while the horn and buzzer peal out. The crowd must think it's for them, but I lock onto the only person it's for to make sure she knows. The girls around Indi jump.

Between watching Kingston and Hourra attempt a sack race on the locker room TVs and riling Indi up over text messages makes intermission end swiftly. We somehow fend off Montreal through the last period, despite how distracted I am from thinking about how to get Fletch out of the room for the night. Wade does it for me. "Fletch, my boy! To the bars! We're gonna pull some French-Canadian le cul tonight!"

"You failed elementary French, didn't you?" Fletcher groans but agrees anyway.

The locker room is chaotic with post-game press, but I manage to get out unscathed. No one asked about Pall or the case. I don't know what Indi said or did for that to happen, but instead of sweats after a shower, I change back into my suit as a thank you. A treat from me to her.

"Gonna treat me to her, more like." I snicker and mumble to myself while making my way to her.

My impatient steps halt abruptly to blow a sharp exhale out, attempting to reel in...*everything*. Wade was right. I'm so stupid for this girl. But how can I not be? I know her rules are specifically put in place to prevent any sort of attachment. But Indi has my whole heart even if she doesn't want it. Which makes the sound of her distant giggle cut like betrayal.

What the fuck?

I seethe, gritting through my teeth when my eyes drop to Sutton's hands on my girl. He's holding her fucking hand, touching that perfect stretch of her back that's only for me.

"Sutt!" I undo the suit jacket button, slowing my pace as I close in on them.

Indi's eyes stretch wide in surprise.

"Landy!" He opens his arms in greeting.

"I see you've met my lawyer." Emphasis on *my*.

I nearly miss her awkward introduction. "Indira Davé."

"Damn." Mack has the fucking audacity to look back at her.

I switch my glare from Indi to him. My old teammate backpedals, picking up the death threats I'm throwing his way.

I refocus to Indi. "Ms. Davé. A word?"

Too shocked to protest, Indi obeys and shuffles next to me down the scuffed tile of the corridor. My hand at its rightful position on her lower back does nothing to quell the march of my pulse, the artery on my neck threatening to burst. A headache looms from how hard my jaw clenches.

"What happened to talking?" Indi whispers through her teeth.

"Fuck talking," I hiss back.

Nobody's here to see, but I have to be sure. We turn right into another hall, this one narrower than the main.

"Let go, Radek," she warns, the whisper angrier and louder than the last. I'm not afraid of her. But she should be afraid of me.

I swing her around into a nook, pinning her to the white-painted cement blocks so she's facing me, palms locking into the wall on either side of her. "Are you trying to piss me off?"

"I'm sorry. What?" The look of utter confusion Indi throws back is laughable.

"You were flirting."

"*Flirting*? You should know better than anyone that I don't do that." She gives me attitude by the bob of her head. "I literally met him—"

"He was holding your hand." My hand to hold. "Touching you." Mine to touch.

"Barely. He was introducing himself. McCri—"

"Nope. Not happening." I grab her hand from where it hangs at her side and pull her toward the exit. "I don't wanna hear another man's name from your lips."

"*Woooow*," she sings from behind. "For being friends, you're being awfully possessive."

Friends? She's gotta be joking. I glance over my shoulder. "You have no idea. I don't share."

"You must've made a terrible kindergartener."

"The worst."

On cue, she rolls her eyes. I'm not taking any of her shit today. My threat comes out in a rumbling growl. "Roll your eyes at me again and I'll give 'em something to roll back about." That comment gives me a rest from her sass. For a second anyway. "And I think you know we're not friends, Indi. You're *mine*."

She scoffs. "Yours? And when did this happen?"

I don't buy her denial. Indi hasn't attempted to free her hand from my clasp. I thread our fingers together through the darkest lane of the parking lot, far away from security cameras and other people. She doesn't resist it either. Her grip tightens.

I stop and let her catch up with me. "Since you sucked me off while wearing my jersey and nothing else. *No*, before that. Since that first night you drank *my* red wine and told me no one has touched this sweet pussy. Remember that? I'm the only one who knows how soft and warm your cunt is, the only one who knows how stunning you are when you come. You listening, Indi? I'm the first and only."

And you can be sure as fuck I'll be the last.

"Look down." I drop my gaze. "You're wearing my jersey, *my* name and number on your back. You're. *Mine*."

Indi wrenches her hand from mine and tips her chin up, defiance streaking through the fire in her eyes. "Get off. I'll do whatever I want. I'm *nobody's*. If I wanna talk to Sutton—"

What a brat.

My teeth grate. "The fuck you will."

She wrinkles her face, visibly disgusted with this side of me and fights my hand off.

"Hell, I'll talk to Hunter. He's cute as hell. I'll flirt with Montreal's whole damn team if I want!" Her arms fold across her chest.

But I'm too fired up to fixate on how incredible the round tops of her tits look molded against my jersey.

The last working nerve my control hangs from short circuits. "That's fucking *it*. We're getting out of here."

I bend to toss her over my shoulder. Gear bags give me less trouble than Indi's flailing limbs as we walk to the Range Rover. She's like an unwieldy bag of flour that kicks.

"Landon! Put me down!" Strong fists pummel my back, her hands pawing at the bottom hem of my jacket.

"No." I give a harsh squeeze to the back of her thighs with my forearm. "Keep it up and someone from security will come over. Is that what you want?" Her kicking ceases. She pops her head up, arching her back.

"And where are we going?"

"To my car. I'm taking you back to the hotel." I dodge a halo of light to stay out of view.

"And what? Spank me?"

We sidle up to the black Rover and I slide her down my front. Her mouth parts with a gasp when I pin her hips and arms with mine, sandwiching her into the passenger door. "If that's what you want. I'll make your ass so red, you'll come until you can't think of anyone else. Screaming my name 'til it's carved into your throat."

Indi blinks three times. "You realize how toxic that is, right?"

I press into her further. "Ask me if I care." My palm lowers to unlock the door behind her, then shifts her to the side to whip it open. "Add a new rule."

She sits without protest, but I can't take the chance. I knock down the child lock and slam the door shut before locking it from the outside.

Indi raps on the glass. "You locked me in here?" She bounces in the seat, continuing to bang on every surface of the door. "You little piece of shit!"

I hold onto the top of the car and lean into the glass. "I think you know better than anyone that there's nothing *little* about me. Now be a good girl and stay in the car. Cut the dramatics." She listens but crosses her arms as she leans into the seat. "If you try to get out, the alarm will go off. Security will catch us. And those bastards gossip more than old ladies at teatime."

I pat the car twice before jogging back to the players' entrance, scanning the halls for McCrimmon. He's where I'd expect: hitting on a young reporter straying from the media horde and sees me heading his way.

"Landy! I was hoping to catch up."

"Excuse us." I tug him by the arm, spinning him away from her and curve in the other direction.

"What the fuck is up with you, man?" His back gets slammed into the cinder blocks without a trace of patience for his fake innocence.

"Touch her again and I'll cut your fucking grubby fingers off with my skates."

He struggles to remove my forearm from his neck, voice strangled by the pressure. "Who?"

"Indira Davé." I shift my feet to dig in further, but he escapes and gasps for breath, tapping the side of his fist into his chest. "She's off-limits."

Sutt straightens and lifts his hands in surrender. "Whoa, dude. I thought you said she was your lawyer."

"She is. She's also my friend." I glare, wringing his sweatshirt collar in my fist. "If you look—*no, think*—about her again, I'll shove your beloved stick so far up your ass you'll look like a scarecrow shitting his guts out."

"*Jesus.*" McCrimmon blows out an *oof* but doesn't fight back when I throw him into the wall again without another word. Remembering his hands were on her makes me fucking crazy.

And now I have to deal with the smartass waiting in the car. Indi's all huffy, nostrils flaring, and lips curled.

I fire up the engine, reverse out of the spot and rev toward the lot exit. "Put this on." My black hat plops into her lap.

The burly security guard pumps his eyebrows in silence upon seeing my turned-around, slouching passenger hiding her face under the bill. I smile politely and put a finger to my lips. He gives me a thumbs up and open-mouthed wink before zipping his mouth shut and throwing away the key.

Montreal's confusing ass road rules almost get us lost through Indi's pouty silence. I hold off until the need to touch her is unbearable. My arm stretches across the center console and palms her clothed thigh. "Mine."

"Calm down, caveman," she mutters, but doesn't move my hand away. "I'm not an object to be owned." A harrumph follows.

"No, but you're mine," I say with a firm squeeze to the tensing muscle, moving to the inseam to cup her between the legs.

She stares at the road ahead, seemingly stoic. Whatever point she's trying to prove is negated by the excited rising of her chest.

"Tell me again you're not and see what happens."

My middle finger presses into the taut denim. Indi jolts and squirms, trapping my hand.

Idling at a stoplight, I finagle the pesky button and zipper open and sigh at the warmth of her covered pussy against my fingertips, those soaked panties dampening them through the fabric. Her head writhes to the side, a tiny whimper muted by her closed lips. One hand wraps around my wrist, but not to resist. It urges me on.

"Landon." Her begging my name somehow hardens my cock and melts my insides into a giant puddle.

"*Fuck*," I rasp, slipping a hand under the soft lace, dipping a finger through the even softer, silken split of her legs. Her hips lift, a wordless cry for more. "Say it." I swipe to be let in, teasing the throbbing, tender spot with narrowing circles. "Say you're mine." Two fingers drive in and curl without further warning, eliciting the most satisfying simper from Indi's throat. "Who made you so sopping wet, baby?" I recede and plunge in again, harder, and faster than the last brutal thrust. "'Cause I know it wasn't him."

The cars next to us move forward when the green arrows light up and I wait for Indi's admission. I yank my hand away as the signal goes full green to turn right into the street where the hotel is.

"You're such an ass." She faces away and buttons her pants as we enter the garage, but I can see her too-pleased reflection in the window.

"You're not fooling anyone with that look, Indi. I think you meant to say, 'I'm yours.'"

While I park, Indi growls and glares before snapping at the door handle, frustrated that she can't get out on her own. I hop out and jog around the back, shrugging off my blazer to place over her shoulders. Like a stealthy pro, she pulls my cap over her eyes and keeps her head dipped.

The door to the stairs next to the elevator bank requires a little force.

The metal clangs open, syncing with a door from above. Rapid steps gallop down, three or four chattering voices getting louder on the descent. We rush underneath the stairwell, hiding in its shadow.

I draw Indi's body to mine, her back to my chest, covering her heavy breathing under my palm and shushing into her ear. My nose grazes her neck, accelerated pulse beating within its column. She smells like my soap, the dry-cleaning chemical on my suit. Like me. The unfamiliar voices trail off and die behind the shut door, but I keep my voice down.

"You smell like mine. Bet you taste like it, too."

Indi audibly gulps.

I pause to ensure there aren't any other intruders. "Let's go."

Rushed footsteps take us to my empty room and Indi lets me hold her hand again the whole way. When she shuts the door behind her, I cross the space to close the curtains, then go back to switch on every light.

She dawdles by the door, clutching the panels of my blazer, her intense eyes only half in view beneath my cap. I lower and recline into the armchair in the corner, unbuttoning my shirt to allow release heat from my anger.

"Lose the clothes," I demand. "Except the jersey."

She listens for once, taking off the jacket and cap and tossing it onto a mattress before slipping out of her sneakers and jeans.

I take in the length of her bare legs. "Bra and panties, too."

She does.

"Good girl." Two curls of my index finger beckon her. "Come here."

Indi doesn't move.

I poke my tongue into the space between my last molar at the heated flesh of my cheek, puffing out a dry laugh of disbelief. It slides across the inner ridge of my bottom teeth as I repeat myself. "Come here." The tone is less of an ask and more of a command the second time.

Indi takes a few steps forward, but it isn't anywhere close as I need her to be.

"Come" —I pat my thigh— "here."

When she nears, I steal her hands to kiss the wrists and rest them on my shoulders, my eyes pleading with her to confirm she's mine. The veins flutter with her heartbeat.

She seats herself on my leg in a straddle. Her pussy weeps through the slacks and into my skin with a sear. *Fuck*, she's so wet.

My fingers claw at her naked ass under my jersey, spurring her hips forward to build friction, voice dropping to a rough whisper.

"Come. Here."

CHAPTER 34:
LET IT BE ME

INDI

THERE'S SOMETHING WRONG WITH ME.

It shouldn't be so satisfying watching a man crumble. I wasn't lying about wanting to see Landon lose his mind, but do I like this? No. Yes. No! Yes, I do. I like it. Being flung over his shoulder like a rag doll might be my new favorite hobby.

I'll have to talk to him about locking me in the car, though. Or where he went for ten minutes while I oscillated between fury and cackling like a power-drunk maniac. Later. I'm too horny to think about anything else right now. A victorious gloat peeks from my expression as we drive to the hotel, but I kill it when he notices. I *hate* that I love the sense of belonging that comes from his possessiveness. *Mine.* I've never been anyone's before.

And what did I say, like a fool? *"I'm nobody's."* A stinging, sad truth. *Rules, rules, rules*, I internally mock myself. *"You smell like mine. Bet you taste like it, too."* I shudder at the recent memory.

"Come here." Landon sloughs off his shirt and smacks his thigh twice, snapping me from the daze and commanding my attention.

My heart sinks, twisting with confusion when his lips connect with my wrists before resting them on his broad, muscular shoulders, the affectionate touch contrasting the harsh grip on my exposed ass. Undisturbed by the arousal smearing onto the wool of his slacks, he rocks me forward, the delicious, grating pressure against my clit drawing a breathy sigh.

"Come. Here."

The pace picks up to tease the orgasm out, my socked toes stretching and curling into the Berber carpet below.

"Say you're mine, Indi."

I bite down to muzzle a needy string of whimpers, lining the inside of my lower lip with blood. Inadvertently tightening around him, my hands circle his neck. His eyes close, head tilting into my palm, nuzzling into it with a restrained grunt.

He likes that? Noted.

Those blue eyes flash open when I stay silent, his guiding hands halting without warning. I gasp out in horror, frustration, and disappointment at the ruined orgasm.

Landon laces his fingers into the sweaty hairs attached to my nape, then fists them, wrenching my head back and chin up. The pain of whiplash feels too good and leaves me breathless. Speechless.

"You're so mouthy out there." His other hand dives under my sole piece of clothing and finds the sensitive bundle between my legs. Calluses rub over the tender flesh. I moan at the sensation. "But I love how quiet your noises get when I touch you." Two of his fingers slip into me, swift and effortless from how soaked I am. My walls close in around them. "Now say it. Whose tight fucking pussy is this?"

Fingertips tap and curl against the tender spot inside. The combined pressure with his thumb flicking across my clit is so unbearable, pleasure shakes through my limbs.

"*Yours*," comes out in a gasped whisper. My forehead falls to his, noses slotted as I shamelessly pant onto his tensed mouth in sync with his thrusts. "Yours, yours, *yours*."

"Good girl." Landon delves deeper, fingers slapping into my wetness faster. "*Fuck—yes*—drench my hand." The peaks of his knuckles slam against the sensitive rim of flesh.

I cry out his name, my entire body clenching and clutching him at every place we connect: hands at his sinewed neck, legs around his hand, sweaty, wrinkled brow on his.

He continues, extending the orgasm ripping through me until I lose my vision. His arms wrap my limp torso, delicate kisses caressing the column of my neck as our labored breaths peter out.

"Say it again." Landon nips at the shell of my ear, voice heavy with a husky murmur. "That all this sweetness is for me." He swipes through the slick remnants of my release.

Goosebumps prickle my skin, on high alert in the aftermath. My cloudy, orgasm-addled brain has yet to catch up and obeys with a nod. "I'm yours."

He returns a sighed groan, massaging my nape until my eyes flutter open, hazily taking in his beautiful features. "That's right, baby. *Mine*."

Our lips brush together in a near-kiss with my next breath and immediately snatches it away. Time drags out the next second, feeling like minutes. Landon suppresses a harsh exhale with puffed cheeks, then whisks me off his leg. The spinning motion lands me with my hips on the edge of the chair and him kneeling between my feet. Leaning forward, he flips my jersey up to expose my breasts, nipples rapidly shrinking as he thumbs and mouths them one after the other, his pleasured noises making me wetter by the second.

I arch into the light grazing of his tongue as it changes to a fierce suck before he lets go and falls back to his haunches. Plush, dampened lips capture the tops of my feet and dote on my ankles, traveling up the curve up my calves to kiss the crease of my left knee while I gasp for air.

His eyes roil and simmer, honed on mine as his tongue laps up the cum slathered over my inner thigh. He pries my knees apart and places them over those sculpted shoulders while a content hum vibrates from his chest and through me.

"So let me taste what's mine."

Landon covers my soaked core with his open mouth, nose rubbing and burying itself at the cleft of my splayed legs. Languid, upward sweeps of his tongue leave me whimpering. My hands tug at the silk strands on his head from the root, nails tearing at his scalp.

"*Fuck*," he drawls through a groan. The pleasure builds quicker this time, climbing and climbing with every punishing lick. His lips pucker around my sore clit, wet smacking and dizzying suction pushing me to the brink at lightning speed.

A high-pitched whine rings in my ears as the warmth of his hand on my parted leg disappears. It almost drowns out the metal jingling as he undoes his belt and the hasty whir from unzipping his pants.

I lower my eyes when he moans and dips his tongue into the needy flesh, gasping at how he strokes from the thick base of his hardened cock to the reddened head. Veins on the back of his hand bulge from the vice-like grip.

The glimpse is gone too soon as my eyes roll back. His devouring gets messy, sloppy as he chases his own release. My hips buck into his face.

"I'm so close, *fuck*." Landon hums and moans as he pumps faster.

"Are you—gonna come—before me?" I say, unraveling with every shallow breath, surprisingly lucid enough for one last jab. "I thought you said you were 'a nice guy.'"

His hand abandons the rigid, floating length, a rumbling, choked-back groan rolling from his chest as he returns to the post on my ass, clawing into each cheek. "I can't stop myself. It's fucking *aching* for you."

I writhe against his mouth, hoping to erase the agony from his desperate tone. Our unabashed moans goad each other on, the repeated lashing of the tip of his tongue on my clit taking me to the peak a second time, mumbling nonsense. "Oh, God. Oh, holy *fuuuuuck*."

My heels dig into his back, feet arched tight as the climax hits, an unbridled wave of pleasure jolting through me. "*Landon!*" I scream out for him, every overstimulated nerve shot to hell. That unrelenting tongue of his has me seizing through the receding orgasm.

My hands relax from their tense fists, shifting to remove the sweat dotting my hairline. Landon beats me to it, brushing aside rogue flyaways and kissing the flushed tops of my cheeks.

"I'm yours," he says with a shush, straightening to his full, upright position, bringing his big guy to *its* full, upright position toward my mouth. "It'll only take a minute to show you how much." His demand paired with the urging hand on my collarbone has my needy pussy crying again. "Get on your knees and open that pretty mouth."

Landon's thumb guides my lips apart and directs the wet head of his cock between them, inching it in slowly to allow me to adjust to its size. "*Mmf.*"

I draw a breath through my nose, hollowing my cheeks in a sharp suck.

"Oh, my—*fuck*." His head drops back, then snaps up to peer down at me through lazy, hooded eyes and those thick lashes. "Take it. I know you can." The low carpet chafes my bare knees as I bob, pulling him in further. "Gorgeous fucking girl." My eyes water. "All of it. Just like that."

Ruthless thrusts follow as he supports my head, tipping it back to lodge himself deeper.

The defined arcs of his hips rock into my palms as I hold on, letting him fuck my tear-stained face as he likes. The merciless movements cease suddenly as Landon groans, neck straining from edging himself out. "You take me so fucking well." He drives in with another thrust. "Feels so fucking good."

I choke, eliciting a delicious, trembling moan in response.

"*Goddamn.*"

Moving his firm grip from my jaw to my throat, the pad of his thumb caresses his length through my cheek, then presses my windpipe where the swollen crown of his cock throbs. "I can feel myself here." His dick grows at the sensation. I gag again. "*Fuck*, Indi. I'm yours."

The speed of his rough thrusts fires up again and one of my hands falls from his hips, disappearing between my legs to rub my clit furiously. It's raw but I don't care. This man makes so fucking horny I can't stand it.

"Hell fucking yes," he encourages. "Play with that greedy clit. Filthy girl. You get off choking on my cock?"

I answer the gritty question by coming so hard, my mashed-potato brain is thoughtless except for him.

Landon. Landon. Landon. No one else, like he promised. Men? What men? There's only Landon, the orgasm whisperer.

He twitches and roars out a low moan, the climax wracking his body and sending hot streams down my throat, my own release dribbling through my fingers and down my thighs.

His cock softens as he removes it from my throat. Sweat trails every chiseled crevice of his immaculate torso. I'm tempted to lick it all away. Before I can act on it, he scoops me up, still cradling my neck.

"I'm yours," he says through an intense sigh. "And you're mine. That's it."

Landon backpedals us, practically dragging my useless body to the bed. I don't fight him when he lays me down and crushes me into the mattress with his weight. He's like a two-hundred-pound blanket. I don't fight the next fifteen minutes of sleep we share.

Wispy sweeps of his fingertips over my cheek and jaw wake me.

Rueful blue eyes stare back, his arm tightening around my midsection. He wets his lips. "I'm sorry."

My mouth gapes. The apology is unexpected.

"I know. I'm an idiot and I'm sorry."

"It is pretty ridiculous to demand I never say any other man's name again."

"I know, baby." He kisses my nose. "Seeing you with Sutton made me want to explode." His fingers lace through my hair, finding a comforting spot where he massages the back of my neck. "I'm not threatened by Sutt, but he touched you." Landon's pained expression makes my heart whir. "And I got scared because it seemed like you liked it."

I gulp. A pause hangs.

He gulps, too, his terrified eyes darting between mine. "Did you?"

"It was different," I explain. "I'm not used to it. Getting attention from someone like that." I correct myself, "Other than you, I mean."

"Just don't get it from him," he cuts me off, detangling from my hair to cup my chin with his index finger and thumb. "If you want attention, I'll give you all of mine."

Landon holds my gaze in the hypnotic depths of his affirming eyes. His hands grasp around me tighter, closer. "If you wanna be touched, have your hand held, let it be me."

The same hands thread through my fingers, stretching our arms above our heads. "If you wanna be fed and cuddled, let it be me."

Mouth dropping to my ear, he rolls his hips into mine, a raspy whisper pleading for a promise. "If you wanna be tasted, kissed, worshipped, *fucked*, let it be me."

I gasp. He groans and repeats the thrusting as my legs widen beneath him. "Please, baby? Let it be me, Indi. No one else."

"No one else," I parrot with a nod, ignoring how my mind reels at his vulnerability. "New rules. Exclusivity. And holding hands and aftercare is allowed."

One of his eyebrows rises.

"It's nice." I pull my lips into my mouth before the confession. "I like it."

Landon smirks, glee apparent. He's fucking reveling in this. "You do realize we've already been doing that?"

"Whatever." I roll my eyes. "Do you accept it or not?"

"Accept." He casually plops a kiss onto the corner of my lips.

My heart. My poor fucking heart. It goes wild.

"Now what?"

"N-n-now..." I stammer, then clear my throat, faking confidence. "Now I get dressed and meet my friends."

"Sounds good, baby. Can I drive you?"

CHAPTER 35:
KILL THE CHEATING PIG

LANDON

INDI CRUSHES THE SECOND BOTTLE OF WATER, downing the last gulp with a content *ahhh*. She scoots up to toss it into the makeshift trash bag hanging from the passenger seat, then pauses to rest her cheek on the side of the driver's seat, chin on my shoulder. "Question."

"Yes, Ms. Davé?" My lips stretch to a smug smile at our little driver-passenger game.

"How'd your car get here? Didn't you take the bus up with the team?"

"I did. Trevor drove it up for me."

The cutest wrinkle forms between her brows. "Why?"

"If you didn't come to the game, I was going to head back to see you."

"But you have a game on Sunday. In Winnipeg." Her eyes narrow.

We idle at a light behind a line of stopped cars. I take the chance and kiss the bridge of her nose. "Yep. We fly tomorrow at noon."

"If I hadn't showed up, you planned to drive down and back here within twelve hours?"

I lift my shoulder, closing her gaping mouth until her teeth clack together. "Maybe."

"You're nuts."

Indi crosses her arm over my chest. I keep it pressed over my heart and she pulls aside my hoodie to leave a sharp kiss onto my neck. I shudder.

"But you make up for it by being the *hottest* fake Uber driver," she murmurs into my ear, sliding over the leather into the back-row bucket seat. I clear my throat and compose myself, readjusting the black hood over my black baseball cap.

The pack of Twinkies hidden in my front pocket crackles when I shift in my seat, tugging at my crotch. To distract from visualizing the filthy last hour in the hotel room, I rip open the thin plastic and stuff one end of a cream-filled cake roll into my mouth.

"What are you eating?"

"Twinkie," I confess with a full mouth.

Indi hums. "You know, I've never had one." She extends her slender arm to swipe the remaining piece from my loose grasp before shimmying back into the seat. "Let's see what all the fuss is about. Gotta scope out my competition and all." Her eyebrow perks. "Here goes nothing."

A single *ha* puffs out and I almost choke as the whole cake disappears between those gorgeous lips. She moans through a chew. "Oh, my *God*."

Balling the plastic wrap in her fist, she drops it into the trash bag. My dick twitches seeing her throat swallow it all.

"It's so soft and sweet. I taste better than that?"

"Yeah, baby. You taste way better." I throw a glance back, poking my tongue into the corner of my mouth. Those cheeks glow pink with a blush. My heart beats faster. We approach and stop at another red light, and I reach back, searching for the edge of her pant leg. Her foot dangles in the air from the way her knees cross and gives me a playful kick. When my fingers find the smooth skin above her ankles, they slide up, tracing the gentle curve of her calf and soaking in all that softness.

Indi drawls, "What are you doing?"

"I like the way you feel," I reply, my voice lowering to a hoarse whisper while checking her reaction in the rearview mirror. "Not being able to touch you is torture."

Goosebumps lift on her legs to meet my fingertips. Indi doesn't flinch or break our eye contact. "It's green."

I blink twice. "What?"

Her tone continues in its flat delivery. "The light's green."

"Okay. *Oh*!" The lull splits when I hit the gas by instinct. I don't let go of her like a selfish bastard, mesmerized by the relaxation her touch provides, and nearly veer off into the next lane.

"*Whoa*. Easy. The map says we're almost there. On the right."

I slam on the brakes almost as hard as the gas pedal, tires screeching to the curb. In neon signage, the word *Muzzy's* lights the awning and

I vaguely recognize the dive bar's orange string lights hanging from the enclosed patio space in front. It's been a few years and I'm sure I was hammered, but I've been here.

A remixed version of Kelly Clarkson's "Since You've Been Gone" streams into the car as Indi climbs out from the passenger side, feet first. She salutes me. "Thank you, my good man." Her head pokes back in through the half-closed door. "Where are you off to now?"

"To rescue Fletch." I wave my phone at her. "Poor bastard's been texting me nonstop."

"Have fun!" she sings.

I lower the bill of my hat. "You, too. Be safe, okay?"

Indi smirks and props a hand on her cocked hip. "Want me to text you when I get home?"

"Yes, please." My lower lip juts out.

She predictably rolls those pretty round eyes. "*Fine.* See ya."

I steer away from the sidewalk and check my phone at the light on the next block.

ME

Where are you?

FLETCH

Some overpacked hole-in-the-wall where the music is too loud, and the women keep asking if I wanna dance. I don't wanna dance.

ME

Name?

FLETCH

Muzzy's.

You don't say. I smile to myself and take the right to loop around the block.

ME

On my way, brother.

The musty hardwood inside Muzzy's holds onto the smell of spilled beer and piss. I find my teammates at the back of the bar, surrounded by a crowd. Fletch looks miserable sandwiched between two blondes, peer-pressured into taking shots with Wade. He winces at the end of his drink as Wade puts on the dramatics, whooping and hollering alongside these puck bunnies. I clap a hand on his back to let him know I'm here.

"Oh, thank *fuck*," he pulls me into a hug. "Get me out of this place. If I have to take another sip of this god-awful—"

"Landy!" Wade shouts through cupped hands over the cheering and music. "Get your ass over here!"

I throw him an acknowledging bro nod and hold a hand up. There's no way I'm taking shots tonight with this fool.

"I need to piss," Fletch grumbles. "If I'm not back in ten minutes, send a rescue squad. It'll mean one of these ladies has cornered me in a stall and I'm fighting for my life." He turns on his heel, disappearing between two large beer-bellied men.

Wade loudly boos my rejection of his offer. "Prude!" His eyes wander to the staircase leading to the upper level. "No way. No fucking way!" He giggles and wrings his hands together. "Your hot lawyer's here. And she's brought hot friends."

Indi, mini-Indi, and Bea descend the steps.

"Shut up." I backhand his chest. "That's her sister and her secretary. I sent her firm tickets." I conveniently leave out the part about eating my lawyer out and fucking her face in my hotel room.

Her sister has the same dimples, same facial structure, but her hair's longer. And her eyes don't sparkle like Indi's. She and Bea vanish when I scan the space for Fletch. Man's gonna have a heart attack seeing Bea in his jersey. Indi pulls back the flirtatious smile she gives the bartender when I linger my gaze on her. Her eyes flick away toward the commotion at the entrance. She shrugs, then curls her hands around three pint glasses.

"Need some help?" I step in front of her and take the beers, fingers brushing during the transfer.

"Thanks," she murmurs from the corner of her mouth. "What are you doing here?"

"Came to pick up my boy."

"Donovan is here?" Her eyes widen with mischief. "Bea's gonna faint."

So is Fletch. Muahahaha!

I set down the beers on a high table. "Yeah, let me find—"

Wade interrupts me, hooking his elbow around my neck from behind. "*Yo*—" he starts, then notices Indi. "*Heyyy*, you!"

I give him my best annoyed glare, but he doesn't budge, switching his glance between us.

"*Um*, can I talk to you for a sec?"

I shake him off. "Go ahead. She's cool."

A nervous smile pulls at his mouth as he leans into me. "I'm about to do something stupid and I need you to back me up."

"What?" My elbow shoves him away. "Don't tell me you wanna fight someone?"

"Not *someone*." Wade looks at Indi again. "That Towers center is here." He points through the crowd.

Kurt Vaughn sits in a red chair against the wall, a petite blonde grinding in his lap as they make out. His hand grips her ass from under her skirt.

Indi's attention falls to the same spot. Her face drops.

Wade's face reddens. "Does that look like Gabe Finch to you?"

He keeps talking, but my focus is on Indi. Those round eyes land on the asshole, mouth tightening into a grim line. Her nostrils flare as the muscles in her jaw tick up a storm.

"I mean, you're right. But why do you care? You don't like her."

"It's fucking rank, that's what. I couldn't care less who anyone fucks, but don't be a disrespectful dick and cheat—"

Before we can stop her, Indi's pummeling through the horde of drunks.

"Shit." I nudge Wade. "Let's go."

"*Kurt!*"

Wade and I shove our way to the fringe of the circle of people clearing around them as the blonde peeks over her shoulder and rolls her eyes. Vaughn straightens from his reclined position and taps the girl's ass twice. She slides off and takes her place at his side, a tanned arm draped over his shoulders.

"What's up?" He slurs the question through bloodshot eyes. Faded bastard has no idea what he's in for.

"What's *up*?" There's not a trace of humor in her dry tone. Her eyes brim with rage as she grits through her teeth, "You little-dicked fuck."

Uh oh. Clenched fists sway at her sides.

"'Scuse me?" Vaughn rises from his seat, intimidating her with his nearly seven-foot build. "Who the fuck are you?"

She meets his threat, pushing her determined chin up to face him. "I'm your fiancée's best friend. And your worst fucking nightmare."

A chorus of *oohs* mixes with muffled laughter from the dozen members making up the audience. Vaughn palms her shoulders and moves her back. My insides burn. The prick touched her. I fight back the urge to beat his face in. There are too many people. Too many witnesses. I can't risk more bad press. Wade pops his knuckles in preparation. I put up an arm across his chest, but it's misdirected. I should've been paying better attention.

Both Wade and I trail to swoop in as Indi lunges at Vaughn with a frustrated scream. Wade blocks us from the asshole while I hold back and lift the fearless hothead, escaping from the taunts and havoc that ensues.

She wriggles like hell, but my arms stay firm around her. I can hardly hear Indi's shrill pleas to let her go so she can "kill the cheating pig," fear pumping adrenaline so hard my body takes in her kicks to my shins and fists to my thighs with stride.

The only quiet corner in the place is by the washrooms.

"Deep breath, baby," I whisper in her ear. Her body shakes with what I imagine is anger. She thrashes once more and then goes limp. "That's it. We're calming down."

"Let go, Radek."

I do. She turns, hateful tears pooling in her eyes, lower lip quivering through every word.

"Didn't you see? That scumbag is cheating on Gabe."

"I saw." My hands give her tense shoulders an affirming squeeze.

We separate when Wade jogs over and joins us in the hiding spot. "That was close," he pants, doubled over with his hands on his knees. "Damn, girl. What the fuck do you think you were doing out there?"

"I was *trying* to beat the life out of the worthless piece of—"

Fletch exiting the men's room ends the conversation.

"*Jesus*, Donovan. I thought you went to take a whiz, not a colossal shit."

Our teammate blushes bright red in Indi's presence.

"There was a line," he mumbles, pointing his thumb over his shoulder.

"I'll catch you up later, Fletchyboy," Wade promises, pulling Fletcher to his side with his meaty arm over his shoulder. "We should go, eh?"

Something sends pangs into my chest. I want to stay but can't with Tweedle Dee and Tweedle Dum in tow. They're wandering off to the exit door, so I take a step closer to her. "You gonna be okay?"

Indi nods. "I need to call Gabe. And find Nik and Bea."

"Text me when you get back to wherever you're staying." I push a short kiss into her forehead as I turn to leave. Her eyes flutter shut, plucking a rogue tear from one corner. I sweep it away. "Promise? I'm gonna worry until you do."

She nuzzles into the light touch. "Promise."

CHAPTER 36:
WMTCOAEYOUCIMM?

INDI

"THE INTERNET IS A BEAUTIFUL PLACE," LANDON announces, plopping his gear bag in the three-by-three foyer of my apartment. "You'll never guess what I found."

"You're right. I'll never guess."

My mood's off for some reason, tone as dry as the fistful of corn kernels I plonk into a pot of warmed olive oil.

He purses his lips with a groan at my inattention, tugging me from the stovetop by the blousing of my oversized chunky knit sweater. His arms wrap tight around my torso, forcing me into a hug.

I soften when he nudges my cheek with the tip of his nose. It's cold from the brisk October evening air.

"Didn't you miss me?"

I nod in response.

Landon sighs a humid breath past my ear, lips tilting upward into a smile against my jawline. "Good," he murmurs. "'Cause I missed you."

I surrender to the embrace, winding my arms around his neck as he nuzzles into mine, speckling kisses onto the quickly spreading goosebumps on my nape.

"My little smartass."

"You came straight here?"

"I haven't seen you since Friday night. And I didn't get to say a proper goodbye." His kisses dot the wispy baby hairs on my forehead.

Words escape my brain. Orgasms aside, this man has so much power over me. His ability to wipe negativity and anxiety from my mind with his touch is nothing short of magic.

A pause in those comforting kisses clears the fog. "You smell like sweaty buttcheeks and bad cologne."

Landon gasps out in horror, bringing the collar of his hoodie to his nose. "Do I?" His nose scrunches, mouth twisting with disgust. "Gross." He takes two steps back and wrenches the sweatshirt over his head.

"Your teammates stink."

"You stink, stink."

"Do not." The sudden popping of corn in the pot interrupts our pointless argument. "Now stop distracting me." I shoo him away by motioning to the couch. "You're gonna make me burn the popcorn."

"The only thing you're burning is this dance floor."

In one hand's grip, his phone plays a video of me dancing at my parents' house from my last visit. I'd posted it on my sister's account in hopes no one would find it. Or recognize that it's me and not her.

Transient embarrassment flees as quickly as it appears. I shake my hair off my shoulders to feign innocence. "That's Nik."

"Nice try. I can tell you apart. That's her in the background. It's you up front." He points at my sister's floating head behind me on the screen and throws me a cheesy, mischievous grin. "You never told me you dance." His eyes rake down to my hips and back up.

My grasp on the pot handle tightens.

I shoot off a sideways glance. "That's because I don't."

"This video begs to differ." He scrolls to another, the Bollywood mashup song clip looping endlessly.

"That's definitely Anika," I say over my shoulder. "*Oop*, and there's Esha." She walks past the camera and ruins Nik's video. "My sisters are the dancers."

I only danced when I was younger because Mom pushed me to. Same with ice skating.

"You're pretty good though."

My shoulder rises and drops with indifference. "*Eh*. I prefer watching."

"Me too." A devilish smirk pulls at his lips as he watches it once more. "An inspiring performance. I saved it to my phone. It's gonna get me through some lonely nights on the road."

He says that so matter-of-factly that I almost miss its innuendo. "That's disgusting."

"What, you don't like the idea of me nutting to—"

"*Landon*," I whine.

"Okay, okay. I'll keep my private-time thoughts to myself." The way his palm squeezes the arch of my hip makes my heart race. I ignore it. "Are you ever gonna give me a live performance?"

"Nope," I say through a swallow, emphasizing the *p* with a *pop*.

Landon shimmies his shoulders and wiggles his hips into my backside. "Maybe I'll dance for you instead."

I elbow him away with a playful nudge. "Please, *no*."

"Give you a strip show." His full-body roll is somehow both stiff and too fluid, kind of like those wacky inflatable waving tube-men that car dealers always have.

I shake my head along with the popcorn in the lidded pot, coating it with any leftover oil. It gets a sprinkling of salt before I transfer it to a bowl.

"You done, Magic Mike? It's movie time."

"Wait, is that what we're watching?" Landon trails behind me, fingers still hooked into my sweater.

"No way. *Mean Girls* is the only acceptable movie to watch today."

"Why today?" He stops at the living room rug.

"This is a safe space, Radek. No need to pretend you don't know."

"I *don't* know."

"Sure, sure. We'll see what's what when your favorite lines come up." I click the play button.

"What favorite lines? I don't know any lines from this movie." Landon sits facing the TV as I relax into the corner of the couch. He moves my legs over his lap, curling an arm around my bent knees hovering over his thighs.

"*Shhh*. It's starting."

We alternate scooping handfuls of popcorn from the bowl resting on my lower belly as the movie plays, fingers lingering at the slight contact when they reach at the same time. It's a far more innocent exchange than we've had recently and has my hormones raging like a teenager. The way his free hand lightly caresses my shin repeatedly almost makes me forget what's coming. The scene approaches and we share a knowing glance.

Landon plays along, asking Aaron Samuels simple question. I recite the famous October third line with a smirk, in chorus with Lindsay Lohan, and eye his reaction. A half-moon dimple appears through his stubbled cheek.

I knew it. No man in this generation with a sister hasn't seen this movie a thousand times.

The sincere, hearty laugh that follows belts from his gut is like the first ray of sunshine warming the morning summer sky. It vibrates against my outer thigh and fills my chest with the coziest sense of comfort.

"How could I forget it was *Mean Girls* Day?" His eyes flick to my mouth, their pupils growing as the blues lessen like an ebbing wave.

"No idea," I whisper. The way my heart pounds whenever he's around is becoming impossible to brush off.

He blinks and clears his throat, looking toward the kitchen. "I'm gonna grab a glass of water. Want some?"

"Sure, thanks."

I watch his round ass bounce as he trots to the kitchen. My mouth waters. I shovel a large handful of popcorn into it, like a salty dam. He pops it back when he notices my gawking.

"Enjoying the view?"

A sheepish blush creeps up my neck and colors my cheeks at my dazed non-response.

"You like that?" Landon flexes, clenching his cheeks together while holding onto the counter, gray sweatpants cinching in his ass crack. "I can twerk if you're into it." He clenches them again.

I blink in equal parts awe and annoyance.

"*Stoppp.*" Chortles sputter past my lips. Doors clunk open and shut as he searches for the glasses. "You do *not* know how to twerk."

"Yes-huh, I do. Wade taught the whole team. I'm one of the better students, I'll have you know—*ahhh!*" A pile of ridiculously-sized bags of Lindt melting chocolate avalanche comically onto his face and forearms when he opens the wrong cabinet. "What...*what is this?*"

I slink under the top edge of the couch, hiding so he can only see me from the eyes up. "They were on sale at Costco."

"*Oooh,* a wholesale girl. I love it." He tosses the three-pound bag between his hands. "I buy Twinkies from there. But this?" His eyebrow perks while reading the label. "This seems excessive even for someone who likes chocolate as much as you do."

"That's not for eating." I roll my eyes. "I mean it is, but not straight up." Not many know about my side hustle, but we've mouthed each other's private parts so I might as well tell him. "I make chocolate bars."

Curiosity peaks in his gaze.

"Custom, *um*, personalized chocolate bars. For special occasions."

"Like you write messages on them?"

"That's pretty much my 'brand.'" I have no idea why I air-quote that word.

"Gimme an example."

I've made a couple hundred of these in the past few years but all I can think of is the "Eat My Ass" bar I made for Gabe earlier this summer.

Landon scoffs out a disbelieving laugh. "You make lewd chocolate bars? That's amazing."

"Is it?"

He pulls his phone from the front pocket of his sweats and types away while smiling. "I gotta tell Skylar."

"Who's Skylar?" I straighten and turn to face him.

"Jaeger's girlfriend—wife," he corrects himself. "They eloped in Vegas but are having a reception to celebrate with everyone. I overheard her complaining to him about finding some funny gifts for her friends that would've been bridesmaids."

"*Mhm*." Nothing is processing at the moment. I'm back to stuffing my face with popcorn while staring at his bulge. Grey sweatpants, thy name is—

"Do you do dicks?"

"*What*?"

"*Dicks*, Indi. Sky's asking if you've ever used, like, penis sprinkles or something to put on top." Landon squints at my astonishment as if this is a totally normal conversation.

"*Uh*, yeah, *uh huh*. Yep, I have those."

Why am I so embarrassed by this? I choke on this man's schlong on the regular, but talking about how I decorate chocolate bars with molded chocolate mini-penises and penis-shaped sprinkles makes me wanna crawl into a hole and die.

"Cool." He nods and types out his response. "Can I give her your number then? If you're interested, that is."

"Yeah, *cool*." The exact opposite of what I'm being right now. "I should be able to take the order."

"Done. She'll text you."

His phone slides into its pocket and Landon returns to the couch with two glasses of water. After a sip, he casually sneaks his arm around my shoulder as we both stare at the TV. Smooth. I slump into it as we slouch into each other. The repeated brushing of his fingertips on the curve of my shoulder send goosebumps down my arm underneath the sweater sleeve. I glance at his hand through my vision's corner, then side-eye him to discover he's side-eyeing me. We refocus on the movie without a word.

Cady babbles to Aaron at the party as they sit on the bed. Landon's hand glides to my nape, blunt fingernails scratching at my lower hairline. I gulp. It's somehow relaxing and anxiety-inducing. When he starts massaging hypnotic circles into my scalp, my face turns to him.

"Indi?" He stares at my mouth. It makes me stare at his mouth.

I give in to him pulling our faces closer. "Yeah?"

They're carnation pink, their color deeper at the seam. His tongue wets the line where they part. Loud buzzing splinters the moment at the same time Cady vomits on-screen. We fly apart as I scramble to retrieve my ringing phone from my pocket.

"It's Gabe," I pant before answering. "Hey, what's going on?"

"Is she okay?" he mouths.

"Uh-huh," I reply to her flat question with a finger to Landon's lips. He smiles and kisses it with a melodramatic smack. "Yep, I'll be there. No problem."

When Gabe goes numb like this, it's the terrifying calm before an even more terrifying storm. "Welp, gotta go." I slap my knees and get to my feet.

"Where are you going?" The honest urging of his doe-eyed expression makes me want to stay. But I can't, because *something—I don't want to say what*—almost happened. Plus, my friend needs me.

"Gabe needs to drop some of Kurt's things to his place. Then I'm giving her a ride to the airport."

Landon stands, too, following me to the entrance as I grab my purse and keys and push my feet into a pair of white sneakers. He lifts his bag over his shoulder as I ready to open the door.

"Come here for a sec."

I sigh through my nose when his lips press to my forehead, eyes falling shut at the soft sensation.

"This was too short."

I agree and apologize before leaving. He lifts his hood and backpedals down the hallway to the emergency exit stairwell as I get to the elevator. He waves and turns at the last minute before knocking the heavy door open. The heaviest breath puffs from my chest as I lean into the elevator wall.

I am in the worst kind of trouble.

———

Without looking at me, Gabe hands over a container holding half a dozen double-chocolate cupcakes. "Don't judge me. I was stress-baking."

"No judgment. They look fantastic." She jumps out of the car when we park at Kurt's, grabs the bulging trash bag she threw in the backseat earlier, and slams the door shut.

Ten minutes later, a cacophony of screamed curses, crunching metal, and shattering glass has me lowering in my seat from where I idle by the gated garage alley entrance. Gabe rushes out, popping the collar of her green army jacket to hide her face as she tugs the panels closed across her chest. She gets into the car, seemingly unfazed.

What have I witnessed? Nothing. I've seen nothing. Heard nothing. Nope. Not getting involved.

"Let's go, Indi. I'm gonna miss my flight."

Streetlights flash as they pass by in her stoic gaze, focusing on the highway through the windshield. We're both pretending nothing happened.

I move my eyes from the road to her. "Anything to say for yourself?"

"You're not my mom."

Ah, so she's mad about two things at the moment. Not that there's ever a good time to cheat, but Gabe gets increasingly irritable and morose in October as her mother's death anniversary nears. I half-wish Landon and Wade had let me give in to the urge to tear that douche apart. Would've been worth it.

"You told me you were going to drop his stuff off while he wasn't at home."

"I did."

My eyebrows jump to the middle of my forehead. "So, you didn't plan to do...the other thing?" I refer to the act of vehicular vandalism that may or may not have occurred.

"No." She scowls. "It just happened, okay? I was leaving through the garage and his stupid, beloved Lambo was sitting there, *taunting* me—"

"*A-tut-tut-tut-tut-tut!*" I cover her mouth with my hand. "I don't want any part of this."

"But I got rid of the bat—"

"I said *shhh!*" I scold, waving her off. "You do remember I'm a lawyer, right? If I get subpoenaed, I can't lie to them. I don't know what you're talking about, and I don't want to."

Her frown turns up into an unapologetic smirk. "Driving me isn't aiding and abetting?"

"Suddenly you're an expert in criminal law!" I throw my hands over my head, letting go of the steering wheel for a few seconds. "For fuck's sake, Gabe. You know I'm on your side. He deserves much worse. Hell, I'd prepare his grave myself if it didn't mean my career going up in flames. But I won't let you throw yours away, either. Not over some disrespectful piece of shit like him."

She says nothing in response, averting her eyes to a line of trees on the horizon. The exit for the airport approaches and I veer onto the ramp during the silent pause. "Where are you going, anyway?"

"Kitchener to spend the week with my dad." The fight in her tone sobers, hands fidgeting, thumbs dawdling in her lap. "I was gonna go home for Thanksgiving weekend anyway. Took extra days off."

I hum and nod while we wait in queue for the passenger drop-off lane.

"I left the ring," she admits softly. "On the nightstand."

A sigh escapes from the ache in my chest. "You should've sold it."

We pull up to the curb. Gabe's reflection in the window tuts with a cringed face.

"Nah. I don't want anything of his."

"Fair point. He *suuuucks.*" My arm crosses the console to palm over the tangle of her fingers. I really am the worst at consoling. "I love you."

She lets me hug her before stepping out of my car, then squeezes my outstretched hand through the open window. "Love you, too. I'll text when Dad picks me up."

"Let me know if you need anything done here that's not illegal."

Gabe snorts. "I'll send my minions to do my dirty work. Don't worry."

"Seriously?" I glare at her. "You *gotta* stop telling me stuff like that."

She winks and chuckles, blowing me a kiss before striding through the sliding double doors. Knowing she'll be in good hands with her family leaves me with a sense of relief.

It's short-lived, however, because my period decides to appear a week early.

———

This first half of the workweek is a string of Mondays and doesn't help my hormone-driven snippiness. An untimely shitstorm brews as Bea's down with a respiratory infection she caught in Montreal, Thomas's borrowed assistant is clueless, and Pall's lawyer left a voicemail to say they have proof Landon made promises to Annalise but won't answer the countless phone calls we make asking for it.

Landon getting back into town after four days away is the shiny cherry on top. My message notifications fill the screen with his filthy texts. So far, I've managed to evade him during the worst few days of the past two cycles. An extra-long blowie and spooning him after did the trick last month.

Not sure I can do that this time without having a total meltdown. I'm not the cool, calm, collected Indi I was last week when he came over to watch *Mean Girls*. Who am I kidding? I wasn't cool then either, but now I know why. The impending blood battle in the ol' cooch had me out of sorts.

I swing from wanting to flip my desk over to hiding underneath it to cry myself a river. Of course, I can't do either and have to be a professional through the horrendous menstrual cramps. These heels add to the constant ache plaguing my lower back. Brief moments of respite where the incapacitating pain isn't so bad are rudely interrupted by lightning striking my butthole.

When I finally escape the office, a bhinda craving hits and comes along with a need to cook it myself. The Indian grocery also offers fresh, locally-made rotli and I snag a packet of those, too. I do my best to slice the okra into thick rounds, soaking the cut pieces in a bowl of water while taking a shower.

The universe seems entirely against me when there's only one tampon left in the box. There's no way I'm leaving this apartment to face society right now. I'll likely get committed.

Clad in a pair of super baggy sweats and the largest, most worn-out t-shirt I own to allow for bra-less freedom for my sensitive chest, I shuffle towards the kitchen for a late dinner. The excitement and sense of pride vanish when realizing the okra has turned into one giant, slimy mass. I make a domestic emergency FaceTime call.

"Hello?" Mom's voice is sleepy.

"Mom? Did I wake you?"

"No, I dozed off while reading." She sniffs and rubs her eye under her glasses. "Is everything okay?"

I stifle tears. "No, everything is *not* okay."

"What happened, betu?"

Pushing the phone against the backsplash, I show her the bowl, sinking my fingers into the bhinda goo and stretching its slime. She gasps.

"You put cut bhinda in water?"

"Was I not supposed to? I always saw you put cut shaak in water."

Her shock turns to laughter. "Not for bhinda! Oh, God. Rahul!" She calls for Dad off-screen with a wave of her arm. "Look what our daughter did!"

"Mom!"

It's not her fault she has no idea how delicate my emotional state is. Dad joins in on the teasing, face-palming at my stupidity. They're still laughing when I've had enough.

"I hope you enjoyed yourselves. Good night."

I hang up, drain the bowl's contents into the sink and turn on the garburator. A regretful frown wrinkles my face at the bare cupboards and moldy bread in the fridge. Plain rotli is no good on its own unless it's fresh. I chuck the packet aside. I've lost my appetite anyway. A good, messy cry is far overdue, but no tears come. My phone dings on the counter.

GYM GUY

WMTCOAEYOUYCIMM?

ME

No, thanks.

GYM GUY

Please? It's been four days since I tasted that pussy and I'm fucking dying.

Too bad it's out of order and doesn't flutter at the suggestion.

ME

Maybe another day.

GYM GUY

What's going on? You've been ignoring me all afternoon.

ME

You don't wanna know.

GYM GUY

I absolutely do want to know.

His niceness fuels my irritation. I mash out a harsh reply.

ME

Please leave me alone.

The text shows *read* but there's no response. Instead, he calls. "What?" No use hiding the anger. I asked him to leave me alone and he did the exact opposite.

"Indi."

I don't care for his stern tone.

"I thought we were past this. You can talk to me—"

"Okay, you know what?" I snap. "Let's talk about it. I've had unbearably long days at the office and I'm fucking *exhausted*." My voice trembles with rage and disappointment through the phone. "I tried cooking my favorite meal because I miss my family and totally ruined the bhinda nu shaak I desperately wanted for dinner and would've been the only thing I would've eaten all day. And I'm bloated like a scared frog because my cramping, swollen uterus is on a murderous rampage. *Also*, I'm out of tampons, my boobs feel like lead and my lower back may never be right again. Is that what you wanted me to talk about?"

A silent pause follows my rant.

"Poor pussy," Landon says with a tut. "Want me to come over and kiss it better?"

My jaw hinges shut through gritting teeth. It's like he wasn't listening. "*Goodbye*, Landon."

"Aw, don't be like that. I was joking—"

The next breath is long and harrowed. I rub the throbbing space between my brows. "I'm fine, okay? I need some space. I'm *fine*. We'll talk later this week."

"Later this week? I'm traveling again on Saturday."

"Sorry. We'll text."

Ending the call before he can say anything else is the best option. He's already seen me at so many embarrassing and absurd moments, but surely this version of me will have him running for the hills.

In an attempt to redirect my unstable emotions, I shroud myself in a blanket burrito and plop down on the couch. A syndicated version of *The Office* appears in my mindless channel surfing. Kelly Kapoor's fatigued face as she explains her juice cleanse hits hard.

As the episode ends, the kitchen trash can gives up on life, no longer able to sustain the weight of its contents. It keels over and spills three-day-old takeout sauce onto the floor.

Don't cry, Indi. Clean it up, throw it out and go to bed.

I go to the door, looking and feeling like the tied garbage bag in hand.

When I yank it open, Landon stands in the hallway, a ready fist in the air about to knock. His arms overflow with a million brown paper bags.

"Hi." He hands over a fragrant bouquet of peonies. The white ones. My favorite. They smell incredible.

The white trash bag lands on the floor. "What are you doing here?" I wave him in, shutting the door behind him. "I told you, I need—"

He places the bags on the kitchen counter. "To eat."

Flipping open one paper bag releases a delicious, familiar spiced aroma. "I lucked out and India House was still open. There's bhindi masala and roti. And some saffron and pistachio ice cream."

My stomach growls.

"And I went to the drugstore and picked up some things." Each bag gets unloaded as he lists out the various items and lines up their boxes. "We've got Cadbury Dairy Milk bars, we've got Smarties. The Twinkies are for me—*an extra boost of energy*—while I'm taking care of you." He winks, then continues. "The trainer always gives us these heat pad sticker things when our shoulders are tight." Landon taps on the box's picture. "I figured you could stick them on your back or lower belly. They didn't have any electric heat pads for some reason."

I gape at the next box. "You bought me tampons?" Tears well but don't fall. I still can't believe he brought all this stuff I complained about earlier. I was such a jackass.

"Sure, you said you were out. And then I found the craziest thing— do you know what a menstrual cup is?" The small box looks smaller in his large hand. "It's like silicone and reusable and medically safe and eco- friendly and—"

Surprise morphs into an overwhelming sense of gratitude for this sweet fucking human, despite him mansplaining feminine products to me. Unceasing tears stream down my face, ugly sobs wracking my chest as I launch myself onto him.

He catches me, adjusting my arms over his shoulders and legs around his waist before propping up my ass and carrying me to the couch. "Aw, no. I didn't want you to cry. You don't like it?"

"I do! I like it." I cry harder, muffling the unattractive gasps of air into the crook of his neck. "No one—has ever—done anything—like this—for me—ever. And—this week—was the worst—"

"Tell me about it," he says, nodding. "You had me so worried, baby." Soothing strokes on my back help relieve the held tension. His patience is truly astonishing.

My shoulders jolt through the last of my sobs, shallow breaths lengthening as I calm. "Why are you—so good to me? I'm so mean—to you?"

Landon forces an attentive gaze by palming my nape. "It's not mean to say what you feel in the moment. It's sincere. I know you, Indi." His thumb draws small circles onto the back of my neck. "You're anything but mean."

A swallow pulls at the column of my throat. I brace myself around him once more, burrowing my face against his warm chest, and hope that he's right.

CHAPTER 37:
BRIGHT LIKE A DIWALI TREE

LANDON

INDI CALMS IN MY HOLD, THEN LIFTS HER HEAD AND grimaces at the black streaks staining my sweatshirt. I tip her chin up with my forefinger. "Do you forgive me for the lame joke?" Giving her my best puppy dog eyes, I jut my lip out.

A sniffle putters through her nose. "Yes. Even though you've ruined my makeup with your niceness." The back of her index finger swipes at the dark smudges below her eyes before she asks for my opinion. "Better?"

I leave an encouraging scratch on her lower back. "I've never seen anyone more beautiful."

"Liar," she says with a sarcastic sneer. Her hands settle under my jaw and draw out our mirroring smiles. "But an exceptionally handsome one." Head tilting right, she leans in with a lingering kiss to one cheek, pressing those soft lips against the bristles of my stubble. "Thank you."

I exhale, eyelids drooping from the tender contact. My chest fills with a warm sense of comfort, though the goosebumps on my skin say otherwise.

"For dinner. For being thoughtful," she whispers. "For being here." She switches sides, the next kiss to the opposite cheek lasting longer.

A sigh hums through my nose. Indi pulls away but I bring her back. My eyes struggle to stay open under the sedation of those delicate kisses.

"I can't think of anywhere I'd rather be than here: you sitting on my lap, being sweet to me." Take it back! my dick screams. Say you'd rather be rearranging her guts! He-Man twitches in rebellion.

"Sweet? I'm *sweet*?"

"You are to me."

Rueful eyes flutter as she rests her forehead onto mine. "I still can't believe you'd do all this to make me feel better."

"Don't you know, Indi? All the things I'd do for you?" Anything. Everything. I'm so tempted to kiss her. Dying to kiss her. "Up, baby." I pat Indi's round ass to pry her away before she notices the one-eyed delinquent on the move. "Let's get you fed."

Her scarfing down a meal is one of the hottest things I've ever seen. Every bite brought to her mouth with her bare hands and how she sucks the fingers clean only spurs on my cock's stubborn need to remain upright. She grabs the chocolate next. Smarties scatter across the tabletop. She scours them, collecting the orange ones in one cupped palm and popping a couple into her mouth every few seconds.

"What are you doing?"

Cheek bulging mid-chew, Indi lowers her gaze. "The orange ones are the only ones I like."

My mouth purses, stifling a laugh. "But they all taste the same."

"Wrong. The orange candy coating tastes *orangey*. Kinda like those chocolate oranges they sell during the holidays."

"They're your favorite, eh?"

Indi affirms with a nod.

"Then I should get to work." I dump out the rest of the box and sort through them, sliding all the orange ones to her side of the table.

She pouts. "*Landon*. You're gonna make me cry again."

"That's okay, baby." I flex a shoulder. "This bad boy isn't only a resting spot for your knees. It's very good at absorbing tears."

Her foot connects with my shin under the table, but it's not hateful. "Do women really fall for lines like that?" Cold, pointed toes climb up my calf.

"Works on you." I reach down to grab the teasing thing to place in my lap, then rub down the length of her arch until a sigh escapes from her mouth. When I lighten the touch, she gets ticklish and kicks me away with a playful curse. I take care of the mess and trash the take-out clutter in the kitchen as she does a slo-mo belly flop onto the sectional.

"Here," I offer, ripping open the box of adhesive heat pads. The backing takes a second to peel off, partially because it's slippery, but mostly because my eyes keep wandering to her swaying ass trying to get into a comfortable position. How am I supposed to pay attention to anything but that?

"Put it on for me?"

My eyes drop to the two dimples straddling her spine when she lowers the waistband. A perfect place for my thumbs to push into while she's on her hands and knees and I'm pushing into—

"Landon?"

"*Uh*, yeah. Yes. I can do that." It transfers to her skin easily.

Indi rolls onto her back and lets out a muted groan while rubbing her stomach.

"Still crampy?"

She nods.

I straighten her legs and crawl onto the cushion, putting a knee on either side of her and willing my dick to go into turtle mode. Let me take care of her in peace, villain. He has no intention of listening. Especially not after the way she responds to my thumbs massaging circles into her swollen lower belly. "Feel okay?"

"*Mmm*." She nods again through a lengthy exhale and closes her eyes. Her hips arch into the motion, mouth parting and releasing these sounds—*fuck*—all those content noises are too close to what she sounds like when—

"Landon!" Indi gasps, her hands reaching up to clench around my forearms. "That feels—"

"G-good?" I forcefully swallow the firm lump growing in my throat.

"So *good*," she gushes.

"Fuck, I love hearing you say that."

"Don't stop."

As if I'd ever. I increase the pressure until she squirms below me. Her head tips back, soft whines crescendoing into pleasured moans.

"*Please*."

"I love it more when you beg." I groan, savoring how she unravels.

"Landon—*oh, God*—I'm so—"

No covert exit for He-Man. He sets up shop and thrashes about, trying to poke between her legs in search of friction. A breath hisses through my teeth. "Let go, baby. Come for me like a good girl."

The simple praise sends her over the edge, short nails biting my skin as her body tremors through the high. I'm as out of breath as she is.

"Holy crap." She throws an arm over her eyes, panting through a chuckle. "You made me come by man-handling my uterus." A sated smile peeks out. "And so quickly. *Whew.*"

I unmask her flushed cheeks and cloudy gaze, shifting my hands until they're above her shoulders. "You're incredible, you know that? I didn't know that was possible."

Indi scoffs out another laugh. "Me either."

"So much for not having any of my firsts."

Her cheeks glow with the proud smile reaching her eyes, hiding a trace of worry. They say more than she ever has: that she wants this, wants *us*, even if something still holds her back. One day, I hope she trusts me enough to tell me what that is. My puffed breath matches hers.

"I'm gonna need a few minutes to recover. Or a trip to the toilet."

She eyes the hand over my painful bulge. "Am I supposed to pretend you didn't ask to have a wank in my washroom?"

"What can I say, baby? Getting you off gets me going."

Leaving Indi gets harder and harder. Every time we part, something gnaws at my chest, widening the void of her absence into a gaping hole until I can fill it with her again. I've never experienced this with anyone before. Sure, I missed Sierra when we weren't together, but this is a much stranger feeling: ache and need combined. Maybe it's because there was no doubt Sierra would be waiting for me. There was a surety, a security. Indi and I agreed on each other—*she's mine and I'm hers*—but I don't and can't have all of her. Not knowing if or when I ever will plucks every last, living heartstring.

We share the longest goodbye while loitering at her door, twined fingers loosening but not letting go, wearing matching lazy, satisfied smiles. Mine goes sullen when realizing our schedules don't line up again for another week.

"You can't come to my game in Toronto?" I bring her knuckles to my cheek stubble and nuzzle the back of her hand, our palms still clasped.

She tilts her head with a sorry frown. "I'll be in Brampton, but my parents will chop off my head if I'm not home for Diwali. They're allowing fireworks at Westwood Mall again. I already missed Navratri. I didn't mind not having to do all the ridiculous choreography my sisters come up with" —she rolls her eyes in sync with a tongue-click— "but Nik sent me a video of the whole neighborhood dancing in the street in eight degree-weather and I got *so* jealous." Indi thumbs over my pouting lips as I let out a grumbly whine. "Rain check for the next one in Ottawa?"

———

Three days later, after the worst game I've had in years, I slump into a deep squat against the stark, white-painted cinder block until my ass hits the mildewed carpet in Toronto's CIBC Arena. The heels of my palms dig into my covered eyes but don't relieve the sting.

None of the team said anything, but their silence was loud enough. Getting benched in the second period was the last nail in the coffin. Under other circumstances, losing the first game of the regular season wouldn't set the team up for failure, especially when we're not on home ice. But this year, I feel like a huge letdown.

Sketching doesn't help ground me from the gut-churning disappointment. A sad attempt at a doodle crumples in my fist and gets lobbed across the empty hallway, ricocheting off the opposite wall and bouncing against my shin before dropping to the floor. Can't fucking do anything right.

Not having Mom or Dad at the game didn't help. They provide emotional support, unlike Delaney, who'd been a bitch and flipped me the bird every time I missed a shot. I try to visualize somewhere serene, calming. My mind takes me north, back at Indi's cozy apartment, sprawled across her couch as she kisses my face and neck. Or me kissing *her* bratty little face as she pretends to not enjoy it. Smartass. *My* smartass. That pang in my chest intensifies. I rub my shirt over my heart and reach into my suit jacket pocket for my phone.

ME

Can you meet me?

GYM GIRL

Now?

ME

Please. It's an emergency. 911.

GYM GIRL

Tell me where.

About an hour passes before Indi's cool hand on my elbow pulls me from the train of self-hating thoughts I've let myself stew in. "Landon?"

Darkly lined brown eyes search mine from where she squats in front of me, cocking her head. I get lost in their concern for a moment. She claps my bicep and boosts herself to stand, offering a hand. "Come on. I'll help you up."

I take it and immediately pull her to me, crushing her into a hug. She smells different, something flowery and sweet in place of the usual warm cinnamon.

Instead of resisting it, she eases into the hold, fingering through the hair at the back of my head and scratching my lower back underneath the jacket. "What's wrong?"

"I needed you." My lips drop to her jaw, brushing that soft skin. "Needed to feel you. I don't know what happened tonight—"

Indi hums, seeming to understand and stretches her head to one side, welcoming my onslaught of the neck kisses. "I followed the game. Those refs were clearly biased. And anyway, it's only the first game, Radek—"

"Can we not talk about it right now? Let me hold you."

"Okay."

Crisp silk wrinkles against the rough texture of my palms. "You make everything better." The fabric feels so foreign, and I inch back to make sure this is my Indi and not some imagined ghost.

A rich emerald drapes her curves—*except for the maroon shawl on her shoulder*—the gold pattern woven into it highlighting the honey hues of her eyes and skin. Crescent-shaped earrings dangle from her ears, matching the pendant hanging from a thick, decorative gold chain and resting on her perfect rack. My hands pass over the clinking bracelets on her wrists as I put more distance between us.

"What's all this?"

Her lips tug to one side. "Bangles. Jewelry."

"No, no. What the *fuck* are you wearing?" Indi's so gorgeous I can't process it. A goddess. That's what she is. She scoffs and smacks my arm, mistaking my admiration for a derisive comment.

"Excuse you! It's a sari. I was at a Diwali party. I do have a life outside of work and stroking your..." Indi fumbles for words while doing an in-air jerking-off motion, "...ego."

It's officially a tie. I like sweet Indi and grumpy Indi equally. And one side makes me want to fuel the other. I hum and smirk at her. "I know you didn't say that to me."

"I did. And by the way, it wasn't any party—*whaaa!*"

In one swift scoop, Indi gets hurled over my shoulder, sari-wrapped side-ass sidled to my face. My feet propel forward, one quick stride after the other to prevent her from any sort of escape. Though I'm not sure she wants to. She's not fighting me. Not physically, anyway. "I've had it with you and your sass in this *sari*, you called it?"

"Landon! You're gonna tear it. This is Banarasi silk! Do you have any idea how much—"

Her mouthing off gets me hard every time. I'm starting to think she could do anything, and my dick would be full-mast. "Don't you worry about that. I'm gonna unwrap you so slowly, my little Diwali gift. I've been a good boy. *Muah!*" My audible kiss to her butt seems to anger her more.

She growls and elbows my back. "No, you haven't. And that's *not* how Diwali works."

We turn the corner and approach a black metal door. "You can tell me all about it after putting that smart mouth to good use. Want you to scream my name until your body lights up, bright like a Diwali tree."

"Again, that's *not* how Diwali works." Her head pops up and turns side-to-side. "Where are we going?"

"Trainer's room."

The door gives under my heavy hand down as we barrel through, triggering the motion-sensing fluorescents. I release her to the floor and lean on an extra-large exam table, eyes raking over her hourglass figure once more.

Indi smooths down the pleats below her exposed mid-section and fires a spiteful glare my way. "You have *got* to quit doing that."

"I will when you quit enjoying it." Jacket shrugged off and discarded to a nearby caddy, I roll up my shirt sleeves before grabbing her bare waist and wrenching her to me. She squeals.

"You're a Neanderthal, you know that?"

"Whatever you say, baby." My lips move over the ridge of her cheekbone. "Now tell me how to get you out of this."

Indi glances at the side housing a pile of folded fabric, then pivots, tapping her left shoulder blade. "There's a pin there. Careful not to poke me."

"Not a problem. I have great concentration and dexterity."

"I meant this." She grinds her ass to my groin, doubling my semi.

"Don't...don't do that. I swear to God, Indi. If you don't cut that out, I'm gonna have to whip it out and shove it down your throat."

"Sounds fun." She laughs through a slight smile, evil as they come. "Just unpin the thing, Radek."

It takes some effort, considering it's tucked underneath this cropped blouse-thing and the fabric is surprisingly heavy. The silk glides away from her rounded shoulder, giving me an insane view of her front. "Goddamn, baby."

My mouth travels across the naked skin at the crook of her neck, fingers tracing the edges of fabric on her tits. They curl around and pull at the silk. I groan at what I see. "How am I now finding out you weren't wearing anything underneath?

"I don't know," she gasps. "The tailor sewed in the cups."

"Wise, wicked tailor," I add between open-mouthed kisses at the delicious spot under her jaw. "Fuckin' genius." Kneading her chest in my palms sends her knees buckling. When she heaves out a breathy moan, I can't fucking stand it any longer.

"Fuck unwrapping. I'll take you like this." The padded table creaks under my weight as I hop onto it, undoing three shirt buttons below the top one.

She lets out a squeaky sound of disbelief. "What am I supposed to be doing?"

"You're supposed to bunch all that up."

Indi bends slightly to lift the bottom hem off the floor, freeing her mile-long legs from the many layers. She cocks one knee, the sari hanging at mid-thigh.

"And take off whatever skimpy thing you've got on underneath. Leave the heels." They're glittery gold and strappy, unlike the red-soled ones she usually wears.

With a roll of her eyes, she wiggles until a tiny piece of lace floats down, then kicks them off. "Now what?"

The vision of Indi brightens as my eyes dilate. I hoist her onto me by fisting the gathered fabric at her hips until her knees flank my waist, then recline. "Now you scoot up and sit on my face."

She looks back at me, frozen in awe, her gaze switching between my torso and face, where a single finger taps against my lips.

"What are you waiting for?"

"I—*uh*—I have no idea what I'm doing."

"Don't go shy on me now, baby. I know the filthy things you read." My fingers divot the flesh of her toned thighs to slide her up my chest in one effortless pull. "Here's a refresher: scooch up, sink down until you can't anymore. Please, Indi? Take my mouth. I'm fucking starving for this sweet pussy."

The rough texture of my beard stubble dots her inner thigh with goosebumps, her supple skin pursing against my lips. She clears her throat and shivers. "But how will you breathe?"

A whine groans through my short laugh. "If I'm meant to meet my maker with my tongue buried in your pretty cunt, so be it. And anyway, I plan on drowning before suffocating." My upward glance is half-convincing. Indi edges closer, bolstering the silk higher. "Open wider," I hoarsely whisper. She drives one of her hands into my hair for support. "I wanna see how wet you are."

Indi listens, and *fuck*, is she wet. That dark cunt glistens. Feeling drunk before having a taste, I lick and suck the flesh leading to the apex of her legs, letting out moan after pleading moan. "*Please*, Indi. Sit on my fucking face already."

A quivering giggle follows. "I love it when you beg."

"I want you to use me," I urge on, sweeping my tongue inward. "Ride my face until you come all over it."

A second hand joins the other in my hair, threading the strands in a death grip before sliding herself into place over my mouth. "*Fuck*, Landon."

I take a deep breath in case it's my last, cherishing how warm and slick Indi is against my mouth. My tongue swipes impatiently, licking and lapping in long strokes as her hips find a rhythm. They buck and grind, eliciting guttural, pleasured noises from both of us. This woman takes me to paradise between her thighs every time. Indi rips at my hair when I lash over her clit, prodding and sucking between devouring dips into her pussy. Her arousal spreads, seeping past the seam of my lips and dripping over the hill of my chin, gravity trailing it down my jaw and neckline. I groan at the sensation of sticky streaks and prod the tip of my tongue into the pulsing sensitive spot, wanting more. Needing more.

"*Yes.*" She mewls.

I repeat the motion and receive a similar response. Her hips drive harder and faster, taking everything I give while chanting my name through ragged breaths. My erection strains against the zipper, dickhead so wet it's probably going to leave a stain at the crotch of my suit slacks. Lifting my hips only makes it worse, the friction more and more unbearable as Indi's pussy readies to explode. My own orgasm rolls forward. There's no stopping it now.

The knot of spiraling pleasure at the base of my spine tightens and tightens, like my palms on her firm ass. She's replaced crying for me with a string of high-pitched *ohs* but if she says my name one more time—

"*Landon!*" Indi's thighs clamp my ears shut, muting the sounds of her climax. The way her fists tear at my hair dulls any feeling other than her juddering and jerking. A wave of her cum flows onto my tongue and I stiffen, unable to stop my torso from curling forward, eyes shooting back while I come harder than I thought I could.

Senseless, dazed, and satisfied to no end, I open my eyes and catch my breath, not knowing how much time has passed. Pinned by the shoulders, I'm greeted by a line of slickness between my neck and stomach where she sits. I sigh, a dopey smile splitting free. Indi's feather-light fingertips cross my sweaty brow and comb through the damp strands of hair.

"Are you okay?"

"Me?" I laugh. "I'm fucking fantastic."

Her dewy, flushed face calls for my touch and I give in, pushing away a rogue hair that escapes her bun. She leans into it, cuddling my palm.

"Did you finish in your pants? *Again?*"

"That did happen, yeah." I sit up and catch Indi as she tips back, cradling her nape and holding us together. My swollen lips tingle as they inch to hers. "Nothing gets me off like getting you off."

Mischief flashes in those dark eyes. "You in a betting mood, Radek?"

"Always."

"I have an idea. An incentive, let's say. Remember when I said I'd come to the next game?

"I can't fucking wait to see you in my jersey again." Her humid breath reaches my lips, and they twitch, restraining themselves from kissing her.

"I'll meet you at your place afterward. For every goal you make, you get to make me come."

My jaw drops and I pull my mouth into a smile before it hits the floor. "Deal."

Indi winks and scoots off my lap, then jumps off the massage table.

I take a peek under my waistband at the mess Indi's made and then at the sexy culprit, who hums and innocently repins the pleats onto her shoulder. The flimsy lace panties from the floor get shoved into my pocket as she scoffs and tries to retrieve them. "Nope, these are mine now."

She crosses her arms and lifts an eyebrow. "So, where's my souvenir?"

I motion to my pants zipper, where my dick is down for the count, snoozing away, covered in his own excitement. "Lick me clean."

"How is that a souvenir?"

The space between us vanishes in one stride. "You'll be so wet after, you'll think of me every step you take for the rest of the night."

Ten minutes later, I fiddle with my shirt sleeves as I pull them through the arms of the blazer, running a hand through my hair, smiling to myself about how Indi used my face as a saddle. The dreamy stupor breaks when Wade flings the metal door open with a clang and marches through.

"The fuck was *that*?"

I didn't realize anyone was still around. I'd told the GM I'd catch up with the boys back at the hotel. Immediately after the shutout, we all went back to the locker room without a word, except for the chatter of the press doing individual interviews. I guess Wade finally felt the need to say something.

"Sorry, bud," I say through a sigh, adjusting the panels of my jacket. "I blew it tonight. I don't know where my head was—"

His brows pull together. "What are you talking about?"

"The game." I squint one eye. "What are *you* talking about?"

Wade shoots off a glare and clenches his jaw, then calls out the propped open door. "Jaeg! Get in here."

He's here, too? The hell is going on?

Derrick bulldozes past Wade and slams the door shut.

"You saw what I saw, right?" Jaeg gives a solitary nod to Wade's question, but his eyes bore into mine. "See? We saw, Radek."

"Saw what?"

"That pretty lawyer of yours leaving this room."

Fear replaces the confusion on my face.

"Looking like a sexed-up Indian queen."

Wade groans in disgust at the too-obvious admission. "You're fucking her? *Jesus.* Isn't that illegal? A conflict of interest?"

"It's not like that." A weak defense if I ever heard one.

"First the PR chick, now *her*?" he rants on, arms waving wildly. "I get they're hot, but how stupid can you be?" Wade stiff-arms me, setting me back two steps. "And what happened to Gym Girl?

"She *is* Gym Girl," Jaeger grumbles.

Wade gasps and spins to Jaeg and back to me, head sagging to the side with a disappointed expression. "*Ugh*, no."

Fuck my life. They've figured it out.

"It's not what you think it is. We're not fucking around—"

"Dude! Stop *lying*. I literally saw her leaving" —his hands dramatically point to the door then scamper over his head— "hair all, like—"

"I'm in love with her."

And there it is. I didn't mean to say it, not like this and definitely not to these two. It fell right out of my mouth like it was the most natural thing in the world and now...I love how it tastes.

Wade's hands drop from the air to the top of his head, fingers spreading, then gripping his hair. "Fuck." The angered shock on his face turns pained, as if his whole world is falling apart.

Jaeg slaps a hand across his eyes and groans, muttering something under his breath. Probably cursing at me.

I'm in love with Indira Davé. And from how easy it was to admit, I think, *maybe*, I always have been.

CHAPTER 38:
A LITTLE EXTRA MOTIVATION

INDI

SHEENA CAN'T STOP LAUGHING.

Citing a work emergency didn't quite take, especially since my legal secretary arrived at Malti Aunty's house before I returned from downtown. The girls demand more stories about the mysterious Gym Guy.

"Hold on, let's go through this again," Sheena says, her lifted index finger telling me to wait while she swallows the gulp of falooda. A scoop of vanilla ice cream melts within my red Solo cup, pooling atop the simple rose-flavored milk. My friend is a falooda purist, taking her sweet time to chew the gummy, soaked vermicelli and tukmaria seeds.

Meanwhile, Bea stuffs a third gulab jamun into her cheek. Like a hamster.

"You cut up okra into little rounds..."

"Uh-huh."

"Submerged them in a bowl of water..."

My sisters snicker behind their drinks. I glare at them and elbow Nik in the ribs. She chokes. Deservedly.

"Yes."

"And then proceeded to take a shower?"

"Yep."

"*Bahahahahahahaha!*" The muffled laughter bursts into outright cackling. The three of them are bent over, hands on knees, uncontrolled guffaws echoing in the front room.

"Oh, come *on*." I roll my eyes and stand akimbo. "It's not that funny."

"How did you not know you can't do that?"

I tighten my palm in the air to slap Sheena across her shaking shoulder, biting down on my lower lip. "Don't laugh at me! Your mom taught you how to cook."

"We have the same parents, Didi," Nik adds. "You don't see me turning water into bhinda goo."

"Stop! *Stop!*" Esha waves an arm around, crossing her legs while holding her sari pleats at her crotch. "No more. I'm gonna pee!"

I shove her hard enough that she stumbles a step forward. "Keep it up and I'll make sure to miss Navratri next year, too. You two can find someone else to force your silly made-up garba steps onto."

"*Didiiiiii,*" Nik whines. "Don't be like that. We need you."

"Shoulda thought of that before."

Sheena sets her cup down on a decorative corner table. "Sorry, I'm done now. What happened after?"

I lower my head and lean in. They form a huddle, listening intently to my recap of the worst day ever: how I gave up on cooking before snapping at Landon when he called, and how he showed up with dinner, chocolate, and all the things I never imagined any man buying for me. The familiar warmth rises in my chest as I talk about him, even anonymously.

Nik and Esha get pulled away by Karishma to meet one of her future cousins-in-law at the juiciest part of the story.

"Sheena," I whisper. "He rubbed my cramps away."

"*Awww.* That's *so* sweet," she coos, swooning. "He sounds so great—"

"It felt so good I came."

Her jaw goes slack, long, dark lashes cartoonishly blinking five times. Behraz nods in agreement. Surprised at her lack of involvement in this conversation, I turn to see she's moved on from gulab jamun to scarfing down soan papdi. "I *know*! Isn't that the craziest—?"

"He's in love with you." Eyes wide with glee, her face tears into a bright white smile.

My heart jumps up into my throat, pounding up a storm.

She pumps her eyebrows once. "You heard me, Indira."

"*Pfft.* No, he's not." I wave her off. He's not. "We're just *friends.*" I've been telling that lie to myself for so long, the sting it leaves on my tongue doesn't hurt anymore.

"Nope. Sorry to break it to you."

Her comforting pats on my shoulder do nothing to soothe me.

"He's in love with you. After all that, how are you not in love with him?"

All blood drains from my face as my poor heart descends to my belly.

Waves crash in my ears, vision going blurry as Sheena rephrases the question. It comes out sounding like she's underwater. "Are you in love with him?"

"Girls!" Mom shrieks through the entryway of the room. "Look who I found."

Gabe appears next to her, clad in a classic white and gold Anarkali gown. "Thanks for inviting me, Anju Aunty." She hugs my mom before she leaves to make her a plate. "Happy Diwali, ladies. Indi looks like a ghost. What'd I miss?"

Sheena goes to answer but refocuses across the room, where Akhil motions his eyes to the door. "*Ooh*, I'll let her explain. I gotta go."

"Where are you going?" I pout.

My best friend winks and blows us kisses. "I'm ovulating and Daddy's ready to roll."

Bea snorts, sending a spray of soan papdi on the floor.

Gabe and I cringe.

"*Ew.* Please don't call him that in front of me ever again." Grabbing both of her shoulders, I spin her around and push her toward her waiting husband. "But good luck!"

"You're not off the hook yet." Gabe throws me a suspicious glare before Mom interrupts us again, guiding us into the large foyer where a few others do rangoli on the marble floor.

"I'm gonna watch from over here." Bea points toward the grand stairwell. "I'll probably trip and send the colors everywhere." The zari work on her Parsi-style sari catches the lights strung from the curved banister as she makes her way to sit on a step, her chest controlled by the high-necked blouse worn underneath. Gabe joins her. Bea murmurs something in her ear while glancing my way.

"Indi, we need to talk." I don't like Gabe's stern tone. I'm a lawyer, but she's a reporter. Her investigative powers match mine.

"Uh-huh, sure. What about?"

"Yeah. What do we need to talk about?" Esha pipes in, gracefully sweeping a white outline of a petal in the larger flower pattern she and

Anika work on. Two girls behind us create a mandala design with paisley. I shush my sister.

"Nothing. I'll fill this section with rani pink. That purple will go well next to it." No back talk for once, because I'm right. The chit-chat quiets to allow for concentration on our art, but my mind is anything but focused. It wanders through Sheena's question, *Are you in love with him?* and replays conversations from earlier in the night.

"You gonna tell me how Diwali works?" Landon kissed the exposed skin bordering the shoulder seam of my blouse as I neatened up my sari. This man wore me like a hat and now he wants to know more about Diwali? What is my life?

"It's not like Christmas," I said, bending my neck to indulge him further. "It's Hindu New Year. Jains and Sikhs celebrate, too, but for different reasons. And there are five days. We decorate our homes and make special foods together as a family."

Landon hummed and nodded, stopping the kisses only for a moment to help fix my skewed necklace.

"There's no Diwali tree," I continued. "No gifts under it, either."

His hand crossed the tense flesh of my stomach, goosebumps returning in the gentle touch's wake.

"There are gifts, usually new traditional clothes. Or cash for good behavior."

Pillowy lips traced the column of my neck up to my ear as I screwed the chandrabali earring tight. "And what's considered good behavior?"

I laughed at his suggestive tone. "It's, like, an understood rule. If you bow down and touch someone's feet in reverence and wish them a happy new year, they place a hand on your head and give you an envelope of cash. A blessing for your respect."

"Interesting." Landon rounded my hips until he faced me, rough hands sliding down the silk silhouette of my legs while lowering to his knees. Long fingers reached under the bottom hem, their light touch crossing the straps of my heels. Eyes roiling with adoration, he revealed a carefree smile, one dimple pushing into his cheek. "Well, Indi? Aren't you going to bless me?"

"You bow to your elders." My hand cupped his jaw. "I'm younger than you."

He circled my wrist to drag it onto the top of his head, closing his eyes while my fingers stretched through silken threads of his brown hair. Landon sighed from his nose before they reopened with renewed mischief. "Bless me anyway."

"Didi!" Esha whisper-screams at me, halting the mindless pouring of the rich pink powder into a single flower petal's design.

"Sorry." I cough. "I spaced out."

Nik clicks her tongue as she drops a series of dots along the border, then flattens their peaks with her fingertip. "If we lose the competition this year, I blame you."

"Don't be too mad, girls." Gabe palms my sisters' shoulders while matching Bea's knowing grin through the iron spindles lining the stairs. "Your sister's mind is occupied."

A fistful of rangoli powder lifts above my head in threat to my obnoxious friends. I should release a chalky cloud upon their smug little heads. But they're not wrong. Landon has burrowed his way into my thoughts, whether he's around or not. The man is infuriatingly sweet, despicably hot, and turns my brain into squashed bananas in his presence.

Oh, my God. I'm in love with him.

My face heats at the thought. I go upright. "I need to use the washroom."

"Indi." Gabe looks repentant, but she has no reason to be. She was telling the truth.

Unlike me. The lie is starting to hurt.

"Come on, we're messing around."

"I know." I play it off. "I'll be back."

Hands clasping the edge of the sink, I count while taking deep breaths. Up to ten, down to ten. The initial panic settles. This is exactly what wasn't supposed to happen. I study my reflection in the gaudy, gold, ornate mirror. Hating him was easy. Adoring him from afar was easier. I spent years denying it, bludgeoning the idea to death because it would never be real. But it's real and scarier to admit.

I've loved Landon Radek for fifteen years.

Like a dormant seed, the love was never nurtured, neglected long before anything sprouted from it. Yet the roots held strong, too stubborn to give up.

Three knocks rap on at the door. "Indira?" My mom's voice isn't as hushed as she thinks it is. "Are you okay? Is it your stomach?"

"No, Mom." Not embarrassing at all. "I'm using the—"

"Because remember last Diwali when you ate too much khandvi? You were on the toilet for so many—"

"Mom! Can you stop?" Unbelievable. "I'll be out in a second."

"Okay, sorry. I didn't want you to miss Aarti. We'll wait for you."

It's not my gut I should be worried about anyhow. My heart's the one shitting itself.

Our hectic schedules put a few more days before Landon and I see each other again, giving me enough time to retract my heart from my sleeve back into the locked chamber of my chest.

———

My heart is a disobedient asshole. It nearly has a myocardial infarction every time Landon's eyes find mine during warmups at the game against Vancouver. Bea chats up the drunk bachelor party next to us and doesn't seem to notice. At least not until the game starts.

Radek goes after the puck, tearing from the Bears' defenders and scoring within the first seven seconds with the fastest snap shot I've ever witnessed. The crowd bursts with surprise. He glides away on one knee, pumping a fist in celly. The team surrounds Landon in a hug, laughing and tapping on his helmet with their gloves. He skates off after, skidding to a stop before looking over his shoulder and mouthing *one* in my direction.

"Huh." Bea scoffs. "Why'd he say that while looking at you?"

"What?" I blink, frozen in my own stupidity.

"He said 'one' while staring right at you."

"*That?*" A nervous chuckle putters out. "We made a bet. I made fun of him because he couldn't score last game."

"And?"

"*And?*"

"What'd you bet?"

There's no time to answer. My eyes follow him across the ice making another breakaway, every stride a crossover, driving him faster and faster toward Vancouver's goalie. Bracovich pulls forward, bracing himself in the crease, but Landon fakes him out and knocks the puck in, right over the unprepared tendy's left leg. The team roars along with the fans, coming in for round two of congratulatory cheers. *Two*, he mouths, holding two fingers up and smiling so wide, both dimples peek between his helmet straps.

Four minutes later, Olsen hip-checks the opposite center, who loses possession and Landon takes it. The Bears catch up, blocking any direct shots, but Radek circles behind the net and drops the puck in, lacrosse-style.

The foghorn blares over the announcer's excited tone. *"And he scores! Bracovich took a snooze and Radek woke him right up!"*

Everyone in the place is on their feet, beer spilling as they jump and scream. Landon goes horizontal on the ice and does three push-ups across his stick. His head pops up to mouth *three*. By the time his teammates circle him, he's all laughs.

My tongue pokes into my cheek. I maniacally laugh inside my head.

Three orgasms are a charm.

The internal gloating is cut short by the end-of-period buzzer. Bea takes a bathroom break. I tell her to go on, armed with the excuse of not wanting our seats to be stolen.

ME

Not bad.

GYM GUY

I'm not done yet.

GYM GUY

And why aren't you wearing my jersey?

I peer down at the black Regents hoodie engulfing my torso.

ME

Didn't want to distract you.

GYM GUY

You realize there are consequences for your actions, right?

ME

What kind of consequences?

GYM GUY

Smartass, I'm gonna make five more goals tonight.

A single *ha* bursts forth, gaining the attention of the people around me. I clear my throat and apologize, bringing a can of beer to my suddenly-dry mouth. When the team returns to the ice, Landon throws me a challenging look through his visor. Donovan and Szeczin back off, passing to him when they can and otherwise staying out of his way. Every point scored is taunted back to me.

Four.

Five.

Six.

And that's before the second period ends. Butterflies nest in my gut.

"This is such a great game!" Bea whoops through cupped hands. "Look at the man go! What on earth did you bet—"

Seven.

Landon scores again, triggering the horn, followed by the buzzer signaling another period's end. Someone a few rows behind us gets so excited, they lose control of their fries, launching them from their container and sprinkling them onto our heads. One of the guys from the bachelor party yells back at him, exchanging a torrent of curses before he goes up to fight. Intermission passes as security struggles to keep two decent-sized drunks from assaulting one another. Eventually, the parties get led out of the arena to the neighboring crowd's heckling and jeers. They settle as both teams skate back into the rink.

The usual starters are on the bench. With the way the game's going, Vancouver doesn't stand a chance. Wade had only let two shots in out of their twenty-five attempts.

Bea stuffs a hot dog into her mouth, chewing through the giant bite. "Who is playing right now?"

"Rookies and dusters, looks like. We've got a good lead. Maybe they're letting the other guys get some low-risk playing time."

Radek gnaws at the protective guard hanging from the corner of his mouth, goofing off with Wade and Donovan. My face heats when they switch out, climbing over the boards for the last few minutes of the game.

"Are you okay, Indi? You look like a tomato, if a brown girl could look like a tomato," Bea comments. "On a scale of one to breaking hockey sticks into pieces, how mad are you?"

Not mad at all. I'm terrified.

Every goal scored reddens my cheeks deeper and deeper, blood sending a pulsing warmth to the furthest edges of my body and the lowest spot at the split of my legs.

Eight.

Nine.

Ten.

The crowd goes wild as Ottawa clinches the win ten-two. Ten goals. My pussy grieves in advance.

Bea elbows me. "You still haven't told me what you bet him—"

"Look, there's Gabe!" I point by the players' exit.

She's got a puffy mic in Radek's face. The interview is barely audible over the pounding of my pulse. Her eyes light up with an in-awe expression, which is saying a lot, considering Gabe isn't easily impressed.

"I'll say what everyone is thinking: *wow*! A ten-goal game is your personal record, not to mention you're broke the record for most goals in one game by any single player in the league. What a difference from the last game against the Sky. What changed?"

Landon shrugs and laughs on the Jumbotron, gaze scanning the lower bowl section we sit in. "Y'know, after that loss, there was nowhere to go but up," he pants through his reply. My heart plummets as he catches me gawping. "Let's say I had something to prove. A little extra motivation." The smug bastard smiles back at Gabe as she thanks and congratulates him once more, then disappears through the gate.

The camera pans away to an interview with the Vancouver captain, but Gabe keeps my attention. Wade Boehner approaches her with a dopey smile and goo-goo eyes. My friend shakes her head and turns away. A disapproving noise tickles my throat. What was that?

"Crazy, crazy game." Bea rants on as we join the beeline of departing fans. I almost miss a cement step when Landon's text pops up on my phone.

GYM GUY

I'll be home in 2 hours.

GYM GUY

You better be naked in my bed.

CHAPTER 39:
SCANTILY CLAD SUPERHEROES

LANDON

LIKE A DRILL SERGEANT, WADE PACES IN FRONT OF the team's rookies, doling out the last of his judgment. The undone clip of his ratty maroon overalls clicks against his lower back, where his hands are clasped.

"Men, the theme of this year's Halloween party was to dress up as the given names of our forever friends: our third legs." All eyes follow to and fro with his calculated strides. "Masturbator!" he barks.

"It's Masterson," the rookie forward mutters.

"Silence! Fuck are you supposed to be, eh?"

Masterson clears his throat, adjusting the bright red foam racecar costume hanging from his shoulders. "Lightning McQueen."

"Lightning McQu—" Wade's eyebrows shoot up into the middle of his forehead, then settle down, unimpressed. "Your dick is a speedy little stock car that always finishes first?"

Fletch shakes his head next to me with a disapproving *mm-mm-mm*.

"Negative fifty out of ten. Get the fuck outta my face." Wade's meaty prosthetic hands jiggle as they swat Masterson to the side. His loud clap rings in my ears. "Okay, who else we have here?" He skims over Olsen and Szecze. "Thor and Hulk. How predictable. Five out of ten. Combined." Narrowed eyes study our center, tugging at a fin. "What's this, Fletch?"

Fletch peers through the mouth of a massive whale costume. "I'm Moby Dick." Stifled laughter in the background eggs him on. "He's a giant sperm whale."

Hand slapping his forehead and pulling down his face, Wade groans.

"Fucking hell, Donovan. Even your cock is a literary character. Seven out of ten for pun potential, though."

I'm next. He grimaces at my near-naked get-up. "Not sure you can call it 'He-Man' if your prick can fit in those tighty whities. Eight out of ten, though. Very realistic. Nice wig." One of those hefty silicone hands fluffs the blond, pageboy bob.

"Hands off. You'll mess it up."

I smack his hand away with my sword. He smacks my chest plate in return. Our hands flap at one another, a full-blown slapping fight breaking out after I drop the plastic sword.

"For fuck's sake. Will you two grow up?" Jaeg rumbles midway through a burp, half-sitting atop the edge of the sectional.

I slap Wade one more time. He elbows me in the gut and stomps over to where our captain is. Skylar cuddles protectively around him, head-to-toe in a glowy green. "You call his dick 'Superman?'"

Sky giggles and presses her nose into Derrick's cheek. "Man of Steel."

"I expected something more original." Wade growls out a disgusted noise. "Why aren't you Lois Lane?"

Skylar nuzzles further as Jaeg brings a beer to his mouth, then drops a kiss onto his neck.

"I'm his Kryptonite."

He lets the trace of a smile slip.

A chorus of *awws* echoes. Wade glares back before gagging. "Fine. Seven out of ten."

Fletch intones a swoony sigh, lifting his tailfin to plop down beside them. "Should've been eleven. You guys are so cute, it makes me wanna sleep on the highway tonight."

"What are you supposed to be, Boehner?" Olsen grunts and crushes a beer can in a fist.

Wade's eyebrows knit together. "You live under a rock or something?" He shows off his costume: an orange, plaid Henley, torn overalls, fake oversized hands and feet, and hair styled in a messy mop. "I'm Wreck-It Ralph." He flexes his arms above his head, puffing out his chest. "I'm six-foot-four, I weigh two-hundred-and-ten pounds. I wreck pussy, professionally. I'm very good at what I do. Probably the best—"

Groans of disbelief and boos reply to his macho display. "*Ah*, fuck off.

No shots for you losers. Stick to the keg beer over there."

We call out his bullshit. Wade can't help but entertain. This year we've got a lineup of vampire shots made of whiskey and vermouth, werewolf shots of Jägermeister and chocolate liqueur, and these spicy Fireball shots he calls Dragon's Breath. Within half an hour, we've all had two rounds of each. Or was it three? The Rocky Horror Picture Show plays from a projector against the bare wall on the far side of the top floor. A DJ starts his set in one corner as women enter from the front door.

"Who are these girls?" I mumble to Wade. Groups of three to five of them keep joining the party.

"Friends," Wade says through a greedy smile, rubbing his hands together. "Everyone on your worst behavior. Except you, Olsen." He points to the defender, who throws his velvet cape over his shoulder and swings Mjölnir around. "Don't harass the nice ladies."

The women descend like lemmings upon the team, all touchy-feely and encouraging us to take shots from various naked body parts. I wasn't against partaking in the past, but now? Indi takes up every spot in my heart and mind.

When a Playboy bunny gropes my ass, I let out a girlish shriek. She titters out a *whoops* and I backpedal with a stern wag of my index finger. "No, thank you!" My body is Indi's and no one else's.

Fletch whines and cradles a few beers in his arms, backing into the spot I'd been eying behind the DJ booth. Hiding in the washroom is the next-best option. I scratch my calf under the furry lining of my boots, then pull out my phone from the pocket built into the chest plate. My most recent message displays the headless mirror selfie Indi sent earlier that evening, showing off her fitted Beyoncé-style black bodysuit and fishnet leggings in the mirror.

ME

How's the party at Giachetti's?

GYM GIRL

Boring. Bea got way too drunk, and I took her home.

GYM GIRL

> I was gonna ask how the team party is going, but you're texting me so it can't be that great.

ME

> It's nuts! Wade knows how to throw them, but the puck bunnies are out for blood tonight.

GYM GIRL

> Aww. How sad for you.

ME

> I knew you'd understand. I hate it here.

GYM GIRL

> Do you need me to come rescue you?

A body slams against the washroom door, followed by a shrill voice. "Open uppppppp. I need to peeeeeeeeee!"

I stick my tongue out toward the interrupter behind the door. "Almost done!'

ME

> Yes, please. I parked the Rover at Argyle and Bank.

GYM GIRL

> I'm across the River. See ya in 10.

The cat-eared brunette tumbles into the washroom, loose curls dragging across the tile as she crawls toward the toilet. Christ. I attempt an escape through the kitchen.

"Landy! Where are you going?" Wade calls over the remixed version of Jeremih's "Put it All on Me." The aforementioned Playboy bunny touches her toes while Wade practically dry humps her from behind.

My hands form a megaphone around my mouth. "I have to go walk my fish!"

Ten minutes seems like forever. I downed the water bottle I grabbed on my way out of the party within thirty seconds and can't stop fidgeting while waiting for Indi. The briefs keep riding up, the furry boots are making my feet sweat and this wig is insanely itchy.

I'm about to text her for an ETA, when there are light raps on the window. I mindlessly push open the back door and slide to the other end of the seat to make room. "Hey, ba—*Ahhhhhhhhhhh!*"

Ghostface greets me, shrouded in black and wielding a large chef's knife. "*Fuuuuck!*" I kick my feet, backing into the door, hands fumbling at the handle.

A familiar throaty chuckle rings out. "What a scaredy cat."

"Indi?" My hand flies to my chest plate, tapping on it to calm my heart. She lifts the mask and props it atop her head. "Trick or treat?"

"Baby," I heave through a shallow breath, placing a hand over her shoulder. "You scared the fuck outta me."

"That was the point, silly man. You miss me?" When she leans in close, a sliver of light from the windshield slashes across her face, splitting her mischievous smile in half.

I tip up my chin to drop a kiss onto her forehead, then hold her softened gaze. "Always."

The corners of her eyes crinkle as she looks me up and down. "How is your costume skimpier than mine?"

"I'm He-Man." I straighten and broaden my chest to give her the best view. "It goes with the theme."

Indi raises an eyebrow. "Which is what? Scantily clad superheroes?"

"Close. We all dressed up as whatever we call our dicks." A stupid lopsided grin forms across my mouth.

Indi tosses her head back with a short, hearty laugh.

Best fucking sound I've ever heard. Maybe second best to her moaning out my name.

"That's ridiculous."

I wanna keep hearing her laugh, so I tell her what the boys dressed up as, slowly tugging her onto me. She wipes tears away by the time I describe Wade as Wreck-It Ralph. Her hands nestle around my neck, legs in their rightful place around mine.

"That sounds like a much better party than the one I was at."

Her dimple calls to me and I answer with another kiss. "I think I like it here best."

The black robe draped over us is a hindrance. My hand bunches at all the extra fabric. "This isn't what you were wearing in the pic you sent me."

"I can't wear that to a Halloween party thrown by my boss." Another smirk pops out. "It's underneath."

A sudden rush of alcohol relaxes all my muscles, except the ones gripping her to me. My voice drops to a hush as I press her forehead to mine. "I'm ready for my treat. You gonna show me?"

Her hands lift from my shoulders to reach behind her neck. I shake out a breath when she undoes two of the Velcro closures.

"You smell like whiskey and cinnamon."

I swallow. "Blame the fancy shots at Wade's."

She returns a breathy giggle.

"You smell like cranberry and vodka."

"I did have a couple of those. Heavy on the vodka. *Ow.*" She glances at her leg. "What poked me?"

I open my mouth to respond.

"And don't say 'that's what she said.'"

My pinched fingers zipper across my lips.

Indi releases from whatever her robe snagged on and holds it at my eye level. "Why do you have zip ties?"

"Skate lace emergency. Equipment manager gave them to me." I'm fucking horny and not above begging. Something tells me she knows it, too. "Forget all that. Show me what you're wearing." My hips urge her on with a quick thrust up, bouncing my phone out of the chest plate pocket. It lands on the seat beside us, lighting up new texts from Wade.

WADE

Get back here fucker!!!!!!

WADE

You better not be with Indi right now

Indi's eyes fall to the lock screen.

Uh oh.

Her head pivots to me. "Landon."

I gulp. Before I can stop it, I'm word-vomiting how Wade and Jaeger cornered me after they caught her leaving the Toronto game.

"And you admitted to it?" Her emotionless response and how steadily she moves my hands from her body are unnerving, sending my rapid pulse into a tailspin.

"There was no way around it, but I promise, they won't tell anyone."

Her hands grip my wrists, keeping them away. Too far away from her. "They better not."

I reach for her, but the grip holds strong. "Can we talk—"

"What's done is done." She clicks her tongue, disappointed. "You broke the rule."

"I'm sorry, baby. How can I make it right? I'll do anything."

"Oh, you *will*." Absolute depravity glints in her eyes. Without another word, she lowers the mask. Hiding from me. I don't like it. "Stay put."

My head pounds with fresh fear.

"Baby, please. Let me see you."

"In a minute." Her hands jostle mine above my head and over the headrest. "You trust me?"

There's no hesitation. "More than anything." The thought ends abruptly when she secures a zip tie around each wrist and the metal rods of the headrest. She slides off me to do the same for my ankles around the seat supports, then clicks a belt across my torso, pulling it as far as it can go before it locks so I can't move. Indi rests a knee on either side of my bare thighs and slots her hips into mine.

"Do you like scary movies, Landon?" Her rasp muffles under the mask.

The prop knife's blade runs the edge of my tensed jaw, trailing down the thumping artery against my throat. "They don't always have happy endings."

I should not be this turned on. Her tearing the Velcro apart and flinging the robe away is no help. The tight onesie thing is better in-person. Way better.

"Fucking look at you," I say through a sigh, straining against the plastic ties. Everything strains against her, especially my big guy below.

She looks to my groin, suede briefs ready to burst. "Look at that. You *enjoy* being tortured by me?"

"I enjoy everything you do to me."

Indi laughs an evil laugh while dragging her fingertips across the curved seam of fabric on her chest. She toys with it, teasing me for a never-ending minute before lowering the cups to flash that incredible rack.

"You're the fucking hottest thing I've ever seen." I groan. "Your tits are perfect." Pulling at the restraints again is useless. "Let me go so I can touch you."

"Not a chance." She rolls her hips, moving herself over the engorged length of my dick. Her face tilts with a hum.

Another alcoholic surge burns through my veins. "Does it make you wet, Indi?" A brazen question. "Seeing me like this?"

"So needy and hard?" There's an obvious smile in her reply. "I don't think I've ever been wetter."

My body clenches, unable to move anything but my bent knees. I'm not sure I want to with the way she's perched over me. "Then keep grinding that little pussy on me. I wanna feel it against my cock."

She does, rocking and grinding at a crushing, patient pace. My head knocks back into the headrest, twisting and groaning louder at the pleasurable torment. Delicious, intoxicating torment. "How's that?"

"Fuck, *yes*. I'm" —her warm cunt rubs over me— *"desperate"* —she sinks further with another thrust— "for you."

The meshy mouth hole of her terrifying mask presses onto my lips with a hot, boozy breath. "Scream for me."

I want it. Her mouth on mine while I show her exactly what I feel. I want to feel her everywhere. And I want her to feel the same. So *fucking* badly. "*Indi!*"

Her hips continue without relent, tits bouncing at my eye level. My mouth roots over air, hoping to snag a taste of those hardened nipples. She reclines, removing them from reach.

"*Please*," I whine, writhing under her and making the most inhuman noises as pleasure rockets through me. "You own me." The liquored confession draws out another. "I've dreamed of you for so long. In my bed. On your couch. You riding me right here, taking my cock so hard I can't see."

Indi's hips circle and increase the pressure.

Muscled sinews of my neck stretch through a frustrated growl. "I'm dying to flip you over and fuck you against this console, fill you up until you can't feel anything else. Can't feel anything but me."

She doesn't stop, doesn't change her speed. Her hands drop from my shoulders to my chest, fingers curling over the plate while she stifles a whimper. Those soft sounds trigger me, the oncoming orgasm playing a horrible game of hide-and-seek.

Like a rabid dog, I grunt and snarl, practically foaming at the fucking mouth for release. The ties slice into my wrists, seat belt cutting into my bare skin as my whole body goes taut when she drives over me again. "Ah, *fuck*. I'm gonna—please don't make me come on myself again."

"*Oh*," she moans, but cuts herself off. "Careful what you wish for."

The contact disappears, building pleasure replaced with the excruciating, unreleased weight of my balls. I grumble and wince. Indi kneels in the seat next to me, the cold silicone of the mask grazing my ear.

"There's nothing scarier than not getting a happy ending." She unlocks the door, reaching for the handle.

Breathing is a chore. "*Fuck*, Indi. I'm sorry."

She shushes me, holding a safety pin in front of my face. "I'm not mad." It does something to the tie, and it loosens, finally releasing my hands. "Honestly, I feel better now." She frees my ankles, too. Indi snorts, making me fall in love with her all over again.

It happens daily, like a dreamy version of Groundhog Day. I didn't know falling in love like that was possible.

"Is He-Man gonna be okay?" She motions to it with a downward flick of her eyes.

Don't talk to me! my dick weeps. I hiss with a shake of my head. "A kiss might make it feel better."

Another glorious laugh. I swoon and pretend to faint on her shoulder. "Next time, eh? I should get back before people start asking questions."

"You're really not mad? I didn't mean—"

"I trust you, too." Her hand warms my thigh. Comforting. Grounding. "If you say your teammates won't rat us out, I believe you. And besides, I'm like, this close" —she pinches her index finger and thumb together— "to having everything we need to settle the case out of court. We have to be more careful until then."

Indi cocks her masked face in my direction, pausing the conversation. "Sometimes, I think..." she mumbles, drawing nervous rounds into her thigh.

"Indi, *um*, I—" A lump in my throat strangles my words. "Do you ever—"

Her hand slips away before I can hold it.

She peeks under the mask, eyes hiding something between regret and longing. "Don't say anything else, Landon."

Too soon, she's gone. The mask is on again and the door clicks as she pushes it open. It swings shut, ending the conversation with an uneasy finality.

She might as well have reached into my chest and slapped my heart. Indi has to know that it already lives and beats for her. But what about the tremble in her voice? Maybe she knew it would change everything.

Or maybe I misunderstood. Maybe she wanted to save me the embarrassment because she doesn't feel the same.

Indi made the rules. She made it so clear, so easy. So clean-cut. She didn't want anything beyond friendship and orgasms. And though we agreed we're more than friends, the minute I think we're moving beyond that, we take two steps back. And me? A fucking sap if I ever saw one. I'm so fucking in love with her, if she told me to go fuck myself, I'd be ready with my cock in-hand.

I sigh and harshly rub my face. The distance feels worse than before, like I've lost her when I haven't had her yet.

Multi-colored lights strobe through the windows of Wade's upper-floor unit as I glance skyward through the tinted glass. There's no way I'm going back up there. I grab my phone from the floor of the Rover and text the group.

ME

Everything under control? I'm out.

FLETCH

Lucky. I wanna go home, too!

JAEG

Done walking that fish, eh? Sky and I are leaving too. See ya tomorrow morning.

WADE

You guys suck filthy ol man balls. Fletch, get your ass out here. I'm drowning in tits.

FLETCH

No thanks. I'm good here.

ME

Can I park here overnight? I'll come get the Rover in the morning.

WADE

For sure.

The night creeps on. My mind switches from fantasizing about Indi to overthinking every word exchanged between us. I'm not in the habit of hiding what I feel, and I won't start now. I don't want to let her go, to give up. I don't want it to end. But I have no idea whether I should keep trying to convince Indi that this could be so much more than what it is.

CHAPTER 40:
IT'S NOT NOTHING

INDI

YOU KNOW HOW BOOKS AND MOVIES RAVE ABOUT those sparks between couples? They depict grand, romantic gestures while fireworks go off in the background.

They're real. And I've only felt them with Landon Radek. They jolt through the taut netting of my Halloween mask during our tipsy non-kiss, pricking at my lips and sending electrified goosebumps down my limbs to the tips of my fingers and toes. Like the sparkling of a lit firecracker wick.

If I'm honest, they come up more and more whenever he's around. Like when he carried my limp body to the oversized tub to bathe me and wash my hair after doling out ten orgasms. His touch was so tender, and those fleeting kisses left my clean skin too quickly.

The same sparks simmered in my gut watching him change the bedsheets as I lounged in his warm robe.

They're still there the morning after, lingering in the sheets as I woke up in his empty penthouse to an envelope on the nightstand with a handwritten note. It contains the years-old doodle he'd drawn of me beating up Bryce Bennett.

> *This is yours. Just like me.*
> *PS - I made you blueberry protein pancakes. They're in the toaster oven. I don't know how to make fancy coffee, but an iced latte should be there soon.*
> *Landon*

I laughed, but I wanted to cry. He was too good to me, his friendship so much more than I deserved. More accepting, more intimate than anyone before him.

Forget about Landon carving windows in the walls surrounding my heart, the sweet man managed to dismantle them entirely. All that's left to protect the stupid organ is my rapidly weakening resolve. It's ready to sacrifice itself, setting partner track aside.

Admitting the truth somehow makes it tougher to swallow. I don't have time to overthink what it all meant or if I'm blowing off my only achievement in life for a chance with him, because the doorbell rings with the arrival of my coffee delivery.

And what do I do in return? Leave the poor man with blue balls in the back seat of his car in the middle of the night.

For the first time since we started this...this *thing*, I wonder how different it'd be if I wasn't standoffish and distant. How Landon would react if I let him know about the space in my heart that he takes up—the one he's always taken up.

ME

Are you home from practice?

GYM GUY

Getting off the massage table now. Helga didn't mess around. I feel like a new man.

ME

Wanna come over?

GYM GUY

Absolutely

ME

Leaving the door unlocked.

Nervous butterflies flit and pace in my gut as I walk circles around the living room, muttering a pep talk through the last bite of a Ferrero Rocher truffle. Its foil wrapper shrinks in my sweaty fist hearing a *creak* from the apartment's entryway.

"Indi?" Landon whispers through the cracked door. He flattens himself, slinking between the two surfaces in his usual disguise, as if anyone could miss his six-two, two-hundred-pounds-of-pure-muscle frame.

A held-back breath hisses between my teeth as he clicks the door shut. "Hi."

When he removes the hood, revealing an easy smile and those softened blue eyes, the bubble of my heart's restraint bursts. I rush the five steps and launch onto him.

He falls back onto the wall, open-mouthed in surprise, but relaxes into the unexpected embrace. His grip tightens around me, arms doubling until his hands squeeze my waist.

"Hi, baby." Landon nuzzles at the hairline below my ear. "You miss me?" There's a sincere need for confirmation in place of his usual cockiness. I give it to him.

"Yes." My heart rattles inside my chest as it presses into his, weight shifting between my tiptoed feet in an awkward slow dance. "Are you surprised?"

"Very surprised." He strokes my nose with his. More sparks ignite in the half-inch gap between our lips. A sultry breath against the delicate skin there beckons goosebumps.

I inhale near his mouth where hints of artificial vanilla linger. "Did you just have a Twinkie?"

His soft smile stretches into something more devilish.

"*Ooh*, busted."

"I'm not ashamed of enjoying an appetizer before the *main course*." His brows waggle.

I narrow my eyes. "No way you said that out loud."

"That's why you called me over, isn't it? Happy to oblige."

"That's not why."

"No?"

My pussy clenches. "I wanted to hang out."

Landon purses his lips, considering my reply. "So, this isn't an ambush to see if I ended up watching that movie?"

"*Hera Pheri*?"

He nods in response.

"And since when do I ambush you?" His eyes flick to our locked hug and back up. "Fine. But you watched it?"

"I finished it on the road. Four out of five stars. Subtitles didn't help as much as I thought, but the shticks were top tier."

"Okay, Hotshot." I lean away from the hold, but keep my elbows draped over his shoulders as he knocks off his sneakers and walks us into the living room. "What was your favorite part?"

"See, I knew there was gonna be a quiz—" His hands loosen and slip into the butt pockets of my jeans.

"Stop trying to weasel your way out of it."

He fakes a fall to the couch with my playful push and in our tangle of limbs, I'm forced forward. "The Star Garage/Star Fisheries mixup."

He did watch it!

Landon's hands slide down my legs and back up, guiding one knee onto the cushion after the other to straddle him. "When someone called the garage asking about the fish quality that day, and the guy in the thick glasses—"

"Babu Rao. Played by Paresh Rawal."

He snaps and points. "Yes, *him*. When he said he fried 'em up and ate the fish, I almost pissed myself. Wade heard me wheezing and made me restart it so he could join." His tongue wets his top lip, fingertips skating across the strip of skin above my denim waistline. I stop him by the wrists and place his open hands on my thighs, ignoring how his touch sears through the worn fabric.

"Seriously, that's *not* why I called you over." Here's your window. Now or never. "I happen to like having you around."

One of his eyebrows perks.

"I do. I'm not good at showing it, but I care about you." My gaze casts downward for a moment's hesitation before courage drowns it out. I cup his face. "Ask me how much."

"How much?"

The column of his throat tenses under my lips. He sighs, dense lash lines fluttering as they close. Quickening beats of his heart thud through the hoodie's thick fleece and my palms. "So much."

I kiss the corner of his bowed mouth, the broad plane of his smooth cheekbone, and the angled corner of his unshaven jaw. Memorizing and favoring each spot as he offers encouraging, content hums. "You mean so much to me."

Those thick azure rings of his eyes shrink as the pupils dilate, staying connected to mine when I position his hands around my neck to gather the hair away from both shoulders. His hardened length stirs beneath me. He gulps again on my descent to the floor.

"Say it again."

My hands pull down his chest. "You." They glide over his thighs. "Mean." My knees wedge between Landon's feet. "So much." A groan rumbles from his chest when I lean over to graze the stretched, tented inseam of his sweatpants with an open mouth, blowing a hot breath through the material. "To me."

"*Fuck.*" Drooping lids halve his eyes from where I glance up, drunk with the power he feeds me.

"Want me to show you?"

Landon puffs out a shaky breath as I uncover him with a slow, deliberate movement. His heavy, engorged cock fills the *o* of my fist until my middle finger and thumb no longer touch. He shivers when I spit on the swollen head and stroke down.

"Oh, my God," he laments, eyes wrinkling shut.

Both of my fists wrap his cock, corkscrewing around the base in opposite directions. Landon groans again with his next exhale. "Oh, my *God.*"

The solid sheets of muscle making up his build tremble when my tongue swirls around the tip. I mouth him and retreat with a wet suck. His lower lip quivers, the once-twined rope of control unraveling by its frayed ends. Landon stutters a protest, hands gently yanking me off by the hair threaded between his fingers. "N-n-n-n-n-no—*please.*"

I still. "No? You don't want me to?"

"I mean—fuck, *yes.*" His hands nudge me forward, brushing my coated lips against the head.

I part them, pulling him in and bobbing off, tracing the underside as he throbs against my tongue.

"Can't get enough of this perfect mouth of yours."

I moan at the praise and take him further, bracing for impact as he hits the back of my throat. A frustrated guttural noise from Landon spurs me on. "Baby, *please*. If you keep going..."

Tears blur my vision.

"I—can't" —he pants, hoarse and ragged— "it's No Nut November."

Retreating with a cartoonish pop, I smirk. "And?"

"And I've got fifty *k* on the line." His head writhes against the couch cushion. "*Stupid*," he mutters under his breath.

"You bet fifty *thousand* dollars that you wouldn't come *all* month?"

"Not just me—the boys are in on it, too. The whole team's raising money for prostate cancer research." One of his hands harshly runs over his face, partially masking his exasperation.

Something inside me rebels. A particularly filthy thought takes root. I dampen the seam of my mouth in prep, twisting my hands around his still-hard shaft. "Don't be a cheapskate, Radek."

He shudders and peeks through his fingers. "*Indi.*"

"It's for a good cause." My lips pucker to blow a cool breath onto the head of his dick.

Landon's body goes taut, eyes wide once more. "We can't have people thinking you're stingy."

I bring his hand to my throat. He follows my cue and latches on, thumb pressing into my pulse, grip threatening to strip me of air.

"*Goddamn*, I love seeing you like this." His jaw ripples with a tick. "Fucking take me."

I gag on him three times before he finishes with an animalistic groan, his release streaming down and providing an intoxicating sense of satisfaction.

Sweat dots the long stubble of his mustache. It tickles my lips when I rise to kiss that perfect corner of his mouth again. His grasp on my neck tightens, keeping me hovering over him. "You've ruined me."

I putter, brushing off the comment with a swat to the chest. "Fifty *k* is a drop in the bucket for you, Mr. Eight Figures."

"That's not what I meant."

An immovable lump forms and I try my best to swallow it down. It doesn't budge. The way his thumb strokes the delicate skin on my throat has me melting. His mouth readies to say something. I wait and pace my excited breaths, but the moment fades quicker than I expect. I don't want it to end. The moment, I mean. I want to be close to him forever, his hands on me and mine on his heart. But Landon's post-orgasm dazed expression is clouded with another emotion I can't place. Warning sirens go off in my head, but I silence them.

"I have a 5 a.m. flight tomorrow."

———

As if I'm not good enough at hurting my own feelings, Landon doesn't text me back for *three* days after landing in L.A. I'm starting to think he's either been kidnapped or somehow got sucked into a heist. Maybe he charmed the hell out of the badass matriarch secretly running the whole crime organization and now they're in love. Damn, I've been reading too many of those mafia romances before bed.

Focusing at work is impossible. My mind trudges through the rabbit hole of doubt and fear as Bea drones on in the background. "...I've got the meeting all squared away. The judge signed the motion with his butthole..."

Butthole?

I blink twice. "Excuse me?"

Bea shoots me a knowing smile. "And here I thought you weren't paying attention." She puts her pen down and folds her hands over one another. "What's up?"

"What do you mean?"

Her head tilts to the side. "Lay it on me. You're so spacey this week. I'm not ready to enter the alternate universe where I'm the more focused one."

I puff my cheeks and drop my head forward in resignation. "Fine. Gym Guy ghosted me."

"Ah."

"It's making me crazy."

"*Mmhm*, mmhm." She taps her lips with a finger.

"It's weird not hearing from him."

"Why don't you go to his place and see what's going on?"

Yes! Why don't I?

"Yeah!" I stand from my chair abruptly, making Bea jump in her seat. "I'll go over there and confront him." Determination surges through my veins, all logic thrown in the garbage bin like my lunch leftovers.

Who the fuck does he think he is, ignoring my messages? After making me fall in love with him. How dare he!

Bea looks like she regrets ever suggesting the idea. "I didn't mean right at this moment."

"Too late!" I shove my laptop into my work bag and throw it over my shoulder, grabbing my wallet from the bottom drawer before locking it. "I'll see you at eight tomorrow. Unless I've turned to a life of crime after discovering this shithead with another woman."

"Slow down, El Capo. It's probably nothing."

I make my presence known in Radek's penthouse by jostling through the door and stomping across the floor. The temperature in the place alone has me breaking into a sweat by the time I near the living area and see the lumpy figure on the couch. A familiar soft melody plays in the background.

It's not nothing.

He lies there, his balled body swallowed entirely in a fuzzy blanket. It's cinched together under his chin like a cozy hood, only the outline of his darkened side profile poking through from where his head rests on a pillow. Countless crumpled-up tissues surround him.

The piano intro continues as Saif Ali Khan and Preity Zinta walk hand-in-hand across the big screen in the heart-wrenching scene from *Kal Ho Na Ho*. He sniffles out a soft sob.

"Landon?"

His head turns to me, not in shock at my sudden appearance or shame for being caught watching my favorite Bollywood movie without me. No, he simply looks miserable. My anger cools.

"It's so sad!" he wails. His handsome face warps with grief. "Aman tells Naina to marry her best friend Rohit, even though he loves her, because Aman's dying, and they can never be together!"

His cries disarm me. I'm stripped of every hard emotion, my insides molten at his frailty.

"*Uh-huh.* I know this movie. We watched it together, remember?" I inch closer, posture softening with each step, and drop my bag on one end of the sofa.

"Thank God you're here." He blows snot into another tissue with a honk, looking especially pitiful in his blanket burrito. "But not too close,"

Landon's nasal voice warns, shifting his legs slightly to make space for me. "Coach benched me until I get rid of this disgusting cold." The breath he takes through his clogged nose confirms it.

"A cold?" I sit a cushion away. "You should've told me."

"But how?" He frowns, no jest in his question. "*How* could I have told you, Indi?"

I recognize the exaggerated whine. It's not any cold. It's a *man*-cold. "I dunno, your phone? I texted you. So many times."

"You did?" His lower lips juts forward. "*Aww.*"

"Yeah."

"You worried about me?"

"...Kinda."

"I'm sorry." Landon swipes at his reddened nose with a fresh tissue and grimaces while pinching the bridge. "I couldn't reach it."

"Where is it? I'll get it for you." I pat his foot twice.

He weakly points to the side table, a mere six inches from his limp hand. "There."

I fail at holding back my laugh. "Damn, Radek. You're a big baby when you're sick."

"Help me," he croaks. "My nose is stuffy, my head's ready to implode, and I'm achy all over."

Older sister instinct kicks in and I roll up my sleeves to dab the back of my hand on his clammy forehead. "Not feverish." I get to my feet. "Be right back. I'm gonna make you some tea, okay?"

"You're an angel." Landon curls further into the couch. "My sweet, sweet, angel baby."

The stupid grin I wear doesn't leave my face while I collect a knot of ginger from his fridge and grate it into a small pot of boiling water. I strain the tea into a mug, squeeze a splash of lemon juice and add a pinch of turmeric before stirring in a spoon of honey.

Landon whines. "Am I gonna die?"

"You're not gonna die. How are you more dramatic when you're not feeling well?" I shake my head and hand him the mug. "Here, drink this."

He takes a noiseless sip and sputters out a cough. "Why is it spicy?"

"Just drink it. It's ginger tea. It'll clear all that congestion right up."

"If you say so."

"I do say so." Retrieving a small container from my briefcase, I poke around the kitchen drawers for cotton twine and cheesecloth, ordering him to a steamy shower after he finishes his cup.

We meet outside the bathroom. I don't think I'll ever tire of seeing newly-showered, shirtless Landon.

"You were right," he confirms. "Cleared the snot right out."

"You sound better already."

"Cleared the whole system out, actually." His hands wave in circles above the defined abs cutting across his stomach.

"Thanks for the visual." I toy with the item in hand, hiding it in my palm from a brisk sense of embarrassment.

Landon gazes at my fist. "Whatcha got there?"

The makeshift necklace with a tiny satchel pendant hangs from my middle fingers.

His eyes squint in curiosity.

"It's a desi herbal cold remedy. There's ajmo—ajwain seed inside the pouch. You wear it around your neck and breathe in its smell."

He takes a step closer. Warm hands guide mine by the wrist. "Put it on me." When I slip the string over his head, he gathers my fingers between his and keeps them on his chest. "Will you stay until I fall asleep?"

"Okay."

Landon lowers his torso between my legs, the weight of his head resting against my belly, toned biceps on my thighs as his arms tuck under the pillow I recline on. Fistfuls of his damp hair airdry as I finger-comb through it, massaging the scalp until we're both lulled into a deeply relaxed state. He intones an exhale when my hands drop to his naked back, nails lightly scratching up and down in languid strokes. "Fuck."

Hard muscles ripple as his goosebumps rise to my fingertips. Landon moans into my hip. "That feels so fucking good, baby. I love this." He groans out a low, sleepy hum. "Can you stay forever?"

I shush him, but my heart stops. It restarts with a new heaviness.

When his soft snores replace long breaths, I go home with a crack in that stupid heart of mine, more sure of what I want from him than when I got there, and less sure of what the hell I'm supposed to do about it.

CHAPTER 41:
THE SWEETEST SECRET

LANDON

IT'S NO NUT NOVEMBER AND I HATE MYSELF.

As if tensions weren't high enough in the locker room, I have to deal with Wade's shit-eating grin and Derrick's disappointed glare when I shove my IOU slip into the glass NNN jar. Explaining myself after the Diwali incident had gone nowhere. They still think I'm fucking myself over.

Fletch whistles and claps a hand on my back. "Damn, brother. Fifty *k?* You couldn't save a wank for three weeks?"

I jostle him off. "You're one to talk. You dropped ten on November third. At least I lasted seven days." Our playful elbowing gets more and more aggressive until I've got him in a headlock on the floor.

Wade strolls by. "Now, now, boys. You both have big dongs. Calm down."

Donovan extends his leg and trips Wade, who belly-flops to the ground. The locker room erupts in laughter, except for the stern face of our tired captain.

Before it turns into a full-on riot, my phone dings.

GYM GIRL

> Feeling better, I see. Great game, Radek.

ME

> The snap you sent helped.
> You're my good luck charm.

> **ME**
>
> I'm gonna need you to send one of those before every game.

> **GYM GIRL**
>
> Some would say that's obsessive.

> **ME**
>
> Call me obsessed, then.

Fletch fixes his bowtie next to me. Wade flicks it. They bicker like an old couple.

"You're so fucking annoying."

"I'm not the one wearing that dumb bowtie." He flicks it again. The bow goes crooked.

Fletch's voice goes up an octave, imitating Jack Black. "Don't be talkin' 'bout my bowtie!"

> **GYM GIRL**
>
> When are you back?

> **ME**
>
> Tomorrow evening

> **GYM GIRL**
>
> FaceTime me when you get to the hotel. I have a surprise for you.

Like clockwork, at 11:15 p.m., Fletch falls asleep with a book on his face. Tonight, it's *Kingdom of the Wicked* or something. A few pages whiffle with every one of his exhales.

Expecting Indi to step up her phone sex game with a visual addition, I slip my earbuds in and pull the sheets over my head. But what pops up on my phone screen is way better. She flashes me a dimpled smile.

"Ready for your surprise?"

"Yes," I whisper.

The camera flips to the front. It pans to her hand using a set of tweezers to drop white letters onto a still-warm chocolate mold.

I M-I-S-S Y-O-U

"Aw, *baby*." My heart floods with a gooey, sunshiney warmth. She's so goddamn cute, I can't stand it. I take a live photo, saving it to rewatch over and over again. "I miss you, too—"

Indi lets out a short *ha* and keeps adding letters.

I M-I-S-S Y-O-U-R C-O-C-K

Her giggles turn into snorts and the need to assault her with endless kisses grows. I settle for riling her up from afar. "You think you're so funny now. Wait until I get back and give it to you. I'll fill your throat up so good. Doubt you'll be able to laugh then."

"*Landon!*" she admonishes.

"That's what you want, right? Your mouth around my cock?" Her hand on the counter edge tightens with a curl, in sync with mine within my boxers. "Flip the camera back, Indi. Lemme see that gorgeous face." She does. The blush on her is so fucking magnificent I would've come into my hand in about two minutes if it wasn't for my teammate sputtering awake. Indi ends the call upon hearing the ruckus.

I cough, "Asswipe."

Fletcher squints. "What did I do?"

"Cock block," I mutter, rolling to face away from him.

"Stupid No Nut November got everyone's balls twisted," he grumbles.

I throw a pillow at him and hold one over my head until sleep takes me under.

———

Six hours on a plane with these buffoons would kill any normal person. I love the dopes, but between Fletch kicking our asses in poker round-after-round, Wade belting out the most horrific, incorrect lyrics about wet ass pussy, and Olsen loudly scratching his balls every five minutes, it's enough to have me committed.

The second my feet hit the tarmac, I hoist the gear bag over my shoulder and book it to the Rover. I've never been so excited to see Indi and despite it being seventeen degrees out and the AC blasts on high, I'm sweating like a pig in summer. I park, then wipe a handkerchief down my face before taking a few deep breaths and getting out of the car.

No receptionist greets me. I weave through the unoccupied desks to get to Indi's door, knocking three times before throwing it open and shutting it behind me. She spins around from her desk and gasps, dropping the phone in hand to the floor, then relaxes her surprise into a coy smile. "Hey."

My love stands in front of her desk wearing the tightest fucking black dress. It fits like a glove, highlighting every beautiful curve. Breathless, I clutch my chest, then fall to my hands and knees.

Her eyes go round, widening with concern. "Oh, God. What's wrong?" Indi hurries toward me.

I hold up a hand, lips twitching to suppress a smile. "I'll be okay. I'll be okay."

She manic-searches my shoulders with her hands. "What's happening?"

"You, in *that*..." Air whines through my wheeze. "You can't wear this dress and look like *that* and expect me *not* to go weak in the knees."

Indi smacks my arm and rolls her eyes. She straightens to cross her arms across her chest and curses under her breath.

I scoot forward on my knees in quick succession. "And now I'm on my knees. *For you.*"

"Super cheesy."

"You like cheese. And you're already standing." I study her from the ankles up, until my impish grin meets her unimpressed gaze. "Might as well take advantage."

She smirks and peeks at her wristwatch. "I guess I have ten minutes."

"You know I'll only need five."

"You're relentless." Indi cups my cheek. "Did you come here straight from the airport?"

I kiss the warm surface of her palm, scraping my grown-out stubble against it. "Yep. Tell me how much you missed me again."

Her face lights up with a smile before she helps me to my feet. Long arms circle my neck in an embrace, letting me do the same over the stiff fabric. It's not the only thing stiff against her hips. "The chocolate bar said, 'I Miss Your Cock', and it was for a customer."

I move my mouth up her collarbone. "You smell fucking amazing." Like home. "I could eat you up."

"Is that so? You don't want to make good on that threat about shoving yourself down my throat?"

"Fuck yes, I do."

She turns us, guiding me backward around her desk until the backs of my knees hit the seat of her chair. I drop into it.

"No one's out there, right?" The pink tip of her tongue wets her full lips. I nod rapidly.

"I've always wanted to do this." Indi ducks under the desk and pulls me toward her. Her hands skate over the inseam of my suit slacks, fingers tracing the bulge against my thigh.

My grip on the armrests clenches. The button and zipper melt under her touch, my overeager dick as wet as I imagine she is. She reaches under the elastic waist of my boxer briefs to stroke and pump me, spreading pre-cum before exposing me to her warm mouth.

"My dirty fucking girl," I groan as she suctions around me.

When she gags, I can't help but throw my head back. Sweat resurfaces, a fresh trail dripping between my pecs and downward. The chair squeaks with every bob, taking me closer and closer to the brink.

Wood slams against the wall. "Why is it that I'm always halfway home before realizing that I forgot—"

Indi and I freeze.

"Mr. Radek?" A helmeted Bea purses her lips. "I didn't see you come in."

Stretched brown eyes peer up from below, mouth still stuffed with my pulsing cock.

"You weren't at your desk—"

Bea takes off the bike helmet and twists her mouth to the side, humming in wonder. "It must've been when I went to the break room to grab my lunch container."

"Must've been," I echo with a nervous chuckle. Indi's tongue lashes side to side and my thighs clench. So does my asshole.

"I meant to come back here but...why are you sitting in *that* chair?"

She glares at me, then scans the office. "Where's Indi—Ms. Davé?"

My eyes fight the panic, staring straight ahead at the closed washroom door. Look sharp, Radek! "*Uh*, well, she had to..."

Indi slowly licks me, and I turn the muted groan that escapes into a throat-clearing noise.

"...Use the washroom. Her chair looked comfortable."

Excited stars appear in Bea's dark eyes. "Isn't it?" She puts a finger to her lips and lowers her voice to a whisper. "Don't tell her, but I sit there when she's not around. The recline is chef's kiss."

"It reclines?" A crooked smile tugs at my lips. "Like this?" I tip back twice—*squeak, squeak*—choking Indi under the table. My balls recoil.

"Yes! Fun, right?"

"Yep, *ha ha. So* fun." Sweat beads drip past my temples.

Indi glares back at me.

"Anyway, have you had a chance to look over the availability chart I sent over? We'll need to go over some things with you before meeting with Ms. Pall and her attorney."

"I haven't, but I'll have Trevor get back to you."

"Perfect." Bea goes to leave, but facepalms and sputters. "I almost forgot again." She rummages through her bag. A file folder drops onto the desktop with a smack before she flips the helmet hanging from her fingers atop her head. "Gotta go before the road gets too icy."

"Stay safe, eh?" I return the wave she gives me, then wrench myself away from the desk with a backward roll.

Indi pops her mouth off and rises to her feet.

I tuck myself in. "*Christ*, woman. We almost got caught."

"'*Stay safe, eh?*'" She scrunches her nose, posting a hand on each of the armrests. "What was that all about?"

"I don't know!" I wave an arm around. "What was I supposed to say? 'I can't think clearly because your boss was sucking me off so good before you barreled through?'"

Something mischievous glimmers in her eyes. She straightens and goes to the door, locking it with a loud *click*. I stand, too, but don't get far before she returns. "Now we won't get caught." Her fist yanks at my tie, bringing my ear to her lips. "You have no idea how wet I am right now."

It's not long before Indi takes her seat and I find out. She guides my hands to remove her soaked panties, then swipes my fingers into the wetness.

I gasp. "You want my mouth, baby? Show me where."

Those garnet-painted nails trace a line up her stretched inner thigh. My lips follow their trail to the glossy space at the cleft of her legs as she spreads wider for me. "Here." Two fingers part her slick pussy and tap her clit. "Right here."

I gorge on her, impatient and noisy. Kissing and lapping at this drenched cunt as her knees settle on my shoulders. Licking and sucking until her hands tear at my hair and pleasured whimpers cry for me, heels digging into my back as her arousal trickles down my chin. My lips swell around her throbbing clit, sending her off the edge with a strangled scream when my finger curls against that sensitive soft spot inside her.

Indi whines when I moan and clean her satisfied pussy with my tongue, coating her over every surface of my mouth. My dick's died and gone to Heaven. She sighs and glances over at me with groggy eyes. "You have a little something—"

The pad of her thumb sweeps against my bottom lip from where the remnants of her release drip. I push it across the upward curve, spreading it like Chapstick. She stills in the swivel chair. Mirroring the switched position she had me in earlier, I get off the floor and lean in, hovering over her mouth. "Wanna know how you taste?"

Her lush lips part before closing. The flush across her cheeks blooms. "No kissing," she says, sounding less convinced than ever.

I grab her throat, gripping the hinge of her jaw. "Who said anything about kissing?" Her cum gathers on my tongue, mixing with my saliva. "Open that pretty mouth wider." When I spit into it, Indi moans and snaps her legs shut with a judder.

Fuck me. I shake my head through a laugh, then draw back to my position over her lips. "You taste like the sweetest secret."

An obnoxious knock on the door brings her back to life with a jolt. I press my forehead to hers, pinning her to the spot, not ready to lose the moment while trying to transfer my thoughts to her brain. I don't want us to be a secret anymore.

"Ms. Davé? It's Wally." The knock peals out again. "I need to take the trash."

Her hand clutches my shirt in the space over my heart, flattening the palm smooth for the shortest time before gently pushing me off. "One moment!"

My mind refuses to accept defeat. Not when Indi offers me glimpse after glimpse of who she really is. Loyal. Brilliant. Kind-hearted, but reserves it for those she fully trusts. And I want nothing more than to keep being one of them.

———

Before warmups, I unload my gear bag and sneak away to meet Indi. No one will bother us in this corner of the arena. Or so I thought.

A hushed voice grows louder as I near. "*Wow*. You look great." After a pause, another voice replies.

"Aren't you married?" Indi asks.

"Almost *not* married." He chuckles. "Down if you are."

"You're *disgusting*."

"Oh, Indi. You don't believe that."

My steps hurry in their direction, ready to tear whoever it is limb by limb.

"Ms. Davé?" I call, hating how informal and distant that title sounds.

Indi hugs her slumped torso, wrinkling my jersey. It's a shadow of her usually confident, proud posture. Terrified eyes peer over her shoulder before she turns back to the jerk facing her.

It's the Dallas Comets' newest risk. Russ Kleinmann's a notoriously dirty player. I haven't seen the guy since he got back from playing in Europe. "Kleinmann."

"Radek." He scoffs. "See you on the ice." His eyes slide to Indi, who flinches when he reaches to touch her elbow. "Maybe we can catch up after the game."

No, you fucking can't.

Kleinmann slinks away.

Her eyes gloss over with a layer of held-back tears. Rage stews deep in my gut. I retract it, trying to maintain some composure. "You know him?"

Indi clasps herself tighter, shrinking from me. I can't let her fade away now. "He...in uni..." She gazes at the damp cement floor in the once-path of the Zamboni.

I connect the dots. My teeth clack together, the veins at my temples filling with angry blood. A single tear rolls off her chin. I catch it and rub it into my palm. "What did he do?" When she doesn't respond, I lead us into an unlit nook and hold her sweet face between my hands. Indi's body eases up. "Tell me."

If it wasn't for the pure fury burning inside me, my heart would rip in half hearing what this sleazy motherfucker did. Indi goes numb recalling how he tried to sleep with her. How he couldn't get it up and made it seem like her fault. Made her apologize and humiliated her.

My knuckles crack as my hand turns into a fist when she says he leaked private pictures of her across campus.

She seems to sense the storm brewing and grabs one of my suit lapels, but I'm too far gone. Even her touch won't calm me. "Landon, don't do anything you'll regret. Not for me."

I cover her hand with mine and release myself from her grasp. "Go to your seat."

Earbuds and a stoic expression keep the boys away while I get dressed. Once the rink opens for warmups, I tune out, shifting my narrowed eyes from Indi to that scumbag on the other side of the red line. He laughs and skates around, missing almost every practice shot into the empty goal. I want to murder him but settle for accidentally bumping him on my way off the ice. He slides into the glass. "Watch out, asshole."

Kleinmann throws his hands up. "What the fuck, man?"

Luck pairs us at the faceoff circle.

"I've heard things about you, Kleinmann."

The bastard huffs and smirks.

"Name suits you. Kleinmann: little man," I chirp.

He doesn't bite. "Whatever."

"Little man, little limp prick. Heard it's broken."

His mouth guard goes loose from his snarl. "Where'd you hear that?"

"Word travels."

"From that wannabe puck bunny, eh? Gotta steer clear of those."

My pulse drums in my ears at a deafening volume, nostrils flaring and sucking in shallow gusts of cool air. Everything else mutes: the crowd, my confused, angry teammates. All I hear is coming from his stupid fucking mouth. Murder. Murder is a good option now.

"Fuck you. Let's go."

The whistle blows.

"Did Indi tell you how desperate she was to be my cumslut?"

I get rid of my stick and gloves. So does he. There's no going back. I clinch his hockey sweater with my bare hand, falling for his baiting. No one talks about Indi like that and walks away clean. My fist crashes into the side of his head, knocking off his helmet. His jaw crunches from a jab as we spin and slide across the ice. He swings aimlessly, missing me several times.

"Too bad the bitch couldn't suck cock if her life depended on it," he laughs through my hits, blood spilling down his cheek. I topple him over with a roar.

"Piece of shit!"

His hands fly to cover his head.

"Tiny dicked" —my fist lands on his eye— "motherfucker!" His cheek and chin take the next blows until the refs and captains pry us apart. Jaeg shoves my gear into my hands as the ref pushes me toward the penalty box.

"That's enough. Go cool off, guys. Five minutes for both of you."

"I should know," Kleinmann keeps going. "The bitch opened that big mouth of hers for me anytime I wanted—"

Breaking free from the ref and tossing my shit aside, two strides close the distance between us and tackle him. "You're fucking dead!"

In the scuffle, he manages to land one on my lip. I hurl bloody spit in his face before we both get thrown into the sin bin.

The flames of outrage continue to lick at my insides and my stick takes the brunt of the outrage, breaking into pieces from my rough slamming. When I look for Indi, her spot is empty. *Fuck.*

Coach yells with a threatening fist to the glass. I don't hear a damn thing he says. Kleinmann's filth repeats in my head.

"Go fucking do your job!" I scream back. He benches me for that.

Halfway through the first period, Kleinmann checks Wade behind the net. I have to be held back from jumping over the boards to help Jaeg, Olsen, and Szecze. They knock him around and end up in the box, too.

At intermission, I complain about not having played even a minute and almost throw hands with the GM. "One more fucking outburst and I swear you'll spend the rest of the night in the locker room."

"Send me fucking home," I seethe. "Ask me if I give a shit."

"Get it together, Radek," Jaeg pipes in. "The fuck has gotten into you?"

I get in his face. "You didn't hear what he said about—"

"*Landon*." He cuts me off, saving me from outing myself and calmly puts space between us. "You're fucking out of line. Sit your ass down."

I warm the bench the rest of the night and skip press to hit the showers. Indi never comes back to her seat.

ME

Where'd you go? You okay?

Her car isn't at her apartment building. I wait for thirty minutes before getting shooed from the curb by a meter maid. I drive back to my place and pull in next to her Audi.

"Indi?" My footsteps thud through the penthouse. "Indi!" I sigh with relief at finding her curled up under the covers in my bed. In my jersey. Just how it should be. "Baby?" I climb in next to her.

She casts a pained look in my direction.

"Say something."

"I didn't want to go home."

"That's okay." This can be your home, too. I want to be your home.

Her sorry eyes fall on my busted lip. "You're hurt."

I wince when her fingertips meet the open cut and force a dry chuckle. "You should see the other guy."

"*Landon*." Indi tuts. "What did you do?"

"You didn't see?"

She sinks her teeth into a corner of her lip. "I couldn't be in the same space as him."

I've never seen Indi make herself so small, so timid. That fucking idiot crushed her sweet spirit by showing up.

"You didn't miss anything. It was a shitty game. Mostly brawls." I don't know if it's okay to touch her right now, but I'm dying to. "Can I hold you?"

"Please." She arches her waist from the mattress to allow my arm to slip under. "Did you win?"

"By a penalty shot."

"Ouch."

"Doesn't matter." I pull her to my chest. She slots against me, notching her bare legs between mine. "I couldn't let that prick talk shit about you."

Indi hides in my neck. It melts away whatever remains of my anger.

"What'd he say?"

My lips rub against her hairline. "I'm not gonna repeat it."

"Go ahead." Her eyes shut and brows raise. "Can't be worse than the truth."

CHAPTER 42:
YOU'RE NOT SUNSHINE,
YOU'RE A DARK, FULL RAIN CLOUD

INDI

LANDON FEELS LIKE HOME.

He's a safe haven, comforting in an expected, familiar way that sates my anxious soul. Like the reassuring, cozy welcome of your own bed after long hours at work or many tiring days of travel, the much-needed, if not slightly forced, embrace from loved ones after time apart, or the clean snap of a perfectly tempered favorite brand of chocolate.

The hardened shell of my heart has been chipped away by his unceasing affection. And the more I surrender to the belief that what we're doing right now is temporary, the more he shows up for me. The more he proves himself as above and beyond any dusty notions of love I'd resigned for myself. I tell him the truth.

"He's right. I was desperate." Shame and guilt wrack through me. "Of all the women on campus, he'd chosen my dumb ass."

"Stop that." A wispy stroke of his hand across my cheek sends goosebumps down my spine. "I hate when you talk down to yourself."

"I believed the lie, you know? Not initially, but he wore me down. Flirty study sessions, stopping by my dorm room with puppy dog eyes. I thought he really liked me." The stubborn, growing lump in my throat grates at my voice. "For a thousand bucks, he had to prove he got the campus prude to go down on him. He took a picture, saying he wanted to remember me like that forever. His friends thought it was photoshopped. So, he invited me to a party, convinced me to get on my knees in the bathroom, and conveniently left it unlocked so we could get caught."

"Fuck."

"I'm sorry I left, but I couldn't handle being in the crowd. It took me back to watching him play junior hockey league games in uni."

"It was worth decking him." Landon sighs. Stormy blue eyes searched me as the muscle in his jaw rippled. "Did he force you?"

It's a hard admission. "Only the first time."

His eyebrows dip dangerously low. "That's one too many."

"I didn't know any better." My head shook. "Thought that I'd done something wrong."

"You have nothing to feel guilty about. He's a pile of shit." An angry rumble rolls from his chest.

"Well, I'm not exactly sunshine and rainbows."

"So, what? That means you're allowed to be treated like that? That you don't deserve respect or consent? That's bullshit, Indi." He brings his leg over mine tighter, drawing our hips together, nothing between us except two scrappy sheets of clothing. "No, you're not sunshine. You're a dark, full rain cloud, ready to burst. You wring yourself out and pour into others."

Goosebumps on my back spread like wildfire, searing my insides in their wake.

"You deserve it all. Everything you want." His first finger traces the number on my chest in an unspoken act of possession. One. Two. Twelve. "I hate that he took advantage of you. I wanna undo all of it. I wanna erase him from you, Indi. You're mine."

Landon spends the next eight hours cradling me to sleep. Nothing sexual. No suggestive movements or lines crossed. Exactly what I needed. I woke before him, and his peaceful, handsome face has another admission dancing atop my tongue. *I love you.*

I return to my apartment in near tears and go straight to the shower. But his smell still kisses my skin. As I ready to head back out into the cold, his text appears.

GYM GUY

> I hate not waking up next to you. Wanted to feed you breakfast.

ME

> Had brunch plans with the girls. Raincheck?

ME

Had brunch plans with the girls. Raincheck?

GYM GUY

Literally anytime you want.

ME

Maybe after we settle with Pall.

———

A line of gray and black suits chatter quietly outside walnut double doors: Landon Radek, Cooke Wagner, Jules Tryon, the team's GM. Reps from the Regents' PR team whose names I can't remember. Which is fine because Theresa's got it covered. She whispers to a nodding Wagner.

Bea fires up her tablet, testing out the documentation software. She and I stand out like injured thumbs. While Bea chose a tan, almost-gold suit that makes her creamy skin glow, I opted for a favorite: my maroon power suit.

Some of the men sniff through nervous breaths, straightening their ties and fixing shoelaces. Some unbutton and rebutton their jackets or fiddle with their fingers at their sides. I check my phone one last time before silencing it. Notifications on the family group chat catch my eye and I can't leave them unread.

DAD

Good luck today, love!! YOU'LL SMASH IT!

ME

Thanks, Dad

MOM

Call us after. Best of luck we love you!!!!

ESHA

She doesn't need luck. Her litigating skills are SUPERIOR

ME

Nice try, Esh. Stay away from my green lehenga. Find something else to wear for your Winter Formal.

ESHA

DIDI PLSSSSS

NIK

It's too late for all that. You already opened up the blouse to fit those big boobs.

DAD

Lalalalala I'm not hearing this

ESHA

YOU LOUDMOUTH

NIK

You're right, you're not hearing it. You're reading it.

MOM

Don't talk back to your father!

ESHA

Why'd you have to say boobs in front
of Dad! RIP

ME

I can't with you guys.

Sliding my finger across the screen to power the phone down, I tuck it into my purse and hand the bag to Bea. Landon stares ahead, his usual kind eyes cold and glossy. I choose my words carefully in my approach. Can't risk any raised brows.

"Feeling okay?"

He blinks away his inattention. "Yeah. You?"

"I'm good." A polite, professional smile will have to suffice. "This is almost over. You trust me?"

"Yes."

"Good. We'll stick to the plan," I address the rest of the crew and motion to the doors, tightening my grip on the briefcase handle. "Time to go."

Annalise Pall and her legal team await us inside. Oliver Coffey, the greasy bastard that's her attorney, stands beside her in a gaudy, but expensive tawny suit. Like a glorified car salesman. I've never had the unfortunate luck of facing him in court.

"Ms. Davé," he calls, extending a hand across the enormous mahogany conference table. I give it a solid shake in return. "Glad we're finally getting to meet."

"You can thank Judge Packard for that. Shall we get started?" The nerve of this guy. He only showed up because we got a court date.

"Please." His hand opens to the chairs surrounding the table. We all take our seats. Landon and Theresa flank me, while Bea sits behind. My briefcase opens with the clapping of its metal closures. I remove three folders and line them up on the tabletop before handing the empty case to Bea.

"Our offer to settle is straightforward," I announce.

Pall fixates on her nails, seemingly bored. She's beautiful in a socially conventional way that I could never be, and I have to stop the jealousy buzzing inside my brain.

"We require a public apology by your client."

Coffey scoffs with a sneer. "I think you've got it twisted, Ms. Davé. If anyone is owed an apology, it's Ms. Pall."

I nod, my mouth turning downward with fake surprise. "Is that so?"

"Her reputation has been sullied by—"

The *smack* of my folder harshly flipping open interrupts him. I pass a stack of clipped-together papers to him across the table.

"What's this?"

"We obtained it from the cellular phone company. It documents the texts exchanged between your client and Marshall Langley in the first two weeks of January. He's a photographer for the Daily News. Ring any bells?"

Coffey shrugs a denial.

"It's the publication that first posted the private picture of my client on June fifth. Other print and internet media sources circulated it in the weeks to follow."

I let my findings sink in.

"As you can see, she initiated the conversation. I've highlighted the important parts for your convenience."

Pall scans up and down my torso. "You're pretty." She glances next to me, a disgusting, sugary grin stretching her mouth. "Your lawyer is *very* pretty, Landon."

I don't know what she's playing at, but it won't work. She doesn't know him. Addressing him to make it seem like it makes me wanna slap her silly.

Theresa chimes in with a gruff command. "Coffey."

He responds by placing a hand in front of his client and shaking his head with closed eyes. The ring on his pinky finger glints at me with every page turn. Emotionless, he leans to the side and whispers something in Pall's ear, then faces me again.

"That doesn't prove anything."

He must think I'm as incompetent as he is.

"It proves intent." I brace myself for the next question. "Is there anything you can provide that proves your client's claimed promises from Mr. Radek?"

A pause passes.

"Don't worry, I've got you covered. Last page of the packet shows that my client had never used Ms. Pall's contact in his phone after entering it. That's not really conducive to having a conversation, much less a relationship."

"Relationships can be secret," he retorts. "Your client made sure of it."

Landon tenses and straightens in his chair.

"There's not a trace. No emails, no clandestine meetings. In fact, I have several eyewitness statements from the Regents organization. Prior to the night when the photograph was obtained by Mr. Langley, my client had only met Ms. Pall three times, and only at team events where many were present. They attest the two had little interaction."

"They had a verbal—"

A hiss escapes through my teeth. "Unfortunately, that's hearsay. It doesn't hold up in court."

Another set of papers gets pushed across.

"Let me catch you up to speed, Mr. Coffey. On January fifteenth of this year, Ms. Pall transferred five thousand dollars from her LLC—*that's her business account in the U.S.*—to Mr. Langley."

Pall gasps as her green eyes go wide. "How did—"

He cuts her off. "Don't say anything." Coffey's eyes lower with a twitch to the signed statement with the receipt of funds.

"Two weeks later, after a tough game, Ms. Pall showed up at a bar that the team frequents, sidled up to my emotionally vulnerable client, and took the opportunity she'd planned with Langley."

I shift my gaze from Pall to Coffey. The color of her face doesn't hide her seething.

"Your client hasn't been truthful with you. She hired Langley to take this photograph and agreed to split any profit he made from selling it. And she waited six months to do so. At the perfect moment when my client was at the peak of his game and had everything to lose." My finger taps the tabletop, pointing toward the papers in hand. "Page five shows every payment made to Langley from various publications. Page seven shows that half of every payment was wired to your client's account the following day."

Landon fights a smile. Theresa props her chin atop her clasped hands. Wagner and Tryon raise their eyebrows and share a knowing look.

Coffey drops a loud gulp in the noiseless room.

"I don't know how good you are at math," I continue. "But I'll make it easy for you. Ms. Pall earned four hundred thousand dollars off of that single photo in a month." Pall's nostrils flare at me as her lawyer murmurs in her ear once more. "That's twice her *yearly* salary while she represented the Ottawa Regents."

Her fists clench on the conference table as Coffey loosens his tie and wipes his upper lip. "I have a counteroffer. My client will pay fifty grand to cover emotional damage and loss of possible wages earned."

The absolute gall. I return a series of disbelieving blinks. "You're *joking*, right? Is that supposed to cover the losses my client and his team bore? The disruption of their playoff streak cost Mr. Radek the potential of two hundred thousand dollars alone. Not including the harm to his privacy or marring his otherwise spotless reputation as the Regents' alternative captain."

Rising to my feet, I lean on my hands and jut my chin forward. "Lucky for her, my client doesn't need or want Ms. Pall's dirty money. There are only two options, Mr. Coffey. Your client will make a public statement to the press within thirty days, redacting her previous allegations and admitting they were lies with the intent of tarnishing Mr. Radek's image, and she'll donate her earnings from the photograph to the charitable organization of my client's choice. Or we can go to court, where I guarantee" —by the harrowed look in Coffey's eyes, the threat isn't lost on him— "you'll see firsthand how good I am at winning."

Pall protests quietly as she and Coffey discuss in the corner. Landon beckons with a finger, but all he can mutter is a *Goddamn* toward my ear before Coffey agrees to our terms.

Confidence rolls through my chest as I accept congratulations from my boss and Landon's reps before we exit the space. Even Pall scowling at me while being ushered out can't bring me down.

On the walk toward the curb, that same confidence pounding through my heart is replaced by renewed fear. It could be us, me. We may not have a relationship, but we have a trail of damning evidence of what we've done. What we're doing. Shit, shit, shit.

The group splits: Wagner, Tryon, and the PR reps in a car, Bea and Theresa in a cab, while Landon leads me to the limo his team arrived in.

"Walk. I told them I had to speak with you in private." He greets the driver, casual as ever.

My chest is about to fold over on itself. How can he be so calm?

"Hey, Patrick. Mind taking me home?"

Patrick lifts two fingers in a silent *message received*.

"What're you listening to these days?"

"I tend to stick to holiday music this time of year, sir."

"Perfect. Have at it, my man. Turn it up as loud as you'd like. There's something I need to discuss with my attorney." Patrick nods from the rearview mirror's reflection and hits the button to lift the soundproof divider.

My eyes burn and I shut them tight, willing the onslaught of emotion away.

Landon's broad palm on my leg slows my runaway breaths. "That was brilliant. I knew you were smart, but, *fuck*, baby. You're spectacular. Seeing you in action..." He puffs out a breath and reaches to clasp my hand.

"I'm scary, eh?"

"Not even close." His hand pulls mine into his lap, shifting it over the blatant, stiff bulge. "It made me so hard." Barely giving me time to gape, he pivots to the limo floor, sinking down until he kneels between my bent legs. "Watching you put those assholes in their place was hot as fuck." The deep pink point of his tongue swipes at his full bottom lip, a devoted gleam in his lust-filled gaze. "Took my fucking breath away."

My thighs go stiff under his feather-light caress, his nose grazing up the inseam of my pants. He stops at the clip holding the suit slacks closed. "Can I take yours away now?"

I blame the stress for saying yes, and before I can rethink, my pants are at my ankles, my knees are hooked over his shoulder, one hand buried in Landon's hair and the other's wrist straining within the limo's hanging overhead handle. His hot mouth ravaging my wet center sends me barreling through an orgasm, so explosive and unrestrained, I go limp in his arms immediately after the high ends.

Landon kisses the sweaty baby hairs framing my forehead and wipes me down with one of the complimentary hot towels. I fix my hair and makeup in the dropdown mirror as his kisses continue down my neck. He only stops with a short peck under my jaw when we pull up to his building. "I'm gonna need you to come upstairs" —his groan wafting past my ear, hips lifting to adjust the scrunching of his pants— "and suck the life out of my cock."

I do.

His arms twine around my hips as I check our calendars for the next week. "You've got road games until next Thursday and I'm out of town for a long weekend."

"Where ya goin'?"

"Snow tubing with the girls." I toss our phones next to where Landon sits at the edge of his bed. "We always do something adventurous to celebrate Gabe's mom."

"Sounds fun. It's her birthday?"

"Death anniversary. Or it was a month ago, but Gabe wasn't able to get away."

"Oh."

"It's a tough season, you know? Fall and winter have all the holidays. She has her dad, and she was really little when it happened, but still. There's, like, family stuff going on everywhere and we get together at Diwali, but I've been planning these trips every year since we roomed together at uni."

Landon lets out a content hum at the inadvertent strokes my fingers leave against his beard-covered jawline.

"It gets harder to coordinate as we get older, but I don't wanna give up the tradition yet."

"I admire you more today than I ever have." Blue eyes soften into mine. "And I don't know if I've said so, but you were already up there."

———

An unpredicted storm traps us at our lodge on the Adirondacks. We lucked out and arrived the night before it hit, but they won't open the slopes until the snowfall slows.

Gabe pokes at the fire, which hisses and crackles in reply. Sheena hands out spiked hot chocolates in the cabin's campfire mugs to Gabe, then Bea in the leather armchair. She sheds the serving tray on a side table and gives me a mug before settling into the opposite end of the L-shaped couch.

After the first sip, I feel watched. And I'm right. They're all staring at me. "What?"

They exchange suspicious looks.

"This is an intervention," Gabe begins.

"Intervention?"

"About your sex life."

"My sex life is fine, thank you very much." I take a larger, guilty gulp of my drink.

They roll their eyes in tandem.

Hey, that's my job.

"Uh-huh."

"Yeah."

"Totally fine."

"Glad we cleared that up," I sass back, but almost spit onto the sheepskin rug when Sheena throws out a question.

"When were you going to tell us you're in love with Landon Radek?"

"Sorry?"

"You thought you were so sneaky," she says. "I've known you forever, Indira. You took on Landon as a client and, what? Coincidentally started a situationship with the mysterious Gym Guy? After not giving any man a single second of your time for the past seven years?" Sheena scoffs.

Gabe and Bea hide knowing smiles behind their hands. Traitors! The whole lot!

"Do you know what you sound like when you talk about him? Your voice goes all gooey, the same as it did when we were twelve. It's not like with anyone else. Not Manu Varma or Griff in high school, not Russ Kleinmann at uni. It's always been Landon. It's never been anyone but him."

"*Wow,*" I intone. "For someone who sobbed out Hanuman Chalisa at the first sign of turbulence on our flight down here, you're getting bold."

Bea chokes on her sip of boozy hot chocolate. It splatters onto her chest, staining her fair skin and neckline.

I clap my hands together in prayer, scrunch my eyes shut, and imitate my best friend. "Jay Hanuman gnan gun sagar! Jay Kapis tihu lok ujagar!"

She fumes. "You're so annoying!"

"Who are you, anyway, The Great Nurse Detective?"

"Enough!" Gabe butts in. "You think we couldn't tell between the lovelorn look in your eyes and the 'client emergency' in the middle of that Diwali party?"

I take a flabbergasted swallow. "You knew, too?"

"Please. *Pfft*. I figured it out after that two-on-two game at Fit365. How stupid do I look? '*Sucks that we didn't run into Gym Guy.*'"

Another guilty gasp escapes me.

"I guessed it when he threw those heart eyes at you while playing against Vancouver," Bea adds. "I still wanna know what you bet? Was it blowjobs or...?"

"*Fuck*! Fine!" I halt the onslaught with a held-up hand, then cover my eyes. "I can't believe you all knew." The whine I force out is childish and desperate. "Is this what you wanna hear? I'm stupidly in love with him. We *were* messing around, but he's so good to me and perfect and I love him. I love him, okay?" I take a long breath before crumpling into the sofa. "What am I supposed to do now?"

Bea clears her throat, breaking the momentary silence. "You're supposed to tell him."

CHAPTER 43:
THERE'S CANNABIS IN THIS?

LANDON

GETTING A CALL FROM YOUR LAWYER'S SECRETARY after hours is never a good sign.

"Mr. Radek—er, Landon?"

"What's up, Bea?"

Her chuckles staccato. "Not much, not much. It's..."

I take a generous gulp of water while waiting for her to finish the thought.

"We, *um*, we have a *situation* on our hands."

The chilly marble counter cools my post-shower skin as I lean against it. "What kind of *situation*?"

"My tummy feels funny. Like a sauna." Indi's groggy voice in the background sounds off whining sirens in my head.

My pulse skyrockets. "What's happening?" I leave my water behind and pace around the kitchen island. "If it's something to do with Indi, you have to tell me. *Now.*"

Surprisingly, it's not weird being this informal with Bea. I thought anyone finding out about us would force me to take daily blood pressure medication, but relief washed over me when Indi told me her girlfriends figured out I was Gym Guy.

"So" —Bea takes a deep intake of air— "I may have had far too many rum and Cokes at home last night, which led to a marathon baking session at a godless hour. And when I woke up in the morning, since there's no way I could eat all those brownies on my own—*it'll go straight to my hips*—I brought them to the office to share, and everyone *loved them*. Like, really, *really*, loved them. They were such a hit, at least until things started getting wonky and then I realized I've done something horribly, terribly wrong." She exhales.

"Wrong? "

"I, *um*, have the *slightest*" —her voice squeaks— "*vaguest* recollection of maybe, possibly, very probably baked something special into it."

"Something special?"

"Yeah, *special*." Her words go static like she's cupping over the phone with a hand. "I put weed in it."

"What?" The blood drains from my face.

Indi gasps, panic apparent in her tone. "Behraz! Holy shit. There was cannabis in this? Oh, God. Oh, God. I ate two."

"Two?" Bea calls away from the receiver.

"Yes, two! Count my fingers: one, two!"

"Bea? Bea! Hello? Stay with me." I snap, but it's no use.

"That's *two* many," she addresses Indi. "*Ha, ha*. Get it? T-w-o, too many?"

My fingers pinch the bridge of my nose before hauling ass into the bedroom to get dressed. What a fucking disaster. I try not to laugh, but it's too ridiculous. This girl served her entire office pot brownies.

"This is no time for puns, Irani! How am I supposed to drive? You're gonna have to give me a ride home!"

"*Um*, I don't have a car anymore, remember?"

"Indi? Bea? Anyone listening?" I switch to speakerphone and scramble into a few layers of shirts to brace for the cold.

"Uh, *hiiiii*." My girl responds from the other end of the line.

My call to her is muffled through the sweatshirt I'm pulling on. "Hi, baby. What's going on?" The neck of my hoodie finally releases the headlock it's got around my skull, allowing blood to pump to my brain again. "I'm worried about you."

"*Welllllll*, my carless legal secretary fucked up and I haven't eaten anything all day except for those two pot brownies and now I'm high— *which is legal, by the way*—and can't drive—*driving while high is definitely not legal*—and Gabe didn't pick up her phone because she's an airplane right now."

"Gabe's an airplane?" I scratch my head.

"Yes."

Bea wails as I stuff my feet into sneakers. "There's not an Uber available for the next forty-five minutes. Likely because everyone in the office was tripping balls and took them all. *Shit*! I'm gonna get fired!"

"You're not gonna get fired! I won't let them. But, Landon, you sweet angel, hockey bro of a man."

I snort. She called me a hockey bro.

"Listen to me. Listen to me carefully. I'm already feeling strange, and if I wait forty-five minutes, I might wander off before the car gets here and end up taking a swim in the river." Indi audibly facepalms, then whines out a groan. "Can you...can you pick me up?"

Without looking, I snatch a set of keys off the rack, leaving the rest clanging on their hooks. "Of course. On my way. Does Bea need a ride, too?"

"No, she's going home on her *bicycle! Bicycle! I want to ride my bicycle! I want to ride my biiiike!*" Indi falsettos Freddie Mercury, then cuts herself off with a grumble. "The little druglord didn't eat any of her own marijuana goodies."

"Okay, good. That's good. Have her stay until I get there."

Driving the Porsche wasn't part of the plan. Actually, nothing about any of this was part of any sort of plan. Thank God, they've cleaned the roads from this morning's snow. The tires squeal and shriek through every turn on the slick roads.

I call Bea to let her know I'm at the curb. She and Indi trot out in pea coats and scarves, arms hooked, avoiding the dark patches of ice. Indi's work bag's strap crosses her chest, bouncing at her hip with each step. She's in better shape than I expected. She's got balance. She's got grace. Indi straightens as they draw near.

"She's all yours." Bea nudges her closer and pats me on the shoulder. "Good luck."

Indi's head lolls to her friend, eyes glazing over. "You're a beautiful, magnificent lamb."

"Yes, I know. You're lucky to have me. Thanks for coming. Text me when she's safe at home." Bea waves us off as she walks to the bike rack.

Indi drops her raised hands into fists at her hips, glaring at me. "And what" —she points a rigid, gloved finger to the white car behind me— "is that supposed to be?"

I shake my head, swallowing a laugh. "It's our ride. Let's go."

"No. *Way*. There's *no* way you'll fit in there." Her head sways, then halts. "And don't say 'that's what she said.'"

Don't say it. Don't say it. Don't say it.

The goofiest grin splits my face. "That's what she said."

In a huge, melodramatic wave of her arm, she smacks the side of her head with a palm, knocking her center of gravity off-kilter.

I catch her, pulling her upright against me until the shell of her ear brushes my mouth. "And if you're talking about something else, Indi." My breath freezes in the air. "I promise you, I'll fit."

"Okay, Mr. Smartypants." She pushes off me and wobbles to the passenger side. "Take me home."

I salute her, then open the door before she can, sliding the bag from her shoulder before buckling her in. "Good?"

She blinks three times and gives me a dopey smile.

"I can't tell if that's a yes or a no."

"I spelled it out with my eyes. Y-E-S."

Oh, boy.

"Thank you," she says meekly once we pull away from the curb. Removing a glove, she threads her fingers through mine and rests the joined hands on her thigh. I internally swoon, color rushing up my neck and face. Indi belts out an operatic note in place of what I think is meant to be a sigh.

Her eyes follow the trail of passing light outside. "*Whee!* Look at all the colors. So pretty!"

I hold back a smile.

"*Beep! Beep!*" She presses her finger into the glass. "I can almost taste them." Indi smacks her lips.

It's so wrong, but my shoulders shake with laughter. "You're hilarious. I love you." My breath immediately hitches.

Indi gives me a slow-motion, open-mouthed smile of shock. "*Whaaat?*" Her free hand whiffs at the air as she pshaws. "Olives are disgusting."

Fucking hell. This is not how I wanted to tell her.

She goes silent again for the last few minutes of the drive, running a hand over her nose, cheeks, eyebrows, and chin, as if she's only now discovering them.

I offer to help when she struggles with the apartment door. "Okay, schpoopy," she sings, wagging a lazy finger at me. "But no funny business. Keep your hands" —she holds up her palms and wiggles her fingers— "to yourself."

Indi starts a tilted descent down the wall.

I prop her up with my body, pinning her to the door as I unlock it. "That's not what you said when my tongue was in your tight cunt last night."

A blush slathers itself across the apples of her cheeks.

"I believe your exact words were, '*Please*, Landon. Touch me—'"

"*Shhhhhh*—shut up, you naughty! The neighbors will hear."

The door gives as I turn the handle and my hand lands on her lower back to prevent a fall. "Don't kid yourself, baby. Guaranteed they've already heard you."

We go vertical again and she drops her bag and coat on the hardwood as the door snaps shut behind us. I get down on one knee and move her hands to my shoulders.

"Hold on. I'm gonna help you out of these shoes." The zippers on her boots are frozen and it takes a minute to lower them enough so she can step out.

Indi cracks her ankles and sighs, slumping her shoulders. "Am I naked yet?"

"No." My hand finds hers. She squeezes it. "But I'll get you some water and help you into your pajamas."

A soft whine buzzes against my neck as I finish buttoning her flannel top.

"My head hurts. And my nipples told me I'm cold."

She shudders and doesn't protest when I scoop her up. Mollified after I tuck her into bed, her eyes droop.

"You're going now?"

"I don't have to. You want me to stay?"

Please, for fuck's sake, say yes.

I move a few messy strands away from her face. The stark, angled cut grew out since we met this summer. Her waves are in full flood, effortless and as gorgeous as she is.

Her hand grasps my wrist, holding it in place over her jaw. "The truth or the lawyer lie?"

"The truth. Always the truth."

"I want you to stay. I want you to stay so much." She nuzzles and leaves a tender kiss in my palm. "And that's exactly why you can't."

"What do you mean?" A laugh exits my nose while pushing her hair back onto the pillow with my fingers. "Of course, I can stay."

"That's so tingly, but you can't. Because if you stay tonight" —Indi's body relaxes further— "I'll end up kissing you. And I'm afraid if I kiss you, you'll kiss me back and I'll fall in love with you."

Sounds good to me.

Her eyes tug downward in the corners, keeping a fresh coat of unreleased tears at bay.

"I'm afraid of wanting to fall asleep in your arms every night and waking up there every morning. I'm afraid of telling you all that because then you'll say this was all fake. That it was a joke."

"*Baby.*" My heart clenches painfully in my chest. "It's not fake. It's not a joke."

She hums. "Faking jokers say stuff like that. You don't fool me."

"It's nothing like that." Resting my forehead against hers doesn't seem to help ease her fear. "Tell me what you want. I can almost promise it's what I want too."

The murmur is ignored. "I'll be humiliated, and it'll hurt worse than when you leave tonight. So go, Landon." Indi shrugs my hand off. "Go, before we both do something we can't take back."

I don't move. I don't want to take anything back. I want to move forward. To fall asleep with her in my arms and wake up next to her drooling on my shoulder. "You're breaking my heart, Indi."

Her eyes hang closed. "Better yours than mine."

"You don't mean that."

She returns a soft snore in reply. My head and heart battle, not knowing for sure if that was genuine or not. I stand from my squat to cover her with a heavy comforter, then pad across the apartment to fill a glass of water for when she wakes.

I check the door lock as I leave, regret sobering in my gut. My head knocks into the back elevator wall.

Indi probably won't remember this whole conversation in the morning. And I don't know how I'm supposed to forget.

CHAPTER 44:
BEST PART OF MY DAY

INDI

"THIS IS SO WEIRD."

Gabe, Sheena, and Bea's faces float within boxes on my iPad screen. The continent-wide blizzard halts my travel back to Ottawa and leaves us all in different cities: Gabe stranded on the West Coast, Sheena in Chicago, and me in Brampton with my parents.

"There's a first time for everything, I guess. Were you able to rebook your flight from Calgary?"

"No." Gabe stretches her neck side-to-side.

"You found a polka band in a U-Haul van?"

Sheena snorts.

Gabe glares. "Hilarious. More like a stuffy bus alongside walking, talking, overactive sweat glands with swamp ass and four shared brain cells." She shakes her head at our inability to catch on. "We hitched a ride with the Bears back to Vancouver and drove across the border to Seattle."

Bea pops the jet-black visor on the motorcycle helmet open and whines, completely ignoring my brilliant comedic delivery and Gabe's disgust. "*Lucky.* I want a big hockey boy to crush me like a weighted blanket."

Gabe rolls her eyes. "I was *working.*"

"Same." Sheena adjusts the curl of her lash line, then turns to face us once more. "Twenty inches of snow doesn't stop babies from getting sick."

"Damn," I chime in. "It's like you never left Canada. They're having you come in?"

"Perks of being essential medical staff. The hospital doesn't have enough nurses as it is."

Snap. Snap. Bea's visor clacks as she flaps it open and closed. She stops when we fall silent, realizing what she's been doing, and lets out a sheepish smile. "Sorry."

"What is that thing?"

"It's a motorcycle helmet."

"And why do you have one?"

She tips it up onto the top of her head. "My brother gifted it to me. Apparently, I'm too clumsy to be biking around in winter unprotected. No trust in me, these people."

The rest of us intone in a somewhat-agreeing chorus. "It *is* kinda dangerous."

"Yeah, the roads get so icy and slippery—"

"I'm *fine*," Bea responds, waving us off. "I got a set of those snow tires and everything. Parwaz caught me switching out the wheels and gave me the helmet, ranting about how if I wasn't gonna listen, I could at least be safe." She flips the visor a couple more times. "It's kinda fun, though."

"And we love that for you. Okay, what else?" Sheena taps her watch by the camera lens. "I gotta leave for my shift in, like, ten minutes."

Leave it to Little Miss Organized to keep us on-task. Before I can bring up everyone's holiday schedule, Landon's FaceTime request interrupts. I hum, swiping the notification away. She notices.

"What's going on?"

"Nothing. Radek's trying to call, but I declined."

"*Nooooo!*" Bea laments. "Why'd you do that?"

"You should add him here." The surprise from Gabe's suggestion writes itself across my face. "What? Radek's sweet. There are a lot of assholes in professional sports. Like Boehner." Her eyes slide to the right, glaring at the thought of the Regents' goalie.

"What's he done now?"

"Stop deflecting!" Bea erupts in a chant. "Add him! Add him! Add him!" Sheena laughs and Gabe agrees, joining in the antics.

I give in, throwing my hands up. "This is the first time he's dealing with you vultures all at once. Be cool, eh?"

I send a warning text, letting Landon know it won't be a private call. He's a fucking saint for putting up with me after the Pot Brownie Debacle. The whole night was a barely-pieced-together fever dream.

"It's not fake. It's not a joke."

"Tell me what you want. I can almost promise it's what I want, too."

And did I really tell him if he stayed we'd kiss and I'd fall in love with him? I'm afraid to ask and find out for sure.

"*Please.* You underestimate us." Sheena tosses a few glossy, straightened strands of hair over her shoulder. "We're the *coolest.*"

"Ladies!" Landon sports his classic, dimpled smirk. "How are we doing today?"

The girls titter through their replies, even calm, collected Gabe. Her blush peeks through those freckled cheeks. So much for being cool. Landon Radek could charm the pants off a tree, if trees wore pants.

"What's new?"

"We're doing a virtual brunch because of the storm."

"That's adorable. Hey, Gabe. Behraz." Landon does a weak salute and pulls a hand over his chin, the long beard hairs sending a scratching noise through the call. "Wait a minute, who's this? The infamous Sheena?"

"That's *me,*" she sings, batting her lashes. "Nice to finally meet you. And thanks for following me on Instagram."

"For sure. My sister loves you."

"Wow, really?"

And she says *my* voice goes all gooey. I glare, then call into the phone. "Akhil! Come get your wife! She's flirting with a ridiculously handsome professional hockey player who makes a hundred thousand times more than you do—"

"Ridiculously handsome, eh?" Landon's tongue peeks from the corner of his smirking mouth. I ignore the reaction. "Tell me I'm not the only one who heard it."

Gabe confirms with a snap, waving an accusing finger like a gun. "She did say that."

"He's on-call, you troublemaker." Sheena's eyes roll. "*Anyway,* I almost forgot to ask about everyone's holiday plans. Akhil and I are with family both weekends and working in between."

"I'm taking my dad to Miami." Gabe reclines, miming putting on large sunglasses and tilting back as if lounging on the beach. "There aren't any games to cover on Christmas Day and he deserves a break from the nursery after the holiday season. He's been wanting to go to a flower show there for years."

"*Aww*, that's sweet," Bea adds. "We're leaving for Tanzania the day after tomorrow to celebrate my grandmother's ninety-fifth birthday. What about you, Indi?"

"Nothing for me," I say with a shake of my head. "My parents are in Leicester for my dad's friend's daughter's wedding." The ladies share a giggle at my long-winded answer. "And my sisters are driving to spend the weekend in New York with some friends. I'll probably watch *The Holiday* and *Elf* on repeat in my pajamas while scarfing down chocolate-drizzled popcorn until I pass out."

"Alone?" Landon tuts. "Unacceptable."

I shrug. "It's not a big deal."

He runs over the top rim of his mustachioed lip with an index finger, humming. "My family's getting together at my grandparents' farm in Bala. You should join us."

"Oh, *uh*, I—" My soul circles the pit of my stomach.

Bea drops the visor closed. "*Bum bum bum, bum pa dum, bum pa dum...*" Her voice deepens to bellow out Darth Vader's theme song intro. She hangs up without another word and the other two follow suit.

"Silly me, I lost track of time. Gotta leave for work!" Sheena announces. Her box disappears.

"Would you look at that? My grilled cheese dinner went cold. Guess I have to remake it." Gabe waves demurely. "Bye!"

Cringe. I wrinkle half of my face. "Sorry, my friends aren't discreet."

Landon perks an eyebrow. "Did she say 'grilled cheese dinner?'"

"Yes. Yes, she did. She makes the most wicked grilled cheese sandwich. Crispy, crunchy crust and perfectly melted cheese." The thought makes my stomach growl.

Landon beams with a smile and my heart beats itself into a puddle. "That's funny."

"What is?"

"All I'm saying is, let's hope Wade never finds out. Bro is obsessed. He'll fall in love with her or something."

"You're joking, right? She'd never feed *anything* to that guy. Except maybe poison. Those two hate each other."

"I wouldn't be so sure. Sometimes I feel like they enjoy giving each other shit."

"Maybe Boehner does. Gabe on the other hand..." Landon's inattention has me trailing off. "What are you doing?"

His thumbs tap on his phone. "Sending a text to the family group chat to let 'em know you're coming to Babi and Děda's."

I wince. "I don't know if that's a good idea. How are we supposed to explain—?"

Without looking up or missing a beat, Landon states, "They already kinda know about you."

"They do?" Ex-squeeze me?

"Yeah, I told them before the season started that my lawyer was an old teammate. They know we're friends."

More than ever, I hate that word between us with a fiery passion. I wanna murder it with a broken plastic spork. "Right." My gaze drops to these nervously dawdling hands against the countertop. "*Friends.*"

"Don't do that." Landon pulls my focus back up. "I know what you're thinking, but don't you dare. We're not *just* friends, Indi. They don't need to know that. I'll tell them whatever you want, as long as it means you'll be there with me."

It doesn't take much convincing. Christmas on a farm with Landon sounds perfect. "Okay."

"You'll join?" I nod and he punches a victorious fist into the air. "*Yes!* It's gonna be great, I promise. Delaney sucks, but everyone else is cool."

"Everyone? Who's everyone?"

"My parents, Dad's boyfriend, Steve, Del and her husband, Seth, and the kids. Plus Uncle Phil and his wife Natalie, Uncle Toni, and Aunt Nina. And my cousins, Gary, Mike, Crawford, Addie, Clara, Mags..."

"That's a lot of people."

"Don't back out on me now. If you're worried about them figuring us out, I suggest you keep those wandering hands to yourself." Landon pulls the panels of his zip-up closed, splaying a hand over his chest as if clutching pearls.

I return a dramatic eye roll. "Let me write that down so I don't forget."

"Indi," his voice drops, nearing the camera. "Sassy girls get spanked," he warns, the naughtiest smirk stretching across his lips. "Or is that what you want?"

I gulp. It's not *unlike* what I want. "No." My thighs clench. "So, I'll see you on Saturday?"

"Can't wait."

———

Slush squelches into the rocks beneath the rented Jeep. An arched metal sign reading *Jezera Cranberry Farms* hangs above the entrance, creaking with every swing from the blowing wind. Distant rooftops of a barn and another building glitter with snow, the various frozen lakes and ponds on the property looking more like glass than ice. Like a winter wonderland.

Landon responds to my text by gunning through the white hills in a blue pickup truck, idling it when he jogs up to unlock the side gate. His classic gray toque atop is expected, but the camel-colored Carhartt coat layered over a blue flannel and work boots catches me off-guard. And don't get me started on the white Henley peeking out below his neck. He gets back into the truck and waves for me to follow, then motions to stop while he parks in the clearing by the barn.

When he hops into the passenger seat, I'm still gaping at how he fits right into the countryscape with his rugged brown beard and outgrown hair. "Welcome to the farm, baby." He leans over the console.

My pulse swells. "Thanks," I whisper, unable to tear my eyes away.

"How was the drive?"

There's a lag in my thoughts.

"Indi?"

"Yeah?"

"You're staring."

My jaw snaps shut.

"It's so cute." He half-chuckles and flicks one of the two poms on my winter hat. "Fuckin' adorable."

"*You're* so cute." The snappy retort rushes out before I can stop it and it doesn't bite as much as it was supposed to.

Landon's wind-burnt cheeks flame as he accepts the compliment with an easy, lopsided smile. "I know." Two taps on the dashboard signal for me to drive ahead. "Go that way. I'll show you around."

This place isn't *like* a winter wonderland, it *is* a winter wonderland.

While they're closed the week between the holidays, Landon explains, the winter season is usually packed with customers. We pass a series of ice-skating ribbons looping around the property and a walk-up cafe stall. The shop where they do wine tastings and sell the farm's cranberry pastries and jam looks like a shut-down Santa's workshop in the light of day.

"Wait until you see it at night," Landon says. "You'll feel like a kid again."

Tucked into the far back corner of the farm lot, behind a line of evergreens, is a pristine white farmhouse. Holiday wreaths decorate its windows and white Christmas lights are threaded across the soffits. The narrow path to the left goes to a smaller house about a thousand feet away. Landon guides me to the shared driveway. He points left.

"Babi's got you all set up in the cabin. My dad got it renovated recently. You'll be the first to use it." Once he drops my weekend bag off at the smaller cabin, Landon doubles back onto the shoveled walkway to the main house. "Come on. I want to introduce you." His excitement would be infectious if I wasn't an anxious wreck.

Solid wood stairs and the boards that make up the front porch whine as we climb them, and the strangest feeling pulls at me when I step inside. I've never been here before, but a nostalgic scent and warmth welcome me. Landon leads through the spaces in a quick tour. The thirty-person table in the dining area does nothing to distract from how perfect his ass sits in those worn jeans.

"Mom? Babi?" he calls.

Quiet chatter and laughter get louder as we approach the hearth room in the back. It peters out when Landon claps his hands together to announce his arrival. "There you are." A low sound grumbles from his throat. "*Great.* Del's here, too."

I gulp as he moves aside, stilling his hands mid-air from moving me forward by the lower back. Instead, he pushes them into his pants pockets. Is he nervous, too?

"This is Indira Davé."

Goosebumps rise under my heavy layers.

The two women get to their feet from the plush couch facing a wood-burning fire, their gazes softening from Landon to me.

"Hi. Nice to meet you," I force out as they exchange glances. "And everyone calls me Indi."

"Mom? Hello?" Landon shakes his head as the awkward non-response lingers.

His mom blinks. "Daisy. I'm Daisy." She takes my extended hand and doesn't let go. "Sorry...you look...have we met before?"

"I was thinking the same," his sister adds with a curious smile. "*Huh*."

"Oh, *uh*, I don't think so." I turn my head to Landon, silently asking for help with widened eyes.

"*Jesus*," he mutters under his breath and rubs a hand over his eyes. "Where are your manners, guys? What happened to 'Hi, how are ya?' or 'Merry Christmas?'"

The eldest of the women places a fist on a hip and cups her cheek, tilting her head at me. "*Hmm*. They're right. Something very familiar."

"Not you, too, Babi." One of Landon's arms drapes over his grandmother's shoulders. "You're supposed to be the normal one."

She grabs my other hand between both of hers. "Never mind. I'm Jana. Welcome!" The same mild smile as Delaney's creases around her mouth. "You must be hungry after that drive. Come, lásko. I made sweets."

Landon pouts. "I thought *I* was your lásko."

"I can have more than one lásko. Don't be a whiner." Babi beckons us, shuffling toward the kitchen and complimenting my gray peacoat before Daisy puts it away for me.

Landon sloughs off his coat, too. I fix the hem of my sweater where it bunches at my hips, losing my focus on the task from him folding his sleeves up over his forearms. Drool.

"Where's everyone? I was hoping to surprise the kids."

"Seth and the dads took them to check out the new routes. They'll be back in a sec," Delaney explains. She knocks the back of Landon's head with an open palm while he's chewing on the last of his pastry, causing him to choke. "And that's for sneezing onto my pillow and turning off the light while I was getting ready this morning."

He pokes his middle finger into her eye, still coughing.

"*Oww!*"

"Will you two behave?" Babi scolds. "If not for us, then for our guest, at least. Or you could make yourself useful and help me prep this bramborový salát."

His sister sticks her tongue out at Landon and joins her mom at the sink to peel potatoes.

"No svíčková?" Landon asks.

"Tomorrow. Traditional Christmas dinner tonight."

Amidst my large, graceless bite of a buttery apricot kolach, the front door slams open. Two sets of footsteps pound across the floor, shedding miniature snowsuits as they barrel toward us.

"Uncle Landy!"

Landon turns from the island and raises an eyebrow. "Do I know you?"

"It's us! Sadie and Gunnar." The girl takes off her knit hat, her blonde hair sticking up with static. She does the same with her brother, revealing another head of mussy blond hair. "See?"

"*No way!*" He gasps, bending over with his hands on his knees to get to their eye level. "The Sadie and Gunnar I know are still babies."

"I not a baby!" his nephew protests.

"Not a baby, eh?" Landon palms the entirety of Gunnar's head as tiny fists fail to meet his thigh. He scoops up the little guy and throws him over his shoulder with a roar. Sadie jumps and tugs at his pant leg, screaming to be lifted. He gives in, tossing her up with one hand, then pelts them with noisy, growled-out kisses as they squeal and giggle, wrapping their tiny arms around their uncle's neck. "You're still babies to me."

Ow, my ovaries. They're exploding.

"Who's that?" His niece points in my direction.

Landon's smile brightens. "That's Indi. Wanna tell her your names?"

Gunnar curls up into a ball against Landon's chest, going shy.

"My real name's Sarah, but my *nickname* is Sadie." She places a hand on her brother's back. "And this is my baby brother Gunnar."

"It's nice to meet you both."

Sadie cups a hand over Landon's ear and attempts to whisper. "Is she your girlfriend?"

I redden.

"Sadie!" Daisy chides.

"Well, she is a girl, and she is my friend, but no." He winks. "Wanna know something, though?" Landon murmurs something into his niece's ear that evokes a giggle.

"Me tooooo," Gunnar whines.

"*Uh-uh*," Sadie denies. "Issa a secret." When she smiles at me, a dimple forms on her cheek, mirroring the one her uncle wears.

"Alright, that's enough." Delaney pries them off of him. "You two still need to wash your hands." She herds them toward the washroom.

Landon straightens as two men walk up. "Indi, this is my dad, Leon." Leon leaves a kiss on his son's head, which is the sweetest thing I've seen since the interaction with his niece and nephew two seconds ago.

"His partner, Steve. Del's husband, Seth. And here comes Děda."

His grandfather is almost as big and broad as Landon. He removes a glove to silently shake my hand.

"Thanks for hosting me for the weekend. You've got a beautiful home."

"Can you believe he designed it? Helped build it." Pride and admiration weigh in every word. "Děda was an architecture graduate in Prague before moving here. Then Babi fell in love with the farm—"

"The cranberries reminded me of those in the Jeseniky mountains—"

"—And the rest is history."

Děda nods at Landon's conclusion as he joins his wife on the other side of the kitchen.

"Barto, do you recognize her?"

His frown deepens, declining with a grunt.

Leon snaps and taps Steve's chest with the back of his hand. "Hey, I thought so! Where would we know you from, Indi?"

"I mean, she's a pretty big deal," Landon brags. "You probably saw her on the news during that case with Senator Pearson."

"Maybe," his dad ponders. "*Ah*, who knows? The ol' noggin ain't what it used to be. Maybe you've got one of those faces."

"Yeah." I chuckle. "Maybe."

More of Landon's extended family arrives, aunts and uncles and cousins. He introduces me to each one and they respond with Christmas greetings and give unexpected bear hugs, before messing around and harassing Landon and Delaney.

The joy in their reunion is a bittersweet reminder of being apart from my own family. I slink away down a hallway behind the kitchen and through a door, hoping to wallow in isolation, but don't get far. Landon appears behind me and turns on the light. What I thought was a washroom is actually a walk-in pantry, organized in labeled glass canisters like something out of Pinterest.

"What's going on? You okay?"

"Just missing my parents and sisters, I think." My arms hug my torso. "I don't know if me coming here was a good idea. This is your family's Christmas. I don't really belong—"

"That's not true," he cuts me off. "You belong here. With me. You can't go now." His eyes search mine, frantic and pleading. "My family likes you."

"They like me?"

"Yeah. They're being weirdos about it, but they do."

"They don't even know me." I step back, cutting the temptation of touching him by another foot of space. The wall behind me doesn't give me any more room.

"Whatever they know, they like. Same goes for me." Landon closes in, propping his arm over my head. "And I want you to stay."

"Okay." I glide my eyes to the shelves on the right. "Whoa. This is a nice pantry. "

"We can't mess around in here, my family's right outside." Landon teases out a smile. "*Indira*," he chides, "you have such a dirty mind."

"That's not what—I do *not*." I totally do.

His gaze flicks to my burning, stretched cheeks. "Then why are your dimples out?"

"I like when you say my name."

"But I say it all the time."

My teeth snag the corner of my lip. "Not my full name. Almost everyone calls me Indi, but only those who I'm closest to call me Indira."

Landon takes another step, straddling my feet with his own, the heat from his body enveloping mine, but he doesn't let us touch. "No one's gotten closer than me, hey?" Someone calls his name in another part of the house, and he laughs, dropping his head back and pushing off the wall. "Guess we should get out there."

We emerge and wander toward the living room. "Hold it right there, Landy! Caught under the mistletoe, bud," his cousin—*Gary, I think*— baits us.

We both look to the ceiling at the green sprig hanging in the entryway.

"Rules are rules. You gonna man up and kiss her, or what?"

His eyes land on my lips and mine on his, my face heats again. For the first time, I don't feel like it's a bad idea. But when our breaths meet,

Landon tears himself away, slicing the tension away. "Fuck off, Gare."

"Why don't you make me, eh?"

Landon turns to me for a moment. "'Scuse me. Gary here has chosen violence today."

They take off and chase each other around until Landon catches him. His cousin is taller, bigger, but slower. A couple of the others move the coffee table aside in time, before the two wrestle each other to the living room floor with a loud thud. Sadie and Gunnar stand by the ten-foot-high Christmas tree in the corner and cheer them on.

Babi sighs and shakes her head at the ruckus. So does Daisy. "Every year. Without fail."

Delaney waves me over and hands me a glass of wine. "Welcome to the shit show."

"Thanks." I laugh away the nerves through my first sip, clasping the edge of the counter where I lean. "I didn't want it to be weird, but I remember when you used to pick Landon up from practice. I know it was a really long time ago, but—"

"Oh my God, that's it!" The sudden recognition lights up her eyes. "You were on his team. You two used to sit on the same bench."

"Yep. That's me."

She crinkles her nose. "You guys were so *cute*. And now, look at you. Gorgeous, crazy successful lawyer."

I can't help but blush when Landon's dad chimes in. "We can't thank you enough for your hard work with Landy's case."

"Of course. It's my job." I nod. "And you can thank me when Ms. Pall publicly retracts her statements."

Delaney puts on a mischievous grin. "Now all he has to do is stop sticking his pee-pee where he shouldn't."

"*Laney!*" Her parents say in chorus.

"What? We're all adults here. And it's the truth."

"You're scaring her." Daisy motions to the dining room. "Wanna get away from the chaos for a second? I'm gonna set the table for lunch."

It's a nice escape. She holds back a smile every time our eyes accidentally meet. Hers aren't blue like his, but just as warm. And seem to know something I don't.

Landon catches me yawning after one too many chlebíčky and offers to walk me back to the guest cabin. He turns on the fireplace on his way out and loiters on the front steps, keeping his hands in his jacket pockets and flapping the panels. I angle against the doorframe, crossing my arms.

"You have something to say?"

"Yeah." He chews on his lip. "My family does gifts on Christmas Eve after dinner."

"Uh-huh."

"And we usually play a friendly game on the big pond Christmas morning. Did you bring your skates?"

"They're in the car." If there's something that makes me more nervous than meeting Landon's family, it's playing puck with him again. "No stick though."

"No worries. We have extra. And, *um*...I got you something."

A ridiculously large smile splits my face.

"It's not a big deal..."

"I got you something, too."

"You did?" Genuine surprise reaches his eyes.

"I'll bring it when I walk over tonight." A ripple of excitement bubbles in my chest. "I hope you like it."

He scoffs out a laugh to the side, then takes two strides to meet me at the door. "I like everything that has to do with you."

Dinner plays out like a dream. I divert myself by gorging on my meal, savoring the breaded, fried carp, creamy potato salad, and tart cranberry wine, but between Landon looking completely delicious in a cable knit sweater and the way he runs his eyes over me while chatting with his family, I'm on edge.

Babi has us sitting next to each other and every slight brush of our hands or thighs under the table and not being able to actually touch him is torture. When I accidentally drop my fork and bend over to get it, he palms the corner of the table, so I don't knock my head on the way back up.

Everyone gathers around the tree after. It's decked in golden string lights and traditional red ornaments. The scent of fresh fir and burning wood from the fire blankets the room with comfort. It's not long before presents are passed around. The adults show off new hockey gear, rave over gadgets and pass around wine as the kids tinker with new toys and books.

"Here," Landon whispers, sliding over a glossy, dark red gift bag.

I pass him the neatly wrapped rectangle from next to me. It was supposed to be subtle, while everyone was busy in their own worlds, but the room goes dead quiet.

He goes first, face paling, then flushing at the items. "A sketchpad and Staedtler pencils? *Wow*," he says through a sigh. "Thank you."

His mom and sister throw each other a look.

I stumble through an explanation, trying my best not to be obvious. "'Cause you like to draw. And I figured you haven't in a while."

"That's sweet," Babi coos. "What a thoughtful gift, Indi."

"What'd you get her, Landy?"

Tissue paper rustles as I remove the item from the bag. "Oh."

"*Socks*?" Delaney asks. "You got her *socks*?" She shoves her brother by the shoulder. "You *suck* at giving gifts."

"Shut up." He shrugs her off by his elbow.

"No, they're nice." Which isn't a lie. The knit slipper socks are thick and have a plush fleece lining, but they're not exactly sentimental. "I like them."

"They're grippy on the bottom so you don't fall."

"Thanks. I'll get good use out of them." I hide my disappointment with a forced smile. No one seems to notice.

"Time for bed, you rascals," Delaney calls to the sprawled-out kids on the floor. She and Seth carry Sadie and Gunnar up the stairs, waving sleepy good nights. Others get up to do the same and I take the cue to head back to my cabin.

GYM GUY

Your feet are always cold.

GYM GUY

It's adorable.

GYM GUY

They're for when I'm not around to keep them warm.

Any doubts I have about how well he really knows me vanish with his texts. My eyes water for a few seconds and I suck in a sniffle before pulling on the gifted socks.

ME

I'm wearing them already.

GYM GUY

Perfect.

GYM GUY

Anything else on your wish list for Santa?

ME

An orgasm would be nice.

GYM GUY

Same. Wanna trade?

GYM GUY

I'm not beneath begging.

ME

Goodnight, Landon.

GYM GUY

Night, baby.

GYM GUY

> If you need me, I'll be in bed stroking my
> cock to death.

I toss my head back and cackle, kicking my feet at our immaturity.

ME

> You're ridiculous.

GYM GUY

> You love it.

I love him.

ME

> I said good night!

An hour or so later, I replay the green flags of the day in my mind. They warm me better than the cloud-like down comforter I'm tucked under. Bragging about me to his family. Telling me I belong with him. Saying my name. Stopping me from hitting my head. The socks. It all cements the truest thing I know in my life so far: I've fallen so hard for Landon Radek, and I don't want to get up.

"Tomorrow," I say to myself, readying to doze off. "Tomorrow, I'll tell him."

———

Putting on my hockey skates is way harder than I thought. Bea drags me and Gabe down to Rideau Canal at least once every winter, but those are always rentals. The pair in hand are *mine* from fifteen years ago, dug out from basement storage at my childhood home. The hand-me-downs weren't going to last much longer, and Dad bought these brand-new, in a size up, with the expectation I'd continue playing. Instead, we moved, I quit and didn't get to wear them except for the two summers spent working at the Mississauga rink.

I dawdle on the cabin stairs, blankly staring at the entrance to the skating ribbon. Airy voices carry across the distance of the quiet farm, which means some of the Radek's are already on the lake. My breath clouds as I sigh.

"Merry Christmas, Indi." Landon saunters over in classic hockey boy strides, skates tied together over the shoulder of an all-black, limited edition Regents jersey. "Forgot how to lace up?"

"Merry Christmas. And *no*." Pride takes hold and I quickly switch out my utilitarian winter boots for the skates, but they don't feel right.

"Can I help?" He drops his pair to one side and kneels on the step below me.

"I do like it when you're on your knees."

His dimple-topped smirk matches mine. "Don't I know it." Strong fingers slip under the unfinished lacing. "Your laces are good and flat. Let's see if I can remember how you like them."

My head tilts, curious and unsure.

"Kick your heel back."

I knock both blades into the wood riser.

Landon counts the eyelets and pulls horizontally at the laces by my toes. "First and second, really tight." His fingers move up, the sear of his touch through the leather-like fabric making my feet go sweaty. "Three, a little tight. Four and five, super loose." He taps against the skate. "Now, six will be really tight again." Every tug is more satisfying than the last. "And these top two are gonna be snug."

A fantasy teases, dragging me away from the moment. What if I kiss him now?

"A nice solid knot up here to finish you off..."

Yes. Please finish me off. "We'll adjust the tongue..."

Tongue, definitely. But before that, I'll tell him I love him and he'll kiss me back and say, "Indi, forget about the stupid game. We're going inside and staying there."

And then I'll say—

"How's that feel?"

"*Hmm?*"

"The skates. Stable?"

We lock eyes. "Perfect." I'm not talking about the laces, though it's true. "How'd you remember that?"

Landon takes a seat next to me, gaze dropping to his fists as he ties on his own skates. "We were so sloppy with our laces. Me, all of us guys." He repeats the lacing pattern. "Coach got so pissed when he saw how we rushed through it. He told us to get serious and watch how you do yours. I don't know if any of them listened, but I did. And I've never gone back."

My insides go molten. Landon Radek paid attention to me—laces his thousand-dollar skates like I did as a kid.

"Ready to go?" His fingers fidget against the thighs of his grey sweats.

"Yep."

Every incessant, nervous thought swirls and expands until the moment we step foot at the mouth of the route. The ice beneath me mutes the internal noise. But not the external.

"Wanna race?"

I slide my eyes to the side in Landon's direction. "Not everything is a competition."

"Isn't it though?" He waits for a response.

I give him one. Without counting down, I take off.

"You're such a cheat!" He huffs while catching up.

"Losers always say that when they're *losing*." I try to shove him into the snow barrier, but he regains balance and narrowly escapes around the sharp turn. Frozen cranberry bogs flank us and disappear. We share childish laughter while rushing down the last stretch to the big pond. I strain through inhales at the bottom. "I win."

"Yeah, right. Cheaters get disqualified."

The aunts and uncles linger at the opposite bank while Seth and Delaney hold Gunnar's hands on one end. Sadie teeters about nearby as others set up the nets. One of his cousins uses a passer to practice. They're all wearing different Regents hockey sweaters and pommed toques. Daisy and Babi wear his Michigan ones while standing to the side. His sister wears Jaeger's jersey, probably to piss him off.

I stick out like an obvious outsider in my simple puffy jacket.

"Crawford!" Landon asks for sticks and gloves with grabby hands. His cousin tosses two sets over, and he heads back to offer one to me before returning to the middle.

I slide on the extra gloves and get acquainted with the weight of the stick, testing the various movements.

Gary shoots a puck into the t-bar with a loud *ping*.

"Nice snipe, asswipe!" Landon yells through a cupped hand.

"*Language!*" Daisy and Delaney yell back.

"Blow me." Gary barges over and shoulder-checks him.

"Didn't I say *language?*" Delaney's scowling face goes bright red.

"I thought you own a gym. Ever tried using it?" Landon pokes him in the chest with the butt of his stick. They continue to antagonize each other as everyone else groans.

"Enough horseplay." Landon's uncle pries them apart. "If I wanted to freeze my ass off while watching grown men bitch, I'd have stayed at work." He whistles and calls the rest of the adults over.

"It's like no one cares that I keep saying '*language!*'"

"Shut it, Delaney!"

"You know the drill. Sticks in the middle."

I end up on the same team as Landon's sister and Dad, and his least-favorite cousin. He, his brother-in-law, and two more cousins, Addie and Clara—*I can't tell the sisters apart*—are on the other side.

"Yes! Indi!" Gary holds up a hand for a high-five. "My team."

I offer a weak slap in reply. "Oh, *uh...*"

"Heard you played with Landy back in the day." He nudges me with his elbow.

Landon's jaw ticks from across the way.

"I did, but that was a long—"

"Bet you'd like to kick his sorry, cocky ass, eh?"

"*Hmm.* That is enticing." I tap the stick on the frozen surface and flick my eyes over to Delaney, then Landon. "Let's do it." She winks at me.

Her brother narrows his eyes, smile going downright evil. Uncle Phil readies the puck and Gary and Landon face off in the middle. I hang back with his sister.

"Pond rules: Four *vee* four. No goalies, no slap shots. You shoot it, you get it. Sticks down, heads up. Watch out for the kids, and don't be a cherry-picker."

Everyone nods and gets into position. When the puck drops, Landon breaks away and goes for a goal by skating a circle around us. It goes right in. He moonwalks in celly.

Delaney rolls her eyes. "Show-off." She smiles my way. "Watch this."

We lose the next possession, but Delaney tricks Seth into passing it to her while Landon argues with Gary. Leon gets control of the puck and I tap it into the net. Landon realizes too late and holds up a gloved finger. "That's the only one you get."

"We'll see, *Landy*."

The satisfaction from the goal is short-lived. His team wins the first game, fair and square, before switching up players. I take a few minutes to keep an eye on the kids with Dêda while Daisy gets some playing time.

"I'm glad you're here." It's the first time Barto's said anything to anyone this weekend, at least within earshot.

My mouth stays hanging open as he continues.

"He's the most loved, the youngest Radek." His crossed arms tighten, never taking his gaze off the game. "I haven't seen him this happy in some time. There's a light in his eyes. And if I were to guess, from the way he looks at you, it's because you two are closer than you're letting on."

A lump swells in my throat. "How does he look at me?"

His slight grin pulls at the silver goatee portion of his beard as he focuses across the pond. Babi furiously waves, boasting a giddy, joyful enthusiasm at her husband while showing off her stick handling. "Like she looks at me."

Sadie's yelp from losing her balance interrupts us.

"You okay?" I call out.

She nods and rolls over to pull herself upright, taking wonky steps until she plops herself between us.

"You're doing pretty good out there."

She huffs and pushes her helmet up from where it falls over her eyes and squints at me. "It's hard work."

"I know, eh? That's why I'm taking a break." I lean into her. "I can show you a trick if you want."

Her ruddy face sparks with a nod.

I skate backward from the edge so she can see. She toddles after me, walking one foot on the ice after the other. "Now try it like this." With bent knees, I push off my right leg, releasing the weight from my left, and then switch, resulting in a series of glides that aren't nearly as much effort.

Sadie doesn't look convinced.

"Here." I offer both my hands. "Hold onto me while you try. Don't be afraid to push me."

Her strides get longer and quicker as her confidence grows, and it's only been a few minutes.

"I'm gonna let go, but I'm right here, okay? And you can hold your stick if you want."

"I'm doin' it! Look!" She laughs and awkwardly turns after a dozen feet.

I clap as she returns to me. "You *are*! Awesome job." I lower to her level and lift a hand for a high-five. The sweet girl gives it to me.

"I'm gonna show my Mommy. She said she'll let me play when I'm five!"

"Before you go, can I ask you a question?"

"Uh-huh."

"What did your uncle tell you yesterday?"

"That we're still babies?" Her confused expression makes me chuckle.

"After that. When you asked who I was."

"*Ohhh*, what Uncle Landy whispish in my ear?" The loud volume of her exclamation has Landon abandoning the game and hustling over to us. His teammates complain loudly.

"Aw, come on! Where ya goin'?"

"He said he *really* wants you to be hi—"

A black glove muffles the rest of her sentence as Landon cuts her off. *"Nananananana!"* He spins her until she's behind him, out of my sight. "Kids, eh?"

Sadie protests from behind, smacking her stick between his skates. *"Heyyyyy!"*

"Don't 'hey' me, young lady. Secrets are supposed to be *secret*. 'Scuse us." He skates her away from us, tapping his stick on her helmet. "You tryin' to get me in trouble?"

"Nuh-uh! I was—"

Landon shushes her. The thorough glance he takes over his shoulder at me has my heart racing.

His grandfather backpedals upon the prodigal grandson's return.

"Where you off to, Dêda?"

"To clean off the shed behind the cabin. Last snowfall was heavy." He nods upward at the graying sky. "It's supposed to snow again tonight. Can't risk it collapsing."

"I'll take care of it." Landon's chest puffs. "Anyone wanna see the Snowmaster at work?"

Delaney scoffs. "No one calls you that."

Her kiddos have the opposite reaction. "*Meeeeee!*"

"What about you, Indi?" He motions to the skating ribbon. "Come along. Get a taste of farm life."

I follow without question, but not without a jab. "Sure, Radek," I say. "Maybe you'll actually beat me back to the house."

Landon lifts a ladder above his head through the waist-high snow surrounding the shed. "Y'know, this drift reminds me of a story."

His sister makes a rumbly disappointed noise.

"A story?" Sadie asks.

He blows out a sharp breath as he sets the ladder against the roof. "There's a place they call Copperhead Creek, in the Deep South of the United States, right in the heart of the Carolinas."

Gunnar gasps. Delaney grimaces. "This better not be a spooky story. They're too young and last time—"

"*Shhh.* You're ruining it." The ladder clangs with every step of his boots on the rungs.

She pinches between her eyebrows. "I swear to God, Landy, if they grow up to be little psychopaths—"

He ignores her and continues, shoveling snow down the slope of the roof. "Purple wisteria already blooming through the pines, no one expected the Great Blizzard of *wlahhhh!*"

Our eyes travel in an arc as the rest of the snow loosens, releasing a sudden avalanche and launches Landon back into the fluffy snowbank, shovel comically flying off to the side.

Delaney sighs and pats the kids on the shoulders. "Show's over, kids. Nothing to see here."

"*Awww!* I wanna hear the rest of the story."

"Maybe next time." She herds them toward the main house. "You got him?"

I nod and trudge through the snow, then peek over a Landon-shaped cutout. "Need some help?"

"Is this Heaven? I think I see an angel."

"*I* think you've hit your head. Grab my hand, Radek."

He does, but my foot slips and I tumble forward. A layer of snow piles onto us. Landon goes to brush it off my shoulder and misses, his glove coasting across my cheek instead. "My head's fine." His steely eye contact steals my breath as the sky grays, clouds looming overhead. "Indi, can we go inside?"

––––––

The dryer whirs in the background at a steady rhythm as the fire crackles and hisses. I cinch a woolen blanket around me, bringing my knees to the thermal undershirt covering my chest. Other than the pair of cotton briefs I have on, it's the only clothing that didn't get wet. Somehow the snow had gotten inside my coat and soaked through.

Landon pads over in his own blanket, the red tinge from the fireplace highlighting the cut muscle on his shirtless torso. They disappear as he joins me on the rug. I shiver.

Panels of flannel open to let me in. "You're cold. Come here."

"What happened to 'no touching?'"

"We've broken lots of rules, Indi. What's one more?" He scoots closer. "If you're okay with it."

I agree. When he lifts and places me sideways over his lap, I melt into his warmth. It feels right. *He* feels right.

His scruffy chin sits on my shoulder. Gold flames dance against the blues of his gaze. "Did you have a good Christmas?"

"Yeah, I did." My thoughts speed by. To tell Landon, what to tell him, how to—

"What was the best part?"

"*Ooh*, tough choice," I intone. "Definitely watching the shed snow take you out. Highly entertaining." It's a snarky attempt to lighten the tense air between us. "What about you?"

"You." His eyes dart between mine. "Always. You're the best part of my day, every day."

Am I supposed to be breathing?

"Every moment we're together, Indi. It feels like winning."

"I—"

"Just listen, okay? I've been holding on to this for so long, and every chance I get to tell you, it doesn't seem like the right time."

"They weren't supposed to be there."

I return a blank expression. "Who?"

"The boys. Our teammates. After the last practice we had together." Landon's hands clasp behind me. "I thought they'd leave, and it'd just be us. But they stayed, gave me crap and you overheard them. I ruined it."

My lips part in preparation to say something, but he keeps going.

"I wanted you alone—*no Newt, no Bennett, none of them*—so I could ask you to the year-end dance at school." His head tilts. "*God*, I liked you so much, Indi. I wanted you to myself, away from those idiots. I wanted to see what you looked like dressed up, to see if it'd be the same as I dreamed. I wanted to hold your hand."

He hides his eyes by lowering them as his fingers push between mine, laughing through a soft smile and shaking his head. "I practiced how I'd ask you in the mirror. I thought—*or hoped, I guess*—at the end of the night, maybe you'd let me kiss you."

There's no air in my lungs or brain or anywhere in my body. Every last iota has been stolen by Landon Radek.

"You don't think you have any of my firsts, but you do. You were my first crush. There's a slice of myself that I kept for you. I didn't realize it until we met again, but it's always been yours."

Landon releases our grasped hands, guiding my palm onto the left side of his chest, as if showing me exactly which part of him is mine. "I love you, Indi. I loved you—*wanted you*—when I didn't know what it meant to truly want or love someone. I still want you. So *fucking* much."

He lets go of my wrist to run his knuckles under my jaw. "And *goddamn it*, I need to kiss you before I fucking lose my mind."

"Do it."

Landon's as surprised by it as I am. "You *want* me to kiss you?"

"I've been denying it, telling you the exact opposite of what I actually want. Hell, six months ago, I didn't believe anyone could ever want me—and definitely not you. Then you show up for me over and over and I'm tired of lying to myself, to you, about what I know is the truth."

The spread hand over his heart presses down in confirmation. "I love you."

Relief in his exhale encourages my admission. My legs shift to straddle him, blanket sliding off my shoulders and piling behind me.

"I loved you when we were twelve and didn't know better, I loved you when we were sixteen and I hated you too much to give you my number when you asked. And I love you now, after you proved me wrong for thinking I was unlovable."

My hands reach for his cheeks, the bristles of his beard tickling my palms. I slot our faces together, rubbing my nose against his for a final confession. "I have always, always, *always* loved you. It's always been you. So, kiss me. Kiss me like—"

The moment stalls before the hand cradling the back of my head shifts to grab my throat, robbing the rest of my sentence by Landon crashing his mouth into mine like a fierce wave coming in to kiss the lip of the shore. There are no fireworks, only an unexpected and much-needed calm. I sink into its power, letting it deepen and deepen until I drown.

Landon pulls away, but I keep hanging from his lips, parched from the loss of their touch. "Indi." He keeps his eyes closed as his forehead drops to mine. "My heart's beating so fast."

"Me, too."

"I can feel it." He presses his thumb on my pulse. "This all for me?"

"Kiss me again and find out," I challenge. "With tongue. Use it like you do on my pu—"

No hesitation on his part this time, every surface of my body wakes when our mouths connect once more, and his tongue sweeps over mine. I moan against it. His smile stretches.

"Remember what I said this summer? You owe me a grand."

I laugh out a scoff. "You're such a little shit. Shut up and keep kissing me."

My fingers tug at the roots of his hair while I steal the next kiss, this one somehow deeper. The moan he returns...*shit*. I'm so wet.

"*Fuck*, baby. We can make out all day and night if that's what you want."

"That's what I want," I say through a nod and another tongue-filled kiss, savoring how his hand wanders into my hair and arm cinches around my waist. "And I want you to fuck me while we do."

He freezes, something other than the fire blazing in his eyes fueling every ounce of courage it takes to ease from his grip. I take my shirt off over my head. I get rid of my bra, too, slowly dropping both on top of the rug next to us. His Adam's apple wobbles while switching focus between my bare chest and face, but he doesn't move.

"Did you hear me, Radek? I said—"

My breath is snatched away again by his mouth, muscular arms pinning us together as he scrambles to stand. "I heard. Taking you to bed," he says between short kisses. Those large hands squeeze my ass and fix my legs around his waist while walking us across the cabin. "Can't fuck you on the floor."

I get plunked onto the mattress with an animated bounce. I'm wetter now.

"Not today, anyway."

Propped on my elbows, I gnaw at my bottom lip watching Landon stroke himself over his boxer briefs. He stops only to mutter a *fuck* when I shimmy out of my panties, then crawls over me, threading our fingers together in a clinch above my head. His mouth is on mine again as he rolls his hips between my legs. I spread wider, wanting more. A low chuckle rumbles from him as he breaks the kiss, tugging at my lower lip with his teeth. "I'll never get sick of seeing you under me."

Goosebumps trail behind his slick mouth. It drops to the line of my jaw, collarbone, and chest, swerving through open-mouthed kisses. Those calloused fingers skim over the taut peaks of my nipples, groaning as he licks and sucks. I arch at the delicious friction from his prickly facial hair and clench *everywhere* when he lowers, tongue dipping into my wetness, lips circling my tender clit. "You're so fucking wet. I'm gonna slide right in."

"*Mm.*" It's almost amazing that any coherent sentences follow. "Yeah? I hate to feed your ego but you're...y'know." Forget what I said about being coherent. "Really *big*," I emphasize with widened eyes. "Most days it's a struggle to take you in my mou—"

Landon shuts me up with a sweltering kiss, the taste of my own arousal on his tongue blinding me with pleasure and instantly replacing whatever he's lapped up. "You'll fit. You already fit everywhere else. My hands" — one, two, then three of his fingers glide into my core while he nips at the sensitive spot on my neck— "my mouth" —his clothed dick replaces the space his fingers exit, exactly where I want him. "And you're gonna fit around this, too, I promise. You're fucking made for me."

I mutter, delirious from the building orgasm, heart rate in a tailspin. "Yours."

"Don't—not yet." His teasing touch is gone too soon. I catch my breath as the knot of pleasure loosens. "I want you to come on my cock."

He backs off the bed and in a smooth swipe, fishes a wallet from his nearby coat and takes out protection. Time drags on while he undresses before kneeling on the bed to stretch the condom over his swollen length with a single-handed pump. "*Christ*, I'm so hard." Landon leans over, dragging his massive length up my inner thigh. "You're sure about this?"

I sit up to pull his face to me and nod. "I want it to be you."

His gravelly hum vibrates all the way down to my clit when he kisses me again. "Hold on to me," he whispers.

I do.

Landon doesn't stop kissing me as the firm head of his cock sweeps between my folds, rubbing against my needy clit over and over until I judder. We share a gasp when he pushes inside me. I tense at how good he feels, a whimpering mess against his mouth.

"I know, baby," he says, retreating for a moment. "You feel fucking incredible to me, too. And that's just the tip."

"Oh, my *God*."

"Relax." Plucked kisses sound out as his palms cover mine to join our fingers again. "Good girl." He presses them into the mattress with the next agonizing, slow thrust.

I gasp out hoarsely at the amazing stretch.

"*Fuck*. You're so snug."

"Landon—"

He cuts me off before continuing to delve deeper, every purposeful drive of his hips more spectacular than the last. "You still okay? We can stop whenever."

I vigorously bob my head and my toes curl when he's slotted into me entirely, pulsing against the never-reached spot in my core. "Don't you dare. Keep going." My walls tighten.

"Goddamn, I wanted to take my time—make it so good for you."

I peek up at him.

This beautiful man is trembling, each defined muscle—*shoulders, pecs, biceps, abs*—flexed to the max. I meet his deep plunges by bucking my hips as my lunchtime fantasy comes true.

"But this soaked little cunt of yours feels too fucking *good*."

Those filthy words send my eyes rolling back. My ears ring with a rapid pulse.

"I won't last—need you to come, too." Landon lets one hand go, our breaths between sloppy kisses going ragged as he thumbs my clit at the same unhurried pace as his thrusts. "Please, baby? Come all over my cock."

Brazen, shameless, and swathed in the most erotic and intimate experience of my life, I squirm and cry out his name.

He grunts and groans back. "I need you to be kissing me while I come."

The combined pleasure of his grazing tongue, deft fingers, and hardened cock is too much. It throws me over the edge, nails biting into his shoulder blades and vision pinholing through darkness until it flashes white. We swallow one another's throaty moans as Landon stills to fill the condom with a hot, extended release. The high recedes as we breathlessly pant like dogs in heat, wiping the dewy sweat away from our brows.

"Holy *shit*," I say through an exhale. "That was…"

His head droops into my neck. "Unreal."

A smile escapes. "I was gonna say 'quick.'"

Landon pops his head up and gapes, faking a hurt sob.

I snort. "And here I thought professional athletes were supposed to have stamina."

"Take it back." He crushes me under his weight.

"No." I hazily giggle.

Landon pulls out and kisses the lowest part of my stomach. "What can I say? This greedy little pussy's got me in a chokehold." He steps away from the bed to tie off the condom and throw it away in the nearby washroom, third leg still at attention in mid-air. "We've got time. It's only…" He squints at the clock across the room, "…noon."

Looping back to me, he tangles his fingers through my nebulous hair.

I mirror their position, placing my hands into the sweaty pieces on his nape.

"I love you."

A sultry, mind-melting kiss is my initial reply. "You love me?" I smack his round, naked ass. "Next round, fuck me like you don't."

Dimpled cheeks and mischievous eyes take on my baiting. Somehow—*despite the countless condom wrappers littering the cabin floor*—never once do I not feel loved by Landon Radek. Bent over the kitchen island when we go to rehydrate, wearing my ankles like earrings while on his knees, missionary with my legs to the side. We mean to shower but can't help ourselves.

He sandwiches me to the damp tile, and I can't—*don't want to, either*—resist kissing him. Slippery hands move me up, adjusting my legs around him so that one foot lands on his shoulder.

"Nothing compares, Indi. Nothing tastes sweeter, feels better than this right here: your mouth on me, perfect cunt around my cock."

"Faster," I demand, with a harsh tug of his hair, desperate for another release. He goes rough, slapping our hips together. The smacking sounds echo.

"Eyes down. Look at how well this pussy swallows me."

The caught glimpse of him pounding in and out, in and out, has yet another climax barreling toward me. I scream and shatter around him as he bottoms out inside me.

Landon wets his lips, all red from the hours of kissing, taking air through flared nostrils. "You're stunning like this. All flushed and well-fucked."

My shoulders shake, a silent laugh wafting through the steam. "You know, I'm already in love with you."

He kisses the tip of my nose while letting me find my footing again. "And I plan on keeping it that way."

Wayward snowflakes blur the glass window against the dark sky, not unlike my fogged, post-marathon session brain. A lazy smile pulls at my mouth. "I take back what I said about your stamina."

"Glad I could prove myself." Landon hums, thick-lashed eyes heavy with sleep as he peers up from my exposed stomach. His plush lips brush against the soft skin, moving aside the panels of my half-buttoned pajama shirt. "You're real, right? 'Cause you feel like a dream."

I grab our twined hands and kiss his knuckles. "Sweet man. You're so smooth with those lines."

"I mean it." He buries his face into my fresh panties, the satin material and his facial hair giving him a static shock. "*Ow.* Never wanna leave this cabin." His head rises suddenly with a whine. "Do you have to go tomorrow?"

"Unfortunately, it's already tomorrow."

Landon grumbles while confirming the godless hour. His chin pokes my stomach. "Are you sore?"

"No."

"Liar."

"Okay, a little bit. But it's worth it."

The consistent circles he massages there lull the conversation. It skips a beat as we drift into slumber. As usual, he breaks the silence.

"Indi, you're my best friend."

"*Ooh,*" I hiss and click my tongue facetiously while toying with the silken strands of brown hair atop his handsome head. "How do I let you down gently? I already have three of those, and I'm not really looking for anyone to join the crew."

"Right." He snickers. "Silly me. Can I be your boyfriend instead?"

My throat goes dry, heartbeat thudding with excitement. I swoop those rogue hairs on his forehead to one side, grinning like an absolute maniac. "You wanna be my boyfriend?"

His head lolls sideways, dilated blue eyes gleaming in the dim light. "More than anything."

If I wasn't up to my neck in Landon's love and affection already, I'm spilling over now. The answer is the easiest, most natural thing to give.

"Then, yes."

CHAPTER 45:
SECRET'S OUT

LANDON

I JUST SLEPT WITH MY BEST FRIEND. LIKE, *A LOT*. AND now I'm her boyfriend.

Indi willingly handed me her titanium-encased heart. She let me have the precious thing, then made me hers. I'm *hers*, full to the brim with everything she makes me feel. Happy. Whole. Loved.

The warm tips of her fingertips massage hypnotic circles onto my scalp. "Does that mean I'm your girlfriend?"

My hands twitch against the soft, bare skin of her mid-section, "Abso-fucking-lutely."

She hums. "'*Landon Radek's girlfriend.*' Has a nice ring to it."

"Rolls right off the tongue." I flip over so my back hits the mattress, not giving up my spot against her bottom half. "I can think of something else that rolls off the tongue—"

"Crude." Indi lets out the sweetest little yawn. "Will your family be upset that we missed lunch and dinner?"

"They'll get over it." I'll apologize to Babi and Dêda later. They'll understand. Arms tucking under her legs, I squeeze them around my head and leave a loud kiss on one flexed inner tendon. "I fucking *love* it here."

My cell phone is within reach on the nightstand, and I switch on the front camera to show her. "Check out how cute I am between your thighs." They butterfly at ear level as I pump them twice. Squish, squish.

The screen displays her with eyes closed, those long, pretty fingers mindlessly twirling my hair around, but she's lucid enough to respond. "It'd be cuter if you were face down."

"Damn, baby." I peer up. "You trying to make my dick fall off?"

A groggy laugh sounds out, bobbing my head against her belly.

"You're all talk, you know that? Go to sleep." I kiss the velvety skin on either side of my face. "I'll bury my face in this perfect pussy after you get some rest."

I wake before her a few hours later, unable to stop fixating on the fact that, come dawn, she has to leave. By the time I hear her mewl and stretch, breakfast is almost ready.

"Holy shit," she grumbles behind me.

I glance back, one eye on the skillet so I don't burn the eggs. "Morning."

Indi pads up to me in those green Christmas socks, an unevenly-buttoned pajama shirt, and nothing else. Gorgeous, full waves of her hair sit on her naked shoulder where the collar is askew.

"It has *got* to be illegal," she continues after a deep inhale, pressing her chest against my back and placing her hands on my pecs. "To look that good while cooking...?" Her eyes narrow in question up at me, unable to see over the curve of my shoulder.

"Scrambled eggs, turkey sausage, waffles, and I've got an iced latte in the fridge—"

"To look this good while making the breakfast of champions after spending an insane amount of hours railing your girlfriend into oblivion. Absolutely criminal."

"*Oooh*, what're you gonna do?" I switch off the gas. "Gonna turn me in? Cuff me?" My tongue sweeps over my bottom lip while guiding her by the hips to the counter.

"Tempting." Her eyebrow quirks and lips curve upward, adorable dimples inviting the onslaught.

I bring her mouth to mine, hand on her throat. An excited pulse drums against my palm.

She moans.

"First, food." I don't want to, but I break the kiss. "Then you can do whatever you want to me."

———

Indi adjusts her hat in the visor mirror from the passenger seat of her rental as we turn onto the highway. "This is crazy. You should be with your family. I know you don't get much time with them during the season—"

"I'll be with them when I get back." I give her leg a rub before grabbing her fidgety hand and pulling it to my chest. "It's only two hours."

"One way. That's like half the day."

"I'm your boyfriend, Indi. Boyfriends do stuff like driving their girlfriend to the airport."

She gives in with a sigh, knocking into the headrest. "Fine."

I can't seem to let her go at the Toronto airport's car return. Every innocent kiss escalates, growing hungry and obscene. One small taste isn't enough. I want to gorge, devour. Have all of her. Our tongues swipe and lips swell, hands wandering through the layers of outerwear and sweaters. Indi nips my bottom lip and sucks, pulling it away and letting it recoil with a *splat*. We jolt when the attendant taps on the window with his fist, clearly annoyed for blocking the lane for the past thirty minutes. "Sir, are you returning the vehicle or not?"

I glare at him as Indi blushes and wipes the corner of her mouth with her thumb, then angrily hit the window switch with my index finger. It lowers leisurely. "Here." I pull a platinum, heavy-to-the-touch credit card from my wallet.

He's confused and looks at his tablet. "But there's already a card on file for the rental."

"Radek, let's go." Indi tugs at my coat sleeve.

"Just wait a sec, eh?" I turn back to this jerk. "I don't think you get it. I'm not paying for the weekend. I'm buying it, in hopes that you'll leave us alone."

His jaw drops. So does Indi's. "Sorry, what?"

"I wanna drive away in this. Can you get someone who'll help me make that happen?"

Indi's hands slap to her face with a muted groan.

The wise-ass attendant shakes his head and jogs to the office.

She backhands my arm, which would hurt if her mittens weren't so fluffy. "You bought the damn car?!"

"Yeah." My shoulders lift. "I don't have a Jeep. This one drives well, only has a couple thousand miles on it, plus—" I tip my torso over the console. "If it's mine, I get to kiss you however much I want inside it without Mr. Wet Blanket interrupting."

"Buying cars so we can make out, eh?" Her tone chides me, but the smile gives her away. She appreciates the gesture. "I told you, I'm already in love with you." We exchange two short kisses before Indi thwarts me. "I *do* have a flight to catch, though. When are you back in Ottawa?"

I whine. "Tomorrow morning, but I have an early skate."

"So, I'll see you tomorrow night?" The passenger door clicks open. I step out of my side, too, rounding the back to help with her suitcase.

"Yes. Will I survive without you? Probably not."

Indi rolls her eyes. "You're so dramatic."

"I'll miss you." I pout.

"It's literally tomorrow night." Her thumb pushes my lip back in, retracting when I try to bite it.

"Tomorrow night."

Saying goodbye to Indi is like leaving home. That's what she feels like, smells like. That's what she's become. My home. Watching her disappear between those automatic glass doors at the terminal drops a hollow ache in my chest that lingers until I get back to Bala.

I spot Seth and my niece and nephew on the far end of the pond as I pull into the driveway. Them being out there means Delaney is on her own upstairs. The stairs aren't great at quieting my rapid steps and my sister's door is wide open, so it shouldn't take her by surprise when I leap through and belly-flop onto the bed with a Rambo scream.

She groans out her disgust and pulls at the down comforter. "*God,* you're so annoying."

I cuddle uncomfortably close and force her to share a pillow. "That's no way to talk to your baby brother."

My sister scoffs. "Go pick on someone your own size."

"But the kids are out on the ice."

"Exactly." She uses a weak elbow to shove me, but it's no match for my unparalleled strength. My entire palm covers her face in a gloveless facewash, fingers rubbing over her eyes. "*Ew.* Get those crusty things away from me. Weren't you gonna show Sadie and Gunnar how to make those frozen bubbles?"

"Yeah, I will. Maybe in a bit." A wistful noise sighs from my chest.

Del raises an eyebrow. "On a scale of one to ten for how in love with

Indi you are, would you say you're at an eleven or twenty-five?"

I facepalm. "That obvious, eh?"

"*Duh*. Your face has been dopier than usual. You made gooey eyes at her all weekend, disappeared with her after the game yesterday morning and spent the morning driving her to the airport."

"That's not all we did in the morning."

"Gross. *Stop*." She gags. "Yeah, bud. You're stupid in love."

"Aw, *man*. I know." I cover my eyes. It's not often that Del and I are serious with one another, but she's always there when it counts. "I feel like I'm going crazy."

"A good sign, if not slightly concerning."

I pinch her playfully.

She winces. "*Ow*. For what it's worth, I think she loves you too."

"She does." A loopy grin splits my face in half, memories of last night refilling the void of her absence. "Indi told me yesterday." Best feeling in the world.

"So." My sister widens her eyes for a sideways stare. "You gonna marry her?"

"*Jesus*, Del. We *just* got together."

"What?" Her hands fly up, faking innocence. "You love her, she loves you, Sadie and Gunn need friends, *bada bing, bada boom...*"

"Delaney." It's a sterner warning this time. "Will you cool it?"

"Does she know...?" Her question trails off as I shake my head no. She blows out a long breath through pursed lips. "*Ooh, boy*. Let me know how it goes when you bring it up."

I sneer at my nosy sister. "And why would I do that?"

"Because I'm old and I like piping hot tea."

———

We've only had a couple of days away from practice and my body feels it. The physical toll is almost as brutal as not being able to fill the boys in with the news of the weekend, but I can't yet. Indi and I agreed to keep it to ourselves until Pall holds up her end of the deal.

GYM GIRL

You make it home?

ME

Barely.

GYM GIRL

Finishing my workout. I'll shower and head over there.

Lifting one knee after the other onto the mattress is a fucking chore, and I collapse onto it, rolling to my back to wait for my girl. Everything hurts and I'm dying. I fight a losing battle with sleep, but my ears perk when the security alarm beeps out.

"Baby?" I call out sluggishly. "That you?" My tired eyes slit open.

Indi smirks from the bedroom doorway, arms folded across her chest and leaning on the frame in a gray sweatsuit, her hoodie up and socked feet crossed at the ankles.

"Long day?"

I puff out a haggard breath. "The longest."

She intones with a hum and makes her way to the bed, slinking onto it belly-down. Her body seems so far away. I extend my hand and Indi stretches an arm to my exposed chest, her fingers crawling into the dip between pecs. The way her nails scratch my skin—*so subtly urgent and needy*—brings me back to life. Torso pivoting left, I curl my hand between her legs to cup her, a scooping motion bringing her towards me until our bodies slot together. I push a knee to separate hers while nuzzling into her neck, breathing in all that fresh, clean skin while sneaking my hand up the back of her sweatshirt. A momentary homecoming.

She tilts my face up to drop a short kiss onto my lips. "I missed you."

Her murmur coasts past my ear, sending a shiver down to my dick and waking it the fuck up. I shift and hold onto her waist tighter, loving how tight she's got her arms around me, too. Lush lips freckle kisses over my face, jaw, and neck until I can't fucking take it anymore. I crush our mouths together, greedy for more and more of her. My hips rock and grind into hers, cock doubling from the friction as I release my grip on the back of her neck to push under the elastic waistband on her sweatpants' and grab a handful of that firm, round ass.

Indi mewls, her fingers skimming my abs before landing on my big guy below. She gasps as her eyes lower to my outrageous stiffy. "This is from kissing?"

I hold her palm there by the wrist, using it to stroke myself and groan into the crook of her neck. "Secret's out. Kissing you makes my dick wet."

Indi blushes but mischief flashes in those warm brown eyes. My cock swells to an impossible state.

"Take your pants off," she demands, then sits up, arms raised, as a signal for me to undress her. "Me next."

I didn't know I had it in me, but here we are, buck naked at the edge of the bed with Indi sitting on my cock. Her hands layer atop mine where they grope her tits like a bra. Our lips lock as I move in slow thrusts from underneath and behind.

"I love fucking you like this." Every inch disappears inside her again and again. "Love how well you take it."

Her head droops to my shoulder with a loud moan. The ends of her messy ponytail thrash and stick to the sweat on my back.

"Look." One of my hands wraps her throat, forcing her to face the mirror in front of us. The other travels between her legs, spread wide over my thighs for a mind-boggling view of her stretched, dripping cunt.

Indi shudders and claws at my nape when I compress the air from the rigid column of her neck and toy with her clit, pinching a thumb and finger over the swollen bud. My chest rumbles when I accidentally graze over the top ridge of my cock where it enters her. "S-stunning," I stammer between shallow breaths. "I'm about to come from watching myself slide in and out of this tight pussy."

A heated flush creeps up her neck and face. "Oh, *God*." Her pupils blow wide seeing us in the reflection, framed by the steamed edges of the mirror.

A wound knot of pleasure at the root of my spine is desperate to burst open, my balls aching for release as I pick up the pace.

"Tell me this is as amazing for you as it is for me." With my fingers on her clit moving faster, her cries for me turn to gibberish. "Tell me I'm the only one who makes you feel this fucking good."

She whines out a breathy *fuck*. "*Landon*. Only you."

The bounce of her tits as I pound the living daylights out of her is so mind-numbing, I don't feel the sting of her nails digging into my shoulder blade and thigh, tearing through the skin. "*Fuck*, baby. Let go so I can, too."

She comes with a harsh tremor, spilling onto our legs and leaving behind a slick, sticky mess. I chase the last of my own high with sloppy thrusts until I explode into the condom with a labored grunt, holding her over me to drive as deep as possible. The aftershock has her pussy walls choking my cock and I diddle that tiny clit, prying one more quick orgasm from her.

Indi clings to me, then goes lax while I pull out. I prop her against my chest, swiping two fingers into her wetness. Weighted lids hide her glazed-over eyes as I suck them clean, my dick jealously twitching in response to the taste of her.

She grabs my wrist and molds one of my hands around her throat before drawling out my name. "*Landon*."

"*Mm?*"

"Spit in my mouth."

Sex-addled mind fog takes over as I tease my mouth over hers.

"Beg me for it."

CHAPTER 46:
WHEN THE TIME'S RIGHT

INDI

NEW YEAR'S EVE IS ALWAYS A SHIT SHOW. THE WEATHER is beyond freezing, the slushy streets are packed with hammered clubgoers and there's not an empty taxi in sight to save anyone from the elements.

Any other year, I'd be holed up in my apartment with a bottle of wine, a smutty read, and a buzzy nighttime friend, far, far away from the chaos below. Not this year, though, because the Regents are playing in Montreal again and the only way I'll get to see Landon is if I go to Wade Boehner's private postgame party. Which means I have to wear something other than pajamas, likely with absurdly high shoes, and hope to God I don't fall to my death on an icy footpath.

And I'm dragging Bea along. Gabe will meet us after covering the game, too. If I have to suffer, *we all have to suffer.*

Twenty minutes of multitasking in extra-large hot rollers and I've got Jessica Rabbit hair, a killer winged liner, and a classic matte red lip. While I stare at the new dress hanging in my closet, the front door sounds out with a knock. I squint one eye to look through the peephole. A bundled-up delivery person stands on the other side, holding a package topped with brown paper.

"Can I help you?"

"I've got a delivery for" —the paper rustles as he checks the receipt in his hand— "Indira Davé?"

"Oh." I swing the door open. "That's me."

He pulls the wrapping away and hands me a bouquet of garnet dahlias—*flowers I only recognize because of Gabe's green thumb*—in a vase, gaps filled with green sprigs. I flip open the crisp white card. It contains a single, handwritten cursive word: *Yours.*

That one simple word says everything. Who it's from, who it's for, what it is. Encompassing our relationship—*who we are to each other*—so concisely I can't help the swell of my chest or these watery eyes. I pull it together to send him a text.

ME

Got some beautiful flowers today.
In my favorite color, too.

GYM GUY

Sounds like someone's really
obsessed with you.

ME

I wish I knew who sent them. I'd
totally WHTCOAEMPUICAOHF.

GYM GUY

Me!!

ME

I might let him tell me to
STFUATTDLAGFG.

GYM GUY

ITS ME BABY!!!!!

ME

Whoever it is better get their round juicy hockey butt over here before I finish the job myself.

GYM GUY

Nooo I'm already at warmups.

GYM GUY

Great, now I'm gonna be hard for the rest of the game

ME

I'll take it later tonight.

GYM GUY

That's what she said.

GYM GUY

Send me a pic of that pretty face to hold me over??

I take a duck-faced selfie from the exposed shoulders up, showing off the voluminous curls. I'm not naked, but it's fun to tease him into thinking so by keeping the strapless bra off-camera.

GYM GUY

Fucking hell. You're trying to kill me.

ME

Win for me?

GYM GUY

Always

The game goes by quickly, with minimal fights and penalties, as if the players want it to end so they can go celebrate. I watch while getting dressed as the Regents pummel Montreal, and it's a total shutout. Boehner doesn't let a single puck get past him. He and Gabe pop up on the screen for an on-ice interview right as the last period ends. Wade makes some underhanded joke about the Spears' "spears" being small and flaccid. Gabe's controlled expression has me cackling. Poor girl is trying so hard not to bludgeon him with the mic.

GABE

I cannot believe you're dragging me to that monkey's NYE party.

ME

Remind me to thank you after I get pounded tonight

BEA

Braggart!

I'd already dished out all the sweet and dirty details of the previous weekend, but it was still new. It's okay to keep mentioning the sheer amount of sex I'm finally having, right? Right.

Bea and I drive to Gabe's hotel in record time. It's a fucking miracle my feet haven't gone numb from flooring the Audi the entire drive. I whistle when she opens the room door, black bodycon dress flattering her modelesque height. The high slit lengthens her long ass legs. She politely accepts my compliment and ushers us in while taking our coats.

"Hey, yourself." Her tongue clicks out loudly while blowing a chef's kiss. "Someone needs to warn Radek to keep a medic on hand. He's gonna go brain-dead when you show up."

"You think?" I tug the clingy fabric at my knees and smooth down the gold sequins on the long sleeves. They cover the whole dress and shimmer with the faintest beams of light. "Sheena overnighted it when I said I needed something for New Year's."

"Your tits look *phenomenal*." Bea's gaze fixates on my chest, and I adjust the double-sided tape to ensure no mishaps.

"I can't wear plunging necklines. My titties would be out like Janet Jackson." She gives herself a double chin by looking down at the scooped neck of her black cocktail dress, cinched in at the waist to show off her classic hourglass figure.

Gabe and I putter with laughter, then the three of us take four shots of peach schnapps—*surely a wise decision for women wearing impractical heels and dress lengths in the dead of winter*—before miraculously hailing a taxi.

The relief fades as we enter the lofted club sometime after eleven. I wish for an untimely death to save me from the blaring volume of music reverberating inside. No one else seems to be bothered. Me and the girls are the only people here with their fingers in their ears.

"I'm gonna find us something else to drink," Bea yells from a few inches below Gabe and me.

"Water!" we yell back in tandem.

I narrow my eyes, peering through the strobes and multicolored disco lights.

"There." Gabe points to one of the bars on the floor.

Flanked by his teammates, in a dark suit, the top buttons of his white shirt undone, hair combed away from his face, and ruthless dimples framing a gentle smile hidden by the lip of his glass. My outrageously handsome boyfriend freezes mid-sip when he catches me gawking. "Go get 'em, tiger." Gabe slaps my ass to nudge me forward. I yelp. "I'll be over at that table."

Goosebumps pull at my skin as his eyes rake up and down, their striking blue hue sparkling between the obnoxious flashing. "Hi."

Donovan turns a bright, beet red and retreats into the crowd. Boehner's jaw hangs as he shamelessly checks out my rack. "*Wowza.*"

Landon stiff-arms him without breaking our eye contact. "Pretend you're blind. Get lost."

"Don't have to tell me twice." Wade covers his eyes and disappears in the same direction as his teammate.

One purposeful stride ends whatever distance between us. His arm rounds my waist and suddenly, no one else exists. "Holy *fuck*. You're perfection," he mutters into my ear. My face flares with a flush. "We gotta leave. *Now.*"

"What do you mean?" I whisper-yell through a disbelieving smile. "I *just* got here. Do you have any idea how long it took me to—"

Landon's hold tightens, urgent and possessive. "I need to get you in bed before I fuck you right here in front of all these people." Velvety lips and the coarse ends of his beard brush the curve of my ear, his voice lazy with need. Pleading. "Can I? Can I take you? I don't want anyone else to see what you look like when you come."

We exchange the briefest of glances before I reach for his drink and throw it back in one swallow. The Scotch burns the whole way down. I attempt a ladylike cough from the corner of my mouth and clear my throat. "Ready when you are."

He barrels through the crowd, oblivious to the line of dolled-up women clamoring as we pass. Landon flits them away like annoying flies.

I try to get Gabe's attention from the table she's at, but there are too many people in between us. Including Wade Boehner. "Hey." I stop and squeeze his hand. "What's going on over there?"

The goalie gets close to Gabe and the instinct to protect her kicks in. Gabe sends him a hateful look. He raises his hands but doesn't surrender. My friend straightens. I read an emphatic, "*Leave me alone*" from her lips. Boehner starts talking again and Gabe abandons her martini to shove him by the chest into the nearest wall. When he tries to move, she presses a hand to his throat and pins him there. Her victim's eyes go wide as she snarls in his face, meeting his terrifying height with her heels. I imagine her doling out a final threat before she storms off.

"*Shit*," my boyfriend says through a laugh. "He deserved that."

We're almost to the door when Playboy catches up to us. "Guys, the *craziest* thing happened."

Landon snorts. "We saw, dipshit. Maybe that'll teach you to back off—"

"Back off?" Wade puffs out a heavy breath. "That was so fucking *hot*. I'm hard as a rock." A giddy joy gleams in his dark eyes. "I need to go find her."

"*Jesus Christ.*" Landon rubs his eyes with his free hand. "Don't go and do something..."

He's gone already. Vanished.

"...Stupid."

"Gabe's gonna punch him in the dick."

His chest huffs with a chuckle. "Serves him right."

Adrenaline surges through me during the short, manic cab ride, all the built-up restraint snapping when we enter the hotel suite. Landon's hands encase my jaw and bring our mouths together, tongue sliding between my lips and giving me no time to think or overthink. I return a sultry caress. If a kiss could reach into your soul and snatch it, that'd be the one. We gasp for air when it breaks. The rough pads of his fingers trickle down my bare chest.

"I wanna kiss every inch of you, every strip of this gorgeous skin tonight."

"Sounds good to me." Whatever alcohol lingers on my breath feeds the confidence already set ablaze by his presence. I tuck his hand under the bottom hem. "Start wherever but end here." It rises and rises, his half-lidded gaze growing wide with realization as he reaches the warm split between my legs.

"You're not...wearing..." He struggles to find the words, "*anything...* underneath."

"*Nothing.*"

Eyes flicking over the challenge drawn on my face, they rapidly blink. Landon's brain visibly short-circuits. "Clothes. Off." His breath teeters. "Bed. Now."

My jog isn't fast enough for him, and he impatiently circles an arm around both of my legs, heaving me over his shoulder before setting me down harshly on the bed. I slide the dress off both arms and wince as I peel it away from my chest while he drops his jacket and unbuttons his shirt.

Landon kneels between my legs, kissing the skin left red by the boob tape removal, soothing away the sting with his tongue. "Better?"

I nod and thread my fingers through the neat strands of hair. His eyes flutter closed, and when I wrench his head back in silken fistfuls to go in for another kiss, a growl vibrates from his throat.

I still. "What happened?"

His gaze slides to the nightstand, where a vintage bottle of Moët bathes in a bucket of ice. The naughtiest smile pulls at the corner of those full lips. "It's five minutes to midnight. I almost forgot I planned to celebrate." Landon tears away the foil and uncorks with a ceremonious *pop.*

Cool champagne dribbles over my chin, gravity pulling the lone droplet swiftly downward. A stern hand grips my neck, guiding my head back. "Open that pretty mouth for me." His thumb strokes the ridged column of my throat, goading the liquid down with each of my noisy gulps. Tears gather in my lower lids. Even through blurry vision, I sense the tremble in his breath, signaling the end of his control. He interrupts the moment to steal a punishing kiss and with it, some of the champagne. "Now lie back."

I scoot away from the edge of the bed, dizzy from the senses overload, but relieved to recline onto a hefty stack of pillows. "You're bossy today."

"You like it. *Perfect,*" he praises, pouring more of the carbonated alcohol into the dip of my collarbone before lapping it up. "Can't think of a better way to ring in the New Year."

Landon continues to drain the bottle, pouring and drinking between my breasts, licking and sucking at the nipples until they're unbearably hard and tight. My shock meets the roguish glint in his eyes when he pulls a shot from my belly button and its remnants dribble down. A chesty moan escapes as the chilled mouth of the glass bottle empties crackling bubbles across my skin, flowing over the most sensitive, needy space between my legs, onto Landon's tongue, and past his pursed lips. They catch flesh along the way.

He groans. "Can't fucking think straight when you taste so much like mine."

Everything inside me coils in response. Before I can do something about it, he rolls us across the mattress, positioning me over him until my knees bracket his shoulders. Elbows locked, palms pressed into the pillow beneath us, I brace for impact. And what an impact it is.

Landon pokes the tip of his tongue through his parted mouth, licking up one inner thigh, then the other, the anticipation sending all blood south. His nose lowers between my soaked pussy lips and I gasp as his mouth roots itself in the wetness. He replies with a content hum and widens my stance, forcing me to sink further onto him. My hips buck when his facial hair brushes my clit.

"That's it. Ride my face raw."

"Oh, *fuck*." Fists clenching the pillow cover, my back curves forward at the skyrocketing pleasure of his tongue plunging deep inside me. I sigh and stifle a whimper by biting my lip.

"As much as I love those little noises, be as loud as you want, baby."

I'd be embarrassed if I had any shame left as his mouth elicits the most unabashed simpers and crescendoing screams from me. When it gets to be too much, I dig both hands into the hair atop his head and prepare to unravel.

Landon makes a chiding noise and guides my arms upward, extending them to their lengthiest span above the high back of his bed.

"Hands on the headboard. And keep them there."

Too afraid to lose the momentum of the high, I obey.

"Good girl."

———

The clock in my office ticks annoyingly slow while I wait for my one-on-one with Theresa. She returns from her month-long holiday, ready to talk through responsibility shifts and financials for taking on partnership in the firm.

My head's all over the place. I took on Landon's case specifically to make partner. Hell, I'm ten years younger than those who are usually given the opportunity and most never get this far. Having a name on the office was the goal. Giachetti, Davé, and Associates. Becoming a partner is what I dreamed of, what every lawyer dreams of.

Now all I dream of is Landon.

The clean laundry smell on his skin, the citrusy shampoo in his hair on nights in with takeout, spooning on the couch while watching classic 90s Bollywood flicks, pond skating during holidays at the farm, having reserved seats by the glass at every game, his ring on my finger and his last name hyphenated with mine. A whole future of me and him. *Us.*

Which I've also got to tell Theresa about. My boss announces her arrival with a resounding slam of the door into my office.

"Davé! Have I told you recently what a genius you are?" She points to her phone screen. "I keep watching Pall's statement on repeat. Can't stop, won't stop!" She cackles with a villainous head toss.

"You haven't, but thank you." I tilt my head to accept the appreciation and wait for her to take a seat. "It went better than expected."

"Radek giving his cut to a children's charity was a nice touch, too." One of her legs swings over the opposite knee as her hands gather over her belly. "Reaffirms his golden boy image."

"That was his idea by the way. He's—"

"Either way. You held up your part, and I'm a woman of my word." Theresa straightens and sets her twined hands on my desk. "You're gonna take this firm to the next level, I know it. I'll have my assistant send the email but consider this the official offer to become a partner."

My face gives away my uneasiness.

"Is something wrong?"

"No. Nothing's *'wrong.'*"

"But?"

"Would it be possible to take some time and think about it?"

Theresa's eyebrow raises. "What's this about? Is there another offer? Another firm?" She stiffens her jaw and searches for lies in my expression. "What're they offering?" A lawyer through and through.

"Nothing like that. I want to be thorough before making my decision."

The reply is enough to calm her concerns. "Wouldn't expect anything less than thorough from you. How long were you thinking? There's no rush, per se, but I'd need to be able to report any changes before the end of the quarter."

"Two weeks. Definitely before the end of the quarter."

We agree on a handshake. As soon as she leaves, I pull out my phone and smile to myself.

GYM GUY

You better bounce that ass over here after work.

GYM GUY

> Wanna spend the rest of my day off eating that sweet little cunt.

Halfway through typing a filthy response, a FaceTime request from my parents has me fumbling the phone once more. I put my earbuds in and swipe to accept.

"Well?" My mother's forehead greets me.

"Hey, Mom. Lower the camera." She does. "And hello to you, too."

"*Ayyyyyyy!*" Dad's face appears on-screen sideways.

I hold back a laugh. "Hi, Dad."

Mom smacks his shoulder. "Grow up, Rahul."

"You first, Anjali." He crinkles his nose and gets in her face.

My expression sours. "Should I hang up, or...?"

"Bas kar, yaar." Mom elbows Dad to shape up. He puffs his chest, a fake serious, goofy look on his face. "So? How'd it go? What happened?"

A deep breath exits my nostrils. "Theresa offered me partner."

Wild hollers ring in my ears as the image on my screen blurs with motion. My father goes upright and freezes, then begins a series of movements that resemble an arm wave.

"Oh, my God, Dad. *Stop.*"

"Why? Ask your Mum. I was a helluva b-boy back in the day." He continues to pop and lock his shoulders between grunts. "Unh-unh. You like that? I know she does." His thumb points at my poor mom.

"Yes, yes." She swats him away. "Your promotion is one reason to celebrate. I can think of another." Her brows pump twice into the camera.

"I have a feeling you're about to tell me."

"You're getting older now."

Danger zone!

"And you're all set with your career."

My breath quickens, a deer-in-headlights panic setting in.

"It wouldn't hurt if you keep your eyes open for..." Mom tries to get Dad to finish the sentence, but he shrugs, having no clue what she means. "Marriage prospects."

"*Moooooom,*" I whine.

"I'm serious!"

Another attempt at getting Dad on board is thwarted. He scowls and crosses his arms. "First comes career, then comes marriage, then comes baby in the baby carriage."

"Baby?" I facepalm. I can barely feed myself most days. "Haven't you missed something?"

Mom side-eyes off-screen. "*Hmm.* I don't think so."

Heated blood rises to my cheeks, stomach churning. "What about love?"

"Right, yes. Love is important, but with the right person..."

The sinking feeling that follows is gut-wrenching. I should tell them about Landon. How much I love him and how good he is at loving me. For whatever reason, I stay quiet.

"Anju, stop pestering the poor girl. She's too young to be married. All my girls have a long way to go yet."

"Ofo! We were already married by her age."

Them bickering is better than being mushy.

"Just because *you're* not ready doesn't mean they aren't. If it was up to you, they'd never get married!" Her hands fly up and gesture this way and that. "They can't faff around our house the rest of their lives." Mom steps into the kitchen behind Dad, rant switching to Gujarati.

"Don't mind her, love. You'll find it when the time's right. Your mother and I did."

And what if I already found him?

———

I duck out of the office early, desperate for a break from the inevitable decisions tormenting my thoughts. Landon's is the first and only stop. He's nowhere to be found inside the penthouse, though. A whirring noise from outside has me squinting at the rooftop patio.

Shivering with each step toward the hot tub, I pull my blazer tighter around my chest and fold my arms to keep it closed. Landon hears my heels clicking against the cement and lifts his head from a pink, blue, and purple book.

"Hi, baby." A sole finger bounces on his lips. "Need my kiss first."

I oblige with a short peck that he elongates by standing and wrapping a damp hand around my nape.

"What are you doing out here?"

He points to the open pages and smirks. "Research."

"It's freezing."

"Not in the water." His eyes drop to my forced half-smile. "Tough day?"

My breath ices upon release in a heavy cloud. "Work stuff."

A trace of concern passes across his gaze, but only for a second. He grins wide, throwing an upward glance from where he bobs inside the jetting water. "Take off your clothes and get in here. I'll make you forget all about it."

"You're naked in there? Is that allowed?" The chill in my bones disappears at the thought. "Won't the goods, y'know, get boiled—"

"Just get in." His tongue glides over the pink seam of his lips as the round muscles of his shoulders stretch over the opposite edge of the hot tub, the delicious valley of his square chest coming into view. "Be a good girl and undress slowly for me."

I'll never recover from how empowering Landon makes me feel. The patience is awe-inspiring as I step out of my heels and drop my suit slacks and panties, his dilated eyes fixating on my fingers as they undo every blouse button and bra clasp until all that's left is me, exposed entirely. My already cold nipples shrink further, goosebumps pebbling my skin.

He sighs, then steps to the middle to make space for me on the bench. One of his hands reaches for me underwater and lands on my hip, thumb dragging over the arch, back and forth, back and forth as I lower in the water. My chin rests at the surface. Blue-green water jettisons over my submerged body for the next few minutes.

"Still cold?"

"Not at all."

"Good. Scoot this fine ass onto this corner." He guides me there, splaying a hand across my stomach to lift me out of the whirling tub and positions me, legs spread for balance. The bite of the cold air combined with the searing water coating my skin heightens the sensation of his drifting touch down my leg. "Time to make good on my promises."

From a wooden box on the landing, Landon retrieves a blue ring with a strange ball setting, too big to wear on a finger but too small to be a comfortable bracelet...*oh*. He sucks his first and middle fingers, wetting them enough to roll the ring down to the knuckles.

"Wow, *um*. That is a..." My throat goes dry.

"I'll put it on my cock in a second, but" —he skims the ring from the inside of my knee and up my thigh, the gentle vibrations tensing each muscle— "I wanna see it at work up close."

Hands clinging to his shoulders, I falter from the next kiss when both fingers slip into me, soft pulsing intensifying as the ring nears my clit.

"You been thinking about me, Indi? Is that why you're so wet, so ready for this?"

I want to say *always*, but barely catch my stolen breath before his mouth veers to my neck and breasts. It settles on my clit and those wicked fingers pump and curl and stretch me.

"Take it all. *Fuck*, your pussy grips me so well."

I moan and clench tighter at the praise, face docking to the gray sky overhead.

He edges me, driving me to the peak of pleasure and away from it with every suck on my clit and thrust of his fingers. The vibrating bulb hits the hood of my clit when Landon goes deep, his knuckles rubbing against my entrance.

"Oh, my *God*." My arms and legs gather around him, exploding onto his hand with a muted scream into his shoulder.

As the high peters out, he propels himself out of the water, too. A condom and the cock ring meet at the base of his now engorged third leg, waving at me to join.

"You gonna keep staring at it or come over here and sit on it?"

Onto his lap I go, the haze of my orgasm washing away any inhibitions of being outside. I gasp into his open mouth as he fills me to the hilt. We sink back down into the water, indulging in a series of tongue-filled kisses. My hips rock and circle, desperate to keep the buzzing toy against my throbbing clit.

Three orgasms later, I almost don't remember the reason for my sullen mood. Almost.

Landon helps me into a robe after a rinse in the shower, his embrace warmer than the heated terrycloth. "What's on your mind?"

My mouth tugs to one side. "Sometimes I don't know who I am or what I want anymore."

"What do you mean?" He frees some trapped hair from under my collar.

"Like, who am I these days?"

"You're Indira Davé, badass attorney and bewitcher of a devilishly good-looking professional hockey player."

My eyes roll. "Don't remind me. That's what started all this." I pause. "Theresa wants me as a partner at the firm."

He gapes. "That's amazing! Proud of you, baby."

"Thanks." I frown. "It's what I thought I wanted. Weirdly enough, it doesn't feel right."

I'm good at it. I'm good at making the winning argument. I'm good at advocating for the justice of my clients. Being partner doesn't mean that would stop. So why is it so difficult to accept?

"Listen to me." His fingers find the crook of my chin. "You're so much more than your job. You're insanely smart, funny as hell, and a fiercely loyal friend. You protect and spoil your sisters and adore your parents. You're good at everything you do: reading dirty books, making chocolate bars with inappropriate messages, sucking my co—"

"*Shhh.*" I headbutt his chest. "I'm trying to be serious."

"What? It's true." He kisses the top of my hair. "Sorry. Go on."

"I can't help but feel a little lost. I never expected an existential crisis in my late twenties. I don't know what I want anymore."

His heart beats steadily against my ear.

"Except you."

Landon heaves out a long breath and holds me tighter. "You already have me, baby."

"What if I don't want to be a partner? What if I don't want to be a lawyer?"

"You'll do great at whatever you decide. I'm here to cheer you on. We all are." Those tender pink lips pelt my cheeks, eyes, and nose with silent kisses.

"Thank you."

His thumb grazes the curve of my lower lip. "Is there something else?"

I cringe. "My parents. Now that they think I'm taking the promotion, they want me to focus on getting married. It's, like, a desi thing. The next step in life or whatever."

"*Indi.*" This sweet man chuckles from deep in his gut. It's warm and welcoming and I want to wear it like a blanket while I await his perfect response. He always seems to know what to say to erase my anxiety. "You don't have to worry about that. I don't wanna get married."

Landon says it so casually, so off-the-cuff, he doesn't notice how those six words shatter my unsuspecting heart.

CHAPTER 47:
I THOUGHT YOU KNEW

LANDON

LIGHT DRAINS FROM INDI'S BRIGHT, ROUND EYES. SHE blinks out of it and tries to play it off. "*Very funny*, Duke of Hastings."

"Who?"

"Never mind." A light hand slaps my arm. "I didn't mean get married right this *second*, silly. I meant a year from now or, like, sometime in the future..."

I look back at her with confused eyebrows. "You *want* to get married?"

The air stills. "Why wouldn't I?"

"You made it sound like it was the worst idea you'd ever heard."

"I don't wanna get married to someone they plucked from a giant book curated by a Seema Aunty-knockoff. I wanna be able to tell them about..."

Fuck. I've read this all wrong. "Indi." I swallow, bracing my next breath. "I don't wanna get married, like, *ever*."

Her hold on me stiffens and recedes. "You're serious?"

"I don't see the point."

"The point?" She backpedals and unties her robe, distracting me with all that flawless brown skin. "*You*? The King of Grand-Romantic-Gestures, Mister I-*Love*-Love himself, doesn't believe in marriage?"

"What does that" —I lose my train of thought before her nakedness disappears under flannel pajamas— "have to do with anything? Marriage and love aren't exclusive. You can have one without the other. I learned that from my parents."

"And *I* learned from mine that love is the foundation of a good marriage." The backs of her knees hit the edge of the mattress and she sighs through her nose, drawing her hands together in her lap.

This is not going great. But she's reasonable. Maybe she'll hear me out.

I scramble into a pair of loose pajama pants while eyeing her nervous hand-wringing. Me kneeling between her legs doesn't seem to relax or sway her. "Just because it works one way for some—"

"Of course not! This isn't a judgment about how others want to live." Her eyes scrunch closed and re-open, exasperated. "How many times have we watched fictional brown people sing and dance or cry and fight their way to a mandap?"

More than I have fingers to count. And yet, this is the first time I've considered what it represents for her.

"My parents have that Bollywood, only-in-the-movies sort of marriage," she continues. "I've seen it all my life." Her glossy gaze punches my heart. "I might not be sure of anything else right now, but I know I want to get married." That low voice of hers drops to a whisper. "I thought you knew."

Carpet scratching my knees, I inch forward. "I thought you knew too. I told you about Sierra."

"I assumed you were too young or whatever."

My head drops into her lap to nudge kisses onto her hands. "I was."

They bloom open as she holds my face upright. "You loved her, eh?"

"Sure, I did. As much of what I understood love to be. There was other stuff going on, too. I had gotten drafted. Sierra was ready to move on and I wasn't. But you" —I latch onto her by the hips, bunching the loose fabric— "*this*. Us. It's right." My throat tenses through a painful gulp. "*I love you*—"

The contrast of her thumb's comforting stroke against the anguish growing in her eyes cuts off my words. She nods. "You love me, but not enough to marry me."

"Indi." I pull at her. "It's not like that. I don't want to marry *anyone*."

Glazed brown eyes plead back. "Why?"

The question has me tugging a frustrated hand through my hair. "*Because!*"

Indi flinches at the raised volume but maintains her position.

"Because what happens one day and one of us decides we're not in love and don't wanna be together anymore? My dad—"

"That's different, Landon."

"The result was the same." A complicated divorce left my father suddenly with a new lease on life while Mom bore the brunt of responsibility. She never remarried, *hell*, she never dated. And how could she? Two kids, a demanding job, and a failed marriage with a man she continued to live with wasn't exactly the stuff of dating dreams.

"Are you telling me you're attracted to men?"

"No, but my dad didn't know when he got married."

"Oh, *Landon*. He knew." Her palms part from my jaw and fall to my shoulders.

"And what if it's you, huh?" That deep-seated fear of being left behind—*the one I don't tell anyone about*—rears its vicious head. "What if you wake up after twenty years of marriage and say you don't love me anymore?"

One fat tear slides down her cheek and crushes my heart. Her silent crying makes me want to cut my chest open, but the eerily calm tone of her voice makes me want to die.

"I don't have an answer to that, but I'm not sure that's an adequate reason to not get married."

I'm not below begging. I'm already on my knees. "Indi, *please*. Listen to me." I release her shirt to support her neck, tilting her mouth to mine for a kiss. "I love you. I want to be with you and no one else."

She doesn't answer right away. "I want a ring," she murmurs. "And everything that comes with it—"

"Baby, I'll give you a *thousand* rings—"

"It's not about the ring!" Indi flies to her feet, knocking me back to my haunches. "I want a wedding and a marriage. It means something to me" —she paces around the room, hands miming scenes in the air— "my loved ones covering me in haldi, you searching for your name in my mehndi, for my family to hold your juta ransom, my sisters stopping your car from letting us leave. And more than any of that, I want a whole future with you. For you to introduce me as your wife and to call you my husband. To be able to tell the world that you are mine and I am yours in every way."

I go upright, only to collapse onto the edge of the bed, groaning and digging the heels of my palms into my eyes until it hurts. "Besides the traditions, the last part is already true." Wrenching them down my face doesn't take away the pain either. "The difference is, I don't need a piece of paper to prove it."

My hand catches her wrist as she passes. Indi stops. I force her gaze.

"Any vow, any promise, I can make and keep right now." The slow pulse thrumming at her inner wrist against my lips sends a shiver down my spine. "I love you more and more every day. Can't that be enough?"

A quivering breath fans my face. "I don't know."

My mouth meets the crook of her elbow, pulling a drawn-out kiss from the delicate skin. "Will you think about it? Please." We can work through this. She loves me. I love her. "Stay with me."

Tension looms through our quiet dinner. When we head to bed, the covers hide the shift between us. I cling to her. She melts to me. But it's different. Like candle wax burning and shrinking away instead of holding two pieces of paper together.

"I'm sorry I made you cry," I whisper into her hair. "Can I make up for it?"

My hand roams over the arch of her hip and dives into her pjs, desperate to be inside her. To be as close to her as two people can be. To show her how much she *is* mine and I *am* hers. How we're more whole together than when we're apart.

"Not tonight." She stops me. "I'm tired."

The rhythm of her breathing never slows as she pretends to sleep. I don't blame her. I can't sleep either. When I get up to take an early morning whizz, Indi's missing. I find her tiptoeing through the kitchen.

"Where you goin'?"

"*Shit*," she says through a gasp. "Sorry, I didn't mean to wake you."

"You didn't." My hands furl and unfurl at my sides, itching to hold her, bring her back to bed, and kiss her until we can't think about anything else.

"I'm heading to my apartment."

The acid in my stomach lurches. "But you always stay here."

"You have to go in, like, an hour for back-to-back road games this week. And I should make sure everything there is okay."

I take a tentative step toward her. "What about you?"

"What about me?"

"Are *you* gonna be okay?" Both of my palms support her jaw. "I hate leaving you before we've resolved anything." I peck the tip of her nose. "Promise me you'll be here when I get back."

"I'll be here."

_____

Indi manages to simultaneously keep and break the promise.

The good-luck, pre-game photos are no longer of my goofy, sweet girl. Worst-case scenarios play on a constant loop in my head, affecting my performance on the ice. Fletch and Szecze head up the shots. I barely manage a few assists and a point in over the next two games. My eyes search the crowds every time, but I know my lucky charm's not there.

When I fly back to Ottawa, low lights in the penthouse draw attention to Indi's slumped shadow on the living room couch. "Baby?"

She straightens to the edge of the cushion. "It's not enough."

"What?" My gear bag slides from my shoulder and thuds to the floor.

"One of your rules—you asked me to tell you what I wanted. And I know it hasn't been that long, but it's not enough to be your girlfriend. Not forever."

Every muscle in my legs turns to noodles. I falter to the ottoman across from her. "So, what does that mean?"

Puffy circles darken her under-eyes. Blotchy reds spot her nose, cheeks, and neck. The steadiness in her voice could've fooled me into thinking she wasn't upset.

"It means you should probably take this." She fidgets to grip the handles of the brown paper bag next to her feet and offers it to me.

"What is it?"

"Things you left at my place."

"I don't want it back," I interrupt. I want you to keep it. I want you to keep me.

"It's *your* stuff." Indi pulls her lips into her mouth for a moment. "I don't want this to end either, but—"

In a brash swipe, I knock the bag from her hands to the side. "Then don't let it."

"Landon." Her head tilts. "We can't go on knowing we're not gonna agree about this. *I love you*." She clasps her hands over mine, the touch almost cruel. "I've loved for you *so* long and denied myself for as long. But when I stopped fighting, I gave you all of me. You healed parts of me I thought would always be broken." The pads of her thumbs unsuccessfully circle comfort into my skin. "I'm so grateful for that, but you've also taught me not to settle. I won't trap you in something you don't want and resent me for the rest of our lives. And I don't see a compromise."

My eyelashes stick together with tears. Her logic isn't wrong. Doesn't mean it hurts any less. Some sort of punishment, a cold shoulder, the silent treatment, *anything* would feel better than her acceptance and understanding. I tighten my hold on her hands from underneath.

"Are we still friends?" I know the answer, but I can't help it. I'm curious to see how far she'll go to spare my feelings.

A laugh sighs from her. Her somber smile displays those precious dimples and has my heart caving in. "Yeah, Radek. We're still friends." Lie.

"Will you pick up if I call you? Or respond to my texts?"

"Of course." Another lie.

We lean further toward one another with every sentence. Until there's nowhere else to go. Our foreheads tap together. "I love you so much, baby." I nudge her nose with mine, begging for a kiss.

Indi pulls away. "Friends don't kiss." If words were knives, my chest would be sliced clean open. She stands. "I should go."

"I don't want you to." Words choke and burn my throat.

"I know. But I should." Indi getting to her full height makes it seem final. I'm not ready. It's too soon. My fingers latch onto hers, unwilling to let go. "It's gonna be okay."

When our hands snap apart, so does whatever is left of my heart.

———

Two sleepless nights later, I can't stand it any longer. If she won't talk to me, I'll go talk to her. I barge in through the office door, surprised the name on it is unchanged. She didn't take on being a partner.

"Sir, can I help you?" An unfamiliar receptionist attacks me with a customer-service smile, blocking the entryway toward the desks with her body.

"I need to see Indira Davé." A professional response. I tug at the lapels of my blazer, reining in some feigned sense of control when I feel anything but. "I'm a client."

Her smile wanes as she taps her tablet. "Do you have an appointment?"

"No, but—"

"Bea, someone is here to see Ms. Davé," she says into her headset. "Please" —her hand motions to the waiting area— "have a seat."

Behraz's haphazard shuffle to the front has me springing to my feet. "Landon—Mr. Radek. What are you doing here?"

"Can I talk to Ms. Davé?" I search the office space behind her. "It'll only take a few minutes."

"I would, but...I'm *so* sorry." She guides me out, blowing a few stray hairs from her face and revealing flushed cheeks. Her arms hug her chest, shoulders rising and falling uncomfortably. "She's not here. You don't know?"

A million situations swim through my brain. "Know what?"

Bea lowers her voice to a hush. "Indi took a leave of absence."

My anxious heart rate plummets, draining the blood from my face. I scrub it with both hands.

"I don't know anything else yet." Bea puffs out a breath. "And if I did, I'm not sure I'd be able to say. I'm sorry, Landon."

"Me, too."

If only Indi knew how sorry.

When I get back in the Rover, I hit the screen to make a call. There's no answer. I dial a second number. No answer there either. I leave a voicemail.

"Hey, Mom. I can't remember if you're working tomorrow or not, but I've got a day between games, and I'd like to come home."

———

My mother greets me in the foyer with open arms. I find security in her matching Regents sweat suit and messy hair gathered into one of those jumbo clips that look like a claw.

"Aw, Landy." The embrace is warm and much needed. "How are ya, kiddo?"

"The little fuck-up's done it again." Delaney ruins the moment by huffing from the doorway behind us.

"Why are you here?" I snap.

"Laney, have some sympathy. Look at him. He's heartbroken."

My head whips between the two. "Wait, you both know?"

Mom's worried smile goes sheepish. "I mentioned you were coming over. Delaney said you and Indi split up."

Laney takes her coat off and tosses it onto the banister. "One day, Indi and I are laughing over that picture of you as a five-year-old yanking on your tiny penis and how not much has changed—"

I stomp behind her into the family room. "Hey, my penis isn't tiny! It's the opposite—"

Delaney puts up a hand and keeps going. "And the next day she leaves me on *Read*. It doesn't take a genius to figure it out." Her legs swing onto the couch as she sits, leaving no room for anyone else. "What've you done?"

"Don't you have anything better to do? Where are the kids?"

"They're with Seth's parents. Now 'fess up so we can fix it."

"There's no 'fixing' anything." I draw out a long breath and plop onto the opposite armchair. "She wants to get married."

My sister groans and presses her head into the cushion. "I told you this would happen."

Mom shoves Laney's feet away to make space for herself. "You've only been together a short while. What's the rush in getting married?"

Delaney perks an eyebrow and gives me her classic side-eyed stare-down. "You gonna tell her, or should I?"

A sigh blows from my flared nostrils. "I don't want to get married."

"So don't." Mom shrugs. "What's the big deal?"

"He doesn't want to get married *at all*." Laney's arms fly up, exasperated. "Fucking idiot."

Narrow eyes study my guilty expression. "Never? Why?"

My sister widens and rolls her eyes. "I'll give you two guesses, Mom."

She purses her lips and furrows her brows in response. Pensive until realization strikes. "Because of me and your Dad?"

I shrug. "I don't want to mess things up."

"Too late," Delaney mutters, eliciting a back-handed smack to the thigh from her couch neighbor.

"Honey." Mom shakes her head. "That's completely different. Leon and I...it's too bad you two got caught in the middle. Your dad didn't choose to be gay. But we chose to be a family."

"I don't know. I love Dad—"

"But?"

"It's not fair! He found Steve. You never got a second chance—"

"For what? Love? Sweetie..." she intones. "I promise, I had plenty of opportunities. I didn't want to date around. I had other priorities. I love being a nurse. I love my friends and family. I have so much love in my life. I never felt I needed more." A soft pat on my hands confirms her words. "Love is out there for whoever wants it. I'm too blessed to be greedy about it. There are so many ways to have happiness."

"Sure, of course." Why didn't I think of that? Here I was, thinking my mom had been left jilted and heartbroken when it couldn't have been further from the truth.

"Leon and I love each other. Your dad's my best friend, you know that. But we were never meant to be."

I lift my head from where it hangs. "And how do you know if it's 'meant to be?'"

Delaney and Mom share glances. "Nothing in life is for sure. But let me show you something."

She leads us to my old bedroom, since repainted a sage green and filled with desks to craft on. A sewing machine in one corner, a Cricut in the other. Some scrapbook paper and stickers that look like Sadie and Gunn have gotten into them.

"I was doing some cleaning and consolidating after New Year's." Mom drags a cardboard box out from the closet floor. "When Indi gave you that sketchpad and pencils for Christmas, Laney and I figured out why we recognized her."

After flipping open the lid, she removes a tangle of various hockey medals. "From playing puck, I know."

Delaney pokes through some items. "You're about to feel really stupid."

"*No*, not hockey."

A pile of folders stack against Mom's arms and before reaching the craft table, they slip from her grasp. Loose papers in all different sizes fly out like confetti. We bend down to gather them and I turn one over. And another. Then another, until a mosaic of sketched faces in various stages of completion stares up at me from the floor. My eyes grow, jaw going lax at the sight.

"It's Indi." My sister lets out a muted squeal of delight into her sweater. "They're all her."

"*They're all her*," Mom affirms. She points to various dates. "You've had her on your mind for years."

Unbelievable. Eyes poring, I scan through all the spread sketches. It's a slightly younger version, as if I'd imagined what she'd look like grown-up. Rounded eyes, strong brow, the curves of her cheekbones and pretty lips and chin, the angles of her nose and jaw. Some sketches smile with perfectly pitted dimples, pricking saltwater from my eyes. Scooping the drawings up and hugging them to my chest sets off a teary catharsis. The image of her has been my respite and solace from anxiety since we met.

"*Landy.*" Delaney kneels next to me and stretches her arm across my shoulder. "I can't make fun of you when you're like this."

"*God*, I fucked up."

"Totally."

Mom clicks her tongue at my sister. "Have you tried talking to her?"

"Probably too much." I show them the evidence on my phone, scrolling through the dozens of unanswered calls and unreplied texts. Except for the last one.

GYM GIRL

> I want to be your friend, but I need time and space.

"Ouch." Delaney grabs the phone from me and bends one knee up with a wince. "Gimme that. No need to fixate. I'm gonna get us some Moose Tracks ice cream."

I sniffle and swipe my runny nose. "Any chance it comes with a side of therapy?"

"Sorry, bud. Not this brand." Her hand musses up my hair as she uses my head to propel to her feet. "But Seth knows a guy."

CHAPTER 48:
CHASING JOY

INDI

TWO MONTHS OF TRAUMA-RELEASE EXERCISES AND home-cooked food don't heal me entirely.

Neither does indulging my sisters by joining their daily ridiculous dance choreo to post on TikTok or changing my chocolate bar side-gig from dirty messages to popular Bollywood lines to accommodate Brampton's needs, despite the success of my *Kuch Kuch Hota Hai* collection. "*Tu si jaa rahe ho? Tu si naa jao*" is especially popular.

The heartache isn't worsening, which is good, but the wound won't close either. Most days I'm chasing joy to replace the high of being with the man of my dreams. I try to find it within myself, but the melancholy chorus of Rahat Fateh Ali Khan's *Main Tenu Samjhawan* plays in my head on repeat through daily chores and routines, providing a sad soundtrack to my Landon-less life. The swell and yearning in the Qawwali singer's voice threatens a mental breakdown at any moment, a painful reminder of what I had, and I lost.

I sniff and regain focus as mustard seeds sizzle in hot peanut oil. Mom lids the pan to avoid the spice from jumping out and landing on my arm. Learning to cook is my newest hobby.

"There's two types of rai, big and little. Always buy the little ones," she explains. "And wait for the popping to slow and stop before adding the jeeru."

I scoop a tiny spoonful from the masala dubbo to add to the oil.

"Good. See how they dance? That's how you know the oil's hot enough. Add some haldi, too."

Her instructions are straightforward, except for the proportions—

440

everything is annoyingly approximate—and I'm grateful she and Dad are patient with my slip-ups. As if watching their successful daughter throw her career down the drain wasn't enough, my poor parents ate the oversalted khichdi I made last week wearing a smile, complimenting the flavor. My sisters weren't as gracious.

"Sauté the onions until they're translucent." Mom motions to the forgotten wooden spoon in my hand. "Then stir in the potatoes and peas."

"Shocking." Esha strolls into the kitchen popping gum between her teeth. "No backtalk? No sarcasm? Who are you anymore?"

My eyes glide to her in a glare. Mom loudly shushes the bratty sister behind me. She's not wrong. I have no idea.

While in bed that night, my phone dings with a text. I'm almost glad I didn't change his contact from Gym Guy. It gives a layer of distance between us, less intimate than his name appearing on my screen, which would surely send me spiraling.

The message is a live picture—*a screenshot he must've taken while we FaceTimed*—of me placing letters on poured chocolate, spelling out the last of the words *I Miss You*. Tears gather as three dots flicker on his side of the message.

GYM GUY

I'm sorry.

I muffle a series of ugly sobs into my pillow, phone dropping to somewhere on the bed. It's not as subtle as I thought because my sisters sneak in and sandwich me in an embrace. When I quiet enough to show his recent messages, I tell them everything beyond what they knew about my once-sneaky link: how wonderful he is and how we fell in love, and how he pulled the rug from under my feet with this marriage hang-up thing. Everything except his name.

"*Screw him!*" Esha twists her face, yelling through a whisper. "Just wait 'til Karish's wedding. We'll find you someone better."

"Mom and Dad are already on it," Anika adds. "I overheard them the other day."

"Oh, *God*." I cover my face with both hands.

"You don't have to say yes to any of them. Date around."

My face scrunches. "Sounds annoying. And it's not dating."

"Close enough." Esha shrugs. "Fancy meals, dessert, coffee, flowers. Sit back and let them try to win you over. They have their work cut out for them, though. My Didi is not easily impressed."

Anika glances at my phone. "Gym Guy must have been outstanding."

"Don't remind me."

Her thumb scrolls too far up, eyes widening as she reads. "There are some spicy texts here."

"Lemme see!" My youngest sister peers over her shoulder. "*Whoa.* Man's got a mouth on him." They giggle.

"Gimme that!" I swipe it from them. "That's enough. Out of my room."

"Nope." Another sandwiching embrace follows, squeezing and swaying until we topple over and squish together in the queen-size bed. "We're staying right here."

———

An encore of Mohammad Rafi's "Baar Baar Din Ye Aaye"—*captained by my father and encouraged by my mom's older brother*—is one of the most ridiculous stunts I've ever witnessed. I down bites of German chocolate cake various family members feed me. We take turns exchanging hugs after they stuff my face as they comment either on how thin I've gotten, or how impressed they are with my Gujarati or the string of suggestions.

"Indira, I know someone *perfect* for you!"

"Leave her be." My Nani playfully smacks the shoulder of Pallavi Aunty, their flat's nosy neighbor. "My turn." Nani slices a big chunk of the two-layer cake piece with a fork and mimes for me to open my mouth.

I lean forward to receive it, then bow to touch her feet.

"Ayushmaan bhava, saubhagyavati bhava." Her wrinkled hands stroke through my hair, the blessings for my longevity and a blissful wedded life drawing tears to my kohl-lined lower lids.

"Not you, too," I say through a sniffle, wrapping my arms around her neck as she squeezes my waist and pats the cheek that isn't smushed into hers.

"Saaru, saaru. Havey hun kashu nahi bolun." Nani zips her lips, bony fingers tremoring along the path. "Not another word."

We take a cheesy selfie. On my part anyway. She looks as graceful and ageless as ever. I kiss her temple and she kisses both dimples. A rich sense of contentment fills my insides. Maybe this trip to India was what I needed after all.

I hide in the guest room after my sisters and cousins chase me around attempting to smear my face with the coconut, pecan, and chocolate icing. My phone buzzes in hand. I expect a threat from one of my siblings. It's worse.

GYM GUY

Happy birthday

Something in my gut tightens, but I feel the need to respond. I can do this. We can be civil.

ME

Thanks

GYM GUY

Can we talk?

The door swings open. "Aha!"

"*Nooooooo!*" I cry, locking my knees to stop them from moving me, but the tiled floor provides no traction. While they hold my arms and the back of my head to smash my face into whatever is left of the cake, the phone clamped in hand rings, and I break free to answer.

"It's a work call!" I lie, scampering back into the extra room. This time I remember to lock it. "This is Indira Davé."

"Oh, my God. *Hi.*"

My heart floats out of my chest for a moment. I check the screen. It is him, after all.

"Hi."

"Hi," Landon repeats with a sigh.

"You said that already."

"Right, sorry." He chuckles, the deep rumble rushing blood everywhere. My face, my arms, my pu— "How are you?"

"Good, you?" See? Perfectly civil.

"We got knocked out in the first round."

"I saw."

"You were watching?"

"No, I saw some highlights." Cheers and questions about my whereabouts call beyond the teak door. "Is that why you called, or...?"

A yelling rickshaw driver and a honking truck sound out from outside the window.

"Where are you?"

"Mumbai."

"Mumbai, India?"

Someone obnoxiously knocks on the door. "One minute!" I move away from it and towards the AC unit where the conversation is less likely to overhear. "Seriously, Radek. What is it? We haven't spoken in months, it's ten p.m. on my birthday, and my cousin's getting married in four days. I'm sorry you guys lost, but I don't know what that has to do with—"

"You weren't there. You're my lucky charm."

"*Landon.*" I huff, rubbing the suddenly throbbing point between my eyebrows.

"And we haven't talked in months because you didn't want to. You wanted time and space..."

"I *still* need time and space. How am I supposed to get over you when you're texting and calling me constantly?"

The conversation skips a beat as the line goes quiet. Landon's voice lowers. "I don't want you to get over me."

"Clearly!" I throw a hand up, accidentally grazing one of Nani's money plants vining from above. "But if you truly want to be friends, you have to let me move on. That's why I'm here. My family's looking for someone for me. To marry."

His throat clears. "And you agreed to that?"

"Yes." I roll my eyes, both at the situation and at the man who shouldn't care about anything to do with my future marriage. "Who knows? Maybe I'll find the love of my life."

His teeth grate and grind in my ears. Even from seventy-five hundred miles away, the man gives me goosebumps. "None of them are as good for you as I am."

"Well, they actually wanna marry me, so..."

That elicits a wince. His voice softens. "Don't do it, Indi. *Please.*"

The headache spreads and I can't deal with it any longer. "You robbed me, Landon. Maybe it was too soon, but I had a whole life—*an actual future*—imagined for us. I would've waited. *You* didn't want it, so don't try to make *me* feel guilty."

He whimpers in response.

"You broke my heart. Stop trying to fix it."

The window seat receives my thrown phone as I hang up to make myself presentable again. Tissues dab away any smeared makeup remnants. I straighten my shoulders, take a deep breath to push down the pain, and rejoin the party, abandoning my phone entirely. The ruckus calms, but the group is scheming for sure. They sit around in the group of sofas and armchairs.

"What about Ashutosh Vyas?" Mom suggests, not realizing I'm seated behind her. She startles when my arm drapes across her shoulder.

"Who's that?"

"You know, Ashutosh. Ash." Her fingers wave in a circle. "Anika's friend Shalini's older brother."

Nik whips her head over from where the rest of my cousins sit at the mention of her name. Spying. "Do I know him?"

"He's the one who got Anika her job."

My sister blushes. I don't think I've ever seen her do that. "Oh, yeah?"

"Yeah, *uh*—he's sorta my boss."

"And he's in Mumbai right now." Mom's brows dance. "They're here for another wedding. I can talk to Shalu's parents."

"Nik." I beckon her. "What's he like? Show me a picture."

Our parents and aunts and uncles continue to discuss him and his family. I can hardly get a few words out of my sister. Another first. Her thumbs dawdle, fumbling to get to Instagram. When she finally pulls up his profile, I'm surprised.

"*Hello?* He's kinda cute," I whisper to her. "How tall is he?"

She shrugs and glances back to Esha and our cousins, who pull out a carom board. "Taller than you, I guess."

"What's wrong? Is he weird?"

"No. *No.*" She shakes off the daze. "He's not weird. He's nice. *Really* nice, actually."

"Tell Shalini's mom I'm open to meeting him."

"That's my girl." Dad snaps and points a finger gun at me. "*Ay*, Bhanu," he addresses the house help. "*Ek aur?*" He wiggles the empty bottle of beer in his opposite hand.

"I got it," I offer, rising to my feet.

"Thanks, betu."

"Be right back."

The stupid handle of the bottle opener bites my palm, but I manage to claim victory after a few tries. Nik corners me, shoving me into the far side of the galley kitchen. "What the hell?"

"*Shhh!*" She puts a finger to her mouth. "Keep it down." A last look over her shoulder ensures no one else is headed this way. "Please don't say yes to meeting Ashutosh."

"Why not?" I study her face. "What's his deal?"

Her eyes slide to the floor before returning to my steadfast gaze. "We're together." My mouth gapes. Her behavior makes sense. "I *know*," she adds, slapping a hand to her forehead. "It's not totally allowed at work, but I've liked him since he visited Shal at uni and..."

"*Wow.*"

"Didi, it's serious."

"How did I not know about any of this?"

"I dunno, you have so much going on. We hung out more after I took the job and started dating, like, four months ago. I was afraid to bring it up while, y'know..."

"*Anika.*" I pull her into a hug. "You didn't have to do that. I can handle it. I'm a grown woman."

She hugs me back.

"Enough mush and gush. We gotta tell Mom and Dad!"

The return to Canada is filled with new excitement and joy. With some support, Anika confesses to dating her best friend's brother and boss—*the romance novel practically writes itself*—and we did a small gor-dhana to make the relationship official.

My mother is plagued with the wedding planning bug worse than the bashful bride herself. By June, I'm ready to rip my hair out from boredom and flee a home visit from the local florist Aunty to go for a drive. When the retro sign for the Mississauga Sports Arena shows up, I turn the Audi left into the lot and park. Its classic blend of damp carpet, sweaty hockey gear, and the plasticky smell of artificial ice are a welcome distraction.

The stands are old, but sturdy, and whine under my weight as I climb steps and choose a spot. There's something calming about the empty ice. So many memories flood back.

"Ma'am, open skate is at rink three."

"Oh, sorry." I scramble to my feet.

"No worries."

My face breaks into a smile at the stout figure across from me. The gray streaking through the sides of his hair is new, but the kind, crow's feet-framed eyes are the same.

"Hey, Coach."

He squints and gives me a once-over. "Indi? That you, kiddo?" His head shakes as he mirrors my disbelief. "It's been ages."

"It has." We do an awkward dance: I extend a hand when he comes in for a hug, then he and I switch. We settle on a fist bump.

"What brought you out today?" His torso turns to the ice.

"I'm not sure." We both take a seat. "I've been staying with my parents for a bit. Needed some air and ended up passing by."

He hums and nods. "Do you still play?"

"Not really, no."

"What do you do?"

"I'm a lawyer. Though I got a chance to play on a lake a few months ago and I wasn't terrible."

"Muscle memory is wild, eh?"

I agree with a laugh.

"You were pretty good if I remember correctly. Bet you're a better lawyer."

An unintentional scoff sputters from my lips. "One of the best in Ottawa."

He whistles.

"To be honest," I intone. "I'm taking a break." The sheen of untouched ice catches my attention again. "I'm *twenty-eight*. I should know what I'm doing with my life by now, but I have no idea."

"What are you talkin' about? You got the whole rest of your life to enjoy. Anyone who tells you they've got it all figured out is either lying to you or themselves."

I frown. "Maybe."

The watch on his wrist beeps. "*Shit*. You stickin' around town for a while?"

"Possibly. Why?"

His bearded grin glimmers with hope. "They're startin' an all-girls league here next season. Doin' intro camps over the summer. Could use all the help they can get with the tiny ones."

A groan brews in my chest. "I don't know if I'm qualified for—"

"It doesn't pay big money like a fancy lawyer gig, but..."

I shouldn't laugh but I do. "Coach, with all due respect, I don't need the money." I've made enough to not need to worry about it. "I just wanna do something I love."

"You care about hockey?"

Yes. It's the first thing I chose for myself. Mom chose ice skating. Skill and unfortunate life experiences chose my career for me. But hockey? I fought to play that one season. And it feels like I've been fighting to get back to it ever since. "Yeah, I do."

"You good with kids?"

I nod in reply.

"That's all it takes." He flips through his clipboard and removes a sheet. "There's a meeting for potential coaches Saturday. We do a few days of training before leading camps and forming teams."

"Thanks, Coach."

His sneakers squeak against the steps. "See ya soon."

I follow his exiting path a few minutes later, then head to the rental counter. The smile on my face doesn't budge. Frigid air cools me with every breath when I get to the other rink. And the moment my skate meets the ice? It's the high I've searched for. Pure magic. Serene. Mind-clearing.

It's home.

CHAPTER 49:
WHAT ARE YOU WAITING FOR?

LANDON

"HOW WAS THIS MORNING?"

Otto's foot bobs by his knee, shifting the notepad in his lap. My hand rubs over the stark, tanned line at my bicep. A reminder of too many days golfing at Wade's house in Fort Lauderdale during the off-season.

"Practice was fine, yeah." I recline on the sofa. "Coach talked our ears to death after, but otherwise, I think the team's looking good. They rallied this summer. Jaeg doesn't even hate the rookies."

"Ready for the first game?"

"It's a pre-season match."

"Even so."

Gaze traveling to the ceiling, I release a deflated breath. "I'm trying to stay focused, I really am. And my game is strong, thank God. But my mind wanders."

"To failure?"

"To her."

"It takes time." My therapist is far more patient than I am. His finger dents his cheek after discarding his pen and pad on the side table. "Have you been doing the guided meditations I shared with you?"

"Every day."

"Great! Keep going. And give yourself a grace period."

"It's been almost six months."

Feels like forever. Damn ego. Damn pride. I've wanted to talk to her on so many occasions, but those two pesky critters hold me back. What if she did move on? I couldn't bear to face her.

"In the grand scheme of things, that's not *that* long. You had a history, a deep connection. It's hard to let go."

"*Oof.* Salt, meet wound."

"Sorry, I didn't mean it like that." He sighs. "What I'm saying is: you had a happy life and successful career before her, and it's okay to take time to find it again."

My head sways, not quite buying into the idea I'll ever get over Indi, but what other option do I have?

Directly from therapy, I drive toward Toronto. Laney sent the Acton rink address for Sadie's game, and I follow the directions mindlessly. My sister waves me over from the glass. Seth leans on a railing, seemingly nervous.

"You're late," Laney chides.

"They haven't started!"

"They're on the ice." She glares.

"Barely." I draw a hand to the rink, pointing out the twenty or so kids toddling about. "They're *five*."

"This is a big deal for her! She's been begging to be on a team." Seth grunts in agreement. "The new girls' league is a game changer." She fixes her baseball hat and crosses her arms, glancing toward the players.

"Which one's Sadie?"

"Number fifteen."

My niece is probably the best kid out there, taking smooth stride after smooth stride while keeping her stick down. I call her name and hold up a hand. She turns and wiggles a glove at me. The inattention bumps her into a teammate and knocks her over, before immediately wiping out on top of her. Seth, Del, and I wince together.

"*Aw*, our little star athlete."

"She is, isn't she?" Delaney beams. "Can't say the same about the rest of these kiddos. And this week we have tough competition."

"Oh, sure. *Super* tough."

"Seriously! The opposite team's coach is the league's coordinator. And I know for a fact she's a hardass." My sister wears a smile, but it's hidden with mischief. Seth harrumphs. He has a smirk on, too.

"Yeah, right. She coaches a dozen five-year-olds. It's just fun at this point." A whistle blows.

"*Fun*! That's the perfect word for this situation."

The huddle on the ice and acoustics of the space diminishes the grown-up voice leading some sort of pep talk for both teams at center ice.

"*I am strong!*" The tiny ones yell between pauses. "*I am smart! I am brave! I am a team player! I am respectful! I am good at hockey!*"

"Yet to be seen," I mutter from the corner of my mouth.

"*Shut up!*" My sister hisses. "This is important. You have no idea."

"*I am proud of myself!*"

They raise their hockey sticks and break apart, slowly making their way to their positions. The adult finally rises amongst the little ones, back facing me, rich, dark brown waves of her ponytail swishing between shoulder blades. My heart thuds within its bony cage recognizing the combo of her black sweater, black vest, black leggings—*the ass it highlights is unforgettable*—and white sneakers.

I squint when she gets to the opposite bench and walks through the boards, hoping, praying, wishing that my eyes are playing tricks. She turns. No such luck. Dimples flank her full pink lips and bright white smile, radiating a happiness I had no part in as Indira Davé encourages her players. Dread sinks to the bottom of my stomach.

"See? I told you it'd be *fun.*"

"Leave the poor sap alone," Seth scolds.

They bicker in the background while I drown everything out except her. I don't know what I expected if I ran into her, but it wasn't this. Every ounce of pride and ego melts away. I'll give her whatever she wants and take whatever she gives me. All I want is *her.*

"You're gonna go talk to her after, right?"

I don't respond.

"You *have* to!" My sister orders under her breath. "Don't be a wimp."

I focus on watching Sadie play and take breaks outside between periods. Long ends of my hair get a brutal raking-through, the automatic doors opening and closing as I pace.

"So?" Delaney is such an instigator.

"Let me think," I grit through my teeth.

"When did you get so broody? *Sheesh.*" She waggles a finger at me. "Don't think for one second I'm beyond doing it for you."

"Fuck off."

"*Language!*"

What to say? What to say? The chant loops over and over until the game ends. To the surprise of no one, it's a total shutout. Neither team manages to get a single goal. Zip. Zilch. Nada. 0-0. Doesn't make a damn difference to the kids, though.

Sadie runs to us off the ice, pure confidence in her smile. Her stick falls to the floor when she comes to hug me first—*obviously, I'm her favorite*—and I swoop her up too hard. Her helmet rolls off. Gunnar chases after to nab it.

My face twists at her matted, sweaty hair. "*Ewww.* You stink, Princess."

"No, *you're* stinky!" She retorts, sniffing twice. "Yuck." Rascal. "Put me down, Uncle Landy. I'm a big girl now."

"Oh, ya are, are ya?"

She wiggles free, then peeks around me. "I'll be back."

"Where ya goin'?"

"Sadie!" Delaney calls after her. But the girl is faster on land than ice and disappears around the curve of the rink. I follow but hang back when approaching my niece's final destination. Strong little arms encircle Indi's legs.

"Whoa. Hey, I think you've got the wrong—"

"Indi! 'Member me? I'm Sadie."

Delaney catches up but doesn't see me behind a wall of painted cement blocks. "Sorry, she made a run for it. Also, hi." An awkward wave hello happens.

"Hey." Her shock softens into a generous smile. "That's okay." She lowers into a squat. "Hi, Sadie. Of course, I remember you."

Oh, my heart.

"Wasn't I good out there?"

Indi holds her arms and gives her a little shake. "You were *so* good. Did you have fun?"

"The *mostest.*"

"That's the most important thing." Her head tilts, mirroring Sadie's bashful position. "I'm really proud of you."

My niece returns a cheesy grin. "I'm proud of me, too."

"Thanks, Indi," my sister says. Indi straightens so they're eye-level. "I'm, *uh*...it's good to see you—"

"*Oh! Oh!*" Sadie tugs on the bottom of Indi's puffy vest. "Uncle Landy's here, too."

"What?"

"*Sadie.*"

"*Uh,* well. I'm not sure he'll want to see me."

"'Course he will! He likes you *so* much." She pulls at Indi's hand, attempting to drag her forward. "He told me he really, really, *really* wants you to be his—"

"*Sarah Ann Chambers!*"

"But *Mommy*—"

Panic strikes. Instead of backtracking, I surge forward, emerging from my hiding spot.

"*Finally.*" Delaney rolls her eyes. "Let's go, Miss Thing. You've done enough today."

I almost can't move, Indi's so beautiful. I chew on my lip as we stare at each other. A gulp travels down my throat. "For the record, I'm not here to see you, but I'm glad I get to."

My pesky niece and her equally pesky mother shuffle off toward the locker room.

"Hi."

"Hi."

"So, this is where you've been, eh?"

The most pitiful sigh leaves her mouth in response.

"You look happy."

"I'm learning how to be." Her brows twist as she looks away, chin jutted up. My girl doesn't fold easily.

"Del mentioned it's the only sponsored league for girls in the area."

Indi's head nods.

"You did that?"

She shrugs. "I helped. Negotiating is a lawyering skill. I wanted them to have the type of support I didn't."

"*Goddamn it*, Indi." My palm massages the back of my neck. "I know I said I'm sorry—*so many times for so many things*—but I am." Somewhat relieved to see her empty ring fingers, I groan. "Can we talk?"

Her mouth crinkles to one side. "Aren't we doing that now?"

"No, I mean, *seriously.*" Impatient feet drive me forward, my hands balling into fists to keep from touching her.

"About what?"

Honesty. We started and ended being true with and to ourselves. "About how miserable I've been the past few months. And how happy I was the months before."

"*Landon*." My name on her lips is the breath of fresh mountain air I needed.

"Or maybe how I'm not over you." The pace of my heart spikes to a swift gallop when her gaze captures mine. "How I'll never be over you."

The closer I step to her, the louder the voice in my head gets. Mine. Mine. Mine.

She backs herself into a tight nook.

"Living without you feels like dying."

Her eyes shift to the worn rubber mat under our feet.

"I've been dead to the world."

The line of space between us is so thin, I can taste her breath, take in her smell. Cranberry. Cinnamon. My mind screams. Home. "I can't enjoy my favorite things anymore. Ask me why."

She flattens against the wall as my arms entrap her.

"Why?"

"Because *you're* all of my favorite things."

"What about your Porsche? You *love* that car."

"It's no good to me without you sitting in it, high as a kite so I can tell you you're hilarious and that I love you."

"You said that?"

"I did."

She doesn't back down, challenging me with the intensity of her glare. "What about Twinkies? You're obsessed with those things."

"Not as obsessed as I am with you." My lips hover over hers.

She swallows.

"You taste better, sweeter."

"Hockey?" Her voice quiets, smaller than a whisper. "It's your passion."

"Being with you feels better than winning." My forehead bows to hers. Our noses touch, eyelashes fluttering. "I'm so in love with you."

Indi blows out a controlled breath. "That doesn't change anything."

"I've changed my mind." I pull back, wanting her to see how much I want this. "Marriage may be a piece of paper to me, but it means something to you. And you mean *everything* to me."

"I won't let you go through with something you don't believe in."

My fingers find her chin, to tip it up. "I believe in *you*. In us." Her body relaxes when I lean in again. "You know why I stopped drawing when we got together? It's a nervous habit. An outlet to manage my anxiety. I focused on a faraway dream to keep calm. I've drawn the same image again and again for years."

One hand brushes through the magnetic tension between our bodies and dives into my jacket's inner pocket. I retrieve a stack of sketches and reveal the top one. My favorite one. The one that looks most like her now.

Indi's eyes gloss over, swirling the brown hue like dark clay on a pottery wheel.

"It's *you*. I didn't have to draw anymore because that dream is *you*. I don't care how we do it. Marriage, big wedding, whatever you want. When I see my future, I don't see fast cars or Twinkies or winning the Stanley Cup. I see *you*."

Long, lean arms break from their sides and climb quickly over my shoulders, locking around my neck as she stifles a sob in our hug. Heat spreads from my chest to the tip of my toes.

"How am I supposed to say anything after that?"

"I'll help." I grip her tighter, nuzzling into my hair. "Say you still love me too."

That gorgeous laugh under my ear makes my heart jump. "I still love you."

"Say you still wanna be with me."

"I couldn't accept being with anyone else. I still wanna be with you." The backs of her fingers stroke my cheeks, trim nails scritching and scratching the unshaven stubble. "However you want. I don't wanna be without you either. Married or not."

Restraint unravels as my fingers stretch the taut, tied-back hairs at the back of her head. "Remember how you said friends don't kiss?"

"Yeah?" The end of her nose slots against my cheek, lips parting, waiting for me.

"Don't be my friend, Indi." An unintentional swipe of my tongue wets my bottom lip. "Kiss me and bring me back to life."

Electricity crackles as the centimeter of space between us closes. Her warm mouth and soft, plush lips invite me to keep going and I slip inside to taste every corner. Saltwater taints the sweetness. I wipe the tears away.

"I'm happy," she murmurs with a sniffle. "Don't stop."

Another extended kiss steals both of our breaths. My forehead connects with hers. "Take me home, Indi."

"How can I do that when I'm already there?"

"You *live* here?"

"No, you dummy." She slaps a hand on my chest. "*You.* You're home to me. Also, I can't physically do that. I live with my parents right now."

"Are they home?"

Indi blinks for a second. "Actually, no."

"Oh, man. I'm trying to get you to have your way with me and you keep saying things that make me wanna do *disgusting* things to you at your parents' house."

"What are you waiting for?"

This woman will never cease to challenge me. I wouldn't have it any other way. Hands reaching to cup her ass, I lift her around me.

"Nothing."

"Where are you taking me? Someone will see."

"Don't care anymore." A quick peck seals the promise. "You're mine. Let everyone know."

"Put me down. I need to grab my things."

I pad behind her into the empty locker room to gather her keys and purse, not releasing my grasp on her hand. Never letting go again.

It tightens as we approach the parking lot. Before we get to my awaiting sister, my love elbows me. "Hey, what was Sadie saying? What do you 'really, really, *really* want me to be'?"

"My girlfriend." I poke my tongue between my teeth, passing her a goofy smirk. "It was our Christmas Eve secret."

She stops about a hundred feet from Delaney. "Ask me."

"Indi, *baby*," I start, turning to prop her sweet face with my palm. "Make me yours again."

And she does.

CHAPTER 50:
GETTING RAILED IN A SUMMER DRESS

INDI

LANDON LICKS EVERY RIDGE OF MY SPINE, ROCKETING pleasure from its root up until the hairs on my nape rise. His grip on my throat recedes to my hip, only to let go and spank me. He drives in harder with a grunt. "That's it, baby. Soak my cock."

As if it was possible to be wetter after three hours of getting eaten out by the NHL's top scorer this season.

"*Landon!*" I gasp, looking over my shoulder. The sheets ball under my fists as he hits the spot deep within me again and again. "Not *fair*."

He smirks, the little shit. "All's fair in love and betting your boyfriend on who's gonna come first."

Arms stretching forward, chest lowering to the mattress, I push back on him.

"Oh, *fuck*, Indi." The hand on my shoulder releases and grasps onto the flesh of my other hip, and I moan out when the vibrating toy wrapped around him stills at my entrance. "Now you're playing dirty."

"You knew what you were getting into," I pant, cheek smashed against the plush bed top. "I'm a lawyer."

My knees glide outward, pressing my breasts into the luxe Egyptian cotton sheets. The friction against my nipples as he picks up the insane pace of thrusts—*all while the cock ring teases my clit*—is almost unbearable.

Landon groans, so deep it rumbles through me and a high-pitched whine escapes. "Love when you fucking visit. Love this sweet cunt choking my cock."

He's beautiful like this. I watch him through tangled eyelashes. Warped expression on his handsome face, sweat trickling through the fine chest hairs between broad pecs and an immaculate set of abs. His forearms strain with raised veins as he holds onto me and whatever restraint he has left.

I'm face-down, ass-up, and completely in love with this filthy-mouthed man.

I shift my hips, heightening the curve of my back to optimize the angle. Landon's throat rips out the most unhinged, prolonged moan. Jaw dropped, the sinews of his neck ready to snap like an overstretched rubber band. His hands slip from their hold on my hips and scratch nail marks into my back, a delightfully painful break from the intoxicating level of pleasure.

"Fucking *fuck*." He twitches inside of me, cock stretching my pulsing walls, filling me entirely as the toy lands on my swollen clit. "Indi...*God*, Indi, let go."

My body reaches the last rung of the orgasm with the command and when his hips judder against mine, I do. A combined, inhuman cry echoes through the penthouse as we come together, his shallow, sloppy pumps making the high last.

I sputter through satisfied laughter, breathless and dazed when Landon empties the last of his release. Blood-filled lips caress my back along with those calloused hands, sending delicious shivers across my sensitive skin. Brushing away the mess of my stuck-on, sweaty hair, he groans in my ear, chuckling. "Fucking *phenomenal*."

"So good," I say, nearly senseless. "We'll call it a tie."

"Where the fuck did you learn how to do that?"

One eyebrow lifts lazily. "I read."

My personal sex god pulls out, removing the cock ring and tying off the condom. His still-stiff third leg is awe-inspiring. "Tell me again why you can't move back to Ottawa."

"One—" I roll over and stretch before relaxing into the unused side of the bed. "A tenant lives in my old apartment."

Landon bends to kiss each of my feet, only stopping to crawl over me.

"Two, it's mid-season. We've got practice and games through March."

He whines, plucking kiss after kiss from my shoulder and neck.

"And three, you haven't met my parents yet."

"That's easy. Move in with me." Tongue licking away the sting of a harsh suck under my jawline, he hums. "We can fuck like this whenever you want."

"Tempting. And what will I do all day while you're on the road?"

Landon tuts and pouts. "There are plenty of leagues to coach here. And let's go meet your folks *now*. I have twenty hours before my flight and I'm *great* with parents."

I giggle and pinch my shoulder to my jaw, skin tickled by his grown-out beard in the winter months. "Rahul and Anjali Davé are in India until May."

My boyfriend resigns with a sigh and child-like obstinate kick of his foot to the bed. "*Fine*. Have it your way." He buries his head between my breasts and places my arms around his bare shoulders. "*Don't* come live with me to get babied and have your back blown out on the regular."

"Landon."

"I love you," he mumbles into my sternum, voice lagged with sleep. "No more arguing."

"Or else?"

"Or else I'll have to stuff that mouth shut with my dick."

———

"You're not nervous?"

Landon side-eyes me from the driver's seat. "No, baby. Relax. Why are *you* so nervous?"

"*Um*, hello?" One hand flies up. "I've never brought a guy home before."

"It's gonna be fine. They're gonna love me." His fingers coast over my thigh and settle on its inner seam.

"My dad's scary-protective. He's as tall as you," I count on my fingers, "almost as big, has a dark beard, *and* plays rugby."

Confidence oozes from his smirking mouth. "I can take him."

I drape a dramatic arm over my forehead and eyes. "You're white and a professional hockey player. That's two strikes."

"*And* my parents are divorced."

My best death glare fires toward his stupid, carefree smile. "You're not helping."

"Fine. Have it your way."

The Rover swerves into the right lane before we take the exit to an upcoming service center somewhere by Sharbot Lake. We park at the edge of a lot facing a dense tree line. Landon hits the parking brake and reclines his seat all the way.

"This is no time for a nap!"

He flips his hat backward. "Oh, *no one* is resting." Two fingers meet his licked lips. "You're gonna sit right here until you can't think."

———

We swing our hands on the walk up to my childhood home, anxiety a distant dream. Of course, they'll love him. I love him and they love me and—*shit!*—before we get to the door, my mother swings it open.

"Hi, Mom."

For once, my mother is silent, agape, surprised eyes taking in the man I've fallen for. She steps aside to welcome us in.

Dad stands in the foyer, arms crossed and scowling at the tame PDA. "Hi, Dad."

The more I try to let go, the tighter Landon clasps our intertwined fingers. My sisters run down the curved stairs, freezing halfway when they see us. They mirror Mom's aghast expression.

"Oh, *good*. Everyone's here." A sarcastic lament. "Mom—Anjali, Dad—Rahul. Anika and Esha, my younger sisters." I motion toward each with my palm up. "This is Landon Radek." A noisy gulp sounds out from my throat. "My boyfriend."

"I *knew* it!" Anika accuses and points back. Eyes widening as far as possible, my breath hitches. "He *was* flirting with you at that game in Montreal!"

"*Shhh!*"

Something softens in Dad's suspicious look. His arms fall to his sides, fingers strumming against his jeans. "Landon Radek?"

"Sir." Landon extends his free hand.

My father wags a finger, then snaps. "Hold on a minute. Landon Radek!" His snort concerns me. My mother has the same reaction.

Twin alapadmas blossom from our hands, questioning what the hell his deal is.

A hefty arm lands on my shoulder. "You're telling me this is the same Landon Radek whose stats you memorized in grade twelve?"

I go as red as any brown girl can.

"Didn't you bake a cake or something when he got drafted?"

"*Dad!*"

"And now you're *dating* him? Your favorite player?"

Landon beams. I groan and cover my face. My sisters cackle from the steps, nearly toppling over each other. Nik can hardly breathe.

"You didn't know about this?" Dad asks.

He denies it. Vehemently.

The arm leaves me, wrapping around Landon's shoulders instead as my father leads him inside. "Aw, *mate*. I hate to break it to you, but this girl's been bonkers over you for ages."

"Has she?"

Help! I mouth to my mom. She frowns and shrugs, then interrupts their conversation to serve them water. "Sorry, Landon? You must be hungry from traveling—"

To my horror, he throws me a mischievous glance. Why am I in actual hell right now? "No, thank you. I ate on the road."

Too soon are my family gathered around the dining table, sharing embarrassing stories of my youth with the love of my life. Landon's comfortable *and* pleased, the backstabbing bastard. It could be worse. Nevertheless, I've heard enough and excuse myself to freshen up with a shower.

The steam and the unusually balmy weather call for an outfit change. I decide on the floral dress some fashion startup sent Sheena in a size too big. The square-neck elastic fits around my chest and flowy fabric billows above the knees when I walk, light as air. I could do without the puffy sleeves, but it fits the early summer vibes.

"*Holy fuck,*" Landon whispers at the foot of the stairwell. "This dress." He checks for spying eyes and moves my hair away to kiss my collarbone, inhaling the clean skin. "I'm gonna need to take you on a drive."

We leave with a promise of returning before dinner, the wayward, unplanned excursion placing us in the middle of nowhere. His lips trace my wrist's pulse as we take the Rover off-road, parking in a field of tall, wild grass. Left hand seizing my throat, he draws a tongue-filled kiss. "Get in the back."

Landon joins me and my sudden need for exhibitionism in the second row. I throw my panties at his bewildered face. My naked ass meets the console when I lift the skirt and spread my legs. "Is this what you wanted?"

He adjusts his hips, running a hand down the enormous bulge at his crotch, those clear blue eyes growing hazy with lust. "*God*, yes."

Inching forward, his fingers reach for my knees, but I click my tongue and *unh-unh,* pushing his chest back with my foot.

My heartbeat dances at the adrenaline rush of control. "How badly?"

"*So* badly." His groan fuels the fire sparking in my belly.

"Show me."

Hands scrambling to remove his shirt and undo his pants, he pulls his cock out, the head red and swollen, an angry vein winding around the shaft within his large fist. "Like this?"

Arousal floods between my thighs. My knees connect with the back seat on either side of Landon.

He pulls me into another sultry, open-mouthed kiss while I rub my wet, exposed core against him. "*Fuck*" —he breaks apart our lips— "we need protection."

My palm squeezes his throat, knocking him into the headrest. "No, we don't." Confusion and panic flash through his eyes as he mumbles a why between hungry kisses. "Started BC a week ago."

Landon halts every movement. "I get to fuck you raw?"

"Yep."

"Christ, baby. Ride my cock." His hips grind, sliding himself through my wetness. "*Please*, Indi. I'm begging you."

"I do love when you do that." My hands settle on the rounded muscles of his shoulders after bunching up the dress around my waist. I gasp while sinking down, savoring the fullness.

Landon's head tosses back with a groan.

"How's that feel?" I ask, lifting and lowering again, adjusting to his thick size. The slow rhythm against my G-spot has me whimpering.

His thumb strokes my sensitive clit, in time with my pace. "Like fucking bliss." A firm hand tugs at the fabric on my shoulder. "Pull this down, let me see."

I listen and show off my naked chest.

"Flawless."

My fingers pinch and tease the nipples, feeding Landon's hot mouth along the way. Lashes strike as he sucks and squeezes them in those talented hands. This time, my head lolls, the combined pleasure too much. It whips back up to see my boyfriend nearly going cross-eyed.

"You're gorgeous like this," he praises, encouraging the speed of my hips, wave after wave of pleasure washing over me. "There's nothing more gorgeous than the way you take every inch of my cock."

A toe-cramping, blinding, deafening, life-changing climax tears through me as I clamp around Landon. He catches me, nipping into my neck for the final thrusts, spurts of his cum leaking out onto my thighs.

I'm still recovering when he seats me on the console again, clenching as he licks between my shuddering legs in the aftershock. He goads my lips apart with a thumb and spits in my mouth. "Don't we taste good all mixed together?"

I come again with a shameless, inhuman moan swallowed by the warmth of Landon's tongue.

"One more time, baby?"

I whine through a tired chuckle but don't deny him.

"Greedy, so greedy," he chides, flipping me around, tits out, and bent over on this damn console. Those rough fingers pump inside me, slow and deep. "Can't get enough of this needy, tight pussy."

My eyes screw shut on impact as Landon drives inside me at an incredible cadence, the weight of his balls smacking my worn clit every time his hips slap soundly against my ass. His string of pleasured grunts spurs my orgasm on. A harsh tug at my hair elicits another moan.

"Look at yourself." Our gazes lock in the rearview mirror, mouths parted, faces shiny with sweat. A rogue hair on his otherwise neatly combed-back hair dances across his forehead. "How stunning you are getting fucked from behind."

I clamp around him at the sight, my breasts flush against the rough, black surface, hardened nipples rubbing with every thrust. Landon groans in response, retreating to massage my G-spot from inside, fingers playing with the oversensitive bundle of nerves.

"Oh, my *God*," I whine, teetering on the edge of another intense release. "Landon."

"Yeah, baby?" His delivery is unstopping, brazen. My eyes roll back. "Do your folks know, huh? That their innocent firstborn loves getting railed in a summer dress?"

That tips me over, every spent muscle tensing through the peak as I explode around him. He bottoms out with a sated laugh, adding to the sticky mess trailing down my inner thighs. Not yet pulling out, Landon positions us, my back against his heaving chest, lip-locked in a mind-numbing kiss.

"You make all my dreams come true," he says into the seam of my mouth. "I love you so fucking much."

Dad's welcome upon our return fades quickly, switching a curious gaze between us as I fix my sexed-up hair. Landon clears his throat. We both burst into a furious blush.

"Stop embarrassing them, Rahul." Mom smacks him with a kitchen towel.

"I know that look." He narrows his eyes with an easy grin, curling an arm over his wife's shoulders. "Your mum and I were young once."

My mouth turns and my sisters voice our communal disgust from the formal living room without looking up from their phones. "Yuuuuck!"

"There's nothing wrong with having a snog." Dad pecks Mom's temple, then her cheek and jaw. The last one lingers.

"Yeah, *uh huh,*" I reply. "Caught us. That's what we were doing. Mom, you need help in the kitchen, don't you?"

Nik scoffs. "Not that you could do anything about it if she did."

"Hey, I know how to cook now!"

"Only salty khichdi. *Bleh.*" Esha sticks out her tongue. "Landon, do you know how to cook? Because this one" —she points her thumb at me— "is smart, but not domesticated."

"Mom, do something!" An ineffective protest.

She slinks off to the kitchen, hands over her ears. "*Girls!*"

My dad and Landon *whew* in chorus.

The daily squabbling between the ladies of the house doesn't prevent me from overhearing Dad's suggestion in the entryway. "This isn't gonna end anytime soon. How 'bout I call up some mates and we have a friendly rugby match?"

Butterflies flit and flicker in my belly the entire elevator ride up.

I've been to Landon's penthouse hundreds of times. I shouldn't be nervous, but I am. The suitcase wheels whir across the marble until I stop outside the double doors. Keypad beeps accept the entered code, and my hand twists the handle open.

It's completely dark.

"*Hmm.*" I wonder to myself, positive Landon said he'd be here, then retrieve my phone from my pocket to check the time and turn on the flash. When I locate a nearby light switch, the most raucous sound has me jumping out of my skin.

"*Surprise!*"

The rest of the lights flash on as a gaggle of familiar faces whoop, holler, and blow noisemakers. I spot Gabe, Bea, Sheena, and Akhil, along with the full Regents' roster. A giant, white, *Welcome Home, Indi!* banner hangs behind them. Tears blur my vision, though my face splits into a ridiculous smile.

Landon emerges from the middle, arms outstretched, hugging and kissing me so hard I float above the hardwood. "Hi, baby. Were you surprised?"

"How'd you know? I was supposed to surprise *you*."

I peer over his shoulder at Wade, who forms a halo above his head with both hands. He's the only one on Landon's side who knew. There's something endearing about the goofy goalie. Something beyond this dumb, playboy jock, sex idiot persona he masks behind. I don't want to jinx it, but he's growing on me. Wade is innocent.

But Bea dons a guilty smile. "*Behraz!*"

"Would you believe me if I said it was an accident?"

"No." My forehead taps Landon's chin in apology. "Wish I could've been the one to tell you."

His arms hook around my lower back. "Tell me anyway." A smirk dimples one stubbled cheek.

"I'm moving in."

Landon swipes his lower lip, dipping his forehead to mine. No one else exists in this pivotal moment. "Great. When?"

"Right now. Is that okay?"

"I'm free. Where's your stuff?" He teases one corner of my lips, pleading for a kiss.

"Some in my suitcase, some in the Audi." I steal his mouth like he wants me to. "The rest gets in on a truck tomorrow."

"Can't wait."

Our friends help empty the car as they leave, the night's excitement ending with pleasant, tipsy goodbyes and best wishes for the move back.

"Whatcha got there?" Landon discovers me hiding a dirty little secret in the corner of the living room.

"Oh, nothing."

The brute picks me up by the shoulders like a weightless stack of feathers and sets me aside. He gasps at the sad state of the prickly cactus he gifted last year.

"*Our love plant!*" he shrieks. "You let it *die!*"

He's watched *How to Lose a Guy in 10 Days* too many times. "It's *not* dead!" I roll my eyes. "It's hibernating."

"How could you let our love plant *die?*"

If Landon is anything, it's melodramatic. I arch an eyebrow at his ostentatious display next to the side table, kneeling and doing his best wailing Gollum impression. He cuts it out when I wind up my leg to kick him in the groin.

"I'm joking, baby. I don't care about that thing. All I care about is you being here with me."

"Good answer. I'll ask Gabe if cacti can be brought back to life. I'm kinda attached to it." I thread our fingers together and help him up. "In the meantime, kiss me and take me to bed."

We break in the mattress on our first night as cohabitating adults and settle against one another. The languid rise and fall of his chest as he drifts off lures my sleep, too. A raspy murmur wafts past my ear. "Indi?"

"*Mmhmm?*"

"Marry me someday."

I don't think I'll ever be happier than in his arms.

"Okay."

CHAPTER 51:
I WANNA BE YOUR EVERYTHING

LANDON

THE STEADY BEAT OF AVICII'S "LEVELS" MATCHES MY pulse as Kingston hypes one section after the other with a dance-off challenge. Our mascot waves his arms and twerks the bulky ass of the costume. It's fucking hilarious usually, but I'm on edge.

I uncross my skate from under a knee while palming my stick with both hands, lowering to the ice, and bouncing to stretch the tightness in my groin after a particularly rough pregame quickie with Indi at home. Her whining moans after finishing in my mouth ring in my ears.

I teased her throbbing pussy with my bare, swollen dick head slathering wetness everywhere. "Landon, please. Get inside me."

"What's this, Indira Davé begging for my cock?"

Her nails dug into my scalp, crushing our faces together in a kiss that hardened me further. She rocked her hips, a solid attempt to slip me in.

"Please." She whimpered. "One more before you leave." How could I say no to those noises?

Already both sopping wet, gliding inside her was a breeze. I hooked the back of her knee over my arm, spreading her as our hips slap together. "This what you wanted, baby? Me pumping deep inside this tiny, tight cunt?"

Indi writhed and cried out beneath me as I quickened my pace, every harsh thrust rippling waves in her flesh. "Wanna be so full of my cum, it spills out of you for weeks?"

"Yes!" Her eyes rolled, pussy tightening when I throttled that red clit with my thumb.

"Fuckkkk," I groaned, pushing my choked cock as far as it could go until

it emptied every last drop into her. We panted through laughs and tongue-filled kisses until our breaths slowed. "It's like I've already won tonight."

Except we haven't.

"*Jesus.*" I shake my head and jump to my feet, whizzing past Skylar and Jaeg to the press box.

Gabe's camerawoman shuts the viewing window as I approach and calls out her name in warning. "Finch! Incoming!"

Loud raps from my blade on the plexiglass startle everyone except my girl's best friend.

"What do you want?"

"Where the hell is she? I can't find her anywhere!" The interrogation sounds more like a whine.

"You're *so* needy."

My blade meets the glass again.

"I'm not fucking around!" I yell over the music. "I won't win without seeing her."

Gabe shoos away the stylist fixing her hair and makeup. "She'll be here. Stop wigging out."

I groan through my teeth, frustrated at how close to game time it is.

"Go bother Bea," Gabe dismisses me, pointing to where she sits. "They drove here together. I'm about to go live."

After weaving through my stretching teammates and flicking away a rogue puck right into the open goal, I skate to a stop halfway around the rink. The WAG section is bare, thanks to most of the team's perpetual singlehood.

"Behraz—" Sweetness blankets my words. "Where is my girlfriend?"

She loudly mouths fistful after fistful of popcorn. "Be more obsessed, Landon. I dare you! She went to get snacks." *Crunchety crunch.* "Also—" *Chomp chomp.* "Consider this your warning. If you win this game, don't propose at the end."

"What? *Pfft,*" I deny and sputter. "I wasn't gonna. Sheesh."

"*Uh-huh.* Sure. I'm just sayin'." Bea beckons me closer to the glass and cups a hand around her mouth to amplify her voice. "I think you've watched enough Bollywood flicks to know what she wants. She *loves* the cheesy shit."

"What cheesy shit?"

"*Oooh,* nachos!" Bea's narrow attention span inadvertently saves our asses. "I knew you'd bring me some. *Yummmm*. Extra jalapeños!" She takes a beer from Indi. "God bless America!"

I press my glove into the clear surface, loving the way she swims in my hockey sweater. "Hi, baby."

She holds her hand up on the other side, a hint of pride in her dimples and gleaming brown eyes. "Hey, Radek."

"Alright, here we go," I say, pushing back and tucking my stick in an armpit. "I can't score without a good luck pic. Lemme see what you got."

My fingers form a square to frame her adorable self and I squint an eye through it, miming taking a snap shot of Indi while she places a hand behind her head, tits perky—something she calls the "Madhuri Dixit." Whatever that means. I'll Google it later.

"*Click click*." Polaroid printing noises and a fake arrow to the heart upon seeing the invisible developed photo have the three of them giggling.

"You guys are *so* cute," Skylar gushes.

"And I'm *so* single." Bea wipes a glop of liquid cheese from her face. She fake-cries into her beer. "When is it my turn?"

Indi nudges her with an elbow. "Maybe soon. Donovan's staring right at you." My girl throws a side glance for confirmation. I wink back.

She chokes on a tortilla chip. "Is he, really?"

"For sure."

My parents send me love from the next section over while Delaney glares and mouths *don't fuck this up* as she cheerfully encourages the kids to wave at me.

Jaeg makes a silent signal for us to round up, announcer booming over the PA system, and I leave to join the rest of the team.

The L.A. Suns had a helluva season, and despite our multiple playoff appearances, we're still considered the underdog. They treat us like Toronto or something. Those poor fucks haven't gotten to the Cup in ages.

We skate into position, the crowd electric and buzzing. My breath clouds the icy air as Fletch nods from the face-off circle. I take one last glance at my lucky charm before the whistle trills and the ref drops the puck. She smiles. I smile back, then sneer at my opponent, a Suns winger named Lendegrass. "Showtime, Grassy."

Donovan swipes the puck and I take off, veering around a too-slow d-man. He flicks it over while Jaeg covers the other goon. Szecze circles me, faking a pass, and as the goalie focuses on him rounding behind the goal, I take a shot. Their tendy reacts too late and the puck flies in with a ping, horns and siren going off in tandem.

"Hell yes!" I pump a fist, as the crowd erupts, and the boys huddle up for a quick hug before we break to get back to center ice. "Let's do this!"

L.A. gets possession this time but loses it when Jaeg takes out their winger. There's a gap while the big fellas have a shoving match and Fletch and I take the puck all the way back. The goalie is ready this time, but not ready enough. He tries to block the puck with a skate, but it ricochets off of the blade and into the net. The horn blares as the siren flashes.

We slot our sticks between our legs and gallop past the girls, whooping as if racing horses. Indi covers her eyes with a hand, shrinking into her seat as the camera falls to her section, Jumbotron displaying our silliness. "Yee-haw!" The charade ends in a double high-five before we hug it out and gear up for the rest of the period.

The momentum continues through the second period, too. Indi sends selfies from her seat at intermission. They keep me motivated. Most of us stay free of PIMs, except for Szecze and Olsen. Distracted by a d-man getting too close, Wade lets the Suns score right before the next intermission.

Up by four, we don't make any adjustments in the last period and take the chance to rest and give a few second and third-liners get some playing time. Whistles blow when a fight breaks out. Coach smacks my shoulder. "Radek, you're up!"

One bloody-nosed rookie gets taken back by the medics. It's a hot game, even in the last few minutes. We're going coast-to-coast as the Suns get more aggressive. The Los Angeles coach seems to have spanked a few asses in the locker room.

A couple of possessions later, it's ours again. The Suns don't give up, I'll give 'em that. They're still grinding, fighting for the puck at every corner. We don't make another shot in time for the buzzer, but it doesn't matter.

An almost coordinated celebration bursts, not unlike my heart, alongside an explosion of mitts, sticks, and helmets being thrown away as we scream and cry and cling to each other. More of the team join from the bench until we lose our balance and dog pile, the crushing sensation calming the coursing adrenaline temporarily. The crowd, my teammates, the horns, sirens, announcers, fireworks, every sound fizzles into static.

Hats and scarves are handed out, my family cries through congratulations, but my eyes and hands search for her.

Indi runs out screaming, straight to center ice through the horde of press and staff in that white, gold, and black jersey. My girl wearing my name, my number. That lucky number twelve. The age I met her, and my life changed forever. Being hers? Way better than winning.

I excuse myself from a reporter with an apology. She pounces me with a shriek and crashes a kiss to my lips with the stuff dreams are made of. I prop her up by a forearm.

"I love you so much," I yell. "You'll marry me, right?"

"You wanna be my husband?" she yells back.

"More than anything!" My hands clutch her everywhere. "I wanna be your *everything*."

"What are the chances?" Her head dips to speak in my ringing ears. "You already are."

A maniacal cackle surges from me as I throttle her excitedly around my torso, then drop her when Jaeg passes me the cup. I hold it over my head in victory.

"I'm gonna eat Twinkies out of the Stanley Cup!"

———

"I'm supposed to believe you *wanted* to go on a hike today?" Indi huffs, climbing over a steeply inclined rock. "Instead of staying in bed and fucking me to oblivion?"

"Baby, I can fuck you to oblivion any day. But look!" My arms span to my sides, as wide as they can. "The sun's out. We're in the fucking mountains. It's amazing!"

"Ah, yes. *Nature*," she deadpans. My mouthy, grumpy girl.

I take a long breath of all that clean air. "Exactly!"

"I'll have whatever you've been snorting."

"That's the spirit." Jogging ahead a few steps, hiking boots tracking prints into the soft earth, I stop at a clearing at the lookout, placing my hands on either hip. The view is insane. Tall evergreens and snowy mountain peaks frame Green Lake below. "Don't you remember the last time we were in Whistler together?"

Indi tucks herself under my arm. "I remember you're a sore loser."

I grab her throat and punish her with a kiss for that comment, then soften, stroking lines under her jaw with my thumb.

"And that you love being little spoon. My big baby," she murmurs between our lips.

"Yours." We share another short peck. "All yours."

I crack my knuckles and snap.

Indi whips her eyes to me. If she didn't love me, they'd shred me to tatters. "Did you snap at me?"

"Huh?"

"You snapped."

"Did I?"

A series of horns peal out. "What was that?"

"No idea." We both seek out the source and I shed my backpack before leaping in front of her.

"*Dhinka chika, dhinka chika, dhinka chika, dhinka chika! Re, ay, ay, ayyyyy! Re, ay, ay, ayyyyy!*"

"Oh, *no*," Indi swallows the dismay under her breath as I shimmy in her direction.

The reprise repeats with the boys' entrance, then more and more of our loved ones join. Her parents, sisters, her best friends, my folks, Del, Seth, and the kids. Jaeg, Wade, Fletch, Szecze, Olsen and I leap and turn to flaunt our best assets, alternating the fondling each buttcheek in sync with the rhythm of the words.

I peer over my shoulder to see my girl, hands over knees, gripping her stomach, barely able to watch, in tears with laughter. "Who planned this?!"

We continue the coordinated, flash-mob style dance with hip-thrusts and silly expressions. It's more acting than dancing, as explained by Indi's sisters, but it does the trick. This is the most joyous, lit-up version of Indi I've ever seen, and I hope whatever I do next keeps her that way. She wipes the corner of her eyes, struggling to catch her breath after that ridiculous shenanigan.

I take a knee. Indi gasps from realization.

"I'm so sorry," I say through a smile, popping open a garnet-colored velvet box. The three and a half carat, oval-cut diamond paints mini-rainbows onto the nearby rocks. Twelve smaller diamonds create the band. "I can't think of anything original to say."

Her eyes scan through the group then back to me. "Say it anyway."

"I love you, Indira Davé. I've loved you since we met, and I'll love you 'til we're gone. Wanna get crazy and marry me?"

Her hand spreads over the top of her nose and parted mouth, then rests on her dimpled cheek. "You are the most annoying, irritating, lovable man on this planet."

"But handsome, too, right?"

"Unbelievably so." She steps forward, splaying out her left hand. Steady. Determined. "And my answer is yes."

The ring slides on as easy as it is to love her. I hop to my feet to mold my torso to hers, kissing those lips until I stop to breathe every part of her in: cranberry, cinnamon, and calm.

She tastes sweeter than any win.

Indira Davé tastes like my future, like all our today's and tomorrow's laced together forever.

EPILOGUE:
WHEN YOU'RE READY,
COME AND GET IT

INDI

MY TOES TWITCH IN IMPATIENCE UNDER A HEAVY lehenga. Muted bells lining my payal jingle underneath. Mom adjusts the gajra surrounding my chignon, the sweet smell of jasmine releasing with every placed pin.

"Hold still," the stern makeup artist says, gluing the round tikka on the thick matha patti to my forehead. Cameras click as my mom and sisters pull the dupatta onto my shoulder and drape a chundari over my head.

The air is thick with emotion, and I hold one border in place over my chest while looking up at the loving women in my family.

Sheena, Gabe, and Bea help in counting to make sure nothing is forgotten from the remaining solah shringar, every piece of jewelry and adornment carefully accounted for. Esha applies attar behind my ears and on the wildly pulsing veins at my wrists and ankles. The slightest movement sets off a symphony of delicate, clinking metal.

Their gazes meet mine in the full-length mirror, smoothing down their complementary bridesmaid saris.

"I look like a jewelry store threw up on me."

They deny in chorus, sandwiching me in a group embrace.

My mother shushes me. "You're beautiful. Will you relax?"

"Sure, this is a very relaxing time in my life."

Mom glares and swats at the air.

My heart knots. The contrast between the plush garnet-colored velvet and intricate gold beadwork of the skirt under my fingertips does nothing to quell my anxiety. "Can I have my phone, please?"

Gabe gives me a flat, disapproving look, but hands it over.

"Mom, sisters, we need you downstairs to greet the baraat!" A planner calls from the corner, ushering them out of the bridal suite with rapid swooping motions and muttering into her earpiece.

ME

Hi.

MY GUY

You doin' okay, baby?

ME

I'm a bumbling bag of nerves. You?

MY GUY

I can't wait to marry you.

A smile cracks my worried expression. I take a long breath, at ease from his response.

ME

I sent you a burger earlier.

MY GUY

Aww, Indi, that's so sweet.

MY GUY

But I'm fasting.

ME

Why?

MY GUY

For the ceremony, aren't you fasting?

ME

Yes.

MY GUY

Then why shouldn't I?

MY GUY

Burger delivery confirmed, Wade ate it.

MY GUY

Also, I apologize for what we're about to do.

ME

About to…EXCUSE ME?

ME

ANSWER ME LANDON.

MY GUY

Greetings! Landon is unavailable.
This is Wade.

ME

Wade, what the hell is going on?

MY GUY

Can't tell you.

ME

YOU HAVE TO!

MY GUY

And ruin the surprise? No way.

"*Ugh!*" I groan, my neck and jaw clenched to the max.

"And you've lost phone privileges." Gabe swipes it from my grasp and drops it in her clutch. "Can't have a stressed bride when it's almost time to go."

Sheena grabs one hand and squeezes. Gabe and Bea do the same with my other.

They goad me to the window, which faces the manor's main circular drive. Amplifiers rumble with a thumping bassline, the animated dholi keeping a steady beat. The four of us smile at the animated procession, my future in-laws dancing, their hands reaching to the sky as they take jaunt steps in time with the music. They're encouraged by my extended family with a few classic dance moves.

Then, like the midday sun breaking through the clouds, Landon appears, riding in the back of his beloved white Porsche, convertible top down. The white sherwani stretches across his broad chest and shoulders, its gold brocade print glistening in the autumn sun. His teammates surround the car, cheering and clamoring in their matching pastel green kurtas like true hypemen.

Bea moves the curtain aside as Gabe unlatches the window. The smell of damp earth from the previous day's rain wafts through. Landon's gaze lifts toward me and I shrink back, not wanting him to see me yet. The party whoops from below as my friends wave their arms beyond the open glass.

He says something in Jaeger's ear, then hops out of the car. Wade and Fletcher, Szeczin, Olsen, Jaeger, and his brother-in-law, Seth, throw on dark shades and form a huddle. A raspy, forlorn voice sings from the speakers and the dhol slows to match its taal. The guys stagger into lines, lifting their chins in arrogance, folding their hands over their groins like wanna-be gangsters.

"Sheena, I'm afraid," I admit. "I think Landon got a little *too* inspired by Anika and Ash's wedding."

"You have no idea," Gabe mumbles.

The boys flip, backs facing us, bending over to twerk to a "*hey, hey, hey, hey…*" Song bursting as the boys leap up and turn in unison, they break out into a coordinated bhangra sequence to Selena Gomez's "Come and Get It."

My jaw hangs somewhere by my boobs. They hit every phulka, side pump, and pataka with style.

Landon raises his hands to me and beckons, screaming while bouncing his shoulders, "When *you're ready, come and get it, na na na na, na na na na!*"

An atrocious laugh escapes. I didn't know being loved like this—*so unashamed and sincere*—was possible. He learned how I needed and wanted to be loved, and, in turn, taught me how to accept his love while allowing myself to love him.

"Where—when the hell did they…?"

Anika and Esha peer up through their oversized sunglasses, singing along while double pointing at me to the live dhol beat while rolling their hips. Of course.

My arm shoots out the window as I whoop back, the crowd below roaring louder in reply. A few minutes of dancing warfare between our loved ones peters to a stop when they approach the arched entrance where my mom and family formally welcome the groom.

As they lead him inside, we retreat from the curtained view. The rush of adrenaline has my hands shaking, and my girlfriends apply pressure on them while forcing me to drink water to calm.

"Indira."

It's my mother's elder brother. His mouth takes a downward turn as tears stream down his tanned cheeks. We're both unprepared for the onslaught of emotion and I run to him, unable to think of anything else to do. The bond Chirag Mama and I share is inexplicable. I only saw him for a few short weeks in summer when visiting Mumbai as children, but the amount of care and love he showers is nothing short of miraculous.

He sniffles as the tears slow. "Anjali always called you Mallika-e-Hindustan. Today, you look the part."

I threaten to weep again if he doesn't stop, and he dabs at my cheeks and chin with his clean handkerchief.

Gabe laments upon checking my phone. "We should probably head down."

"Why? What happened?"

Her lower lip pouts through a smile. "Wade texted saying Radek's about to cry. He's jittery and keeps asking if you're there yet."

The assistant nods toward the door. "You ready?"

I'm not gonna cry, not gonna cry, not gonna cry when I see him.

Bridesmaids ahead, we walk under the canopy of strung-together jasmine my cousin-brothers hold over our heads. Yet another wave of emotion rises upon hearing the Mangalashtak, sung by Mom's sisters.

"Your Kalyani Masi is off-key," Chirag Mama whispers.

A good effort at breaking the tension and nerves from everyone's gaze as we stride down the marigold-petal-covered aisle. Somehow my uncle hoists me onto the mandap as the song trails off, forty extra pounds of lehenga and all. Our guests clap and cheer.

"You there, baby?" His voice, shaky, hoarse with restlessness—*and barely audible over the priest clamoring a spoon against a steel dish*—sparks goosebumps up my arms. Tight streamers of white flowers hang between us like a sheet.

"I'm here."

Mom places a garland between my hands in preparation for our first look.

Landon puffs out a breath. I catch a glimpse of his lowered eyes through the shroud. Relieved sobs through laughs wrack through me as they remove the floral wall.

On the other side, the sweetest man alive falls apart, the tears sitting on the thick line of lashes spilling down his face on sight. His nearly-closed, wrinkled eyes hide the pretty blue shade underneath.

I'm not sure because I'm a mess myself, but I think I see Jaeger, Wade, and Donovan shrugging off tears, too. A chorus of *awww* echoes in the tent.

Most grooms playfully evade the bride's offered garland, but Landon? My overeager husband-to-be doesn't wait for the priest's instructions and tucks his head through it. When I feign hesitation and dodge his attempt, he pokes his tongue in his cheek and shakes his head, lowering it with resignation.

"Just kidding," I tease, wrapping my wrists around his to put the varmaala over my covered head.

Nik and Esha loosen its hold around my neck from where it weighs down my chundari.

So much of the ceremony is a blur, despite my best efforts to soak in every moment. At least until we're given the seven vows to read aloud while taking our first steps together as a wedded couple.

I start. "We promise to respect and honor each other."

"We promise to always support one another mentally, emotionally, and physically," Landon adds.

"We promise to be faithful to one another."

My husband wears a naughty smile. "We promise to fulfill each other's needs: mind, soul, and *body*." He emphasizes the last word.

I'll hear it from my mother afterward for rolling my eyes during the ceremony, but I can't help it. I reach for the mic, but he elbows my hand away, continuing. "We promise to create and raise many, *many*, noble and virtuous children who will be *exceptional* at playing puck."

The crowd giggles.

"*Landon!*" I gasp at his off-script commentary. My taut palm meets his shoulder with a slap. "That is *not* what that says!"

He lets me have the mic, stifling his chuckling against his wrist.

"We promise to grow old together, hoping for long lives filled with peace and success."

He wrangles it back from my hand with ease, the big bully, but it's worth it. Because he looks at no one but me when he announces the final vow. "We promise to build a life of friendship, love, and mutual trust. Always."

I melt.

When we stand to receive blessings from our elders, Nani signals for me to bow and touch Landon's feet. The feminist within burns, but out of respect for tradition, I listen.

"Lift your skirt," he murmurs as I straighten.

"Excuse me?" Rage simmers, threatening to spill out through my clenched teeth. He sighs and bends over to pick up the bottom hem, positioning his warm hand over my cold foot.

"Landon, what are you doing?"

"What do you mean? Aren't we supposed to bow to one another?"

My shoulders rise, unsure of what to say. His head turns to the priest. "You said when we're on the altar, Indira and I are the human form of the higher power."

Mom and Dad gape, shocked. My sisters, too.

"If I am her god, then she is my goddess." He refocuses on me, still at my feet, the ocean of his eyes swirling with adoration. "She is strength and sacrifice personified, and there is no one else I'd rather spend my life worshipping."

Approving applause rings out and continues as we exit down the aisle.

"You're the best," I whisper.

"I know." His smile-stretched mouth grazes my cheek as we pose for a photo. "Goddamn, baby. Those red lips. You gonna paint my cock with them after this?"

"That depends," I say into his ear, genuine joy unable to leave my face. "You gonna paint my throat?"

Nose pressing into my dimple, his shoulders shake with silent laughter. "Will you cut it out? I'm already so fucking hard."

My family promised a quick and tear-free vidaai. They crack up when Landon lifts me into the 911, grumbling about why my skirt is so big. Sheena, Gabe, Bea, and my sisters block the front of the car, their hands on the hood. Seth revs the engine from the driver's side. Delaney sweetly bribes them with a few hundred dollars, but they refuse.

"Taking my shoes wasn't enough, eh?" Landon tosses a stack of hundreds at them. Gabe catches it in one hand. "Take it all. All I want is my wife."

We're late, and the ride around the estate is short before we have to get changed for the reception. Landon hasn't let go of my hand since my parents placed it in his. He won't stop kissing me either. The stroking thumb against my throat and sweeps of his tongue at the seam of my lips is too high of a high, the tender cradling of my head becoming more urgent as we get to the suite. My husband seems to be in no rush except for one thing.

He puts up both arms and prevents the hair and makeup team from reaching me. "Nope. Everyone out! I need two hours with my wife. Alone."

"We don't have two hours!" I protest. "Do you know how many bobby pins are holding *this*" —my pointed finger circles my head— "together right now?"

The vendors skedaddle, frowning at Landon's menacing expression. It disappears as they do.

He plops a kiss onto my forehead while unbuttoning his sherwani. "One hour. And don't worry. I'll fuck you out of every last pin." A single arm wraps around me as he walks us back to the long conference table. "Right out of these clothes, too." His rough grip arcs around my foot. "Everything except these anklets and" —he slips a finger underneath the gold chain circling my waist— "whatever this is."

Landon bunches multiple layers of the lehenga in his large hands. "Don't you dare rip it," I warn.

He whines, face dropping into the crook of my neck. "But baby—"

"I'm serious, Radek. This is Sabyasachi. You're not allowed to ruin it."

His grasp on the skirt is strong enough to pick me up with a grunt and throw my ass onto one edge of the table. "Can I tear at what's underneath?"

I reward him with a hungry kiss while peeling away his sweaty white undershirt.

"Absolutely."

———

Naked except for my kandoro and payal, I lean against the en suite's doorway, damp, loose curls sticking to the arms crossing my chest.

Landon steps out of the spacious marble shower and palms a folded towel, every firm, beautiful muscle on his torso rippling as he dries himself. He catches me staring and smirks over his shoulder. "What? Is there something stuck to my ass?"

"No."

"Then what are you looking at?"

"The love of my life. I waited a long, long time for him."

His playful expression wanes, every serious step chipping away at the remaining distance between us. A harsh hand clasps my neck and pulls me into a sweltering, open-mouthed kiss, sending staticky sparks to my fingertips and toes.

"Indi," he sighs. "You need to get in that bed *now*."

I rub a denial into his chest, the beat beneath it drumming into my palms. "We have a reception to get to. People will be waiting."

"Let 'em wait. What are they gonna do, have the reception without us?"

My feet backpedal as Landon discards the towel and stalks after me, cock hardening in his fist. Slick heat pools between my legs. Lust and mischief flicker in his eyes while approaching the edge of the mattress. I splay myself open for him. "Gonna fuck my wife so sore, she won't be able to walk without an ache in her pussy as a reminder of our wedding day."

An hour later, we're in a world of trouble.

"I can't believe you," I scream under my breath as we loiter in the lobby.

Landon pats my hand. "It's gonna be fine."

My best glower meets his softened, carefree gaze.

"Yes, what can I assist you with today?" The poor front desk attendant has no idea what she's in for. I yelp and cower behind him, the white beading of my Indo-Western gown scratching at his navy suit jacket.

"Hi! We're the newlyweds celebrating our wedding here today." He beams, that sunshiney smile tinging her pale cheeks with a pink blush.

I wiggle my glittery engagement ring from where my hand sits on his stomach. *Mine.*

"There's been an incident in our suite." His tongue darts out to wet his bottom lip. "You see, the bed's broken."

"Sir?"

Landon leans over the counter, tutting and hissing through his explanation. "I'm really sorry. We broke the bed. Went a little hard, you know."

Aghast, she asks for her supervisor's help. My shameless husband fishes his wallet out in the meantime, prepared to take on any charges. The hotel manager is more than displeased, red in the face after going upstairs to review the damage. "It's a priceless Victorian-era poster bed frame. How do you plan on paying for its replacement?"

"You know what? Forget about replacing it." The platinum credit card returns to its wallet slot.

"I beg your pardon?"

"I think I'll buy the place." His arm draws an invisible arc in the air, narrowed eyes studying every corner of the ceiling. "What do you think, Indi? Real estate is always a good investment, eh?"

———

Globe lights strung across the tent's clear top sparkle in the background as Landon's forehead rests on mine, my hands at his nape. He hums along with my private rendition of "Jag Ghoomeya" as Rahat Fateh Ali Khan croons over the sound system. We sway in the middle of the dance floor, our wedding reception well underway.

Emotional rollercoaster-like speeches and family skit-like dance performances complete, the night is ours to cherish. My head tilts to one side, offering my temple for Landon to kiss.

From the corner of my eye, Gabe's figure storms down the hilly lawn from the manor. Two beats later, Wade Boehner stumbles down the same path. An entirely different world of trouble.

"Landon, my love." I bat my lashes four or five times, tone changing from sweet to serious. My mouth tightens to a stiff line. "What's happening over there?"

"Where?" He responds, dazed and lost in the moment, a crooked smile dimpling one cheek.

My eyes slide to the left, to Gabe finger-combing her curls.

"Don't 'where' me, Radek! Gabe has sex hair." I tip my chin to Boehner. "And Wade's shirt is undone."

"Baby, his shirt's always open." The caressing hands on my exposed lower back do nothing to douse the anger.

"It is *not*! He had a tie on earlier."

Landon finally looks over to them, a squint morphing into surprise and realization. "*No!* They didn't!"

"They *totally* did."

"B-but Gabe's so sensible, and Wade's so..."

"Juvenile?"

"What the hell?"

I drag Landon from the wooden flooring and poke a finger into his solid chest. "This is all your fault!"

"Me? I don't have any control over what Wade's dick does or where it goes! I already told him to stay away from Esha."

A loud scoff follows. "He hit on my baby sister?!" I growl and ball my skirt in my fists to pick up the pace in my march across the tent. Landon trails behind me.

"Hey, he promised to leave her alone."

"How did you *not* talk to him about this beforehand? Gabe is very delicate right now." My fingers jut into his chest, for good measure. "I am holding you" —*poke*— "responsible" —*poke*— "for that trainwreck."

My husband huffs through his nostrils. We call out our friends' names simultaneously.

"*Gabe!*"

"*Wade!*"

They go wide-eyed and hightail in opposite directions, a confirmation of guilt if I ever saw one.

I scowl through my teeth. "If I'm right, I'm gonna edge you out, then hate-fuck you until the sun comes up."

"And I'm gonna enjoy the hell out of it." Landon practically prances away, glowing with anticipation. "I love you so much."

"I love you, too," I reply. "But this isn't over."

THE END

ACKNOWLEDGEMENTS

Writing has saved me from the brink an insane amount of times. It got me through every turbulent and transitional period of my life: the angst of middle and high school, new adulthood, and the trials and tribulations of marriage and parenthood. While its form has changed, the therapeutic effect of it hasn't.

This book is no different. I wrote it through the hardest times of motherhood as I tried to salvage the pieces of myself that I believed were long gone.

To Nadia Alexander, for being my first friend on this journey. Soumya, your writing made me feel seen after a long time. You led me to writing my own South Asian stories and I can't thank you enough for helping me find my voice.

This story wouldn't have been written without the urging of Aly, my OG critique partner, and incredible alpha readers, Afreen and Reanne. And it definitely wouldn't have been possible without my impostor syndrome exorcists Erin and Leigh, who not only read the first draft and guided developmental edits, but also constantly listened to me rant about this book and its characters along with every big and small decision around publishing. I don't know how I'll ever repay you, but a PR box will have to do.

Lindsey Clarke, my editing angel, if not for you, I'd forever be misplacing em dashes and incorrectly splitting paragraphs. I'm so thankful for our new friendship and your gentle guidance. To the genius artists I've had the wonderful opportunity to work beside, Allie Wygonik and Kell from Little Pluto Design: you brought my characters to life and made what was once only a pipe dream come true. I also can't forget to thank Margherita, who saved me from withering in formatting hell.

To the writing community: thank you for seeing me and hearing my voice in a world where I felt small and unheard. You have given me confidence to take this publishing step. Additionally, a special shout-out to my girl, Tishni. I adore you. This is because of you. This is for you. Throttling and bullying me into publishing worked.

To the South Asian diaspora authors who inspire me everyday: Jhumpa

Lahiri, Rupi Kaur, Nisha Sharma, Monica Arya, Swati MH, and Priyanka Taslim.

And last, but in no way the least, to my husband who has sacrificed so much of our time together so that I could chase something that filled my cup.

ABOUT THE AUTHOR

Ruby Rana is an elder millennial who writes spicy, funny and heartfelt romance about sassy brown girls. She excels in sending messages where autocorrect has gone terribly wrong.

When she's not battling typos, you can find her explaining Midwestern slang to her East Coast-raised husband, being used as a jungle gym by her young children or experimenting with new recipes in the kitchen.

Want to connect further? You can find her on the following platforms:

Instagram: rubyranawrites
TikTok: rubyranawrites
Goodreads: rubyranawrites
Amazon: Ruby Rana

Made in the USA
Columbia, SC
24 September 2023

23340892R00293